Makeshift

Makeshift

Sarah Campion

Introduction by Diana Wichtel
Afterword by Sarah Shieff

RECOVERED BOOKS
BOILER HOUSE PRESS

Contents

Introduction
by Diana Wichtel

We shared a house for most of a decade, on and off, but much of what I would learn about my then mother-in-law, Sarah Campion, came from a bookcase in the living room. The house, perched on a sloping clay section running down to Stanley Bay Park in the Auckland seaside suburb of Devonport, was built in 1956, four years after Sarah emigrated from England with her husband, New Zealander Antony Alpers. She was an author and broadcaster of note back home. He was a journalist and Katherine Mansfield biographer 13 years her junior. They were a literary power couple settling down to raise their son, Philip, in North Shore 50s bohemia.

It was a volatile relationship. There was a story of Sarah throwing pieces of coal at the window of a sea captain's house where Antony was boarding during one of their times apart. But the new house was a joint effort. It was designed for them in the post-and-beam, "elegant shed" manner of the moment, by an architect adjacent to the Group, a midcentury practice determined that New Zealand should have an architecture of its own.

A bold, no-nonsense style that suited a similarly constructed new immigrant from literary London. Sarah wrote about the house and life in it for *Home and Building* magazine, in a column at first rather fancifully named *A Housewife's Diary*. The location—beach and ferry along the path at the bottom of the garden to the left; to the right, the Navy dump and sizable rats the cats would bring in—was idyllic if, like Sarah, a little untamed around the edges. She created a garden teeming with plants that grew like weeds in the Auckland climate—morning glory, wild ginger—unmoved by the fact that they were considered pests in her new country.

I remember running my eyes over the row of books with her name on them when I first visited the house. There were 13, mostly novels, all published in the UK. I was impressed. But then she had made an impression from the start. Sarah was Philip's most accessible parent since she and Antony parted ways when he was still a boy. She came with a backstory that included being born Mary Rose Coulton, daughter of Cambridge don G. G. Coulton, and growing up around members of the Bloomsbury Group. Watch out, a friend warned me, Sarah is a formidable woman.

She blew in from her travels to visit our shambolic student flat in Mt Eden around 1968. She was tall, all angular elbows and knees, her red hair fading to grey. With her resonantly rolled 'r's, her upper-middle-class, cut-glass enunciation, she was arresting, if less daunting than reported, even though Philip said she had described me, with the pitiless precision I came to appreciate in her gossip and her writing, as a "spotty-faced 17-year-old."

After Philip and I married in 1972, we moved into the house in Stanley Bay, with Sarah occupying, after our son Ben was born in 1976, a granny flat built for her under the house. "Danny!" Ben would call down the stairs to her as a toddler. She taught him to relieve himself on neighbours' lawns if caught short on their walks and to stomp the snails in the garden with his little gumboots. I drew the line at the snails.

4

At the dining table Antony made from a native timber door, over a pot of Sarah's preferred blend of tea—smokey Lapsang Souchong and Darjeeling, strong enough to stand a teaspoon up in it—I heard stories that had become family legend. During the Blitz in World War II, she had served tea to Londoners taking shelter in Underground stations. In the early 70s, when we visited her during one of her stays in London, she insisted on taking the bus on outings, when the Underground was more convenient. She was always so fearless. It took me a while to consider the trauma that being trapped underground while bombs fell overhead might have caused her.

In the 30s she had been in Germany, teaching English to the children of Jewish families planning escape. She was expelled by the Nazis in 1937 for refusing to give up her clients' names. These stories opened a door to my own past. Sarah was one of the few people to whom I could talk about my father, a Polish Holocaust survivor who disappeared from my life when I was thirteen and my mother brought my sister, brother and me home to her family in New Zealand. Dad remained in Canada. We lost touch. I never saw him again. Sarah affirmed that mislaid heritage in her inimitable way. "She was a typical New York Jewess," she would intone, of some acquaintance. "*You* will know what I mean, Diana." I met the immigrant circle, some of whom had escaped the Holocaust, among her Auckland friends. She brought me back from Mexico a silver and turquoise Star of David necklace my daughter still has.

There were intrepid stories of her time in the Australian out-back in the late 30s; of going out with a shooting party as a bush cook, gutting pigeons, encasing them in clay and roasting them over the campfire.

She talked about growing up with GG Coulton, subject of her biography, *Father*. He was difficult and demanding, whipping her for her rebellious spirit and, once, her sense of injustice still fresh in the telling, for playing with a ball. Such was the shadow he cast that Sarah and her sister Bridget both married in their 40s, after Father had died. The most moving passage I recall in her writing is from *Father*, a conversation as dawn broke when he was close to death. He spoke of their past clashes and begged her pardon for the worst. "It's all right now, dear girl, isn't it?" he asks her. "I assured him it was all right, and kissed him to show how I meant it," she writes.[1] Wherever she lived there was on the wall a photo of Father, one of Philip and, later, her grandson, Ben: the men in her life.

Her anecdotes informed what I found as I began to read my way along her row on books. There was *Mo Burdekin*, first published in 1941, part of an Australian trilogy set in a vividly evocative version of late nineteenth-century North Queensland: "Down came the rain remorseless as jealousy, awful as deserved doom."[2] The plight of small children swept away in a wet season flood is observed with Sarah's characteristically cool eye, making their fate all the more devastating. In her fiction, as well as in *Father*, there is often an attraction to, and a pushback against, a world run by men.

Into her stories she lobs narrative grenades designed to go off when least expected, to startling effect. *National Baby*, her witty 1950 nonfiction account of having a baby—Philip—under the then-new National Health Service, revealed how singularly self-contained she was. She writes about an evening out in London with Antony. They are living in separate accommodation. She sends him on his way without mentioning that she has gone into labour and takes herself off to the hospital alone.

Various grenades exploded when I first read *Makeshift*, published in 1940, drawing on Sarah's experience in Germany during the rise of Hitler. Charlotte Herz, the book's sharp, maddening

1   Sarah Campion, *Father*, Michael Joseph, 1948, p.228

2   Sarah Campion, *Mo Burdekin*, Penguin, 1990, p.2

narrator, is a young, orphaned Jewish woman making her way in an increasingly dangerous world in which, for a woman of limited means, marrying well is not just a matter of social status but of survival.

Charlotte's struggle for an independent life—there are affairs, wanderings, an interlude with a tramp in a hay-hut—is surprisingly modern, as is the humour. Of a disreputable cousin she muses, "I only know that he played ravishingly on the flute and looked even more beautiful drunk than sober. Which is more than can be said of many of us."

New Zealand, where Sarah would finally settle, is where *Makeshift* begins. Charlotte has left her youth and Berlin behind. She has been ill, and the miasma of a long hospital recuperation is viscerally evoked. Illness does not prevent Charlotte from casting a bitter, satirical eye on her surroundings. Of the unctuous, patronising doctor she reports, "I shall have to pay for that smile...'for Professional Smile, 10 guineas.'"

Makeshift is also about writing, an act, in Charlotte's unromantic terms, of necessary purging. "A basin is brought, you are sick, the basin is taken away and emptied, you feel better. (Forgive these nursing-home metaphors but they are apt.)" She will write, she announces, of her youth in Berlin, "of the things that broke me."

I read the book in my early 20s. It was the manner in which Charlotte walks away, "Unhurried, cold as frost...," from motherhood as an unmarried woman, from her baby daughter, that shook me. Sarah was deeply unsentimental, except about cats, but still. That you judge Charlotte more harshly than you might have a male character is part of the story's particular heft as a portrait of a woman of her times and circumstances. You judge her no more harshly than she judges herself.

More shocking to me, rereading the book now, are Charlotte's observations of her fellow Jews, laden with tropes about cunning and greed: "Let Nature be ever so green, we look at her with a shrewd eye and decide that she is not for us. There's no money in her." Such musings are hard to take with the knowledge of what happened to the Jews of Europe in the years after the book was published.

Of course, Charlotte is equally unsparing of just about everyone she encounters: "The little town was crawling with Americans, who champed their clay-coloured jaws over Wrigley's, darted febrile eyes here and there for bargains..." And she is alert to the mechanics of antisemitism: "The truth is we have committed the cardinal crime: we have survived persecution." As she grapples with her identity, there are moments of deep connection with a collective experience: "...but we live! we live!"

Sarah, too, occasionally talked about the things that broke her, of waking at the remorseless hour of four in the morning, beset by regrets. She would have liked, she said, to have had another child, a daughter.

Sarah's last years were spent in a nursing home after she had a stroke. Before that she lived up the road from the reconstituted family Chris and I had made, becoming "Granny" to a second Ben, my stepson, and to our daughter, Monika. She was a fixture at Christmases, with her mince pies and hard sauce. We would find in our letterbox newsletters from a variety of progressive causes she signed me up to and in our garden violets and jasmine she planted in clandestine territorial incursions. She liked to leave her mark.

She continued to write, mostly bracing letters to the editor, and to work on editing the diary of her mother, Rose, who, as a young woman also ahead of her time, had studied in New Zealand.

I would visit her in her tiny council flat in the late afternoon. She would put down her pen, pour us a glass of her favourite Tio Pepe sherry and offer one of the carefully rationed cigarettes she allowed herself: "I don't inhale." We would talk about writing. She would propose a toast. "Here's to two good working women."

I knew after she died in 2002, at the age of 96, that I would never know anyone like her again, that I didn't really know her at all and that I would always miss her booming voice, mid-anecdote, coming up the stairs.

I'm sure that Sarah would be delighted to see *Makeshift* reissued. The new edition arrives at a time when many of the book's themes—war, displacement, antisemitism, the impediments to women making choices about their lives—seem distressingly current. No doubt Sarah would respond to our moment as she did to hers. She would roll up her sleeves, protest, fire off some blistering letters to the editor, certain that it would make a difference. She would write.

Makeshift

by Sarah Campion

A Note from the Publishers

This book was originally published in 1940. It is a historical text and for this reason we have not made any changes to its use of language.

In Memoriam

J. L. C.

"For human intercourse, as soon as we look at it for its own sake and not as a social adjunct, is seen to be haunted by a spectre. We cannot understand each other, except in a rough and ready way; we cannot reveal ourselves, even when we want to; what we call intimacy is only a makeshift; perfect knowledge is an illusion."[1]

E. M. Forster

1   E. M. Forster, *Aspects of the Novel*.

Chapter 1
Arum Lilies

In South Africa the sluits[1] were full of these disgusting blooms, sprouting riotously and yet with peculiar tight primness along all the marshy bottoms, by the duck-pond, round the dam, in the grass beneath the Monterey pines, in the green shade of the willows that swung over the water-trough. The black feet of the women, coming to wash, trod down the trumpet blooms, crushed and mangled them. I was glad to see that.

I hoped I should never set eyes on an arum lily again, once I had left South Africa. But here in New Zealand they bloom like mad, like the children of pale curates, unrestrained, arriving into the world one after the other with no sense of decency whatever, sprouting pale and unhealthy wherever the ground gives them the dankness they love. There is more wetness in New Zealand than in South Africa: wetness in the lush paddocks under the cabbage palms and the rosetting tree-ferns, beneath the fresh weeping

---

1   A culvert usually formed by or constructed for draining rainwater.

willows. So there are more arum lilies; whole fields full of them sometimes, wholly sickening. Even by the crumbled grey wooden steps of the house near Te Mahia they rear their fleshy leaves and their self-conscious waxy flowers. Each time I went out that way I would nip one, nip it furiously, so that its impeccable whiteness was spoiled. When the wind blew from the southeast up the avenue, the arum trumpets bent and creaked juicily. I loved to see them bruised, browning at the edges, blowsy and undignified. Because, otherwise, they are too loathsomely good to be true as they bloom with all the lustiness of weeds, those pale thick pig lilies.

Some people love them. This morning Mrs. Wyatt came, tiptoeing to my bed. She brought with her a sheaf of the horrid blooms: as she bent to kiss me a whiff of death, no less, floated up from those bleached trumpets. When after half an hour's chatting she was gone I made the nurse put them in the lavatory. For to the lavatory they certainly belong.

So now I am free of them, but their death-smell lurks. The doctor will like that smell when he comes. Lifting his blunt nose, in which reddish hairs quiver, he will cry: "What a lovely scent—delicious—but then you always have such delightful flowers, you lucky woman." And will then drop the same nose to my sweet peas, the idiot, as if the smell came from them. But he knows nothing of flowers, which is for some reason a great joke in the Anglo-Saxon world. Going up to my roses every morning he bawls, snuffing: "What *are* these? No, don't tell me. I'll guess. Never know a thing about flowers, really upon my word I couldn't tell the difference between a cabbage and a cauliflower. But I do know these—aha!—I've got it! They're *linum grandiflorum rubrum!*[2] Ha! Ha! Ha!"

Ha! Ha! What a funny joke. The nurse leans against the wall, quite weak with it: the matron's starch rustles with it. Those braying masculine *ha-ha's!* go booming down the passage, tickling the

---

2 Botanical term for scarlet flax.

ears of all the other inmates of this bedlam, making them envy me my hearty jovial doctor.

Yesterday he came, talked for ten minutes of the iniquities of Mr. Savage and his Social Security Scheme,[3] then perfunctorily of me. He held my hand, told me I had been very ill. "Very, *very* ill, my dear: but we're round the corner now. All we want is a little help from you. We want you to co-operate. Just lie back and think of nothing—or think of lovely meadows with daisies in them. You do have daisies in Germany, don't you? Good! Well, think of them, think of anything pleasant. Relax, eat, sleep, and leave the rest to me."

The doctor-patter nauseates me: anyhow, I never cared for daisies. But why protest? I am to eat, sleep and think of pleasant things. The doctor smiled again, pressed my hand again, and left. I shall have to pay for that smile: it was so luxurious. I await the bill with resignation: "To Miss Charlotte Herz for Professional Services, 20 guineas; for Professional Smile, 10 guineas."

Ah, the long illness, the disgusting days! The agony of crawling back from a dozen small deaths; the hot prickles of the bed; the nursing-home smells, the bed-pans, clinical thermometers, invalid drinking cups stained at the spout by drink of other invalids, hot-water bottles at the feet, ice-packs at the head, eau-de-cologne everywhere. The flowers from dear friends, the dear friends in person hot on the heels of their insufferable freesias, bending their prawn eyes at me from the visitor's chair beside the bed, seeing How I Look. The only one I can tolerate is Adrian, and he, loathing illness, comes but seldom.

I have been here, they tell me, eight weeks in all. All that time the sheets pricked like hot sand, the visitors crept in and out,

---

3   The Social Security Bill put forward by New Zealand Prime Minister Michael Savage and passed by Parliament in 1938, one of the first government social security schemes in the world.

stabbing me with their eyes, voluptuously drinking in every detail of my helplessness. The nurses, ineffably kind, professional angels, coaxed and tended me—me, the carcase from which their living springs. Every day, regular as sin, came the ponderous tom-cat doctor with his blunt snuffing nose, his jests, his loud *ha-ha's!* to hold my hand, assure me I did very well, and recommend me to think on daisies.

Sometimes I read, for they brought me books as well as flowers. Safe books in which there was no excitement since all the characters were dead. Sometimes I ate their grapes, trying to be grateful, for in Auckland grapes cost money. The inevitable pips slid about my tongue like shiny bullets, the skins were as tough as oxhide, the taste like frozen dish-water. Sometimes I talked to the nurses—but why say "nurses"? There was but one, they were all the same, the universal nurse, popping in and out under different pseudonyms, glossy with starch, all nursehood rolled into one bland bloodless nursing machine, efficient to the last safety pin. Sometimes I even wrote letters, for one must be careful not to offend these automatically kind gentile strangers. "Dear Mrs. Robinson, Thank you so much for the delightful flowers, they smell so sweet." ("Nurse! Nurse! take away those damned freesias, they make me sick. Nurse!") "I am much better and hope to be about again soon. I should be delighted if you would come and see me..."

But mostly, in the first few weeks of convalescence, I stayed flat on my back and stared at the ceiling. Neither resentfully nor hopefully, merely blankly. This nursing home is far too efficient to have ceilings with any incident in them: there are no interesting cracks that could be imagined into men's faces, no damp marks the mind could conjure into little cats. Simply a high remote acre or so of impeccable whitewash, faintly changing with the faintly changeful sky. At the whitewash I stared, mindless, till I was pronounced fit enough to get up. Propelled by two nurses, I found myself in a chair. "Isn't that nice?" they said. I murmured:

Yes, it was very nice. In truth, it was no different. Only the walls were now my ceiling. Before, prone, I had goggled at horizontal planes of whitewash, like myself miraculously up-ended. When they got me back to bed again I exchanged one landscape for the other with complete indifference.

The days went on. One bright morning the matron, creaking down the passage like a stout barque in a gale, told me I was well enough to go out. I took the news calmly: it meant nothing to me. They packed clothes upon me while I rocked on my feet and made deprecating noises. Once more on my tired flesh the suspenders rasped: there was the almost forgotten tension of stockings, the hardness of shoes on pale bleached soles, the stranglehold of a woollen sweater, the horror of a hat. They piled these on me, making sounds of encouragement while I tottered: they led me deftly down the passage, through a hall with a brass gong and a bowl of wistaria, out into a garden. They packed me on a seat beneath a flowering kowhai tree[4] dropping yellow blooms: they bade me regard the grass which was, they cried in chorus, "*greener* than *e*-ver!" But I have never been particularly attached to grass. Unpleasant sensations welled up in me, I turned my head aside and was weakly sick over the back of the seat. "Dear, dear!" they said, plucking me up and leading me, gasping like a fish, into the bathroom. Here they hung me over a lavatory pan and waited for more to come. There was no more. They tidied me, straightened my hat, gave me a clean handkerchief, led me once more to the grass and the kowhais. No nonsense *this* time, said their well-washed capable hands as they packed me on to a different seat and stuffed the same cushions at my back. I was to look once more at the grass. All over the garden, muffled in rugs, left abandoned on seats painted a dark green, sat sexless figures looking at the grass. Sometimes a rustling nurse would

---

4   A small tree with yellow flowers, a legume native to New Zealand.

trip across that odious sward with something on a tray; and then one or other of the creatures would be induced to drink, to nibble. But for the most part we merely sat, eyes goggling downwards, a happy picture of convalescence.

Sitting there, gazing also at grass, I knew suddenly what I must do. Thoughts writhed Laocoön-like[5] behind my popping grass-sated eyes. I knew I must write. I cannot forever struggle with myself, forever gnaw serpent-like at my own tail, nor swallow my own venom. There is no mind on earth to whom I can say the things that can be written. Writing is the prime catharsis, the excellent emetic. For once you are delivered of the words, the pencil-and-paper form of your disorder, there is no reason why they should trouble you again. They are gone. A basin is brought, you are sick, the basin is taken away and emptied, you feel better. (Forgive these nursing-home metaphors, but they are apt.) So with writing. I shall never see again what I have heaved into the basin. It is mine no longer. Unlike writers I have known, who with a consuming interest in what they write return over and over to it like a dog to its vomit, I shall never read again what I have written. There, that is done, shall be my cry.

All this I said to myself, nearly four weeks ago, sitting with other mummies in that garden. Now, thought I, here is Charlotte Herz with nothing much to do. The time will come when she is booted out from this smug haven, this escapist Eden, and has to batter and bruise herself once more in the world. But until then she is as rich in time as woman can well be. Time does not so much hang heavy on her hands as slip away unused, leaving nothing.

Common sense put in a weak word at this, suggesting that sick women should not write. What they write must be abnormal: only the normal should interest healthy readers. And Jewish women, said common sense, should not pour themselves on to paper at

---

5   A priest of Apollo who warned the Trojans against the wooden horse left by the Greeks; killed with his twin sons by sea serpents.

all. Theirs only, in the present world, to do or die, muttonish as the inglorious six hundred of whom the English poet sang.[6] Anyhow, we have heard enough about Jews, shouts the world: yes, you are unhappy—yes, you are persecuted—yes, you are poor, homeless, stateless, in truth a very wretched people—but for God's sake don't tell us about it. Because, says the world, all this is your own fault: are you not Jews?

Yes, I am a Jew. And though homeless, stateless, almost bankrupt, I am about to have the imprudence to write of myself, of the things that broke me. I am to be deliberately absorbed in my own re-living, in speculations, interestingly idle, on why I have become what I am, or what I should have become had I turned down this side-alley instead of that, or where I go from here. I have forgotten much, for which I am deeply thankful: but what I remember I see. Comparisons with the cinema are trite but useful: my life clicks past in a more or less ordered manner with the light behind it, a stream of image. Unlike Eisenstein, who had not the necessary ruthlessness, I shall cut one hundred and fifty thousand feet of film down to a mere fifty thousand. Much of it, since I am human, will be romanticised: I am too old to believe in the intrinsic value of stark truth, or, indeed, in the intrinsic value of anything at all. Things are worthy or worthless in so far as I find them so: there is no other yard-stick.

Only in writing about myself can I find sanity. Now I am all my world, for a few weeks I am I and only I, belonging to no one, standing alone looking inward, seeing myself as something that was for ever changing as a tree changes through the year and years, yet forever in essence, in my first wood and leaves, the same tree. Charlotte looks at Charlotte in the light of an unregretting present, without shame, modesty, or reproach, seeing her, as far as she can, not as she would like to be seen but as she in life was.

6   A reference to "The Charge of the Light Brigade" by Alfred Lord Tennyson.

All this went through my head as I sat in the garden of the Welquik Nursing Home and stared at the Welquik's grass. It seemed to me that the matter was urgent, that I must start at once. My race has always been and always will be shamelessly dramatic. We get the foamier, headier flavour of life that way. Thus Rudolf Herz, my father, who died of hunger in the war, drank during that bitter time champagne out of the water carafe. Wrapping the dingy glass about with a dingier napkin (we had little soap) he solemnly poured the liquor forth so that it fell from a fantastic height to froth in the glass. We then drank each other's health in it, commenting gravely on the fine dry sparkle. Anyone watching would have thought we quaffed champagne of a priceless vintage, connoisseurs to our finger-tips.

So now, with this sense of urgency in me, and the sudden most unconvalescent uprising of my Jewish blood, I abandoned myself to drama. When the next angel in starch came floating over the lawn with orange juice, she found me fainted clean away. With my poor head sagging backward over the edge of the seat, my poor mouth hanging open, I hope I looked quite alarming. There lay I, the Woman Who Had Been Taken into the Garden Before She was Fit for It.

The angel saw me, called genteelly for another angel, for a glass of water: between them they revived me. It was all in the day's work for them. When I passed off by easy stages into a fit of hysterics they were not confounded. They like dealing with hysterics, it shows so clearly the power of the calm trained mind. When their calm minds had brought back my flitting reason I was where I wanted to be, once more in my bed staring at the whitewash. Here, a smitten woman, I begged to be allowed to stay. The garden, I shrieked, was full of things. Intoxicated by the drama, I even produced a tear: and lying wanly on my pillows felt with considerable satisfaction that it rambled across my cheek.

They conferred together and said yes, perhaps I was better here, perhaps the garden had been too much for me. Next morning

26

the doctor heard about it from low voices outside the bedroom door. He took my wrist and said, how casually, that he heard I had been out yesterday, into the garden. I closed my eyes and gave him a stunning tableau of the woman who would scream if he said that word again. "Very well," he murmured suavely. "No more garden for this child!"; and his *ha-ha!* rang hollow in the muted air, for once not confident. Another confidential chat in the corridor: I did not need to be told what they were saying. "Her age, of course, and the nature of the illness—hm, some sexual inhibition, I fancy," from the doctor: and a mere look, prim yet fathomlessly knowing, from the matron. Her knowledge of Freud, Jung and Adler lies as glassily over her mind as the starch over her round tight bosom and stomach. She knows all about sexual inhibitions in virgins of thirty-five. There could be no other explanation of my gardenphobia but this. Some shape, some form in the innocent Eden, had brought one of my endless unsavoury complexes to boiling-point: the caterpillar on the leaf, perhaps, had reminded thee of thy mother's grief. Quite natural, of course, said the doctor's and the matron's minds in unison.

Now I lie here day after day with a closed nun's face, as good as gold. When in their infrequent visits they find me writing I tell them with a girlish stare that I am writing letters. "Poor thing," they think, as they murmur: "That's nice." The sooner I get married the better, they think, eyeing Adrian with avid interest when he briefly and charmingly comes. The sooner the better, oh yes indeed. Sometimes, to please them, I begin one of my chapters: "Liebe Tante Lydia," and leave it about for a while so that the night nurse, coyly peeping when she inserts the bed-pan, can see that it is indeed a letter that I write. And then I am left to myself with a faint reading-lamp, and the long busy hours in which I can peer backward, backward along a muddled medley of years.

Even the scent of the arums that Mrs. Rowland brought me today is not unhelpful. It is a wistful scent, and to every woman the lost child who was herself is unbearably wistful. In this aroma, then, the story of Charlotte Herz begins. It begins, not in a neat Auckland nursing-home stinking of arum lilies, but in Berlin. Berlin in that brief Indian summer after the war; that little time, between the occupation and the inflation, when we in Germany had hope. If my memories of it seem heavy with nostalgia, reeking, like these damned lilies, of regret and death, remember that I have left Berlin forever, that my young life died there and I shall never see its grave. There I was young and innocently happy: here I am old and do not, perhaps, pin so much faith to happiness.

Ach Berlin! Berlin! du kleine Stadt! you dear little town in which Charlotte Herz was once so young!

Chapter 2
Im Grünen Wald

Mark how already the capital *I*s stick arrogantly up over the pages, sign-posts to egotism. For this is autobiography, whole-hearted wallowing among discarded selves. Thus wallowing, I find my sister Mitzi at twenty-three, myself at seventeen, in Berlin in 1920. Mitzi was as slim as a rush, war-starved: Tante Heidi, vast in pearls and black satin, used often to nip that meagre little backside and shriek: "*Du!* if we two were rolled together in a bag there'd be enough for three good women!" In the family laugh (Tante Heidi had money) Mitzi joined but wanly: she was sensitive about her paper thinness.

Tante Heidi, on the other hand, incessantly bemoaned her flesh. Now that the Berlin shops were beginning timidly to blossom after years of barrenness, Tante Heidi roamed through them in search of the Figure. In the West End corsetières began to wipe their plate-glass, shovel up the dead flies from the corners where they lay in blueish heaps, and to fill the windows once again. Modern stark-ness was the note in window-dressing, in 1920. A black bowl of wax water-lilies, an expanse of polished wood, one black velvet perch from which dangled one tender pink garment marked "Gelegenheit!"[1] These objects, the ideas they bred of bosoms frail as little apples, were the undoing of our Tante Heidi's financial canniness. She was forever coming back from the Tauentzien to the Landgrafenstrasse with a triumphant guilty look, forever cupping, strapping, lacing, squeezing and buttoning herself into the latest thing in controls. Generally the "Sylphide" or the "Jungeforme" lasted but half an hour or so: then ping! it went. When she found one of stouter stuff the effect was dramatic. Our Tante Heidi was translated from a broad-bellied, slim-legged, slack-breasted matron into a smart pouter pigeon, streamlined as the *Bremen*, erect, self-confident, proud. To those who knew her the tension was terrific: she might disintegrate at any moment, we held our breaths and prayed.

Beside this Tante Heidi, Mitzi looked an underfed schoolboy, her chest as flat as a board. The straightdown-in-one-piece figure, buttons on the dress giving the only hillocks, was not yet with us: Mitzi's figure was ahead of her time. Curves were still the fashion. When in the West End shops there appeared those dainty little false bosoms, twin chiffon rosettes wedded by shoulder-straps. Mitzi saw a sign from heaven. She starved herself for two weeks, amassed twelve marks, bullied me into buying her one. See me, a composed seventeen, entering the shop. In the window hangs the garment "Die Lorelei." The air is filled with a dubious scent. A fair boy with rose-pink lips lolls against the counter fingering cami-knickers. A bangle tinkles on his delicate wrist. Later, when post-war Berlin has got into its naughty stride, he too will buy "Die Lorelei." Later still, in brown shirt, he will lean against the shoulder of a Röhm.[2] As yet in 1920, he is but a gangling apprentice.

---

1 German: Opportunity.

2 Ernst Röhm (1887-1934), leader of the *Sturmabteilung* (SA) or brown shirts, the Nazi Party's first paramilitary wing, murdered on 1 July 1934 in the "Night of the Long Knives" purge.

I buy the "Lorelei." It hurts me to part with twelve good marks for the sake of Mitzi's chicken-breast. But I pay, take the parcel and, avoiding the unsexed eye of the youth, shoot back to Mitzi. In our one room at the Nollendorfplatz through which the noise of the U-Bahn tears a jagged hole once every two minutes, Mitzi strips and tries the thing on. Dressed in nothing but "Lorelei" she spins on one toe, pouting her false breasts at the mirror. She entertains ambassadors, offers cocktails to an English prince, invites compliments from a Russian grand duke. Bowing, smiling, languorously bending, Mitzi is a match for any of them. They pass, casting admiring looks behind. Pulling her face back to normal, Mitzi wheels to where I crouch on an upturned soap-box and says: "Well?"

"Pretty good. Only you'll have to be careful they don't slip. Fancy you wriggling coyly in James B.'s arms and dropping your bosom on the floor!"

"Be serious, Charlotte—will I *do*?"

"Yes, you look quite appetising."

"Charlotte, if I don't bring it off with James this time—"

"You'll manage. Only remember the Lorelei smile."

She practises the Lorelei smile, sitting not on a soap-box but on a rock in the green powerful Rhine waters, combing out hair that is gold and long. Then she takes a needle and begins to mend her last pair of silk stockings.

Whether it was "Die Lorelei" or the Lorelei smile or the surprise of both I do not know: but she landed James B. Baggerlay within the week. He was an American with money. Though in 1920 one American dollar did not as yet spell Eldorado, you could not think of eight thousand such, coming in as regular as rain every year, without watering at the mouth. Mitzi collared all this: her stock went soaring in the family market. But she never lost her head. Though blown with triumph and the thought of things to come she left nothing to chance, and married James B. before the end of March.

Because this chilly forenoon was almost the last time we sat in that miserable room with our common youth still around us, in the free unthinking intimacy of virgin sisters, I remember it sharply. I feel still the scrubby edge of the soap-box under my bare knees, I smell the Sauerkraut and Eisbein[3] which Frau Gaedtke incessantly cooked in the room below, mingling with the sweet stale scent of Mitzi's cheap face-powder. I hear the whine of the window as it swings in the February gale. We stuffed newspaper beneath to keep it tight, but it always swung loose, always the sleet seeped through on to the iron stove beneath, hissing faintly as it landed. Beside the window, under an old cotton dressing-gown spread-eagled over two nails as a curtain, hung all our clothes. The wall was old and wet, the clothes always damp. Sometimes when it was very cold we wore all our clothes at once: otherwise it hung under the dressing-gown, our meagre wardrobe, and we used to take it down, plan wild alterations, sigh, put it back again and decide not to go out after all. Now that Mitzi was bringing up all her batteries to bear on James B. she had commandeered my things to swell the slight variety of her own. I stayed at home, nursing the stove, wearing the oddest choice of garments under father's old ulster. It came from England, that ulster: the Burberry label on its greasy old collar was the first English I had ever learnt. It was made of English wool—and how we loved wool in those winter days of 1919-20. Real wool was the dizzy peak of luxury: we literally clung to it. The ulster clothed me by day and the two of us by night: it lay over our bed, we crept under it, holding our breath for fear of losing warmth, and hugged it to us. All through our childhood father in his English ulster had been winter's sign, as much a sign as the red felt half-curtains that went up in the trams on November 1st. As one of Albert Ballin's[4] promising

---

3 Corned ham hock, a German dish usually served with sauerkraut.

4 Albert Ballin (1887-1918), director of the Hamburg-America steamship line from 1899 to 1918.

young men, father had gone to England and bought the ulster. It may be that he had also shipping business which took him Londonwards in 1888: to us his sole purpose had been to buy the coat we knew so intimately. Strutting in it, when its black was still young and sooty, he had met and married my mother. On keen autumn Sundays, strolling under the twiggy shade of Unter den Linden with one small child, two small children strung between them, the young Herzes had made a neat, brilliant pair. Mother wore her dark green cloth dress with the black ball fringe round the jacket, a fur pelisse from the Blümchen work-rooms over her narrow shoulders: father wore the ulster. The brother who came between Mitzi and me died in the folds of the ulster on a station platform in Silesia during the bitter winter of 1902. They were travelling back from Grandfather Werner Blümchen's house in Königshütte, my parents and the two small children. Ulrich had asthma, choked whenever he was laid flat, coughed his little heart up at the least exertion. The train drew into Oppeln on a black frosty midnight, the snow hissing beneath the wheels in the north-east wind. Ulrich begged to be taken out, away from the engine smell, the soot, the stale cigars. Father wrapped the ulster about them both, cradled Ulrich, feebly croaking, under the cape that was already growing green. The train stayed nearly an hour at Oppeln, waiting for the south-bound express to roar grandly through. When forty, fifty minutes had gone and father was not yet back, mother laid Mitzi down on the long seat, banked her with rugs so that in her sleep she should not roll off, and climbed down the high dirty steps into the snow.

Father stood at the end of the platform with his head tilted to the stars, snow lightly powdering his beard. The child under the ulster was dead, had died in a frenzy of coughing twenty minutes before. Since then father had not moved: he had been showing Ulrich bright-belted Orion when the paroxysms began, he stayed there gazing at Orion still, knowing he had no courage to go back.

Now the guard bustled from the refreshment-room wiping his moustache. He held up the white and green signal: my parents climbed back into the train. Ulrich, wrapped still in the ulster with only his face showing, was laid on the seat foot to foot with Mitzi. For another twelve hours they travelled thus, facing the dead child and the living child, all the way back to Berlin.

Ulrich was buried alongside all the other Blümchens in the Jewish cemetery. Every fourth of January the whole family, clad in a black so profound that it hurt your eyes, went out by tram bearing flowers, stood about the very small grave. Every fourth of January, in the evening, in the apartment on the Elisabeth Ufer, my father sang "Der Erlkönig" in a weak, sweet baritone. Tears were a relief as we listened. The children wept easily, the elders painfully, with little gasping sobs, small sounds of woe that tickled their throats and gave them vague pleasure. We were a family that enjoyed its grief. "*Das—Kind—war...tot!*"—the last words died to a whisper in the hot room, stuffy with the smell of Mandelhörnchen and coffee and thick Sunday satins: away raced Tante Clara's fingers at the piano, chasing the last tinkling wistful notes till they died in stillness. To the children sitting goggle-eyed on footstools among the adult feet, uncomfortably trussed up in sailor suits, velvet dresses or woollen tartans of a violently un-highland pattern, the words seemed to be sucked from our midst by some mysterious draught, sucked into the great blue and white porcelain stove in whose niche a china Hebe poised her china teapot.

In 1915, for the first time, I had no tears at this yearly exhibition. I was an emotional Backfisch[5] of twelve, but I had no tears for poor asthmatic little Ulrich dead under the ulster, for poor father warbling Goethe. His expression of stern sorrow, my mother's gentle snufflings, left me unmoved. Perhaps the war, that new-begun catastrophe, had speeded up by a year or two my adolescent scorn.

---

5   German: Literally, fried fish, but also slang for a teenage girl.

That is the history of father's ulster, under which we shivered and snuggled night after night in 1920. The stove died down inexorably, little muffled crashes coming to us every now and then through the iron door. With each crash of a dying coal the air grew ten degrees colder. Our apprehensions of a worse cold grew livelier. We shivered, rolled in each other's arms, waiting with sick hearts for the last crash of all. But before that came we were asleep.

When we woke the snow had puddled itself through the window-crack, over and about the stove: the air was stuffy, yet like a knife in our lungs. We lay and told each other today was going to be better, and giggled sometimes if we had woken fairly warm. Mitzi had dramatic spasms at this hour: would mimic Frau Gaedtke demanding the rent, the old King of Saxony bawling from the carriage window, "*Macht Eueren Dreck alleene!*",[6] Rosa Luxembourg in Karl Liebknecht's arms imploring him to shave off his beard because it tickled when he kissed her, the Kaiserin trying to sell Queen Wilhelmina her crown in the palace at the Hague. Absurd scenes, fantastic as a child's fancy, shrewd, cruel and malicious with the wit of a young female newly awakened. Making a tent of the ulster and our meagre blanket Mitzi and I lay in the foul faint warmth spluttering with laughter into each other's faces. I laughed into the pit made by Mitzi's thin arm and bosom: little dark hairs tickled me, the smell of Mitzi's pale flesh was thick as syrup in my nose. Above me her voice, Queen Wilhelmina's voice, squeaked in execrable German: "No more than sixty-seven pfennige—I won't give more than sixty-seven pfennige!" and Mitzi's finger traced an imperial crown on my naked flank. This all seemed to us so exquisitely funny that we heaved with laughter, locked so close that our arms and legs were hardly our own, and lay waiting for another day to bring us what it could.

6   German: Do your own dirty work!, the words with which Frederick Augustus III, the last King of Saxony, abdicated in 1918.

A faint smell of chicory[7] under the door gave an edge to the air already heavy with our night's breathing. We smacked our lips, imagining fresh hot rolls larded with butter. Frau Gaedtke flung herself against the door: it crashed inwards, she slapped down at the bed-head one thick, chipped mug from which we drank in turns. Berlin coffee then was said to be made of cow-dung ground up with wood-ash: but it was hot, it slipped comfortably about in our vacant stomachs, and cupping our hands round the earthenware we had a strong illusion of warmth. I wonder how Frau Gaedtke thinks of us now—if she remembers at all? Perhaps as a couple of Jewish asps she misguidedly nursed in her bosom. Then she was too busy for much anti-Semitism: we were two thin excitable young girls, starving on clay-heavy bread, turnips and bad margarine, and she cherished us in a rough spasmodic way. On Monday she demanded the rent, threatened to bring Schupos:[8] on Tuesday she dropped in on us with a cup of nauseating bouillon made from heaven-knows-what tired livestock, told us to forget the money, she trusted us: on Wednesday it was the rent again, no bouillon: on Thursday morning two mugs of coffee and an astounding kiss. When we did pay, handing over some of the precious dollars Mitzi had manoeuvred out of James, Frau Gaedtke demanded fifty marks more, pointing to the window. We had broken the window, she screamed: sixty marks would not repair the damage. A strange, charitable, grasping woman, Frau Gaedtke—but she never grasped that extra fifty marks.

*****

---

7   Chicory was commonly used as a coffee substitute in the hardship after the war.

8   Schupo is the German equivalent of bobby—a beat policeman.

Mitzi married James B. Baggerlay on March 14th. The nuptials were somewhat thrown out of joint by the Kapp Putsch,[9] but no one could have foreseen that. Tante Cosima was blackmailed by the family into lending us her flat on the Fasanenstrasse: apart from Tante Heidi's on the Landgrafenstrasse, which was never lent to anyone, this was the only decent dwelling the Blümchen family, in those lean years, could muster. There Mitzi and I spent the night before the wedding, getting up once or twice to be sick out of pure excitement, and being struck anew, each time, by the grandeur of the surroundings. Tante Cosima's taste, like her nature, was on the warm and lavish side: the place glittered with Louis Seize gilt. It was what James called a "reg'lar love-nest." Many an honest scholar, digging in the political chit-chat of the later nineteenth century for biographical ore, has stubbed his toe on my Tante Cosima. She crops up everywhere. There was never a real scandal, but there might have been a dozen. She had never had any tact: she said what she thought when she thought it, and it took all the diplomacy of various diplomatic circles to untangle her afterwards. We could never believe that she had been beautiful; but there in the Fasanenstrasse apartment, which had seen many an indiscreet whoopee, were the photographs of various ducal and higher heads, and portraits of Tante Cosima in all her stage parts leered and ogled and swooned at us wherever we looked. Cosima Blümchen as Miss Sara Sampson, Käthchen von Heilbronn, Maria Stuart, the Bride of Messina, Minna von Barnhelm, Emilia Galotti, the Maid of Orleans, and Gretchen. This last with unreal flaxen plaits, in the first flush of her career, when the young Cosima had committed her one indiscretion from which no politician could untangle her. In the middle of the play's run she had joyfully, and, as was her nature, openly, retired for two months and borne a son.

9   An attempted coup by right-wing and militarist forces against the German government in Berlin on 13 March 1920.

The father was Georg Melchoir, who played Faust. She may have loved him, but there are limits, as Tante Lydia often said, to living one's part. The baby proved the curse of Tante Cosima's life. He grew from a black-browed child into a lumpish youth with all the little vices: from this, through easy stages, into the family rake. He drank, he wenched, he squandered: he wrote excruciating verse which the Berlin police judged, so far as they understood it at all, to be obscene: he drifted finally to London, was interned during the war, died in 1917, and bequeathed to Tante Cosima, that least maternal of women, a baby daughter whose mother nobody knew anything about. Young Cosima came squalling to Berlin in the hamper of a kindly Quaker woman in 1918, and her grandmother brought her up somehow. I was too young to remember much of the disgraceful Siegmund: I only know that he played ravishingly on the flute and looked even more beautiful drunk than sober. Which is more than can be said of many of us.

Tante Cosima, her own descendants being illegitimate and scandalous, was hardly the one to launch a young virgin like Mitzi into marriage. But hers was the only flat possible to us and she not only lent it but withdrew, grumbling in three languages, to the cramped home of Tante Clara on the Luisenufer. The U-Bahn had stopped running because there was a general strike: I believe she and young Cosima had to beg lifts in brewers' drays, which must have been a new experience even for Cosima Blümchen, but we were all too busy next day to ask her about it.

The Kapp Putsch made Mitzi's wedding hilarious and mad. There were no trams, no buses, and no U-Bahn. As for the droschkies,[10] they were all too busy carrying the everyday street traffic, at fantastic prices, to bother about wedding parties. Onkel Franz Laddach, who was to have called for the bride in a carriage twined with white satin, telephoned to say: "Wait until I come.

---

10   German form of the Russian droshky, an open carriage.

I'll get you something else as soon as I can." But the telephone had also struck, we heard not a tinkle. Mitzi in her white satin, I in my new blue cloth coat and skirt, set out to walk to the Alexanderplatz. I carried over my arm the old ulster, now bottle-green: but Mitzi hysterically refused to wear it. The day entitled her to white satin, if not to a bridal carriage. We had about four miles to walk. Mitzi wept most of the way, not because she minded having to walk through Berlin in a white satin wedding dress on a March morning, but because she was so happy at getting married at all. She was twenty-three, and had been haunted for years by spinsterhood, that spectre of all Jewish women. So she walked and wept, dribbling tears on her satin: and I hopped alongside in a pair of perfectly new shoes which hurt like fury.

At the Potsdamerplatz it began to rain. We stood by the newspaper kiosk and waited for it to finish. There was a regular circus going on at the Platz. People walking to work surged over the roadway like beetles making blindly for their holes: people thrown out of work by the strike lounged and jeered, ripe for any evil. There was a glaze of uneasiness, uncertainty, over all the silly faces. All the resurrected vehicles of Berlin creaked past, filled with people and merchandise that had to be got somewhere somehow. A fantastic red wagon, tied together with blind-cord and barbed wire, ambled in from the Linkstrasse and halted at the tram stop. Painted on its flank, in tipsy capitals, was *Potsdamer Bhf.—Wittenberg Pl. nur I Rm.* People hesitated, suspecting a joke. But the driver sat stolidly above his flea-bitten horse and bawled: "Only a mark. Only a mark! Get you there quicker than the tram!" Finally, like timid hares creeping from their holes, two fur-wrapped women with shopping bags clambered up and sat high on the high-backed seat. The loafers gathered closer. Bright in the cheeks of the two women burned an apprehensive blush, the fear that something unpleasant was about to happen. It was. The loafers shouted for the driver to get down. Not he, not he! puffed the fat one; a hundred guns would not blow him from his seat, no, not if Noske[11] himself were behind them. The crowd tittered, but they were grim enough. They shouted to the two women to get down. Cackle—cackle—cackle! went the indignant hens, putting their faces together and making violent gestures with their shopping-bags. Two or three loafers, leaning now at its side, rocked the wagon. The women let out an ear-splitting yell, stood up, dived into the crowd stomach-downwards. The men caught them, set them upright, advised them to do their shopping on the Leipzigerstrasse and mix no longer with strike-breakers.

Gobbling, a brace of plushy turkey-hens, the women shot off into the blessed haven of the women's lavatory, waddled indignantly downwards into its bowels.

The crowd overturned the wagon quietly, efficiently, men going about their everyday tasks. The driver fell out among them, bouncing like a plump sack of meal. As we came from our shelter and held out upturned palms to see how the rain did, they were setting fire to the gay old red wagon. It burned well, being lined with straw. There was a cheerful warm blaze, the only warmth in view, as we went on to the wedding.

Mitzi had begun once more to cry at the thought of getting married at last. That, with the drizzle, was making her satin look utterly pock-marked. Our stomachs rumbled loudly as we walked: we had had no more than a cup of coffee at breakfast. We hurried desperately on through the street, clutching our waists.

"I can't stand this!" sobbed Mitzi at the Spittelmarkt. "I *must* eat something!" She paused to sniff the air: there is always a delicious smell of roasting coffee round these parts, and it caught us full amidships, making our stomachs rumble more than ever.

"Just a roll and some honey!" said Mitzi wistfully, stroking her satin middle with a very dirty hand.

11   Gustav Noske (1868-1946), the first defence minister of the Weimar Republic.

40

We went into the Café Kühn with our two marks, our few tinkling groschen, and sat down by the central heating. The waitress looked at us avidly, but she had seen some odd things in the last few years and was probably surprise-proof.

"Getting married?"

"Yes," said Mitzi, and started to weep again into her coffee-cup.

"Don't talk to her," I said, "she's hysterical. Have you an umbrella you could lend us?"

"Do I look as if I had an umbrella?" said she, quite indignant.

"No," said I, and she went back to her cash-desk and dug furiously into her scalp with a hair-pin.

Outside it rained harder than ever. The swing-door whirled open, letting in for a second the sound of wetness pouring on asphalt and the plash of wheels in puddles—letting in also a creature in a thick British warm, a lovely thing, a British officer. The entire British army could not have had a more galvanising effect. Mitzi and the waitress stiffened as one woman: I have never seen a girl brighten as that frowsy-smelling bit behind the counter now did. She leaned over so that you could see clear down her V-neck to her waist, and cooed: "Coffee, sirr? Good-day! Good-day!" till it sickened you to watch her.

"Coffee," said the officer, blushing at so much flesh. He sat down just behind Mitzi, studying her white satin back in a stolid pale-eyed surprise.

"Pull yourself together," I whispered, "the army's got its eye on you."

Mitzi giggled weakly. It was anyhow a weak joke. It amused us, the way those khaki, twig-legged creatures bounced around Berlin finding out how much we Germans could pay for losing the war. They were like new schoolmasters, scared to death of unpleasantness, yearning to be loved, yet so bent on Duty that their faces were rigidly odious with it. And they had their noses in all the corners of our life. "You mustn't touch that—the army's

41

got its eye on you!" one of us would whoop if the other took out a piece of bread to gnaw in the room at Frau Gaedtke's. "You can't have that, they want it for the British Museum!" And then we giggled ourselves sick, sitting on the soap-box sharing the hunk of evil-smelling stuff that in those days had clay in it for makeweight, and lay in your stomach like a lump of earthenware.

Mitzi now giggled again, sniffed back some tears, and turned to look at the Army. He blushed furiously, as the English do when you, not they, are doing the staring; switching his eyes to his coffee-cup he studied it as if he could read all wisdom therein. But as soon as Mitzi stopped looking, he stared again, drinking in all the details of her limp veil, her spotted satin, her bouquet wrapped up against the weather in a yellowed *Vossische Zeitung*.[12] He'd never seen anything like this before: you could see him writing it all home in a letter to his mother.

We gulped down the last of our coffee, chased the last crumb of bread round the plate with licked fingers, looked at each other, and sighed. The rain came down now in sheets, venomously spattering: a fusillade of rain blew in at the door as it twirled to admit another customer. Mitzi stared beyond him, dropped her eyes to mine, and winked. Mitzi's wink was the very devil, but nothing to what generally followed it. The last time she had winked at me we had ended up by being put out of the Romanisches Café, politely but oh! so very firmly, by the manager. Now, she put her face to rights, smoothed her hair, arranged her veil. Then slowly, languidly, like a wet lily, she rose to her feet. The pale innocent eyes of the Englishman widened as he saw how slender she was. Mitzi always looked better standing: the line from hip to ankle was beautiful, a firm curve of pure temptation. Leaning now against

---

12   The *Vossische Zeitung* (Voss's Newspaper) was the oldest newspaper in Berlin, dating from the 17th century. Representing the interests of the liberal middle class, it was forced by Nazi censorship to close in March 1934.

the counter, paying the bill with my two marks, she let him have it full in the eye.

Then in English, in her best Lady Windermere manner, she said to me:

"We had better be going, dear, if you're quite ready." The officer smacked his cup down, got to his feet.

"You're English!" he cried.

"Naturally not," said Mitzi coldly.

"She marries an American mister," I put in, feeling that her appearance needed some explanation.

"How—how *nice*," he stammered.

"*Eine Mark zehn!*" barked the waitress, slapping down the change and giving Mitzi a serpent look. But my sister was not to be quenched by all the embittered waitresses in Berlin.

"Yes, I'm getting married today. Such a day to choose, is it not? But we shall manage it. The Alexanderplatz (she sighed, looking at her little muddy white satin feet) "is not so *very* far."

"You're not walking?"

"What else can we do?"

She made for the door, a picture of virginal suffering, though somewhat damp.

"Oh, I say!" called the poor dunderhead, pursuing her. "I've got a cab—I should be happy—I mean, I don't know if you'd care to—"

"I should," said Mitzi briskly; "where is it?"

The driver gaped, seeing the British Army come out of the Café Kühn with a white satin bride draped over its arm. James B. was more impassive. I often wonder what he thought. He stood there on the Rathaus steps, chewing gum, waiting with a certain dry *savoir faire* for the bride he felt sure would come. In spite of Kapp and his Putsch the bride was sure to come. When the bride in rain-spotted satin, a rain-limp veil, tripped out of a droschky on the arm of an English officer, James B. did not bat an eyelid. The Englishman blushed and stammered, but no blood glowed under

James B.'s guinea-yellow skin. His approach to all questions was economic: he had good reason to be pretty sure of Mitzi.

So Mitzi was married, as quickly as possible, the registrar being technically out on strike and not anxious to be caught blacklegging. We went back, in the oddest collection of vehicles, to the Fasanenstrasse. Over the door Tante Cosima had skittishly hung a cardboard bassinet with a celluloid baby in it. The family giggled furtively, eyeing James B.: but that, too, the poker-faced barbarian could take in his stride.

The Englishman was swept into the party fatalistically, as part of the war's aftermath. We spoke all the English we knew, pressed food and drink upon him. Filled with Onkel Franz's precious Moselwein he became positively sparky. His German was of the *Der Hund und Die Katze sitzen nie zusammen*[13] variety, but it went down pretty well. We were all so glad to have the knot safely tied round Mitzi that we would have thought any oaf a wit. When he stood up on a chair between the Ming vase full of pampas grass and a weary Macquartsbouquet much treasured by Tante Cosima, and recited bits of *Alice in Wonderland*, we laughed uproariously. He beamed on us and began all over again, in an even shriller falsetto. But Onkel Franz had started a rival speech in another corner, and no one listened to Alice but myself. By then I was half tipsy. I climbed the chair, laid my head on his khaki shoulder and mournfully chanted the words after him.

> I passed by his garden and marked with one eye
> How the Owl and the Panther were sharing a pie;
> The Panther took pie-crust, and gravy, and meat,
> While the Owl had the dish as its share of the treat...

---

13   German. Literally, The dog and the cat don't sit together, it means the Englishman's German is basic and sounds awkward to the native speakers.

44

There was something further about pocketing spoons, which we both thought very funny, the peak of wit—but I have forgotten how it went. We repeated the first four lines over and over again: they satisfied our maudlin needs. Why, I have wondered since, does the Englishman under an emotional strain dive always for this incomprehensible girl child and her adventures among rabbits? It is a reflex action: perhaps no use to ask them "why?"

After the chanting we both wept. I think he cannot have been much older than I. Anyhow, we wept in bubbling chorus, over the dusty-smelling Macquartsbouquet, until I had to dress Mitzi for her wedding journey. Too maudlin to know that I was losing her forever, I did up numberless little cloth buttons on her going-away dress. The fashion then was for buttons down the back: it must have felt like sitting in a pea-pod. When the buttons were done, the cloche hat rammed down, we clung for a moment and then parted silently, despairing and calm.

It was all over. A droschky, miraculously found, had borne them both away under the leafless twigs of the Kurfürstendamm. Mitzi's hand fluttered from the window clutching a handkerchief I knew was wet. The Englishman's arm tightened round my waist. I expect he called me "little girl"—most Englishmen do. We turned our backs on the awful disorder of the apartment, where the family, weeping heartily, were busy finishing off the wedding breakfast, and went off in another droschky to the dripping Tiergarten. Here we jogged about for almost an hour, clasped damply in each other's arms. He told me his life history: I dare say it was a relief to him, but I forgot it as soon as heard. The bubbling elation of being tipsy ebbed: I was cold, sick and miserable.

At some point in our confidences he learned that I was Jewish. Already bored with me, as I with him, he gave me a scowling red-rimmed blink.

"In England decent—I mean, lots of people—don't like Jews."

"Why should we care? We're the most cultured people in the world."

"Don't talk nonsense: what has that to do with it? You don't look Jewish, anyway."

I chose to be furious with him for thinking me Gentile because my hair was chestnut brown, my eyes blue. Then remembering those typical Jewesses, Berta and Brigitta Seligmann, sallow virgins with great drooping noses, I preened myself. Vanity and racial pride fought their first battle, there in the smelly cab. Vanity won. I smiled alluringly at my Englishman, raised my thick brown lashes in a way I found fetching, and murmured: "Why don't I look like a Jewess?"

"Come to think of it," he remarked coolly, "you do."

We sat on, morose and gloomy. Onkel Franz's Moselle had not been quite potent enough. I have often speculated since on where I might be now if we had drunk another glass or two. I might now be the mother of toothy brats, Mrs.—, but I do not know the man's name. He came and he went, on Mitzi's wedding day: he was no more than a khaki blur who could not carry his liquor. We parted furtively at the edge of the Tiergarten, for he dared not drive up to the Adlon with a German Jewess. Though but seventeen, I had seen some life: I made him pay for the droschky right back to the Fasanenstrasse. It cost him a pretty penny: I lolled luxuriously through the strike-ravaged streets, wishing I knew how to be really sinful.

And now, quite sober, I realised that there was no Mitzi, nor ever would be again. In the flat the wedding litter was piled high: Tante Cosima roved like a vulture among the ruins, groaning of money spent.

*****

The thin big-eyed Mitzi Herz who bought artificial breasts, flirted with anything in trousers, chattered and laughed with me in a small

46

miserable cold room, huddled with me under the old ulster in Berlin, in 1920, has now for nearly twenty years been Mrs. James Baggerlay of Syracuse, N.Y. I have never seen her since. We write affectionately, as parted sisters do, about nothing that really matters to either of us. She has become plump and brisk: we take it for granted she is happy.

When she had gone there was no competition among the family for me, her orphaned sister. Duty pricked forward a few aunts to make tentative offers. Tante Ricarda Blümchen, now Mme. Alfred Doucet, wrote from Paris in a startling violet ink. Blood, she supposed, was thicker than water: feeling in France was dying out: if I learned French properly so as not to offend with a thick German accent, I might go as Haustochter[14] to her for a while. Or I might not, thought I, politely replying. Berlin to a seventeen-year-old was more exciting. The war years dropped like rotten plums behind us, the blockade was lifted, life began to flow. Besides, in Paris Tante Ricarda would press me into the arms of the first possible parti, perhaps some dull suitable poilu[15] with a small black moustache and a passion for economical bouillon: in Berlin I did my own hunting. Each male might be a James B. Baggerlay, less coarse, less crassly gentile, but still the fount of all good things, the universal provider. I began the chase with relish, demurely accepting Tante Clara's kind but meagre offer of the Mädchenzimmer[16] in her flat on the Luisenufer. It was understood that the Mädchenzimmer would not see me for long: I was to marry something rich as soon as possible.

Besides those seductive twins Berta and Brigitta (straight from an Assyrian frieze, the two of them) Tante Clara had a son,

---

14 German: Literally, house daughter, meaning something like a maid or au pair, and often specifically when the individual is a relative considered of lower status.

15 An ordinary French soldier.

16 The smallest bedroom in an apartment, usually given to the maid.

Kurt. The lively girls, plain as parrots and fizzling with energy, ran a marriage bureau on the Nürnbergerstrasse. Like other strident virgins, they burned with a desire to marry off everyone within range. Also with the need to make money: I honestly do not know which idea swelled uppermost in their grasshopper minds. They yearned above all to try their prentice hands on me: I was so much guinea-pig to Berta and Brigitta. Back they came in the evenings to press upon me titbits from their growing dossiers.

"Listen, Charlotte, here's what you want. 'Widower, Christian, with good government position, wishes meet refined young lady view friendship, marriage: two children'."

"I don't like other people's children, and I'll stick to the Jews, thank you."

"Quite right, meine Liebe," approved Tante Clara, for whom I had said it, not caring one tittle in my hard young avarice whether the man I hooked be Jew, Gentile, Buddhist, Moslem or Aztec so long as he were rich. "Quite right. Jewish men make the best husbands. They're so thoughtful, almost like a woman. Look at my Max: when we first married..."

"Oh, Mama, not *that* story again!" screamed Brigitta. "Now listen, Charlotte, here's just the thing..."

On it went: widowers with children, widowers with no children, bachelors of fifty who wanted refined ladies of forty-five, reckless bachelors of forty who merely wanted slim blondes between eighteen and twenty-one. A pitiful troupe. But I was too young to feel pathos. To me it was all natural enough. Deep in every Jewess is the fear of spinsterhood: single, she knows herself a failure. But Berta's lists, Brigitta's enthusiasms, were irritating: the man I wanted and meant to get would not come to me like a sale's remnant, through the clippings of Geschwister Seligmann's Heiratsbüro.[17] I was better-looking than Mitzi. Though they teased me

---

17   German: the Seligmann Sister's Marriage Agency.

about my tawny colouring, calling me Veitel Itzig after Freytag's odious little Jew-boy,[18] I was handsomer than Mitzi. Brainless Mitzi had caught a wealthy American; I meant to use my brains and do better still.

I confess I look back on this young thing, this eager seeking Charlotte Herz, with wistful affection. She was not a lovable child, but she is dear to me now. She had a great fresh appetite for life. Like an innocent night-gowned infant peering through the door-chink at the dishes of an adult feast, she poked a finger into this one and that one, sucking it to try. Nothing that she found in any dish, however horrid, stopped her from trying the next. She had to try everything, so that she might know. Years later when I first saw, in a Mickey Mouse film, the eager Pluto—when I saw him, snout pressed to ground, snuffing up new odours, pursuing that avid nose through disaster after disaster, eternally led astray by that seeking nose, getting it nipped by pliers, in mangles, by saucy birds, I thought: "There is Charlotte in 1920, 1923. The young Pluto, the inquisitive hound." And I yearned back, with a sentimental pain, to that female stripling so blindly sniffing at life.

For which reason, because no woman of thirty-five can look objectively upon her seventeen-year-old self, I do not propose to look much longer. She is dead, young Charlotte, and in death smells too sweet. She was in her time hungry, sated, lonely, socia-ble, discontented, blissfully happy, ready for suicide, fiercely virginal for no cause whatever, wildly loose the next moment with as little reason. She thought herself in love a dozen times, found with pleasure that she was not, that she was free, free to fall in love again. She discovered in herself a frenzied urge to Do Something, and worked awhile with the Quakers relieving hunger with tin bowls of soup, improving her English. Then she

18   Veitel Itzig is a Jewish character and the villain in Gustav Freytag's novel *Soll und Haben* [Debit and Credit] (1855).

must have money, she must make thousands. She hired her-self out to a tourist bureau on the Friedrichstrasse, took gaping imbeciles, mainly American, about Berlin at one mark per head. With the inflation each American head was worth thousands of marks, which in their turn were worth nothing. Despite presents of American soap, American cigarettes, American silk stockings, Charlotte at this time made but a bare living. One or two of the Americans expressed a desire to sleep with her, naturally at her own expense: these and other advances were repulsed. Such affairs do not get a girl any farther. And through it all she stayed virgin, she grew shrewder, she was still very young. Marriage was no longer the only end. It was like woollen underwear, desirable in middle life but not necessary to the young. Not yet, at any rate, thought Charlotte at twenty, not yet. And she went her airy way unheeded by anything save poverty.

*****

I was in and out of love so often in my very young days that no one was much shattered when I fell in love with Cousin Kurt. My other lads had done most of the wooing, Kurt seemed indifferent: but I knew he would succumb. And he was definitely attractive, a lean hollow-eyed cynic, incalculable, moody, with four years' war behind him, a piece of British shrapnel in his body still. Mysterious little bit of metal, cruising around within Kurt! At last, smoothed by its journeyings, it dropped from the back of his mouth, he coughed it forward, rejoiced over it, and had it made into a truly hideous brooch for Gisela. But this was in 1927, when I was no longer in love with him. In 1923 the presence of the shrapnel only made him more intriguing, a kind of bran pie. He had come back from hospital in March to the tiny flat on the Luisenufer: it had been too small when Tante Clara, the twins and I were in it: now, with Kurt sleeping on the sitting-room couch, we were large hens in a small coop. We lived in a state of needful intimacy. Coming back late at night from the tourist bureau I would find Kurt sprawling under the lamp reading Stefan Zweig:[19] creeping off to work early in the morning I passed sleeping Kurt among his army blankets, took care to look the other way (for no one should be stared at asleep, defenceless), and looked back from the door in a spasm of tenderness. He never slept with his mouth open, like Onkel Franz Levin. He would be fine to sleep with, better than any of the others, thought I who had not yet slept with any man, as I clattered down the dank cold steps into the frosty street.

Then on Sundays, blessed Sundays, we had the day together, Berta, Brigitta, Kurt and I. We lay abed till lying bored us, then made weak coffee, took in the rolls from the linen bag hung outside the door, chewed them as we sprawled over chairs or beds reading the weekend section of the *Frankfurter*. Things were desperate, we hardly knew from day to day what our money would be worth. Kurt had lost his first job and could find no other. The state of the marriage market was so parlous that Berta and Brigitta despaired of being cupids. But we were young, we enjoyed ourselves, and let Tante Clara do the worrying. There we sat amongst the litter of coffee-cups, rolls and newspaper: Kurt in his army nightshirt with a blanket upon him for decency, the twins in the newest, flimsiest, cheapest nighties the Tauentzienstrasse offered, I in some wicked black satin things Mitzi had sent from New York. We drank our chicory coffee, gnawed our rolls, read out jokes to one another, roared with laughter, and watched through the wide open windows the lazy clouds go past. It was Sunday, we lazed away the hours, nothing mattered. But round about noon we would go suddenly mad with energy, throw ourselves into our clothes, pack all the food we could find into Kurt's haversack, troop downstairs

---

19   Stefan Zweig (1881-1942), an Austrian Jewish writer whose works were banned by the Nazis.

and out into the Luisenufer. If we had money we went as far as Potsdam on one of the white steamers from the Jannowitzbrücke: more often we had not, and could only muster the underground fare to the Grunewald and back. There were about a dozen of us young ones, recklessly poor, who lived in the sedate old streets of Frederick the Great round the Michaelkirche. Boys and girls who had been babies with Mitzi and me when we lived opposite on the Elisabethufer: young Weissbaums, Kahns, Ludwigs, Grünfeldts, all undernourished, poor as mice, and, on Sundays, hysterically gay. As we flung out of the door into the hot bright sunshine we yodelled up and down the rows of old, grave solid houses. Answering yodels rang out from Willi Ludwig on the balcony three floors up at Number 27: from Gertrud Grünfeldt at Number 40, three noisy Kahn boys on the Michaelkirchplatz, two pretty Weissbaums next door to our old house on the opposite Ufer. They all called down to us: "Wait! Wait! I won't be a minute!" Willi, sunbathing on the balcony in nothing but his night-shirt, popped back out of sight with a flicker of thin legs: Gertrud came to her window in her petticoat bodice, piling up her mat of raven hair. We waited, champing like impatient horses. Shimmering under the sun lay the wide Luisenufer: the young trees were sprouting, the Michaelkirche at the far end already skirted in great bushes of mauve lilac. We shrieked rude witticisms upwards at Gertrud's curtains, at the smallest Weissbaum, who was too young to come with us and dangled with its hair in curl-papers from the iron balcony, imploring to be taken just for today. Now we are all assembled, last of all Gertrud panting stoutly, her hair plaited thick on her kind stupid head. At the Michaelkirchplatz we yodel hideously for Mückichen who squeals back, hopping with excitement, from his mother's balcony on the Engelufer. Mückichen was a small, dusty-haired, spindle-legged child who buzzed like a very little gnat: he was our pet, our mascot, our victim. He had to be kept in order, poor unoffending lamb: never was a child so boisterously bullied. On the U-Bahn: "Stand *up*, Mückichen, and give the lady your seat—Get *up*, Mückichen, remember you're a gentleman!" At the Wannsee station: "Mückichen, carry my rucksack while I do my hair" (a shower of hair-pins from Gertrud, who must have two dozen at least in her plaits). In the wood: "Mückichen, Mückichen! don't drag your feet like that, walk properly!" Luckily, he was a simple child, adoring us all. I wonder what he is now, poor tough rickety little Mückichen with a genius for getting buffeted.

Every Sunday that summer we went out to the Grunewald. Perhaps there were rainy Sundays, but I have forgotten them. When we had a little money we hired boats and rowed hilariously out into the Wannsee, the Havel, then stopped rowing, lay flat in the bottom of the craft mooning at the hot sky, the lovely sun, talking in scraps, or just sleeping. Mückichen was a water brat and splashed about in his tiny striped drawers, hauling himself up over the gunwale when he was tired, clambering in over our faces, shaking himself over us like a perverse terrier. "Mückichen, keep off, you little swine! Get out!" and there was Gertrud with her only summer dress wet and stained from the impact of Mückichen's dripping little bottom. "Take it off," suggested Kurt, and Gertrud, blushing at our jeers, took it off to reveal a white starched petticoat bodice, foaming with Swiss embroidery, a tucked petticoat which must surely have grown up with her grandmother.

Sometimes we all bathed, shrieking and yelling, flinging up our arms and pretending to drown so that the handsome heroes sipping coffee at the Schwedischer Pavillon should plunge in to rescue us. But the only people who paid any attention were the boat attendants, surly unimpressionable men who bawled at us to stop that damned noise and look where our boats were drifting. Then wet, exhausted, drained by laughter, we clambered in once more, rowed a little, lay once more in the eye of the sun to watch the yachts and the steamers plying along the Havel to Potsdam with loads of smug moneyed persons aboard. If only some of them would fall in! we often thought, watching the white steamers go, fixing our evil thoughts on immaculate spooning couples leaning at the rail, seeing in lustful imagination the rail giving way, the smart white-silk flapper and the dandy man in pale grey go flopping to their sartorial ruin. How they would have shrieked and spouted, how we should have laughed! But the steamers passed on, rocking us in their backwash; and no one ever fell in. We lay browning in the sun, raked by the supercilious eyes of persons going to Potsdam, and were gloriously happy.

How cruelly, how ruthlessly, we teased Willi Ludwig and Anne-Lise Weissbaum, who were lovers, very young, very sure that love would last. We taunted them with having slept together; they never answered, smiling secretly at one another, turning from us to the security of one another's eyes: and later, when the sun began slowly to fall behind the dreaming pines, they would wander off hand in hand and be lost to us till next Sunday. Berta and Brigitta sighed after them, mourning lost custom: for of what use was a Heiratsbüro to Anne-Lise and Willi, who had so fatally made up their innocent young minds? Kurt, older than us all, laughed at them gently for sticking so leech-like to one another, for seeing nothing ahead but marriage when they were old enough. Kurt then did not believe in love and marriage: he read Shaw, Schnitzler, Zweig, all the sceptical moderns. The only sensible thing, preached Kurt, was to take one's pleasure as one fancied and damn the cost.

"Variety," he proclaimed, lying on his back with his brown arms under his head, "is the only thing that never stales. You poor mutts, why don't you try it? Now if you slept with me, Anne-Lise, and Willi slept with the twins, you'd both be the better for the change."

Anne-Lise, who had a white-skinned, gentile mother from Hanover, blushed a blueish-pink and turned to Willi, who was plainly appalled at the picture of himself between the lively Seligmann women.

"Kurt, you are *awful*!" squealed Berta and Brigitta, sighing regretfully, "you do say the most *awful* things!"

The rest of us looked admiringly at Kurt, who had come back from the war, knew all about love, and said such awful things. And Kurt smiled slowly, mysteriously, the man of the world, while Mückichen clambered adoring over his feet, draping his ankles round about with flower wreaths. It was a Sunday in June: we lay in a gentle meadow on the Lindenwerder Insel in the afternoon sunlight under lime trees tasselled with sweet hanging flowerlets. Then, the Lindenwerder Insel was not very popular: there were no crowds. There was a little house where we could get hot water for our coffee; a little boatshed, a few dilapidated boats, some hens and a wistful lonely cow. For the rest, the island was no more than grass, a grove of lime-trees, some sedge-fringed pebbles by the water's edge, and beyond them the great calm breast of the Havel stretching away to the farther shore, to the low hills by Gatow. We lay there in the grass, deliberately waiting for Abendbrot till our hunger overpowered us, and lazily teased one another, blinking sideways at the familiar faces in the mellowing light. Mückichen buzzed here and there gathering flowers and grasses for Kurt's adornment. Soon Kurt would look like a sacrificial heifer, garlanded about with forget-me-nots, willow herb, buttercups and tiny salmon-red pimpernels.

"Sing, somebody."

Gertrud began to sing. She had a lovely heart-wringing soprano voice, light as champagne, and hoped therewith to win Kurt's heart. Up sprang her voice in the Swabian melody which we all loved: when she had finished the first verse we joined in with her, humming when the words escaped us, making a great deal of noise because our young stomachs were so empty.

Denn wenn es zwei Sterne wären
Schaute Töffel wohl hinein
Und ich wolt's ihm auch night wehren
Sollt' ich selbst der Himmel sein!
Aber so verstohlen blicket
Man nicht zu den Sternen hin;
Und was mich im Herzen drücket
Ist auch nicht im Himmel drin![20]

"*Ist auch nicht im Himmel drin, ist auch nicht im Himmel drin!*" piped Mückichen to a tune all his own, sticking an ox-eye daisy behind Kurt's ear.

"What do you know about heaven, du Lümmel?[21] Get away for God's sake and stop tickling me!" cried Kurt, flinging the child off with one arm, plucking the daisy from his ear and chewing up the stalk. But as soon as his arm dropped Mückichen came back again, like the little gadfly that he was.

I wished that I dared plague Kurt so. I picked another daisy, leaning over and pushed it behind his ear. Slyly he pulled away my supporting arm, and falling across him I lay there for a dizzy minute on his breast. If I had been Anne-Lise I should have blushed beetroot, but thank heaven my skin is the unblushing kind. While my heart pounded in my ears I got up, managed to laugh as the others laughed and tweaked the daisy to a saucier angle. So far I had been a match for any man I met: not now, not with Kurt.

---

20   From "Blödigkeit," a Swabian folk song:
        For if there were two stars,
        Töffel would look into them,
        And I wouldn't stop him,
        Even if I were the sky myself
        But one doesn't look at the stars so furtively,
        And what weighs on my heart
        Isn't the sky in there either.

21   German: You rascal.

For hours afterwards, against my breast, I felt his hard impact, the hard beat of his heart as it lay for only a minute under mine.

"Why on earth do you keep stroking yourself, Charlotte?"

"I wasn't."

"Yes, you were, you keep doing this—" and Berta laid her plump hand on her plumper breast with a baroque gesture.

"Rubbish," I said, annoyed. I clung to Gertrud all the way home: she would notice nothing. Dear Gertrud, even if my odd fancy were real, if Kurt's heart beat still over mine, hanging there for all the world to see, she would never have noticed. We called her cotton-wool—she was so dense, so safe, so dull.

All that summer we worked through the long grinding week-days, played like children on Sundays. About us the mark surged to fantastic heights; in the Ruhr the French faced passive resistance: Bavaria was a choppy sea of unrest, seething with hatred and envy of Prussia, that stiff bloodless Beamter.[22] The whole of Germany was fevered. We did not know which way to go: we had no light, no sign-posts. All this on workdays, when we were adults trying not to starve: on Sundays, plunging into the Wannsee from our boats, singing as we walked under the thick shade of the beeches, under the swaying pines, we did not give a damn for Cuno, Stresemann or the bogey M. Poincaré.[23] They were not here, in the Grunewald. September came, a sultry September, and the Grunewald began to look woefully old, raddled, tired: October, and the leaves, dry and sapless, fell slowly around us, we marched over dead leaves, dead burnt-up grass, under branches that were suddenly naked. But we could not bear to leave it, to

---

22 A German civil servant with special legal privileges.

23 Wilhelm Cuno (1876-1933), Chancellor of Germany 22 November 1922 - 12 August 1923; Gustav Stresemann (1878-1929), Chancellor of Germany 13 August - 30 November 1923. As Prime Minister of France, Raymond Poincaré (1860-1934) ordered the occupation of the Ruhr on 11 January 1923.

say that winter was steadily coming. Heaven gave us suddenly a perfect Indian summer, a week of breathless tender air, bright sunshine, skies as blue as speedwell. All that week we strained at our jobs, longing to be out and away, fretting at our office stools, our cramped desks, dusty fly-spotted windows. On Saturday night, as the lights of the Luisenufer went out one by one, you could almost have heard breath being held at Weissbaums, Ludwigs, Kahns, Grünfeldts, Seligmanns. Would the weather hold over Sunday—would it? It did. Sunday dawned bland as a baby's eye: the earth was crisply filmed with frost which melted as we choked down our coffee, and lay, when we rushed along the Ufer, in dark pools of wet among the dying chrysanthemums. Our voices rang out on the heady, chilly air. It was colder than it had been all the week, but the sun shone, the air went to our heads; we whooped up and down under Willi's balcony where Willi's mother tenderly sponged her India-rubber plants: we shouted remarks up to Gertrud which brought her furiously blushing to the window with her hair down her back. By the Michaelkirche, under the leafless lilacs, Mückichen hopped from leg to leg odiously caterwauling. He wore his winter cap of scarlet wool, and we knew as we raced towards him that Mückichen's mother was right: winter was here, this Sunday in the Grunewald would be our last. Till next summer, of course: we did not think of change. Next summer would be as this, a string of halcyon Sundays: now here was our last of 1923 and ourselves hurrying to seize it, pouring down the steps into the Neanderstrasse station, crowding into a crowded carriage, dangling on straps and laughing for no reason at all into each other's careless faces.

The Grunewald was lonely, miles of great naked trees to which a few leaves still clung despairing, patches of dark pine under which the air was dank, cold, smelling of slow decay. Our voices echoed in the empty avenues; the sound of our feet crashing through the dead leaves, the broken twigs, rang up and down the little hills. But the sky was tender and miraculous, clear blue: a few very small crisp clouds hung over the dark far shores by the Havel.

We walked all day. Sometimes we sang, sometimes we talked, sometimes we simply streamed in and out among the trees yelling at one another. At home, in Berlin, our old folk were shaking their dewlaps over France, Bavaria, the incalculable mark: but to us nothing mattered now. Passive resistance in the Ruhr was costing us more marks daily than ever the war had done: what did we care? We had not a hand in either. Ludendorff[24] might be up to some dirty work in München but we gave not a fig for him and his plottings. As for Hitler, we had never heard of him, or if we had we had forgotten. Our hero for the day was Smuts of Africa:[25] Smuts who championed us briefly against France. Him we toasted, in terrible coffee, at one of the tiny restaurants near the Krummelanke. "To you, General Smuts!" cried Kurt, raising the loathsome draught in its thick chipped white cup. We stood dramatically, yelling: "Germany salutes the General!" What had he said? It seems mild enough now, but then it was terrific. Remember, an enemy speaks. "In the question of the Ruhr, a very heavy responsibility lies upon France before the bar of history." Just that, no more! Quiet, moderate, sane, in a world full of raving words. The phrase rang through Germany, more rousing than a bugle-call. And standing by the filthy wooden table under the trees, waving mugs of tepid coffee, we cried Prosit! to the General, then sat down flushed and happy to our black bread and our Kümmelkäse.

In the afternoon, still in sunshine, we went up to the Kaiser Wilhelm Turm, that tasteless pile that ruins the little dark green

---

24   Erich Ludendorff (1865-1937), German general who took a leading role in Adolf Hitler's attempt to seize power in Bavaria, the Beer Hall Putsch of 8 November 1923 in München [Munich].

25   Field Marshal Jan Smuts (1870-1950), leader of the Boer forces during the Boer War (1899-1902) and second Prime Minister of South Africa, 1919-1924.

hill above the Havel. The place stood like Sleeping Beauty's palace, dreaming and deserted. The iron tables were tipped on their sides with chairs piled round them: the great hall with its grisly statues stank, squealed Mückichen, bolting from it, of the dead. We bullied the caretaker's wife into giving us coffee: Kurt had newly got a job in Magdeburg and large-handedly celebrated, paying for us all with two marks borrowed from the twins. We sat outside, daring the grim table-strewn spaces that in summer were so bustling and lively. Leaves dropped sadly about us, sleepy insects crawled in the damp branches and dangled on fine threads into our cups. The caretaker's wife, impressed by our temerity and the noise we made, produced an aged apple-cake on a tin plate. It was blue with mould but we devoured it, feeling that this and the grey coffee were fitting salutes to our Grunewald before the winter nipped in on us. We drank to next summer, to a rendezvous here, under the Kaiser Wilhelm Turm, on the first Sunday in May.

"Bring the baby-carriage!" cried Kurt largely to Anne-Lise: then, seeing the poor child's eyes already swimming, plunged into less wounding jokes. That little affair was, like the season, edged now with a wintry chill: Willi too had got a job, in his uncle's hotel in Switzerland; and to Anne-Lise's young mind Basel was as far away as Mars.

It was cold under the trees, cold and rather sad. We shook ourselves, cried farewells to the caretaker's wife, and swung away downhill. Her wintry visage had a smile on it: we had bribed Mückichen with the largest piece of Apfelstrudel to kiss her good-bye for all of us. He took a deep breath, bolted the cake, then sought her out and flung himself upon her in an access of honourable despair. The embrace, though sudden, went down very well: she stroked him with a filthy hand and called him "Engelchen."[26] We

---

26   German: Little angel.

left her, singing "Muss i denn"[27] to her, and turned at the foot of the hill to wave once more, shout one more "Aufwiederseh'n."

The Havel looked so cold and leaden that we shivered at it, remembering our bathes. One hardy fellow rowed across the bay: rather he than I, we thought, waving and shouting to him.

"There'll be a moon to-night," said Berta romantically.

"Bosh! I'd rather have a stove!" sang Manfred Kahn, blowing on his great red fingers.

"Oh, let's stay and see it!"

"What'll we do for Abendbrot?"

"Go without, you greedy swine."

"You can, but my old woman's got goulasch, and I'm going home."

With their lips wet at the thought of goulasch, the three young Kahns left us outside Wannsee station. The rest, trying to be hardy but wishing nevertheless that our families had savoury stews waiting, tramped on round the lake to the Little Wannsee, to the far corner where Kleist[28] lies buried. It amused us always to visit the grave and see the marks of our Tante Cosima upon it. As Käthchen von Heilbronn she briefly had been the town's idol: she cherished still, that old woman of sixty-four, a lush sentiment for the unhappy poet. Every year on his birthday, every anniversary of the day he shot himself and his Henriette, Tante Cosima drove out in a hired car to the Little Wannsee, laid a posy on the green grave. Her great sprawling script on the cards was unmistakable: no one but Tante Cosima, either, would compose such messages to lie over a dead dramatist.

"From the ever-grateful Käthchen to her Creator!"—("as if the thing had been written for *her*!" snorted Kurt, kicking the rain-smeared card)—"Käthchen Remembers Ever!" and a forest

---

27 A Swabian folk song, "Must I, Then?"

28 Heinrich von Kleist (1777-1811), German dramatist and novelist.

of exclamation marks dizzily spattering downhill—"From the One who can Ne'er Forget!"

"Forget what?" demanded Kurt.

"Ssh!" hissed Berta and Brigitta, shocked.

The blooms with this last tribute were (or had been) lilies, than which no flower, considering Tante Cosima's life, could have been more inappropriate. We stood and gazed at them.

"How lovely," murmured Anne-Lise, "to be so fond of him."

We yelled with laughter.

"*Du, Schafkopf!*[29] She never even saw him. Why, he was dead fifty years before she was born!"

"All the same, you can love a person without knowing him," murmured Anne-Lise, her eyes filling with ready tears. We called her "Die Fontäne" and loved her for this gentle feminine wetness, though often it exasperated us beyond measure.

"She's right," said the twins sentimentally, "it *is* rather touching." And they, too, dropped a tear, probably much helped by the bitter wind which made our eyes and noses run.

"My God!" cried Kurt in disgust, "what a ghastly lot of ninnies you are, standing there snivelling over the man's grave without even knowing what you're snivelling for!"

"There's the moon!" cried Mückichen, hopping and pointing, "the *moon*!"

And there she was, rising slowly over the dark wind-bent pines, an enormous orb, honey yellow, soft and terrifying. It was not quite dark: the day's light still hung faint and exhausted over the woods and the water: above it, overlaying it, this strange full moonlight seeped in.

"There!" cried Berta, "I told you there was going to be a moon."

And she gazed at it fondly, like a mother: without Berta, we were made to feel, there would have been no moon this night.

---

29   German: You, sheep's head! An insult.

"We'll walk to the Pfaueninsel."[30]

"Kurt, don't be mad, it's *miles*."

"Not if we go over the hill instead of by the road."

"We'll get lost."

"Not in this light."

"Well, I'm going home," said Brigitta decidedly. Her shoes, she added, were worn through; she had had enough walking for one day.

Willi and Anne-Lise, hand in hand now that the moon was up, were also going home: Willi had to leave for Basel early next morning. Rosie Weissbaum tactfully wanted to go back with the twins: she was a model sister for a girl in love. So Gertrud, Mückichen, Kurt and I were left to skirt the little lake, plunge into the deep dark wood, and forge our way uphill as best we might. It was mad. The Pfaueninsel was miles away, half-way to Potsdam. But there was the moon, high and most brilliant, flooding the air, lying in bright pools at our feet as we pushed on. Soon Gertrud and Mückichen had lagged behind: Kurt and I went on alone to the top of the hill, looked down through pine-tops to the quiet water.

"Cold?"

"Yes."

"We'll run down. Give me your hand. Now run, don't break your ankle over those roots, run, girl!"

We ran, speeding down the steep path, dodging stones and roots, often dodging dark smears that were nothing but moon shadows, inky black. When we got to the bottom our hill speed carried us on, right out from under the dark pines to the narrow sandy shore, bleached by moonlight. Lapped in thin moonlight the water shifted, ebbing with small sucking noises like a baby mouth at the breast, coming to our feet in restless lines of silver,

---

30   The Pfaueninsel is a palace on the shore of the River Havel in southwest Berlin, opposite Pfaueninsel [Peacock Island].

pawing at us, drawing back, a lilting changing pattern. The noise of water was everywhere: we held our breath and heard far back in the hooded hill a little stream, piping its thin tune. The moonlight grew too strong: we stood back in the shadow of a beech-tree. Above in the stripped branches small birds rustled, scratching their feet along the wood. Some creature ran out of the grass that darkly etched the sand: we saw its soft hump, its silver eye: then it ran in again, the grasses shook a trail behind it.

"What's happened to the others?"

"I think they've gone back."

"Even Mückichen?"

"Even Mückichen."

"God, I'm tired; we shall never get to the Pfaueninsel." He flung himself down in the shadow of the beech-tree. As we lay there panting a cock crowed across the water, half-heartedly, as if he knew he was out of season. Lying on my back I held up my hand with sprawled fingers against the moon. Kurt's flattened hand lay on my waist, stroking upwards to my heart.

"Frightened?"

"No, not yet."

"Charlotte, little Charlotte."

Lying under the beech-tree, staring at the silver dappled sky, having time to think: This is what it is like, this, this—when Kurt's dark head, propped on his elbows, came between me and the moon. And once again, far across the water, that insane cock raised his exultant voice.

Chapter 3
Bärbel

Before the war, as children, we spent our summers in Grübl at the southern foot of the Totengebirge.[1] In those days Austria, the Salzkammergut, had not yet been fouled by popularity: there were no foreign tourists in Grübl. It was a place hooked out of the world's reach, a finger of green valley stretched into the heart of those wild and sombre peaks. The finger tapered to a lake, and then nothing but the rock-wall streaked all year with snow. Grübl lay between two lakes: the Grüblersee, really quite civilised, with a steamer coming up it twice a week in the season, and that small, deep, tree-darkened mystery the Kännchen. It was so round, so steep, so bottomless that peering into it was like searching the depths of a tall coffee-pot. Between the Kännchen, where even civilisation petered out, and the Grüblersee, lay the village of Grübl. Going from the reeds and pale shingle of the larger lake,

---

1   The Totengebirge [Dead Mountains] is a range of mountains in the Austria state of Styria.

the road meandered amiably two kilometres up to the top of the valley, to the full-stop of the Kännchen. The village, like most valley villages, ambled crazily beside it without apparent plan, the houses as native in their disorder as marrows sprawling over a dung-hill. Only the meanderings of the road, the deep powerful flow of the stream which came down from the mountains, had had any influence on Grübl's form. Even then you had the sneaking feeling that the houses had decided the voyage of the road, not, as in our newer settlements, that the road had laid down the law for the houses.

Another stream, which had no name, was Grübl's artery. It shot sixty feet from the rock wall, a solid glassy spout crashing into a pool. From there, led by generations of Grübler peasants who had lovingly dug it channels, carved for it pine-troughs and rude overhead pipes on long wooden legs, it fed the village. Harnessed to duty so soon as it left the pool, it fed a water scheme so wide and yet so simple that every couple of Grübl's thirty houses had a scooped trough, a vigorous streamlet spouting from a V-shaped gutter, waste water scampering away by the side of the road through round holes brilliant with watery slime. Grübl's water, the myriad children of that single liquid curve from the cliff, was everywhere. It flowed deep between the parting grasses of the orchards, murmuring under a green arch: through the small gardens where in the tender summer dawns the figures of Grübl's women bent absorbed above their bunchy lettuces, their radishes, turnips, beetroots and dark-feathered carrots: past the church standing like a lonely virgin on a small mound thick with hay and flowers, pointing upwards from its whitewashed hump one pale sharp finger finished in grey shingles: through the rye-fields, the rare wheat patches: tumbling finally downhill across inn-keeper Oskar Prandtl's great hay-field in a dozen small streamlets which abandoned themselves to the deep chalky stretch of Tauben. Tauben is a glacier stream, falling from the upper wastes of the Totengebirge into the Kännchen, coming out again, with its glacier bloom still upon it, in two streams which joined half-way down the valley. I daresay Tauben's legend has become tourist-trophy now in Grübl, paid for with a glass of beer at Oskar Prandtl's inn: then, in the early nineteen-hundreds, it was not yet commercialised. My Amme[2] from Grübl used to tell it to us until we got bored with the tale. There were, she said, two doves who loved one another. One lived in the pines shadowing the northern stream, one among the alders fringing the southern. They visited and cooed happily enough on a branch, but neither could make up its mind to leave for ever its own home shade. It was a discussion that seemed endless—coo-coo—coo-coo: any husband to any wife.

So one Johannisnacht, when the sun turns round to curve back into winter, the northern dove fluttered from its needled shade and sat composedly upon the water, drifting downward to where the two streams meet. To this fork, by a hillocky meadow through which the living rock breaks, the southern stream bore the southern dove. They laid their tender beaks together and, thus pressed bosom to bosom, cooing and murmuring in the muted fashion of doves, were borne swiftly down to the Grüblersee. Since then, so remote a time that it has no date, the stream has been called, not die Taube—a dove, but simply Tauben—doves. The peasants, with their instinct for a neat ending, add that all the doves on the shores of the Grüblersee, all the doves preening themselves and burbling among the branches that droop greenly to the water, on the steep banks coloured by purpled bells of wild clematis, among the bright blue-red pinks, the auriculas springing from a green mat in inhospitable rock crannies—all the doves along the banks are sprung from that adventurous tender couple whose name the Tauben bears.

---

2   Familiar German term for nursemaid.

The valley in which Grübl lies, through which Tauben flows, is never very wide and for the most part very green. Above it, on laps of rock, hang lovely little alps where the flowers riot all the summer. Down in the valley it may be July, but above in the Schneckenalm it is still June: farther, higher, in the two-winged alp they call the Schmetterling it is May yet, and the snow hardly melted. So that Grübl's year lies round it in layers: when the auriculas have died to brown tassels by the Grüblersee they are still lusty, still the colour of egg-yolk, in the higher alp. Next month, edging towards the snows that never melt, they will have taken their last stand on the Schmetterling. Here also is the farthest limit of the Grübl cows: early in summer they are driven through the woods north of the Kännchen, across a desolate moor where only scrub and the tough spires of last year's yellow gentian grow, through another wood where, the snow still lies in soiled heaps, to the snow-wet greenness of the Schmetterling.

All alps are green, but those about Grübl, surely, more green than any. To me they are so. I was a child in Grübl and see it in the colours on which my infant eyes first fed. I was almost born there: Father rented each year a wooden deep-browed house, brilliant with petunias, standing on a meadow slope, and transported us there every May. The family settled in, black with mourning for Ulrich. And suddenly poor Mama, remembering him, remembering in a retrospective panic what a very bad time she had had six years before with Mitzi, clamoured for the civilisation of Bad Aussee, the soothing frock-coats of the doctors. So slowly, carefully, not in Herr Pforrbach's wagon but in a carriage chosen by Father for its springs, Mama and I were transplanted to that delectable watering-place. There, a month later, I was born. However, though I missed being a native, I have Grübl blood in me. From my Amme in the village I drank in the sound of Grübl's cow-bells before dawn, the smell of Grübl's first hay (the loveliest) in June, the colours of Grübl's meadow flowers, the sway of the narcissus, like St. Ursula's eleven thousand virgins, in the slope beneath our Grübl house. We stayed all my first summer there, leaving only in October when the heavy-uddered cows were brought down from the Schmetterling to the byres. When we went Berlin-wards my Amme went with us, but so pined for Grübl that I had to be untimely weaned. Then, like a swallow released, the bright earthy creature sped back to her Salzkammergut, to Grübl by this time under its first crust of snow.

To Grübl we went back each year, each May, till I was nine. Then Father discovered East Prussia, the Baltic, and thereafter blew the family on the wind of his enthusiasm northward instead of south. It was a poor exchange. What were Rügen, Silt, Timmendorfer Strand, compared with Grübl and the tinkling of the cow-bells? However, Mitzi and I enjoyed ourselves well enough for two years until the war came and childhood ended.

Now in 1924, see the return of the native. It was May, spring was very late. The snow was still thick down in the valley. Even in the village, in dirty crusted piles under the overhanging roofs, the snow was not yet melted away. Grübl looked shop-soiled but peaceful as I drove into it on the front seat of Herr Pforrbach's wagonette. It was inflation time and the world, for Germans and Austrians, rocked crazily on a wobbling pivot. In the country the peasants desperately hid all they could, knowing that when things grew worse still the cesspools of Berlin, Wien, München would slop a tide of ravening lunatics over the countryside in search of food. It had been a long hard winter but now summer could be smelt in the air, and in summer things are never so desperate. The inn looked the same as it had looked to me at nine years old. They had built a new Saal in the prosperous summer of 1913: the ghost of four war years dwelt there yet. It was a long bare room designed for gaiety in which no one ever looked very gay. Sitting there in a circle of luggage I heard the Prandtl news. Hanni was married to the son of old Jakob Otzer in Bad Aussee: Leni was not yet married but her cousin

Friedl had been hanging round her all winter and was even now building himself a new house ("with a wash-kitchen!" gloated Frau Prandtl) down by the side of the lake. Sepp, whom I remembered as a tow-headed lad burnt brick-red from May to September, was now managing the farm. He came in as we talked, towered above me, shook my hand and called me "Gnädige Frau."[3]

"And you, Fräulein Charlotte?" asked Frau Prandtl when the family tale was ended.

She looked me up and down, one woman to another, and remembering her own days eased herself more comfortably into her grey dirndl.

"I'd like to stay the whole summer. Can you give me that corner room till September?"

"Naturally."

We haggled politely about prices. The war had made Frau Prandtl, as it had made all of us, grasping about money. After five minutes' brisk talk I had agreed to pay two schilling a week more than I had planned, she to accept two schilling less. Like the ends of a concertina melodiously squelched together, our two demands met. After which we sat and looked at one another, our regard in no way lessened.

"And the little one?" asked Frau Prandtl.

"Towards the end of July, I think."

"The Gnädige's husband will be coming from Berlin to be with her? There are two beds in the corner room."

"No, Frau Prandtl."

"Ah!" she sighed, smoothing the firm dome of her stomach, "what a pity."

Frau Prandtl had run through most of life's phases: she was not easily surprised. Though from now on she scrupulously called me "Gnädige Frau," there was an amused irony in her voice.

---

3   German: Madam, a polite form of address for a married woman.

So I settled down in Grübl to wait for the child. Tante Lydia had helped me to get away: I had stayed two months with her in her beloved Goslar before coming on to Austria. Like Frau Prandtl she had seen too much raw life to be much stirred by it now. I was going to have Kurt's baby—well and good. For everybody's sake I must go to some quiet healthy place and bear the child in decent secrecy. So far she had no interest in the baby as such. When it came she would examine it, exclaim over it, bending her dark marmoset face close so as to miss no details. It would then be added to the human troupe whose acrobatics she observed with such sardonic glee. But until then she was bothering only with the practical problems. She questioned me sharply about the money I had, decided I could do with such and such a sum if I were careful (the proviso was typical of my aunt, who never in her long life had been either careful or prudent), and gave me some old Cluny lace to sell. It had belonged to her unhappy addlepated mother, Rosa Blümchen, before that to great-grandmother Berta Blümchen, who in her turn had had it from a great-aunt in Versailles. The lace, reaching its filmy tentacles well back into the eighteenth century, was handed over to me. "Silly stuff!" cried Tante Lydia, her fingers roaming with passionate love among the creamy mesh, "silly useless stuff. I don't know what people keep this sort of thing for. Better not sell it till you get to Salzburg: there'll be some fluffy-headed American bitch there who'll give you twice what it's worth if only you use your wits. I suppose you haven't thought of having it" (she sketched the embryo with one yellow hand) "removed?"

"No, Tante Lydia."

"Daresay I should feel that way too," said the crone, well satisfied. "Only for God's sake don't have twins: there were none in the family till Clara started it, and there's no reason why there should be any more. Get along with you now before I change my mind about that lace."

With which blessing in my ears I got as best I could to Salzburg.

The little town was crawling with Americans, who champed their clay-coloured jaws over Wrigley's, darted febrile eyes here and there for bargains, and were determined to see how Yurrup had stood up to the war. They bought wagon-loads of curios to take back to Little Rock, Ark. and Des Moines, Ill.[4] There were American Jews, too, who knew what things were worth: these I avoided like lepers. Plying the hotel porter at Die Krone with sex appeal, I got into touch with a Mrs. Hermon Braxon, got her interested in both my lace and me. I was poor but exceedingly noble, the last blossom of a proud Hungarian stem (I do not know why Hungarian, the idea occurred at the last moment and sounded very well): would the Höchstwohlgeborene[5] Frau Braxon care to give me a trifle for my family lace? I spoke English better than she did, but broke it for the game's sake. That, and the fantastic tale bedewed with countesses, marchionesses and references to Marie Antoinette that I spun around the lace got me about three times as much as it was worth. Mrs. Braxon was enchanted, guessed she'd have her dressmaker fix it, wouldn't it just make the cutest little negleedge you ever—"and did you say Marie Antoin*ette*?"

"Yes, gnädige, Marie Antoinette, when visiting the famous nunnery at Cluny—the gnädige knows Cluny?"

"You betcha," said Mrs. Braxon, chewing.

"—with her own hands felt this lace and commented on its—how do you say?—its textures. Gnädige, my great-grandmother, my grandmother and my mother were wedded beneath this veil—I cannot sell it. Your pardon, gnädige, I did wrong to come."

"Here, wait a *min*nit—I'll give you another ten dollars—another fifteen!" cried the alarmed Mrs. B.

---

4   Des Moines is in Iowa.

5   German: Literally, high well-born, corresponding to Most Noble, an honorific originally used for some ranks within the Austrian and German nobility and later extended to civilians of high achievement, such as Sigmund Freud.

I passed one hand wearily over my brow and murmured fatalistically: "One must eat. Yes, gnädige, you shall have my lace."

"Gee, honey, that's swell. I'll give you the money right now. What did you say your name was?"

"Marie-Alphonsine Sophia Anastasia de Kolnagyi," I murmured.

"Gee!" said Mrs. Braxon.

She paid me the heavenly dollars, then hesitated, glancing at me with eyes hungry for more sensation.

"We'd sure like to have you stay and eat with us in this quaint little caravanserai, er—Countess," she cried, disentangling her superb false teeth from the gum in which they were for the moment embroiled.

"Princess," I corrected gently.

"Prin-cess! Waal, waal, will this tickle 'em way back in Nebraska! Now you must just come along, I'd like to have you meet Mr. Braxon and the folks."

I met the folks. They were her aunt, her mother, two reluctantly unmarried sisters and a depressed niece.

"*Ma joi, quelle ménagerie!*"[6] I cried, shaking hands all round: a trifle deranged, perhaps, by the feel of those American notes in the legs of my bloomers.

"What's that, Princess?"

"Excuse, please—home in the family now so afflictingly dispersed we always talked French. Family life, gnädige—"

"That's so," agreed Mr. Braxon gravely, settling my chair, "that's so. The family, Princess, is the spine of national life, no less: the flame upon that sacred hearth—"

"Hermon!" carolled his wife, "there's Schnitzel *again*. Isn't that cute? I do *love* Schnitzel."

We ate Paprika-Schnitzel, salad, omelette foaming at the brim,

---

6   French: My delight, what a menagerie!

budding into red Preiselbeeren,[7] Emmenthaler cheese, American crackers, real butter: afterwards we drank coffee with cream and sugar. I had forgotten such food was possible. Young, pregnant, hungry, I walked into that meal with my elbows out and praised heaven afterwards as the blue smoke rolled deliciously upwards from my good American cigarette. I could not really dislike the Americans who fed me so. Stammering my thanks in quaint, pretty English, I left them, feeling only sorry for the poor vulgar barbarians.

And here I was, in May, waiting for my child. The summer strode on, magnificent and fierce. Each day I woke very early to see the eastern light striking down to the pines above the Tauben, creeping across the meadow to the foot of the inn, to the balcony, to my waiting face. There was a ringing splendour about these May mornings—they were Handel at his best. The sky blazed with a light as fresh and proud as creation: the great shadow of the Kännchen's eastern wall shimmered fierce blue behind a veil of light. Light, after dark starry nights in which the pines themselves were out-blacked, streamed invincible over the whole valley. The valley lay sucking up the splendour of light, demanding more and more. From my bed, facing east, I saw the great hay-meadows shouting with light, the sheeny tops of the grasses blowing in it, the dark pines at the farther edge triumphantly lit with it. And, beyond, the wall of rock blue against a bluer sky. Standing on the balcony with my nightgown plastered against me by the wind which swept up the valley on the heels of dawn, I heard the Tauben singing over its stones beneath the pine branches, the leaning alders and the dipping grasses. I heard the rhythmical juicy swish of Sepp's scythe in the hay at the foot of the slope, Sepp's voice uplifted in the song of the Lustige Bua. Below my window was Frau Prandtl, her grey dirndl and black apron girt up against the dewy drenching of the grass, stooping over her kitchen

---

7   German: Cranberries.

garden. Shut in against the ravages of cattle, dogs and little boys by a low criss-cross fence, laid out with passionate orderliness in serried rows of beet, plumy carrot, brilliant rosettes of lettuce and herbs of every kind, that garden saw Frau Prandtl every morning of its summer life at four o'clock. She toiled in it for an hour or two while Leni and Mariele, the kitchen-wench, went about their cooking in the fly-frequented kitchen. Beyond Frau Prandtl, behind the grassy ridge where the hay-field sloped riverwards, the bright heads of Sepp and Willi the Knecht beat time to the steady swooping of their scythes. From the kitchen rang out the clang of a dropped saucepan and a whoop of laughter from Mariele. Herr Prandtl, in his grey short coat with dark green froggings, his grey leather breeches now greasy-brown with time, strolled out of the inn. Knee-deep in wet grass, one hand against the sun, he spun slowly, thoughtfully, and weighed up the coming day.

Meanwhile the light grew warmer, stronger. The last veil of mist over the Tauben had been twitched upwards to vanish in the blue. A troop of goats, harried by a small loud child in a check shirt reaching barely to its navel, clattered past the benches, under the chestnut trees at the hill's front. In the village doors creaked open, became dark holes in which buckets swam to the surface. The sound of a dozen lusty streamlets spouting down into troughs was broken by the splash of water on a bucket's rim, the hollow sound of water filling empty wood. The cries of the women calling from trough to trough swam up to me on tide of smell: the smell of new-ground coffee breathing out its heart in the Prandtl kitchen. Another day had begun.

At six o'clock Leni, in a fresh blue-and-white dirndl, her shoulders mere puffs of muslin through which the warm flesh shone, brought me breakfast. A Brötchen hot from the cone-shaped basket the baker had just cased from his shoulder to the kitchen step, a pat of butter already swooning in the sunlight, a clear small well of honey. What a feast, to anyone coming from Berlin!

I exclaimed each morning over its beauties, and Leni, standing in the sunlight to watch me eat, smiled indulgently. Our day began with gossip. She always had something to say, something terse, to the point, instinct with life. Gossip was her currency, milled at the edges by a wit as sharp as it was naïve. The life of Grübl, as surprising as the tales of Hoffmann,[8] flowed through my room in those early mornings as she leaned against the door with the sun in her plaits, and prattled on. So my days began with gurgles of laughter, Leni's clear light voice rising in the dialect I had learnt in my babyhood, her brown arms dark against the blazing sky as she mimicked Moz Osterl playing the zither, or Tante Battiger, the village midwife, hurrying to a case.

The days floated me serenely on. Tante Lydia's letters came once a week, bulging through cheap envelopes on which she never put enough stamps. Carrying odd cargo in the shape of newspaper cuttings, fragments of other people's letters, brown juiceless flowers she had plucked on her lonely Sunday walks, they were all I had of Berlin. I read them in the hay-field where they had not yet ravished the rich grass, sitting among the roots while the seeded grass plumes waved about me, sitting like a fat tiger in a jungle. Or, farther afield, I climbed the slope beyond the Tauben and sitting in the eye of the sun glanced up from Tante Lydia's spider-crawlings to the flash of the stream as it curled past the pine trunks. When the sun was falling, falling behind the grey thimble of the Bischofshut I climbed higher to be in it, right up to the house we had once had. Standing at the head of the long steep meadow it was the last house in Grübl to hold the western sun. Long after the valley lay in chilly shadow, long after the Tauben flashed no longer, flowing sullenly beneath its evening mist, our old house stood there in a honey-coloured light, its windows

---

8   E. T. A. Hoffmann (1776-1822), a German writer whose fantastical tales that were the basis of *The Nutcracker* and other ballets.

over the petunia boxes glowing like wine. No one rented it now, there was no money: but the petunias seeded themselves and bloomed again each year. In the meadow, in June, the narcissus flowered. The green slope paled with their frail papery petals and bland yellow eyes. Their stalks dribbled syrup over my fingers as I carried them in armfuls back to the inn. But they did not live away from their meadow: set in Frau Prandtl's jam-jars about the chilly Saal, cowed by the inhuman air, they shivered and withered like ghosts at cock-crow.

I cannot remember ever facing up to my plight, looking it full and boldly in the eye. I was still young enough to be romantic. I saw myself beginning an epic drama: the young mother struggling for her child, nobly self-sufficient, proudly spurning help. The child (a boy) would grow to manhood in a world bounded by this magnificent figure, by the mother who was both parents to him, had brought him up single-handed. What companions we would be, what comrades! Even now, as I waddled swollen between the parting Grübl grasses, I was blazing a new brave trail for womanhood, for single women: establishing the right of every woman to motherhood without any of the boredoms of marriage. After all, why not? If men were sexual free-lances, why not women? It all seemed so simple, so gloriously obvious. And motherhood was so beautiful, no woman should miss it. My eyes swam as I went slowly upwards to the inn: the bright Mayfields, yellow and purple and blue with flowers, melted together under my sentimental gaze.

True, I was disgustingly sick every morning when I first got up, but this was only one more sign of beautiful motherhood—less picturesque than other signs, perhaps, but definitely interesting.

*****

Dreaming along at Grübl, I found myself in the last week of July. Frau Prandtl eyed me sharply in the evenings, and gave me a hand-bell to set by my bed. It had hung from the neck of a respected old cow now dead, and on its leather strap clung still a homely speckling of dung. I used to amuse myself, in the radiant early mornings, by tinkling it gently to and fro, lying on my back with the thing hung in a belfry made of my two thumbs. Faint and wheezy it breathed out its single note, the ghostly essence of all Alpine cows: from the green Alps beyond the balcony, ringing down the far distant pastures, came like an echo the tinkle of other bells on living necks.

Otherwise the bell was never used. A very small wrathful daughter was born, to my shocked surprise, in full afternoon. It was the feast of Mariä Himmelfahrt.[9] Pious Grübl enjoyed itself with beer under the chestnut trees, with coffee and cakes at trestle tables in the newly mown meadow, with dancing in the Saal. The valley rang with sounds of flute, zither, fiddle, concertina and hands clap-ping out the beat of the dance. The first pains exploded sharply within me at noon: lying upstairs in my room above the Saal, waiting for more to come, I thought hazily of the dancers below. The lads in leather breeks, short coats and cocky felt hats knelt, I knew, in a ring: the girls, with dirndls starched to cracking point, old gaudy silk handkerchiefs tucked round their necks, old silver filigree in their braided hair, went round slowly, slowly in the circle, pirouetting as they faced each man, making as if to perch on his knee, then passing on, in the lusty haunting rhythm of a peasant dance. The men's hands, clapping out the time on the frailer pattern of the music, went on untiring like waves on a distant shore, waves beating upon stone.

Now the dance was finishing, a roar of voices and the click of heels almost drowned the hand-clapping.

9   The Assumption of Mary, celebrated each year on 15 August.

Hoch vom Dachstein an wo der Aar noch haust
Bis zum Wendenland am Bett der Saav'
Wo die Sennerin frohe Jodler singt
Und der Jäger kühn sein Jagdrohr schwingt:
Dieses schöne Land is' der Steirer land
Is' mein leibes, theures Heimathland... [10]

And hot upon the last notes, the last clap, rang a yodel from some joyous throat, triumphant as a cock crow.

Frau Prandtl, prinked out in a plum-coloured dirndl, with a cyclamen-pink apron, a purple and silver kerchief, stood by my window fanning the air in and out with a horse-tail of pine. In her, too, the music throbbed: her plump brown arms, the dark pine-plume beat steadily the dance's rhythm. It was very hot. The exhausted afternoon lay swooning on the hay-field where the second crop stood ripe for cutting, on the expressionless pines and the Tauben swollen by the fast-melting snows of the Totengebirge. I stumbled out to the balcony once, and the blaze of sun-bright air was like a blow in the face, so hot, so fierce, so cruel. I remember saying to the woman at the window, who sometimes was Frau Prandtl, sometimes Mitzi, sometimes my Tante Lydia, that the dancers must be mad to go prancing in this heat. But the woman laughed comfortably and told me not to grieve over them. I dare say she thought I should be getting on with this business of giving birth, not brooding over heat and the dancers.

---

10   German: High above the rooftops looking off to the place the [Swiss] River Aare runs
     Over to the land of the Wends/Sorbs in the basin of the River Sava
     Where the milkmaid sings jolly songs
     And the hunter jauntily swings his hunting horn:
     This beautiful land is Styria.
     It is my dear, sweet home.

From the *Dachsteinlied*, the anthem of the Austrian region of Styria.

The dance grew more furious. The men gave wild whoops as they swung their partners from the ground, as the women's white-stockinged legs whirled outward in a ballooning mass of skirts. Bärbel burst into the world in the full tide of one of these whoops, and added to them a piercing poignant noise, more painful than the scratch of pencil on slate. As for me, I was now far away, floating on the Wannsee not with Kurt but with the English officer in his British warm, who offered me a little red wagon as the rain fell about us. On, on, boatless, oarless, rudderless; the rain has turned to snow, the Wannsee to the dirty slush of the Leipzigerstrasse; at my side runs Mitzi in her spattered wedding-dress (is it blood, Mitzi? Mitzi! there's blood on your wedding-dress!). There is a smell of burning, of roasting coffee, of sweat: proud on the waters of the Karpfenteich swims Frau Prandtl with the silver ornaments bobbing in her hair, supporting on her breast a zither, a violin, a concertina. On she floats.

I after her, to a green shade, a dark tunnel, sleep on a misty flaccid tide, oblivion.

*****

The whole business seemed to me so simple. I lay in bed for a week, at intervals with a fierce joy suckling my Bärbel. The village came to see me, in twos and threes, though you would have thought they had all had enough and to spare of the new-born. Outside August blazed on: it was still very hot. The outraged rye rustled brittle and sapless on its stalk, scorched brown, whispering harshly in the noontide wind which sprang up and died down again without bringing relief. Each night the sky crackled with thunder, bright livid flashes chased from side to side of the panting valley. Even the cicadas in the long grass were too dry to chirrup. The flies dustily drifting in away from the sun swam swooning around in the solid air, then drifted out again to haunt the hot shade of the chestnut-trees, the cracked and blistered benches. On Frau Prandtl's face as she bent to stroke the breast on which Bärbel hung coursed a rolling tide of sweat, drop after drop: the drops fell on to Bärbel's thin silky hairs, and Frau Prandtl wiped them away with hands caked in dry garden soil. Only Leni looked cool, in blue-and-white cotton, as she stood by my breakfast tray and sketched the ringing smack which Mariele had just given Willi's face in the kitchen below.

Bärbel was as strange as any baby, remembering things we had long ago forgotten, raising her milky blue eyes as if there were a secret, subtle, shocking, but most amusing, that she and I alone knew. I hung above her and watched new-born thought swimming like a little fish in those opaque waters. When she had lost her early crumples, began to look more human, Frau Prandtl fingered her tiny limbs and exclaimed over them. Though as to most Jewish women, a daughter was but half a child, I too found them perfect. I was not yet bored with fierce possessiveness. She was all mine. For a week or two the cord that had tied us so pleasantly together lay neatly curled on the pink dome of her little belly: then it shrivelled, dropped off as sadly as an autumn leaf, and I wept to see it go.

Now, in late August, the storm broke, the rain came. Down on the inn's roof, during a pitch-black night, the ram came hurtling. The bruised roof rang, every shutter flung back and forth in the flying gale: pallid lightning flickered over the valley. Flickering over the pine-tops, catching a group of pines, throwing them livid and brutally distinct against the eye, it then lapsed, flickered away, dropping the trees once more into the bottomless obscurity of the night. With a ferocity unbelievable even in the Salzkammergut, that rain streamed all night, all next day, all next night, and withdrew sullenly into a sullen purple sky almost fifty hours after it began.

That first morning there was no sun striking down over the eastern crags. The day came a milky grey, the vertical rain still fell. Where yesterday the stream had dropped demurely down its

81

rock wall there was now a tigerish yellow spout. The pool frothed over drenched banks: the scummy froth blew over the meadow, rested in great dirty bubbles among the brilliant grasses. Beside the waterfall a dozen infant jets, filled with débris from the ruined alps above, now raced down the rock. The valley rang with a sound of water. The Tauben flowed bank-high, a sombre pea-soup green, tossing foam, pine branches, shattered twigs on its roaring tide. Under the chestnut-trees the iron tables and benches were sheeted in water on which a few early-fallen leaves dismally plastered. The hot soil of the road was rutted and gutted, cold with rain. Puddles mirrored dimly the passage of a dejected peasant hooded in old sacks, a mule with drooping ears and rain-dark sides, the baker with his bicycle scattering spokes of muddy water, his great basket shrouded in oilskin.

We sat all together in the chilly Saal, forced by the rain to be sociable. We stared out of the windows, which rippled with rain so that the view entered in a series of watery shivers. There were not many of us: two unattached women from Wien, affecting dirndl; a Herr Rittmeister from Passau, whose vast belly was scooped into some kind of decency by the firm squeezing of his leather breeks; a family from Rosenheim; a honeymoon pair from Salzburg. The women knitted socks in complicated twisted patterns, complaining to one another of the wool, which since 1914 had grown steadily more scratchy, more greasy, more impossible. The men smoked, played cards, yawned and drank beer, thus drearily defying their wives. They also yapped ill-humouredly at their off-spring. The poor children did what they could: ran up and down the Saal whooping experimentally until told to stop, climbed on chairs, fell off again, yelled, were ignored, yelled louder, were slapped, retreated hiccoughing into corners and fell to amusing themselves with odd bits of string, window-fasteners, their own little anatomies. At my feet Bärbel slept in her clothes-basket, a curdled line of milk dribbling sideways from her mouth.

Sepp blew in on a gust of wind and rain, dripping at every corner. He had cycled, the vigorous youth, to fetch us our letters from Bad Aussee. There was one for me from Tante Lydia—her weekly gossip. It began: "My darling Charlotte," which was unusual: Tante Lydia seldom trickled into endearments. Plunging to the root of the matter, it went on to tell me Kurt had married our cousin Gisela Gottlieb in Hamburg. Tante Lydia, shrewd, kind, ruthless for my good, wrote this as one family member passing on family news to another. "You'll be as surprised as any of us—I never thought he fancied Gisela. The two of them have kept it pretty quiet, I must say. He wrote to Tante Clara yesterday. It seems that they fixed it all up at the New Year party at the Levin's—you remember my saying Kurt must be drunk, he had such a colour? But she wouldn't marry at once—some scruples about being surer of one another, I fancy. Our Gisela always was a cautious puss. So they said nothing to us till Kurt went off to Hamburg last Thursday and wired back that the two of them were married. I imagine she will keep her job in the Kindergarten if she can: the pay's not much but it's better than nothing. He has given up the Magdeburg place, and will try to get something in H. They'll manage all right, though why anyone marries in times like these passes my understanding.

"Now, my dear child, how are you and the little Barbara? When are you coming back? Herta has gone (God be thanked) to the Kühns at Brandenburg for eight weeks. They seem able to contemplate the long visit with calm, or perhaps it is merely despair. So I have the apartment to myself when I have cleared up H.'s mess. You should see her room: a regular dog's dinner. But when I've cleared it up it'll be ready for you. You wrote that you mean to brave it out, bring the child back and keep only Kurt's name out of the affair. That sounds very noble, but is it practical? And is it fair to the baby? Far better find some good peasant woman and farm her out—you can spend at any rate some time together. I expect you've already made arrangements, being a sensible girl. How are you off for money? I hope you kept as many American dollars as you could: cling to them, they'll be worth more and more. There's that beaver pelisse of your grandmother's still quite good: I could send you that if needed: it should fetch in something. As far as I can see these Rentenmarke aren't the slightest use. The money and the prices still go up and down like a monkey on a stick. If we had honest men to govern us! But we haven't. Everybody is mad!"

And away went Tante Lydia into a frantic diatribe against all economists, scientists, politicians, generals and business men: the sadness and the fury which she felt for me resolving itself into a frenzy against those untouchables in high places who were responsible for the crazy mark.

The rain outside spattered as dismally as ever. I picked up Bärbel from her clothes basket and took her upstairs. The abundant bosoms of the matriarchs from Rosenhain made me ashamed, insignificant: rather than suckle my child under their contemptuous cow-eyes I would exile us both to the dreary mist-filled little room where before the sun had shone so bravely, where now the walls dripped damp despair.

Here I wept for myself, with Bärbel tugging at my breast. The tears dripped on Bärbel's downy head, shifting from side to side as she sucked. Now and then she braced her heels against my lap, her little stomach jerked upwards in a greedy spasm. She was always a fierce grasping creature: from the beginning I had not had enough for her. She strained for more, missed the nipple, flung out her purple hands in a fury, clawing at air: once more her stomach heaved upward, her heels dug in. She would be a great snatcher at life, I thought, watching her hands as they blindly fastened on me once again. This creature, this snatching greedy leech hanging on my flesh, was all I had of Kurt who had married Gisela. All that had been thrilling and romantic was now sordid and loathsome: here was the old fustian story, faintly

84

ridiculous, of an uncontrolled female. One more moonlit night, one more seduction, one more bastard, one more fool weeping. For years this greedy brat would be snatching at me, snatching all she could get, shrilly asking for more. Battening on me, draining me, the creature would grow older, bigger, more able to batten and to drain. I saw us both in Frau Prandtl's crazy round mirror that tilted slightly forward on the chest of drawers. I stared at us, two miserable wretches. I saw the baby as a sucking mouth, a pair of greedy growing hands that seized all I had. Though innocent, she was to me loathsome, as an infant vulture is loathsome while it pecks naturally at rotting flesh. But now in a mad tenderness I hugged my baby vulture, my carrion crow: she was once more the helpless wee thing, my little crumb, my dove. I yearned over her, feverish with sentimentality, till common sense nipped frostily in to stop my tears. Life would not be one long embrace for us both, tenderness crystallised to last. It would not be tender, it would be a struggle so sordid, so compact of small humiliations, annoyances, insults, failures, so filled with the gnawing need to keep alive, to keep sane, that my tears dried to a grim despair. Life in Germany for a battling spinster was even then hard enough: what should I do with a child? Battle for us both, I supposed, until with my still young and personable body I had captured some male sot, less fastidious than most, to battle for us both. After that, a married life begun on shame, continued in boredom and stuffy closeness, made up of lustful unloving nights, nagging days, brats begotten in pure animal fury coming year after year to be suckled, clothed, washed, endured—all on a foundation of my shame and my rescuer's brief nobility simmering down to a reminder of my shame. He would unendingly want gratitude. I hated gratitude then, I hate it still. The thought of it nauseated me, when I had put Bärbel back in her cradle and lay flat on my bed hearing the rain drip, seeing the awful future writ smearily on the ceiling. Though that ceiling was but a few feet from my nose, the future pressed more intimately near. In a few months it would be deep winter, no longer could we live this animal outdoor life, cheap only because air and sunshine were cheap. Soon that money I had would be gone, then my beautiful American dollars, got by lying, would slip away one by one. The end of them would be nothing, nothing at all. Nothing is a ghastly word, even more devastating in German than in English. I said it feebly to myself, feeling the tears come, knowing how useless and silly they were, yet feeling them dribble with relief. And weeping, snuffling puppy-like into my damp pillow, I slept.

*****

When I woke it was dark. The rain still poured, the gutters still spilled in the weary water-worn patches beneath their rusted ends. Everything was as it had been. From the kitchen I fetched water for Bärbel's bath, and there sat Sepp teasing Leni as she darted to and fro over the supper. Not for the first time, my heart murmured that this was a comely young man. He sat there slumped upon himself as peasants do when they ease from the stretch of their working muscles, a little sleepy from the fire's warmth, handsomely flushed, ripe for mischief because he had been today so much indoors instead of pouring his vigour into the juicy swoopings of his scythe. His eye roamed naughtily over both of us, caressing innocently our limbs as we moved. Dishes sang and bubbled on the great stove; the blue wood smoke curled up through the cracks to the rafters, seeped there round herbs, sausages, black puddings and rain-sleepy flies. It was very human, and very warm, so that after supper, remembering it, I could not bear my room. I could not bear the Saal, full of the rain's grim dribble and the families from Rosenheim. The honeymoon couple practised coy tendernesses in one corner: I loathed them as I left them. In the kitchen Leni and Sepp wrangled over politics. What a godsend politics are to women in trouble! Thrashing furiously into these muddy waters, I could forget for a little my grief. I sat beside Sepp on the bench and watched, waiting for my chance. He had been so much in the sun these last hot months that even his eyeballs were sunburnt: as he passionately argued he had an inflamed look. Generally a silent youth, he agonised to himself over rival policies, warring ideal. It seemed to him (not yet old enough to see that one ism is probably no better than the other) that there must be a central idea somewhere giving coherence to the shambles. Now at last he had hit on something. For the first time, far away there in wet remote Grübl, I heard that nasty word: "Führerprinzip."[11]

"But what does that *mean*?" I asked impatiently. "Führerprinzip—Führerprinzip—it's no more than two words strung together—it means nothing."

"Yes, Fräulein, it does."

"Fräulein, indeed!" mocked Leni, with an impudent friendly eye cocked at me. "You call her 'Fräulein'?"

Poor Sepp halted in his politics to blush and stammer.

"Never mind," I cried, pushing away spectres, "explain to me the Führerprinzip."

He explained, shifting restlessly on his bench between the great copper milk-pans. The fine sunburned skin on his forehead shone with soap: he clasped his hands tightly between his knees, afraid that they might betray him, and wrestled with my ignorance, with the Führerprinzip. The names of Alois Drexel, Gottfried Feder, Hitler, Ludendorf, plopped into the hot kitchen air. Leni crinkled her nose at them all, cried: "Psst! you silly big baby!" and finally bounced impatient from the room. He hardly saw her go. His blue eyes grew starry, dark with excitement: he

---

11   The principle that the German nation's leader had supreme power, even above all written laws, which was advocated by the Nazis and adopted by Adolf Hitler in 1934.

plunged his hands through his hair, so carefully wetted under the pump before supper, till it stood up in a crest along his head. He spoke as if he had not talked to anyone for a very long time, as if he had been desperately thinking, shut up alone. Words poured from him in a spate, the hot eager words of a youth explaining an ideal, defending it, furiously emphatic because, deep in himself, he knows he is not yet quite sure.

"I can't understand it even now," I said at last. "How can an independent man give himself to such an idea, delivering himself up lock, stock and barrel to another man, however wise?"

He looked troubled. For the first time I rejoiced, feeling him resist me. This was what I wanted to-night: battle, battle, battle to the grimmest death. Before he had been gentle, merry, acquiescent: now he gathered himself into a hard knot of resistance. My self-respect began once more to bud.

"Ah, Fräulein, but the *man*!"

"What man, for heaven's sake?"

"Hitler."

"That little pip-squeak! You've never seen him, you know nothing about him. He's just a frothy idealist caged up in Land— Land—where *is* it they've put him?"

"Landsberg."[12]

"Huh! in Landsberg then. You can't think much of a Führer who gets himself put in prison for a silly little Putsch that didn't come off: you can't even *call* him a Führer."

"He's my Führer, for whom I fight."

"Did you get yourself mixed up in that München business?"

"I was there in the Bürgerbräu. When the shooting began outside the Feldherrnhalle, I—"

"—lay down like a silly sheep—like your Hitler—in the middle

---

12   Landsberg was the prison to which Adolf Hitler was sentenced following the failure of the Beer Hall Putsch in November 1923.

of the road and waited for them to put you in a nice comfortable prison where you'd be safe."

"Fräulein!"

"Oh, Herr Sepp, I'm sorry. But the whole thing was so—so childish and drivelling, He and Ludendorff and all the rest of them were going to rescue Germany, to save us all; and when the first shot rang out there they were lying on their stomachs among the cobbles, scared to death. All Germany laughed, it was too ridiculous."

"Not to us!" he cried, leaning on the table, beating at the wood, "not to us! Hitler is in prison—yes: and Stresemann can scold Ludendorff in the Reichstag[13] as if the General were a naughty schoolboy—but there are more of us left. We go on working till he comes out again to lead us. Then you will see something. Can't you realise, Fräulein, the only chance for Germany, for Austria, is to have a strong leader? Look what we do, leaderless. Look how we crumpled up after the war: we hadn't anybody, we looked everywhere and all we saw was officers running away from their troops and politicians running away from their people. Now when Hitler is free and Germany has a leader again all will be different."

On the lad spouted, deathly earnest. He was vividly attractive, as he sat there glowing with his ideals, warm with hope and faith. My little blaze of resistance was gone, I felt old and tired and cold, bored to distraction with man's politics. Führer or no Führer, Hitler or no Hitler, what was I going to do? From whom was I to tear a livelihood for myself, for Bärbel? I leaned my cheek on my hand and listened to Sepp without hearing. All that women can do about politics, I thought, is to suffer them. Their struggle goes on, whether or no.

Looking deep into his magnificent eyes I suddenly said: "Herr Sepp, I want to ask you something."

---

13   German Chancellor Gustav Stresemann castigated General Erich Ludendorff in the Reichstag for his role in the Beer Hall Putsch.

"Please?" he stammered reluctantly, checked in his rhetoric.

"What do you think of me?"

"Of you, Fräulein?"

"Yes, of me. Go on, tell me what you think."

"I think you're useless," he said after a struggling pause.

"Useless?"

"Yes. I mean only that you think and think and do nothing with your thoughts. That is what I call useless."

Damn his peasant arrogance.

"Well, I suppose *you* are useful, Herr Sepp. You till the soil, and sow seeds and reap your hay and your rye and cut wood for the stoves. You run the whole farm" (I flung out a scornful hand towards the streaming landscape), "you feed yourself and your family and your father's guests, you talk to women about the Führerprinzip. What else do you do?"

He winced at the female malice in my voice, but went on stoutly enough.

"I didn't mean that in quite the way you do. Only we have seen so many of the thinking people, those who let others do their doing for them, and I have always thought we peasants are better. Better as men and women, I mean. They come here every summer from Wien, the writers and the music people and the actors, and they lie about in the sun watching us hay-cutting, harvesting, and they laugh at our clumsy peasant ways. That's part of their holiday, to laugh at us and feel how behindhand we are in everything. They wear our Lederhosen and our dirndl because they find that picturesque on us and hope it will look pretty on them: but when the holiday is over they pack up the dirndl, say: 'Why don't you do your farm work with machines, it's far less trouble?' and go back to their town. We are the better people: we put our lives into the land and get our lives from it again. They only live on other people's lives."

"They do their thinking for you."

"No, that they don't. We do that for ourselves in our own way. They think that they think for us; but we have a grand laugh over their ideas when they've gone back to Wien and we shall still be doing it when they are rotting. I wish you hadn't asked me such a question, Fräulein, the answer only makes you angry."

"Do you care whether I'm angry or not?"

"Yes, I'm sorry for you."

"Because I'm what you call useless?"

"Partly. Why do you *float* so, Fräulein? You're cleverer than any of us here and yet you do nothing."

"You mean that if I waved my pistol and yelled 'Heil Hitler' you'd approve of me?"

"No," he answered, rebuffing extravagance, "but if you believed in something you'd be happier."

"Happy!" I said bitterly.

Useless I might be, but he had no right to say so. Look at him sitting there, the peasant, with his broad peasant hands and flat peasant wrists jutting out red from his jacket sleeves, his bony peasant knees so aggressively sprouting fair hair. A peasant every inch, rude as the soil under his finger-nails, yet a better man than I. And how warmly, how tinglingly attractive! I shivered for a moment as I looked at him, then looked swiftly away.

Oh, God, I have brought a child into this mess, this litter of personal futilities, this life I can't manage even for myself!

After a strained silence full of reproaches I rose and said good night.

Bärbel was awake, as if she knew her tragedy. She screamed indignantly at me. Walking up and down with her, pausing against the open window to look out on the rain, I felt fever mount in me and was sick at heart. Things, the inanimates, took on a sultry full-blooded significance. The pine walls glowed like the steamy flanks of a stallion, the chest of drawers pulsed, the floor, metres away, had an independent and unruly life all its own. I had an odd carved black tray shaped like an open-mouthed head, with eyes of green sea-shell. Long ago an English governess had given it shyly at Christmas; Maori work, from New Zealand, she said, trying to make me see romance. But the word "Maori" had not then made me feel romantic: I did not care for Miss Bailey. Now the gaping black mouth held Bärbel's safety pins: it was at least useful. It came from New Zealand, I thought, as it leered at me bristling with safety pins. I might go to New Zealand, we might go. Away, away, across seas as blue as heaven and more remote, though under the ship's prow the water peeled intimately away: away past South America, rounding strange comers, gaping at strange sights, to New Zealand. Surely in a new country a new life begins? I was yet young enough to think it. Patting Bärbel at my shoulder, hearing her let up wind, I brooded over foreign lands. They could not all be hostile. What had happened to Papua—was it German no longer? I did not know, but saw myself in a palm-leaf hut accepting bananas from a lithe virgin who glistened like wet coal. Bärbel at my ear ceased gulping and was still: I still patted absently, cloudy-minded, ravished by fever and phantasy. Papua, Papua—there's the place for us, I thought, as I put the child back on her pillow. Outside it rained harder than ever. The valley was a black howling void that dripped wetness. Far away across the scream of the pine-trees the Tauben rushed downwards with a steadier noise. For a moment as I shivered in my night-gown on the balcony there were two stars, watery but bright: the cloud heaved up against them and they were gone. But I clung there still, muttering to the wind that I was useless, that I would go to Papua.

All night was hot with dreams, with the same dream. I stood on the dirty top step of a train drawing into the Friedrichstrasse Bahnhof. Bärbel lay in my arms, Kurt waited for us both with uplifted face. Again and again the train shuddered to a stop, Bärbel breathed upon my arm, Kurt waited, but for nothing, since I never got down. Each time I knew that it was but a dream; the most poignant agony of all is that, when the dreamy self knows that it dreams yet needs must go on dreaming.

Naturally, I had a fever when I woke. The walls, as I stood up and saw that it still rained, shook a little: the floor rose ever so gently to meet them. I crept back to bed with Bärbel. Everything steamed, was fusty as if blown upon by foul breath. Bärbel wrinkled up her nose, mewed like a kitten. Loathing the fretful baby sound, the pink mouth opened, gummily blank, giving out these nasty noises, I clapped my hand fiercely to her mouth. She was at once still, quiet, so quiet that after a few dazed moments I peered at her, and saw how motionless, how still as death she lay. But she was asleep, not dead, and snatching my hand away from her face I fell to kissing her frantically, roughly embracing the poor startled little thing so that she kicked and yelled.

Leni, coming in with the coffee, found us so.

"Gnädige, you will choke the child."

"I'm loving her, my poor one."

Leni eyed me curiously as she set down the tray.

"Did the Gnädige sleep badly? Better stay in bed this morning, there's nothing to get up for."

"Nonsense," I cried, and stood up. The bed-head rose to hit me; Leni, the coffee-tray and the furniture swam together, flotsam on a foul stream: the pillows sucked at me as I fell. Shrill through my head as I dropped rang Bärbel's whining hungry cry.

So I stayed in bed that day. Figures roamed my room: Frau Prandtl with a bowl of something tasting like hot glue, Tante Lydia sitting on a letter, Leni murmuring: "There! there!", Sepp, black-moustached, waving a pistol, Mückichen pattering round and round me asking shrill questions. But no Kurt.

Through it all rang Bärbel's fretful wail. She was sick after her first feed: in a moment of appalling consciousness I saw her throw up the milk over Frau Prandtl's arm. Groaning, I sank once more into my nightmares. Later, when they held her up to me again, she turned away her head and feebly squalled. I pushed her off and dribbled into feeble tears.

"There! there!" cried Frau Prandtl, stroking my head with a heavy onion-smelling hand, "sleep, Gnädige, sleep—she'll be all right."

They drew the shutters to, blacked out the sun that began now to seep through the rain, and left me.

There is no need to dwell on nightmares long since past: the looming shapes, the grins, the heat, the sweat, the clawing hands, the sudden noises which jerk you from a budding doze once more into the horrors which your mind begets. Enough that I had a fever; that Bärbel, turning from me, was fed on cow's milk and sugar, seeming after the first day's distraction to like it very well. When thought came back I knew the last of our bonds had broken: first the expulsion of birth, then the withering of the little cord, now this. She no longer needed me: a cow could be her mother, helped by a teaspoon of sugar. A cow, and sugar from a blue tin with Franz Joseph's whiskered face upon the lid. From a cow and a sugar tin, not from me, Bärbel now sucked her life.

When the fever and the madness had ebbed, I lay for days weak as a kitten. The rain had stopped: in the valley the sun shone again. The flowers straightened, turned their faces upward, bloomed again. There was once more a blue sheen on the rye, though patches of it lay beaten flat, already rotting. Sepp and Willi, in the brave dawn, strode under my window to the hay-field, singing:

Mein Bier und Wein ist frisch und klar
Mein Töchterchen liegt auf der Todtenbahr.[14]

---

14 German: My beer and wine are fresh and clear
My little daughter lies dead on the bier.

Loudly they sang, confident as the morning. Soon the swish of the scythes among the luscious grass came beating up the hill, and the smell of juice in freshened stalks, the sweet smell of wet leaves warming in sunshine. The families from Rosenheim were returning to Rosenheim. The springs of Herr Pforrbach's wagonette creaked under the chestnut trees as the ten of them bounded in. Then a crack of the whip, a protesting brake lifted from the wheel, and away they went. Away, away, sang the scythes in the green juices of the hay-field, away, away.

Wanting no more than death, I said to Leni's gentle questions that I was much better. "Leni, when will Herr Pforrbach be here again?"

"When the Herr Rittmeister goes away, on Saturday."

"I must get back."

"But the Gnädige isn't fit to travel."

"Yes, I am. Bring me Bärbel."

Leni laid her in my arms. "Mutti is so pleased, she says she never weaned any of us with so little trouble."

I hated the child for going gladly from me to the accursed cow. If I could not own my child, she was nothing. I noticed with fury that she looked much the same. Yet the cow's milk, not mine, was even now dissolving in her little stomach.

"You'll be as happy as a lark to be free of her now," soothed Frau Prandtl when I pettishly told her to take the brat away. "It's hard at first, when they've hung on you so, but you'll soon be glad of it."

So Herr Pforrbach's wagon rumbled to a stop under the chestnut trees early on Saturday morning. Herr Rittmeister, more bloated than ever in a town suit, his cocky green felt exchanged for a straw boater of the kind affected by Englishmen, handed me up to the front seat. There I sat, sick and shaken, seeing the kind faces below in a weak haze. Frau Prandtl, imploring me once more to come down and get back to bed, put Bärbel into my arms. Herr Prandtl swung my suitcase in at the back. The family stood waving at me from the shade of the trees, among the leaf-strewn tables, as we rumbled out of Grübl down the hill to the glistening lake. The fountains spouted clear water now, instead of the sandy foam of a few days before: in the orchard by the fire-station the small apples were reddening. I saw it all in a languid mist, holding Bärbel as firmly as I could. The ground swam gently up and down, the woods by the Grüblersee came tiptoeing close, then ebbed, a dark green tide.

In Bad Aussee sauntered tourists, gay creatures in marvellous crisp linens. Our inflation had made everything so cheap: they swarmed to buy what they could with their francs, their shillings and their dollars. Herr Rittmeister descended into the heap of them at the door of the Krone. He bowed as far as his stomach would let him, bidding me good-bye in half a dozen flowery Viennese phrases. I was not too ill to preen myself at this, to think: "I am still charming, though a mother." Then I fell into a faint angry rage, for Herr Rittmeister had paid only a third of the fare instead of half. Against my protests Herr Pforrbach maintained that Bärbel and I were two passengers.

"She's a baby in arms!" I cried when Herr Rittmeister was no more than a dot on the sidewalk. "No one charges full fare for babies."

"Ah, Gnädige," sighed Herr Pforrbach, smiling slyly under his straw hat, "when one travels with babies it is always inconvenient."

His hateful smile, over teeth as black as charred tree-stumps, said plainly enough: "What are *you* doing with a baby in arms, Gnädige, oh, Gnädige!"

What indeed? I drearily thought, holding the child slack against me. Poor little Bärbel, this is but the first of those stings that you and I must share.

The train was atrociously hot. Like all our trains in those disjointed nineteen-twenties it crawled from halt to halt like a wounded beast at its last gasp. I sat faintly in a corner, Bärbel across my lap. In my mind Herr Pforrbach leered still, licking his lips over my unhappy state. There sat a woman opposite me with a little ruddy-haired boy about two years old who tumbled over our feet, sucked the window-strap, got blacker every minute under his mother's doting eye. She smiled at me.

"I hate travelling with them at this age, you can't keep them quiet. Lucky for you yours lies still. What a pretty baby!"

And the usual questions: How old? How much did she weigh? Was I nursing her?

I answered without enthusiasm, forcing the words up my sick throat.

"Ah well," she said, "the first baby's always difficult. You have to get used to being tied hand and foot. Now me, I couldn't have enough, even in these times. He's my fourth, aren't you, my birdling, my pet?"

I looked at her in horror while she seized upon him, opened her bodice and forced his great head into breasts that were already slack and sagging.

"Oh Lord!" she cried, fanning herself while the child, out of pure habit, sucked. "Are we never going to move on? These trains! They say the rolling stock's as old as old—the Allies took all the good stuff. Ai! when one loses a war!"

On my right the Wolfgangsee lay like burning silver. We had stopped at the last halt before the climb over the pass began: no more than a shed, it was, with the wild flowery bank sloping down to the lake behind it, and on the other side the narrow road, the unending pines.

I took Bärbel along to the lavatory. Sitting in that noisome place, faint and sick, I tried to suckle her. She turned away and flapped feebly at me with her little fists.

"Suck, my little one, my dove, my precious crumb!" I whispered with my lips against her warm head, against that tender throbbing pulse between the unjoined bones, "suck again."

Perhaps if she had clung to me as at first she did, fumbled for me, fastened ecstatically upon me, I should have her yet. But she turned away and sent out once more into the fœtid air a thin, nerve-wracking wail.

I paced up and down with her in the corridor trying to stop that noise. At last she fell asleep, and in her sleep grunted as young puppies do. I laid her in the other woman's baby carriage which stood packed into the corner by the lavatory door. The blankets were clean and warm; I tucked them in around her, folded the linen cover over her sleeping face.

The whistle blew, the train began to move. The guard swung himself up from the station hut to the last carriage. Unhurried, cold as frost, I climbed out on the other side.

Chapter 4
Interlude

I walked all that day. It is a lonely enough pass, this high slip of alp between the Totengebirge and the Salzburg valley. When you have left the few villas of St. Gilgen you are not much troubled with humans. There is space enough, and all time, in those wide Alps slung against the sky. Only, every here and there, a hay hut, a water-trough for the kine,[1] a shrine in which the crazed figure dangles, uncouth, loathsome, crucified.

At noon I had left the hay-fields from which the bending peasants stopped in the rhythm of their mowing to wave: I had left the last cluster of houses, deserted save for two pigs rootling in the dock leaves by the water-trough. I drank deep of that water, splashed it over my face, my burning breasts, and went dripping on. In the dark wood the brindled horse-flies gathered on my legs, and bit till blood streamed. In Grübl I had kept them away from Bärbel with a switch of fragrant pine, crooning:

---

1 An archaic expression for cows, collectively.

Alles ist ruhig, ist still wie im Grab
Schläf' nur, ich weh'n die Fliegen dir ab.[2]

Now they bit me while I waved feebly at them, watching the blood ooze. Then I was out once more in the hot, hot sun, going up a valley which closed about me like a hand. Below, the stream roared; an infant stream brawling and tossing over boulders. On either side towered the gaunt lonely hills, as chilly as my bowels. On the last pale pasture moved a troop of goats: their bells' jinglings were single notes struck from an old faint harpsichord. Here the last crumbles of an avalanche blocked the way, dirty earth-browned snow in which torn pine-trees and small bushes lay embedded. At the edge grew soldanella with mauve-fringed bells among strange roots newly come to light, purple, yellow and sour green.

Above me there was now another hay-strip hanging on the mountainside like a dropped handkerchief. Against its clear green three insect figures bent, swayed, rose in the rhythm of the scythe. No use waving to them: for them there was nothing in the world but hay. I looked up dizzily, yearning to be recognised as human, but they could not see me, I was only an insect, infinitesimal, crawling about the valley's foot.

Round a rocky bend, good-bye to the goats, the living creatures in the hay-field. I stumbled, for the path was very rough and reared up like the rump of Herr Pforrbach's horse. The stream and the path were joined, one leading up, the other tumbling with a watery cry downhill. There was so much ice-cold, tossing water, more even than my thirst needed. Stooping to drink once again my bare hand slipped on the rock, into the pool I crashed, lying there a moment with but half my senses. When I pulled myself out to lie wet and shaking by the water's edge I remembered in

---

2   German: Everything is quiet, still like in a grave
                Just sleep. I will shoo the flies off of you.

astonishment that it was I, I, Charlotte, who years ago had done the ghastly thing. Standing apart from her, shaking with the cold drench of the glacier stream, I watched her at it even now. She drew the linen cover over the baby's face: she smiled at it, she opened the door of the train, beyond which the stones and sleepers of the track already slowly moved, and stepped out. There was no release. Whichever way we looked, the two of us, was horror, sickness, fear clawing at the cold stomach.

Now for a brief spell the path dropped downward to a green triangular alp. Here were signs of living again; a whitewashed chapel, an untidy Bauernhaus beetle-browed with balconies, roofed in grey shingle on which a score of boulders comically sat. Here also were three paths: I swayed at the junction, dizzily sun-blinded, hazily wondering which way. In the farm-house, suddenly, a woman sang: loudly, carelessly, as if she knew the wildness of the place and could pour herself out unhindered into space. The singing went on, clear as a challenge, even as I blundered through the half door and groped in the dark passage. On the right was a room hung with pots, jugs, wooden hay-forks, buckets and saddles: here sat a fellow on a wooden stool and dandled over his knee a pink and dimpled lass who boisterously sang. With her head thrown back, her mouth stretched full, she hung against him and carolled as she stared upward. Even as I goggled at them both the man pulled her shoulders against his, planted a kiss on that joyous mouth, and stopped the singing on a chuckle of delight. Then, looking up, the lovers saw my wild face peering.

I asked the way lamely, falteringly. My eyes were sun-glazed and my voice thick from long silence. The woman jerked up from the bare knees that held her, came across the dirty floor, led me without a word into the open, and flung a scornful hand towards the rock wall that closed the valley.

"There!"

She nodded, stared hard, went back into the house. The door

slammed. I was left alone in the valley with the sound of rushing water in my ears.

Hours later, at the top of the pass, I came to a hamlet strung out on the saddle of coarse grass between two rock walls. Here the stream sprang from a cliff above the shingle roofs and began that breathless noisy journey down the ravine I had just climbed. Four goats came from the shade of the rocks to muzzle their heads into my sweaty hands, licking the salt. Under the brows of the farthest house an old woman squatted on a stool mending a wooden hay-rake.

"*Grüss Gott!*"[3]

"*Grüss Gott!*"

I sat there watching her as if she were the first human in my life. Her old fingers, like tree-roots torn from rotting soil, moved stiffly in and out of the wooden prongs. Her old lean bosom was thrust upward under the grey dirndl by some strange device: God knows, I thought vaguely, what these peasant women wear to make them such a shape. Surely not whalebone? But if not whalebone, what else, to force her waist to such a stony stiffness, to force what breasts she has left upwards into such a stiff pouting shelf?

Vividly, as one remembers delirium, I remember now her rasping, dry-throated prattle. They were bringing in the second hay-crop, she said: it had been a good year. They had heard there was no food in the town, but here everything was as usual. Not good, she sighed, not bad. There had been sickness among the goats, since the grass had been very lush and wet in July and the silly beasts had gorged themselves upon it. Though the rain had come after the first hay-crop: both hay-crops had been fine. Back now to where we had begun, the simple circle of the hamlet's thought perfected, she asked me incuriously how I did. The familiar words: "*Wie geht's?*"[4]

---

3   German: From Grüss dich Gott [God bless you]. A greeting most common in southern Germany and Austria.

4   German: How goes it, or How are you doing? Another common greeting.

"*Gut*," I answered, "*gut*."

I asked for a glass of milk and she quickened at once, telling me that it would cost me five groschen. Remote as this straggling settlement was, the post-war spirit had yet seeped up to it: in my childhood, in Styria, strangers were given milk, not sold it. Was there any place, I wondered, still unrotted by the war?

"*Grüss Gott*," I said, paying, getting up dizzily from the bench.

She peered at me as if I were wholly new and strange, as if I had not been sitting there beside her for the last fifteen minutes. Perhaps, I wildly thought, it is indeed so, she has seen no one, talked to no one. Perhaps I am only a voice asking for milk, a voice murmuring "*Grüss Gott*," no weight of footsteps on the grass as I go from her.

"*Grüss Gott!*" she called indifferently after me.

The evening glowed as I went on, the sun now mellowing to a finish. In the valley, deep as a cup below, tiny figures drove tiny cattle along a pale curl of road. A pinpoint woman gathered in her linen from a line strung between cherry trees. As I watched, wondering whether this tiny panoramic life below, so soundless, so remotely clear, lived at all outside my stumbling mind, the first raindrop fell. A dark cloud was boiling up from the south: rain-drops spattered, heavy as cool ripe plums, dropping from the tree. Soon the valley was flooded with thick squall, the rain swept over the hills into the hollow, swept over me as I stumbled downwards. In these high bare wastes before the alps begin there is something gruesome about solitude in rain. My heart beat heavy with fear, terror of something behind or before, it did not matter which, for it was anyhow imminent. The path leapt downward in a string of crazy turns and bends, doubling on itself between the thick scrub, the dark hard-leaved Alpenrosen on which a few small blooms, brown with bruises, still hung: between the boulders covered in dead green lichen, the clumps of coarse dry grass in which the ox-eye daisies looked ghastly pale. There was now not a living thing in sight, not a bird, not a rabbit, not a deer. Only as I ran madly down across the scree a few loose stones came trickling from above, and looking up I saw the bony impertinent hind-quarters of a chamois bounding skywards.

Now the valley swam in sight again, through driving mist, the path grew smoother, less wildly steep. There were sparse trees beside it, a pine bent in a half-hoop by years of wind, a group of pines with naked blasted sides, then a small wood, dark and damply fragrant. Here I heard over the roar of the gathering wind, the stinging slap of the rain, a scudding of footsteps as urgent as my own. Ahead of me, lost for long seconds in the gloom of the trees, behind wet reddish trunks, scuttled the strange figure of a little man, a man with bare muscular calves and a grey fez on his black wet head. He vanished; I hurled myself after down the slope, running from rain and fear: at the edge of a cliff, beyond a tiny patch of meadow and a white shrine, I saw him pop rabbit-like into a hay hut. And after, a wild thing rain-beaten and rain-terrified, I stumbled in, leaned gasping against the wall.

He was short, sturdy, a wiry muscular fellow with crisp hair as black as poppy seed, the ridiculous jaunty grey fez perched well back upon his wool. His black eyes went over me boldly, stripping me as I leaned and coldly dripped against the dripping planks.

"*Grüss Gott!*"

"*Grüss Gott!*"

"You're very wet, Fräulein. So am I."

He laughed outright, eased his rucksack from his back and without more ado twitched from it a concertina. The first faint wheezing notes came dismal as an owl's sneeze: tentatively he played a few bars, eyeing me with that bold sideways stare. Then:

"Let the rain pour!" he yelped suddenly, showing strong teeth. "Let it pour, we don't care. We're from Schwäbisch-Land."

Schwäbisch-Land
O Schwäbisch-Land!
Du kannst es wohl
Nicht widerstand![5]

"Play me something," I murmured vacantly, watching the rain trickle over the open doorway.

"That's good—she asked for it, she asked me to play!" cried the oddity to the damp wooden boards. "It's generally: 'Here's a groschen for you, you son of a bastard, if you'll take that thing round a corner and make your noises there.' Wilhelmine, Wilhelmine, at last we've got an audience."

And he slapped his concertina as men slap the stout backsides of their wives, before fitting his hands in the straps, drawing them apart so that the instrument sighed again, and bursting as a thrush does into clear ringing song.

Warum blickt doch so verstohlen
Mich des Nachbar's Töffel an?
Da er mir doch unverstohlen
In das Auge sehen kann.
Ich muss nur die Mutti fragen
Was er so verstohlen blickt:
Den wollt' ich's ihm selber sagen
Liess es wohl recht ungeschickt![6]

---

5   German: Swabia
                   Oh, land of Swabia!
                   You probably can't
                   Beat it.

6   German: Why does the devil of a neighbor
                   Watch me in secret?
                   Since he can look me
                   Straight in the eye.
                   I'll have to ask Mama

105

And so on, and so on, verse after verse, the consciously arch sentimentality of good old Germany when the beer flowed, and love too, under the chestnut trees in summer: when balmy nights were made for lovers' protestations and maidens' heaving sighs, when kisses smacked like little thunderclaps on rosy cheeks, and bosoms pouted to be fondled. A song of Germany, in short, before the war: that Germany, and those poets who warbled with such hearty coyness about love, are both long since dead, and their loss not too acutely felt, either. However, my Minnesänger[7] seemed unconscious that the lyrical corpse stank: he warbled to its end, rolling his fine eyes, and when the last note died away, when the concertina sighed to stop under his weaving hands, cocked a brilliant eye at me.

"*Siehst du*,"[8] he said, "we're fated. Here we are together in a hay-hut, outside there's nothing but rain, and evening coming on fast. *O weh!* we must spend the night together, there's nothing else for it. The question is, where? It's getting darker every minute, indeed it is. Where shall we sleep, *kleines Fräulein?* In this hay-hut? No, no, there's no hay. What use is a hay-hut without hay? About as much use as a woman without breasts; to sleep on, I mean. When the rain's let up a little, my tender ewe, I shall go out, I, Herman Metzger of Schwabmünchen, and find us a hay-hut in which we can sleep. Don't you think so, don't you think that's a notion?"

"Oh, for God's sake leave me alone!"

"So that's the way it is, the way it is. Upon my word, there's hardly a tune that will fit it. Ah yes, as usual, Johann Wolfgang Goethe to our rescue."

Why he looks at me in secret:
Because I want to tell him myself
Just look at me however clumsy you are.

7   German: minstrel.

8   German: Do you see?

And weaving his concertina back and forth once more he plaintively warbled:

Dann folg 'ich der weidenden Herde,
Mein Hündchen bewahret mir sie,
Ich bin herunter gekommen
Und weiss doch selber nicht wie.
Da stehet von schönen Blumen
Die ganze Wiese so voll
Ich breche sie ohne zu wissen
Wem ich sie geben soll![9]

"Is that how it is with you, my chicken? He's left you and there's no one to pick flowers for?"

Du brichst sie ohne zu wiss—en
Wem du sie geben sollst![10]

"You shouldn't be like that, Fräulein dear. Not one of us is really worth it. Try to think of something else. Would you like another song? You would? Oh, you're the woman for Herman, you listen and weep and let him make the music. What a woman! What a silence! What'll you have? Tannenbaum? Too hackneyed for a rare

---

9   German: I'll just follow the herd of cows grazing.
                   My little doggie will watch over them for me.
                   I came along with them
                   But don't know myself how I got here.
                   The whole meadow is full
                   Of beautiful flowers
                   I pick them without knowing
                   Who they are for!

10 German: You pick them without knowing
                   Who they are for!

107

woman. '*Der lustige Bua?*'[11] In your present state of melancholy, my bird, that might jar. Yes, indeed it would certainly jar. *Der Bua* has no business to be merry when maidens grieve. '*Ach, du lieber Augustin,*' what a mess! But I have it, I have it."

And without more ado he rattled off into "*Mädele rück, rück, rück,*" sang the whole song twice, so delighted was he with it, so loth to let it go; and then, sliding as birds do from one melody to another, he played on—all the old songs of south Germany, melancholy even at their gayest, haunting as the sea on an unbearably lonely shore.

I dozed a little, leaning my back against the wood, my feet stuck straight out along the floor, my wet body marking its shape in an oozy stain. When I woke it was really dark, the rain still fell. Opposite me Herman Metzger had laid his concertina aside and now combed his hair with the help of a mirror propped between his hairy knees. Seeing me awake he whistled a few bars of "*Mädele*" and crossed over to where I sat.

"It's still raining, Fräulein."

Yes, it was still raining. Awake now to my horror, I saw the train going out from the Wolfgangsee station, saw into it as one sees into a bowl of goldfish. There slept Bärbel in her borrowed bed, the linen cover (it had a blue bow embroidered on it) lying lightly over her face. Up went the train, winding painfully as if it had an aching back, up the rainy pass, up and away. Now there was nothing left but rain inside and outside: at the far corner of the hut, through a round knot in the wood, the rain spattered down.

We were startled both, in our wet silence, by an animal, sobbing sound. Past the door a woman ran up the path, a woman woefully wet, decked out in the country dress of dirndl, silk-fringed neckerchief, bright apron, dangling silver ornaments. Her gaudy silks were dark with rain, she hiccuped as she stumbled and never ceased to wail hoarsely on a climbing note.

---

11   *The Happy Lad*, a popular German song of the time.

We both peered out: my own misery, it seemed, rushed past in the flesh.

"What's here?" murmured the tramp, his black eyes popping, his cheek warm to mine, "a seduction? Alas, it's too wet, there won't be one on this dripping path. No need to run so, Mädele, he'll not run after you in this rain. But Lord, how she runs all the same! Women running remind me of fowls, all backside and neck: beg your pardon, Fräulein, but that's what they remind me of."

The woman vanished in at the open door of the little chapel, flopped in one wet movement to her knees. We saw dimly her soles upturned towards us; blown on the wind, her sobbings drifted down the path.

"So that's how it is!" hoarsely whispered the tramp, winking at me, laying a finger along his nose. "I knew there was a man in it somewhere. *Der heilige Christ*, no less. Things must have come to a pretty pass when the man she runs to is a plaster one with gilt on him. Never get that way, Fräulein: you stick to flesh and blood. Religion's the very deuce, indeed it is. I had it once when my old mother lived: she made me pious and believed I was a good boy, the soft old goose. *Das Mutter Herz*," he carolled suddenly, "*bleibt ewig treu! Das Mut-ter Herz bleibt e—e—e—wig treu!*"[12]

At the sound of his mocking falsetto the woman turned, gaped, shuddered at us over her shoulder and ducked once again to her altar littered with tawdry rubbish, her wounded-beast sobbing.

I leaned my head against the wood, longing to sleep again. The rain beat down a maddening chorus to my thoughts. Herman leaned near me, pared his nails with a long knife, and hummed as he scraped. Now the woman came yowling from the chapel and went once more yowling down the hill.

"Good thing she's not in here," said he. "I'd hardly have spirit enough for a chirrup, upon my word. She's a damp one, she is.

---

12   German: The mother's heart remains forever true.

But you—you're different. You positively encourage me by saying nothing at all. What'll you have? 'The Melancholy Shepherd' all over again?"

"I want to sleep."

"So you shall, my blossom, when the rain's stopped. Then Herman'll find us a nice cosy hay-hut with plenty of fine hay to lay us down in. And we'll sleep—ah, how we'll sleep! Like the great Wallenstein, '*Ich denke einen langen Schlaf zu tun.*'[13] Only I hope nobody'll murder *me* in the dark night—eh, my little Buttler? Or perhaps, being a female, you prefer nails as a weapon, eh, my little Jael?"[14]

I got away from my support, the cold door-post, and stumbled out into the rain. He called after me, whistled, yodelled. Soon he was splashing alongside in the gravelly runnels.

"Very well, very well, if you *will* go out, well then, you will. I know a woman of spirit when I see one. Maybe you're right, too: maybe the rain's not going to let up this side of Christmas. Hey, stop a minute, there's a hut—there by the stream. No, no good, the hay's not in yet, though it ought to be. Upon my soul, that Bua'll have some rotten sodden stuff on his hands if he doesn't hurry up and get it in. These Austrians, now, happy go lucky's not the word for 'em. Talk about Wiener Schlamperei[15]—it's a real Schweinerei,[16] to my mind. Aha! aha! there's another hut up there by the pines: and may I be struck down as an infidel, Fräuleinchen, if that hut hasn't hay in it!"

---

13   From *Wallenstein*, by Friedrich Schiller: "*Ich denke einen langen Schlaf zu tun, denn dieser letzten Tage Qual war groß...*" ("I think I will have a long sleep, for the troubles of these last days have been great...")

14   A reference to Jael (or Yael), the Biblical heroine who aids the Israelites by killing Sisera, the general of the Canaanite army, by driving a tent stake through his skull (Judges 4:21).

15   German: Viennese sloppiness.

16   German: A terrible mess.

It had. Herman Metzger's brown legs gleamed wetly as he leapt a fence, scampered through a meadow. With one deft flick he had picked out the two horizontal boards across the opening: there lay the hay piled up inside with stooping room atop between it and the roof.

"In you go, Fräulein—want a leg-up?"

"No."

"Very well, then, in you go. I'll look the other way. Always the gentleman, that's Herman, when females show leg. He has his eyes fixed on yonder snowy peak which he can't see because the rain's too thick. Are you in yet? Good. You must have a light conscience, my little brown Fräulein, to clamber in so kittenishly."

He clambered after, himself as spry as a goat. We stood there knee-deep in hay, breathing quickly. The sound of rain on the roof was shattering: the sweet smell of hay made me sick. Which to be, I dimly wondered: drowned outside, or hay-smothered inside?

"At last!" he cried, treading the hay level; "now we'll have a fine nest. We'll make two little graves, under this bit of roof that doesn't leak. Two nice little graves, my duck, as snug as the real thing but far more interesting."

He bent down: I heard him throwing hay out between his legs like a terrier digging sand. The moist smell of fomenting hay was thick on the air. I never wanted to smell hay again, after that night pillowed on the steaming stuff. The tramp stopped scrabbling, grunted, and crouched in the shadows gnawing at something, staring out over the meadow to where, through the rain, a snow-shoulder glimmered pale.

"Give me some."

"Eh, Fräulein?"

"Give me some bread."

"Women are so improvident," he grumbled, carefully tearing off a tiny crust. "They run away from home in rain-storms with their best aprons on, they get wet and probably catch their death of cold visiting plaster saints, they go for long tramps through the mountains with cotton dirndl and no food whatever. But they come through all right, the bitches. The men see to that: they'll always meet some poor oaf who shares his last crust with them. What *have* you brought with you, Fräulein?"

"Nothing."

"There, you see. Ye gods, here she comes galloping over the alps with nothing, nothing at all. No money, even?"

"No," I lied.

"Well, I daresay *you* know what you're at."

He took his concertina and played again, with a maudlin dribbling melancholy, the herdsman's song. The lachrymose notes died away; nothing now but the rain-beat, the steady plopping of water from the roof to the sodden grass, and suddenly, away up in the dark alp, the hoarse bark of a deer.

"Come to your grave, Mädele. Come to your little grave. You'll sleep well to-night, a woman always sleeps better when she's not alone. Aah—aah! we shall both sleep well, and let the rain rain all night if it will."

We lay alongside in the narrow troughs, in the fungus-damp gloom.

"*Siehst du*," he sighed close to my ear, "wasn't I right when I first saw you there by the shrine and said we two were made for one another? That girl's made for me. I said, seeing you come down the mountain like a bird on your spun-glass ankles."

"I want to sleep."

"So you shall. Listen, Liebling, don't go on to-morrow. I don't know where it is you're making for, but don't make for it. Look, we'll stay here in the hay as snug as little cats. I'll go into the village for some food, you can lie here and wait for me."

"To-morrow I go on."

"Why to-morrow, in Christ's name? Stay here with me."

"I'm going on."

112

SARAH CAMPION

"Ah no, not to-morrow—to-morrow you stay with me."

"No, no."

"Very well, then we make the best of to-night. Are you warm and snug, Liebling?"

Why not, thought I as I heard him scuffling, throwing off his clothes, why not? The warmth of damp hay is not long to be borne, is too inhuman, a fungoid warmth. Clasped now to a naked hairy chest, warm with another close-pressed body, I shivered in reluctant delight, not from cold. We made love as beasts do, because we must. There were none of the refinements of passion in the hay that night: a heated urgency, a rough rude taking, and thrills running fiercely along tired flesh. Later I woke to the smell of hay, to a head snuggling like a baby's in the curve between breast and arm-pit. I laid my cheek along the round head: ah, Bärbel, little burrowing Bärbel.

"*Du—du*—be kind to me again."

"Go to sleep, little one, sleep like that with your head just there."

"*Du—*" he muttered again, pressing closer, yawning full-mouthed against me, "*du—!*" And the voice trailed off into the hay while I lay half-awake thinking, this that I dreamed yesterday was only a dream, brewed in some other mind. Here is Bärbel's head, here is Bärbel's head once more against me.

Dawn was very pale and sorry, shimmering through the pines. It was raining harder than before. The man sprawled, clutching hay in his hands. What did he look like? I had no idea, remembering him only as a hot thick voice in the dark, a pressing body, a round head on my breast.

My hair was full of hay. I pulled at it with stiff fingers, combing out the brittle stalks, distastefully picking wisps from my clothing, my ears, my neck. Ugh! how the stuff smelt—so intimate, so stale, so sweetly breathing decay and a kind of mushroom death.

He rolled over, grunted, flung out a hand to clutch my ankle.

"Ah—dear little one!" he murmured, opening one eye. His face was sodden with sleep, hay-creased, and his thick oily curls stuck through with hay.

"*Lebwohl.*"

"No—no—don't go."

"*Aufwiederseh'n.*"

"*Du—!*" he shouted, clutching. But I had dropped over the boards, landed squelching in the meadow, and was away.

*****

The second day is ever the worst. I remember little but nightmare: lying writhing and vomiting by a stream, among pale grass of Parnassus: drinking icy water, vomiting again. Later, in the road, a peasant with incurious deep eyes hoisted me to the front of his wagon, took me for miles along the road to Salzburg. The landscape floated past, a dirty sea beaten into puckers by the rain. Salzburg was a bank of staring eyes through which I stumbled to the post office, and spent one of my last precious schilling in a telegram to Tante Lydia saying simply and dramatically: "KOMM." I knew she would come, grumbling at nieces as she did so. But, disordered though my hot mind was, I knew she could not come to Salzburg: she had no Austrian visa. So I added the address of the prim, chestnut shaded hotel in München my father always loved, and, this done, stumbled on for Freilassing and the German frontier.

On the third day, as I tramped the hot dusty road towards Rosenheim, the soles of my shoes flapped loosely in the dust, small pebbles wormed their way through to chafe my hot feet, and my mind swung back to and fro slyly presenting arguments for its own comfort. The wild cherry trees heard those muttered arguments, those protestations that I had, after all, done the best I could for Bärbel. What chance had she with me in Berlin? None, cried my mind, exulting in its common sense. So, as I went along,

I saw for myself Bärbel's life as it now would be in some small town at the foot of the Alps, in the simplicity, the pure clean air that even the war had not managed to spoil. The woman had looked like the wife of some frugal Beamter: a railway clerk, perhaps, tidy and affectionate and careful. The Austrians, anyhow, are very fond of children.

Tante Lydia, highly irritated at having been fool enough to come, was in München before me, with the suitcase I had expressed from Bad Aussee to Berlin. She asked no questions, simply listened with a fretful face.

"She's dead, Tante Lydia. Croup. And I'm glad, poor little thing. What chance would she have had? God knows how I'll live without her; but it was hard enough to support myself in Berlin, I couldn't have kept a child as well."

"That's a very sensible reflection, Charlotte."

"But you think I'm a heartless brute for thinking of that when I've lost my baby?"

"Don't look for meanings under meanings, child, you'll be a nuisance to everyone if you do. Now, what are you going to try next? Are you coming back to Berlin?"

Did she believe me? I never knew. One was safe with her. She is easily the most exasperating old harpy I have ever known, but she keeps other people's secrets as well as she has kept her own. With her in München, calming down under her sharp common sense to something like normal, I watched and wondered. It was a blessing to wonder about Tante Lydia, not alone about myself. There were things the family for years had ached to know. What had she done with herself all that time, in the last century, when she professed to be studying art in München, Wien, Florence, Paris? No one knew. Tante Lydia came back with an odious joy in daubing, and a mouth tight shut. As the years went on and her past, whatever its colour, should have been allowed a decent rest, the family's guesses grew wilder and wilder. My imagination now rioted after them, heated by the memories I was trying to stifle. Astonishing that Tante Lydia herself abruptly lifted the veil a little. We hung one fine morning over the Maximiliansbrücke, staring at the Isar. She flowed beneath us chalky green, ruffled with foam streaks, deeply silent. Only when you closed your ears against the rattle of wooden wheels, the shuffle of feet, you could hear the war in her narrow channel strongly whispering, steadily flowing down to the rhythm of her own music. A barge floated through the arch of the bridge, piled high with pine-trunks. A stout brown fellow in faded blue trousers, his chest mother-naked, stood forward and plied a pole to keep his craft in the stream's centre.

Tante Lydia suddenly chuckled. "Bruno thought that looked so easy!" she said.

"Bruno—was he ever here?"

"Not him, for heaven's sake! I mean his father. He was here for a week or two, years ago, of course. He was writing a poem about München: it began:

Ach, du frohes Mädel des Gebirges![17]

And it went on in much the same strain till he ran dry at the end of the first canto. Oh well, a man who doesn't write poetry in his youth seldom does much worth doing later on."

Was I sensitively imagining, or did Tante Lydia's voice caress that word Bruno? I looked at her sharply, remembering Uncle Bruno Blümchen as a pale melancholy man, absorbed in business, wearily patient with Tante Ludmilla. Mysterious, to my young mind, that his tired stout body should ever have housed this ardent poem-writing spirit. He died in the war, of diabetes: now in 1924 he leaned with us, in Tante Lydia's thoughts, over the sunny parapet to watch the bargee poking his cargo out of sight. The brief tenderness passed:

17   German: Oh, you happy girl of the mountains!

I glanced once again at my aunt, who was pettishly picking wax out of her ears, and suggested that we move on. That was all I ever heard of the youthful Bruno in München: the veil dropped down on him again to leave me with Tante Lydia, that shrewd tiresome female, and the gnawing of my own troubles.

When she got bored with München, when our little hoard of money was almost drained, we proceeded soberly back to Berlin, to that rummage bag of an apartment on the Schwalbenufer. Tante Herta was still, thank God, wanly frolicking with her Kühns in Magdeburg: we had time to settle in before she returned to fret us, as she did all her relatives, into a state of hysterical self-pity. Tante Clara yearned to have me back on the Luisenufer—or so she said: but Tante Lydia clung resentfully to me, grudgingly disbursed cash for my meagre wants, and evidently saw in me a bolster, a convenient shock-absorber, against the time when her other stable-mate should return.

By wheedling, by promises of favours which I never gave nor meant to give, I got back my job with the Touristenbüro. The Americans were glad to see me back, having had in my place a toothy, stringy-bosomed Aryan from Pommern who dragooned them into listening to her instead of gazing at her curves (she had few) and letting their minds roam down warm seductive alleys of speculation. Once again, for me, the spasmodic stream of cigarettes, cakes of soap, putative lovers, took up its earlier course. Once again I marched briskly, a dead woman, around Berlin with goggling fools trailing my wake: once again hot hands pressed against my hips, my thighs as we stood in a cluster admiring the Siegessäule, Potsdam's Orangerie or the Garnisonkirche. Mechanically, a woman who has known all this and is now dead, beyond it, I shifted my limbs from the pawing American palms, went suavely on with my account of what Friedrich der Grosse said to the French architect. It did not matter at all, I thought, accepting everything and getting nothing; why should anything matter?

This is a common enough state for the smitten twenties. At twenty-one, twenty-two, I was beginning to live again. I breathed again, I smelt the lime blossom as I went to work along Unter den Linden; my heart lifted a very little (and why not?) at the sight of the trees greening once more in the Tiergarten. Why should not the twenty-two-year-old heart leap at such things, at the sight (down, burgeoning heart!) of a more than usually handsome American man in the tourist flock (who, alas, pressed no hand to my thigh): at the kind but rabidly inquisitive warmth of the Blümchen family? It was natural enough, but I was dramatically ashamed of myself for being once again so undramatically normal. I should have stayed a dead woman smashed by tragedy, but thank heaven I did not. Resenting my new life, I became plumper, though never fat: colour bloomed in my cheeks, my hair shone, my eyes glistened, aunts and other female Blümchens exclaimed at the betterment of my looks. Some of them (for they were mainly sharp-witted) surely guessed at the story of the long summer in Austria, the return of a thin sallow Charlotte to their bosom. But family feeling was too close-knit, too fiercely exclusive, to allow of gossip outside the family circle. No doubt among themselves they chatted in delighted malice, as they had done all these years about Tante Lydia. The aunt had buried her remembrance of things past, I buried mine: we cared not two straws for the family opinion, squabbled as much as ever in the fullness of our mutual regard, and stormily shared the Schwalbenufer roof. How she annoyed me with her thin fretful fussings over household things, over the position of a saucepan in her tomb-like kitchen, the washing of a curtain, the question (perennial as frost and snow) of bed bugs! They swarmed, naturally, in the old rotting house: but Tante Lydia would not hear of them. Tante Ludmilla on the floor below might have them—in fact, said Tante Lydia, she most certainly had, the Russian slut: young Bruno's pale small girls might appear at breakfast mottled by the night-ravages of the loathsome pests—but she,

Lydia, had none. And off she would jerk, muttering furiously, to her own apartment, her own room, there to lock the door, barricade the window and battle grimly with pail, broom and some wholly useless home-made disinfectant against Things in the Walls for whom we none of us dared supply a name. A greedy, warm-hearted, mulish old bitch was my Tante Lydia in these later years when she and I and that poor weak maggot Herta lived near the roof on the Schwalbenufer. We were much together, drawn close by a curious irritation, a common disillusionment. The family christened us the two spinsters, Die Jungfrauen,[18] and teased us about our supposed hatred for men. We cared as little for that as for the other things they almost certainly said. She kept my young mind alive, the young mind returning with a briskness it found indecent from the swamping desolation of its first tragedy.

Under Tante Lydia's roof, upheld by the glitter, so like a wet stone, of Tante Lydia's eye, I met Kurt once again. They came together, the young Seligmanns, to settle in Berlin. Kurt was studying to be a dentist: Gisela had given up kindergarten work for the more important business of motherhood. They could not afford a baby and were now about, blithely, to have one. Kurt was older, soberer, very much the father. He fussed about her with shawls which she waved away, was tenderly anxious that she should not be cold (ah! that chill moonlit night on the Havel's banks!) nor hot, nor bored, nor excited, nor anything at all but a vessel bursting with creation. We met calmly, cousins who had once been fond and were now affectionately indifferent. We discussed the name of the child: Kurt, certain it would be a girl, wished it called "Gisela": Gisela, firm in her belief that her burden was male, insisted on "Kurt." I found the fond dispute nauseating, fled on some plea of business to the office in the Dorotheenstrasse and arrived with cheeks strangely hot, heart strangely cool at this meeting with

---

18   German: the virgins.

the father of my Bärbel. Both now seemed faint and shadowy, quite trivial, as I made up some accounts and considered next morning's programme. "9.30 Mrs. Silas Blumwitzer and party to Schloss. 11 a.m. Colonel and Mrs. Archibald Shafto to Potsdam." This seemed at the time, and mercifully enough, to be important. It seemed more important than Gisela's and Kurt's baby, for that had not yet arrived: and how was I to reconcile Mrs. Blumwitzer at 9.30 with the Colonel and his pinched Scottish wife at 11? These were the things that really mattered, in 1925.

It appals me, looking back, to see how little I thought or knew of the politics that then raged about me. No more Cuno—but Stresemann: and I knew nothing of either. In 1924, Americans made sly, spy-out-the-land references to the Plan of one General Dawes[19]: I had never heard of it, nor wanted to. "Waal, Miss Hurts. I guess you folks'll be sitting pretty now," they said, showing superb expensive teeth, and I smiled, wondering whether these were the kind of men who press dollar tips into the palm, wondering what their smiles were worth to me, Charlotte. In spite of my scorn, to Sepp, how many years ago, a man called Hitler also appeared to be still with us. Those who had their ears laid to the political ground heard him simmering like a tightly-lidded pan: the rest of us vaguely heard the man mentioned now and then, when our ears were unoccupied with weightier matters. Various henchmen of this Hitler got themselves killed in one way or another from time to time. The name Schlageter[20] made quite a little noise, and to us this seemed absurd. So many had been killed: in little street frays, in snipings from dark buildings, with dagger-thrusts outside

19   Charles G. Dawes (1865-1951), head of the Allied Reparations Commission, 1923-24. The Dawes Plan temporarily relieved the impact of Allied reparations on the German economy by stretching out the payments and providing a major loan to the German government.

20   Albert Schlageter (1894-1923), the former German officer executed by French forces occupying the Ruhr for acts of sabotage.

brothels and cafés, on lonely moors: why worry about Schlageter? Thus with the idea of anti-Semitism: it cropped up, as it always did when Germany was in a ferment. It had always been with us as a series of small pin-pricks in our social life. I was German in those days, no Jew. I listened vacantly to political talk when the man I was with would talk no other kind, but afterwards promptly forgot it, which was merciful, since in later years my miserable generation were able to do nothing else. Since that time we have become conscious that whether we like it nor not we are nothing less than Jew: then, before Hitler, we knew it not. Only the old ones, who root out trouble with their aged snouts, were forever urging us to return to Judaism, to cling to Judaism. Rarely, goaded by them, we turned to look for it—and what was there? No more, upon my oath, than a pious vacuum, a vacuum sucked airless by generations of grandfathers, great-aunts and even more remote forebears. In the synagogues there was nothing but a rich heavy-smelling flummery of robes, prayer aprons, men and women divided, not by a flaming sword but by a flooring of old thick wood. In Judaism there was nothing but a once lively faith now grown more than rotten. We young ones turned from it: we were Germans, not Jews. Thus argued Kurt and Gisela, busily founding a little German family who still had Jewish names: young Bruno argued thus, who had fought four years as a German and now went to work in the Blümchen fur shop every morning like any other sober, almost middle-aged and affectionate Vati bent on bringing back worms a-plenty to his young brood. I doubt if his wife Sabine who had been a Grünwald ever felt as Teuton as he: later, when the trouble came, she was the fanatical Jewess, the prophesying Deborah, of our family. Hitler kindled many a flame, but none so fierce as the race-pride which scorched Sabine's heart in 1933 and burned with such discomfort against the mild Aryan kin of her husband and children. Perhaps though, Hitler was not so much to blame as Sabine's Russian-Aryan mother-in-law, a woman who would make the most pious Mohammedan yearn for Christianity, if she preached Mohammedanism. But in 1925-1926 Sabine was silent about her Jewish blood: the Blümchen family as a whole was to the outward eye just another German family intent on earning a living in the political havoc which the war had left us. We went on with our jobs while we had them, searched desperately (desperately aided by all the other Blümchens) for any sort of a job when we had none, and met once a month to talk about the hardness of life while sipping vile after-war coffee. In winter the Romanisches café, in summer the Karpfenteich restaurant at Treptow: Blümchens with their spreading branches and twiglets had done this before the war, which interrupted, but did not kill, the gathering: those of us who were left started again about 1920. Blümchen women had in the last century married Gottliebs, Seligmanns, Bleibtreus, Gottschalks, Laddachs, Herzes: there had been a great many female Blümchens, only a few rather spindling Blümchen men. Now those that were left, and their descendants—all the clan still in Berlin—came together on Family Sunday, met at three o'clock after the midday rest, stayed chattering, squabbling, innuendoe-ing, till eight o'clock or after. The women had knitting, the men cigars. It was an impressive sight. Waiters rushed for us when we appeared thickly massed on the horizon: with an eagerness that grew more mechanical after 1933, they competed for our favours by putting three big iron tables end to end, fringing them with chairs, buzzing respectfully around until the order for coffee was given. We were sensibly frugal, but not of the type which takes its coffee beans and demands nothing of the management but hot water. The Blümchen housewives had enough of coffeemaking through the week: one Sunday a month they yielded up the ritual to the Karpfenteich slaves, keeping, however, a sharp eye skinned to see that the job was well done. We did take our own cakes to the Karpfenteich: that delectable spot gave nothing more stirring than a Sandkuchen which lived up to its name. So each summer

Family Sunday it became the task of one Blümchen woman to bring the food. As children we linked the aunt inevitably with her offering. Our one Gentile relative, Tante Ludmilla Blümchen, had a passion (which her purse favoured) for simple Kranzkuchen; and this she would get only from Kühn's on the Spittelmarkt where, declared my father, they saved up the week's leavings and let her have them cheaply, as remnants. Tante Clara Seligmann's knotted hands always unwrapped Apfel-strudel from the snowy tissue paper: it was put aside for her at Kuchen Kaiser early in the morning, piping fresh: she called for it on her way from the Luisenufer to the tram, and the same baldheaded waiter made always the same mild respectful joke as he put it into her hands. Tante Cosima, descending like a bright-eyed old parrot from the exotic region of the Kurfürstendamm, laid in a store of Mocha Torte at Kempinsky's on her way. Tante Lotte Laddach brought Zitronensahne, which travelled very badly, from Willi Komm on the Gertraudenstrasse. Tantes Herta Blümchen and Lydia Gottschalk, living together on the Schwalbenufer only because they were too poor to do otherwise, brought a rag-bag collection of their own baking: odd biscuits, strange humpy confections, buns in the English style. These last we called Knopf-kuchen ever since the lamentable day when once of Tante Lydia's bodice buttons leapt from her bosom into the mixing bowl and later broke a tooth of Onkel Franz Laddach as he bit cautiously into a bun. Apart from the button-cakes, whose taste and appearance none could foretell, we children knew precisely from Familien-Sonntag to Familien-Sonntag what we were going joyously to eat with our coffee. There were swarms of children before the war: three little Gottliebs, two little Herzes, three little Seligmanns, four little Bruno Blümchens (contemptuously called by us Mischlinge[21] because their mother, Tante

---

21   German. Mixed breeds or mongrels. Used to describe people of mixed "Aryan" and "non-Aryan" ancestry.

Ludmilla, was a Gentile), and young Cosima with no immediate family background beyond her utterly disreputable grandmamma. Not that Tante Cosima was less than enough for any child: like a one-man band she, singlehanded, supplied Cosima with all the noise, emotional crises, petty strifes, vituperations, caresses and bitter reproaches of the average parent-couple.

But in 1934, when through my backward-peering glass I see one of our family Sundays, the young ones were meagre. The parent generation now suffered from ideas: they brooded over the state of the world instead of uncritically going about their job and re-peopling it. By now there was but a handful of children in Berlin to show what the proud, fruitful, lively Blümchen stock had once been. Kurt's three sprouts, David, Käthy and Hedwig. Tante Ludmilla's pale grandchildren, Lore and Gitta; little Sophie Kopje, not a Blümchen at all but the first by Anna Blümchen's second marriage to a gentile Dutchman: six little sprouts of the new generation, no more. Six little Blümchen sprouts, only two of them called Blümchen, and those two girls, were all that the older generation could feast its eyes upon. Now my eyes were upon them too, this breathless afternoon in August. I had nothing to do, no one to knit for: the talk bored me. I had smoked too many ciga-rettes and eaten as much Kranzkuchen as my figure would stand. So I leaned back looking at the nursery end of the table, at the little Seligmann's and Blümchen's, at the single little Kopje. They babbled, they fought, they spooned their coffee at one another, they crumbled Kranzkuchen, snooped sugar-lumps: among them, affronted by the things they did, sat poor little Julie Freudenberg, Anna's first by her divorced husband, born at the war's end and now in the painful half-way house of fifteen.

Kurt's offspring, I thought (and could think it quietly with no heart-pangs) were much the same as other children, though Gisela naturally found them vastly superior. David had the large brown eyes, the bow mouth of the young Kurt: Käthy was her mother's child, blacker, sturdier, more determined. Tante Herta had just made a fool of herself by declaring her to be the image of Tante Cosima at the same age. Tante Cosima, snorting down her over-powdered nose, asked how the devil Herta knew anything about it, having herself been born three years later. Tante Herta, crushed but defiant, slid behind her glasses into the whining apologies, the snuffling incoherencies, which she always used as a refuge from reason. Even gentle Gisela bridled at her: no tender mother would like her child compared to that ageing Jezebel, our Tante Cosima.

I, on the other hand, thought I should not like any child of mine to resemble Anna Kopje's Sophie, that waxen piglet. Here was a child who had been scrubbed twice a day, fed every two or three hours, clothed in the solidest garments that money could buy: a child on whom good money had been unceasingly lavished. The nastiest bit of Aryanism you could find anywhere, she squatted with her chin on the level of the table and single-mindedly mopped up the cake that David had left. She made me glad to be a Jew: for the first time race-pride budded in me, watching this Mischling who was three-quarters Aryan. I looked round the table, with new eyes, at my Jewish clan: parrot-faced Tante Cosima with her gaudy lips; young Cosima already a ripe scowling beauty doomed to quick decay; Tante Clara whose face had gone yellow with the years and whose new wig fitted even worse than the last; Bruno and Georg Blümchen, egg-headed, already getting bald, caricatures, no less, of all middle-aged Jewry; Berta and Brigitta, not only plain but strident; Kurt, with subtle down-dropping nose, mournful eyes that looked always a little wet, full lips; Gisela, pale and blackly browed; Tante Heidi bound into tyre-like bulges by her new brassiere; Tante Lydia despised by all the matrons for being at 78 unmarried (though, said Tante Ludmilla, no virgin either); Tante Herta slobbering uncontrollably over her last piece of Kranzkuchen. My God, I thought, we are a frightful lot: but we've all got something. A restless, deathless vitality, animating even Tante Cosima who by rights should have been under the sod long ago: a vitality which kept Tante Lydia's seventy-eight-year-old mind as keen as a razor blade and fully as merciless; a vitality infusing even Tante Herta's absurdities with more sparkle than there had ever been in the trim pink body of Anna Kopje. They're awful, I thought, regarding my aunts: they sit here like rapacious fowls tearing at the stuff of life; they're awful—: we're awful, but we live! we live!

Suddenly, terrified yet ecstatic as I had been when Bärbel first stirred in me, I felt the quickening of my Jewish pride, quickening and as yet unborn. I was a vessel fearfully filled with rapture. The dark faces of my kin, the colours, the smells, the sights and sounds of that one speck of time—myself sitting at that iron table by the Karpfenteich embedded in the Blümchen matrix yet a separate jewel—glowed like a landscape before a thunderstorm. Everything was crystal-edged, shone with its little life, was proud to be unique. I saw everything at once, all impinged upon a deliciously shocked consciousness. The trees hung round me heavy with late summer, the dark green rich exhaustion which comes in August. Beneath spread the blobby shapelessness of more than a hundred people sitting round chequered squares of tablecloth laden with eating-refuse: the varied, unrhythmical crowd pattern that vexes yet titillates the eye. Down the narrow alleys between tables the waiters added restlessness by seething to and fro, bearing high over their heads trays laden with coffee-pots, milk jugs, blue-white squares of sugar, pale yellow piles of Sandkuchen. Beyond, in the greener, tenderer shade of the willows by the pond's edge, sated families strolled back and forth, large shape-less parent-cruisers attended by smaller, more volatile craft. They strolled, exuding tobacco puffs, or clouds of eau-de-Cologne strongly soured by under-arm sweat: they bent carefully to peer at the carp as lazy as themselves in the dark green waters on which a summer's scum floated: they exclaimed over the yellow water lilies: they fed the ducks. Further still, absorbing the tired eye, sucking it down to cool depths, was a bank of trees, thick bushes trailing in the water; a bank gratefully and bottomlessly green. Against it, forever shifting with the noise of a muddy tide on pebbles, the human stream: peering, poking, absorbing food, exclaiming.

An air of innocent heavy-footed enjoyment was abroad. The Germans, thought I (I, the newly race-conscious) lack our gaiety but balance the loss by enthusiasm. They are always "begeistert" when confronted by that whore, Nature. They exclaim, they point, they shriek epithets. The water lilies are "wunderbar," the stagnant water "zu herrlich," the blowsy ducks "entzückend."[22] Perhaps, in fact these objects are so: but the Germans bombard Nature with expressions of their happiness in seeing her, they deck her with ponderous bouquets of words. She, smiling dangerously, bends her neck for these somewhat musty artificial flora, and remains as much a mystery as ever. We Jews have little real respect for the hussy: we like better the things we have ourselves created. Music, art, drama, the whole fine structure of entertainment, the handiwork of quickening the senses—these are ours. Let Nature be ever so green, we look at her with a shrewd eye, and decide that she is not for us. There's no money in her.

But alas! even for Germans there is in every Eden a serpent. It must be admitted that the midges in this pleasant afternoon were frightful. They twitched through the torpid air in gauzy swarms: now the keen ear, seeking fundamental mysteries, could catch the faint exasperated ping! of the slaps that followed their assault. But they came too late, these slaps: all slaps come too late, it is their doom. The slap on the child's hand, the male's cheek, at the midge's airy body that whisk away unharmed, they all cry: "Too late!", are all but the cracklings of futility, a most futile sound.

---

22 German. Begeistert: enthusiastic; wunderbar: wonderful; zu herrlich: splendid; entzücken: delightful.

A slap rang out now at our table: one insect, surely more virulent than all the rest, had punctured Georg Blümchen's hairless scalp. Leaping like a squib, he slapped agonised at the part.

And at once the crystal roundness of my little scene, so vivid, sensual, tender, was broken up. I saw it no more as a whole. I who had been timeless was now shackled to time by 1934, was gazing through cigarette smoke at Georg, who had just been midge-bitten, and thinking for the twentieth time how homely he was.

"Ge—org!" cried his mother, clawing him back into his seat, "it's only a midge."

"Put some washing soda on it, Georg," suggested Anna calmly.

Her brother glared. "And where am I to get washing soda?"

"Oh well!" She shrugged her massive shoulders at man's unreason. Anna was very trying today: most married women are trying when they come back to the family bosom. A smug odour hung about her, ineffably smug.

"Come here, Liebling, and let me wipe your mouth!" she called to Sophie. I was glad to see the child took not the slightest notice. Nor had Anna really thought that it would: she merely wanted to call attention to it, to her motherhood. It was a shaft aimed at all of us who were not mothers, particularly at Tante Lydia and myself whose spinsterhood the family felt to be a blot. Drawing ourselves up, puffing cigarette smoke, exchanging amused glances, we stood it pretty well. We had not littered the earth with little waxy Aryan swine, not we: nor were we likely to.

"She's very like her father," murmured the doting grandmother.

"I'm glad there's some reason for her looks," replied Tante Lydia crisply.

The two ladies, between whom there had always been a deep mistrustful loathing, glared at one another across the table. Tante Clara at once began peaceably on politics, always a safety valve and now, in 1934, never far from our minds. Leaning our elbows on the littered table, abandoning our knitting, we lapsed into talk of the thirtieth of June[23] (which still shocked us), we wondered about Dollfüss'[24] widow, we whispered of the dead Röhm and then, descending from the large political issue to the small, we talked, also in undertones, of Onkel Hans Bleibtreu.

Now this Onkel Hans of ours was a shocking example of how not to grow old. He had started the ageing process well enough; had seemed all set to become the silver-haired bachelor, the pet uncle, the milch cow of the Blümchens. But then he had destroyed the family legend in the middle years by marrying, in January of this very year, his housekeeper. Among the vivid parrot flock of my relations, most of them characters in their own way, Onkel Hans had had nothing but that rather nebulous good old uncle-hood which was grafted on him by the family. His character, that is, rather flowed through the channel of another's, was moulded into liquid form by someone else's stronger will. He was an amiable watery man, no more, until he disastrously decided something for himself and married Marie Hahnenfuss. That brought him right out of the background for most of us. My aunts said, and they were almost certainly right, that he only married her because he could get her no other way. She was comely, plump, toothsome, and forty. She had a fierce tight virtue which said "no" more than once to the importunate dotard. Even after he had panted behind her with his tongue hanging out for a number of years, he had got no nearer possessing her than a squeeze of her ribs as she passed him in the dark passage, a kiss smearily imprinted on her neck as she bent unguardedly over the washing-up. So he married her on a cold January morning, at a registrar's office: she

23   30 June 1934 marked the beginning of the Night of the Long Knives, the purge of leaders and members of the SA (*Sturmabteilung*).

24   Engelbert Dollfuss (1892-1934), Chancellor of Austria, elected in 1932. Consistently opposed to Nazi demands, he was assassinated on 25 July 1934 by a group of Austrian Nazis in an attempted coup d'état.

tightly solid in a suit of electric blue woollen, himself miserable in a frock coat and top hat.

At the news the Blümchens rose like a swarm of hornets. Marie might have apple-red cheeks and a bosom which made Onkel Hans' joints turn to water when he looked at it, but who was she? She had no family that was not low and disreputable. Who was Herr Papa Hahnenfuss? Marie did not know. Frau Hahnenfuss her mamma protested that she had long since forgotten. Anyhow, even if there had been a Herr Hahnenfuss, even if he had ever had a name (which all the females in the Blümchen, Herz, Gottlieb, Gottschalk and Seligmann families shrilly doubted), what a name to have! What a low, guttersmelling ridiculous name! Hahnenfuss, cockfoot—it was the sort of name which cracked your sides with laughter in the Varieté, it was a loud joke of a name, altogether too ridiculous.

So thus the family, separately and *en masse*, buzzing about the head of our poor Onkel Hans. The truth was that Hans had money, considerable cash: and the mere smell of his marriage upset many a private scheme in the family. Of all the male descendants of that shrewd old fur-trader Egon Blümchen, my great grandfather, only Onkel Hans had any fortune left. Nephews and nieces, the children of his fruitful cousins Anni, Ruth, Clara and Cosima, had been mentally setting themselves up in businesses, educating their children, dowering themselves or their daughters with Onkel Hans' gold for years. We were not mercenary, we were Jews, therefore coldly logical about cash. We needed it for a full life, we wanted to lead full lives (who of us does not?), therefore we must make or get money. Among the Blümchens it was a sensible tradition that the money made by our men (most of them busy, intelligent and honest) should stay in the family. Not to be hoarded but used for the Blümchen good. Reasonable enough, surely. But here was the nightmare unreason of Onkel Hans, glazed with lust, shackling himself and his money to this plump forceful nobody. Why on earth had he *married* her? asked the women, merely rhetorically. Whereat the men, with knowing winks and nudges, coarsely replied that if only old Hans had known a thing or two he'd have got all he wanted from Fräulein Hahnenfuss at a much cheaper rate. At which the women squealed "Du! Georg, Bruno, Kurt, Franz" (whichever the name might be), "you ought to be ashamed of yourself!" Knowing, deep in their shrewd female hearts, that the men were right. He should never have had to marry the Hahnenfuss.

However, marry her he did: she forty, he seventy-nine. Life may begin at forty, but at seventy-nine it is usually on the wane. Onkel Hans had never been peculiarly virile. Sure that he was still a man, eighty years a mere bagatelle, he advanced to the now lawful embraces of Marie Hahnenfuss. Like a boa constrictor binding itself about its appalled prey, Marie wrapped him round. She was quite prepared for him, though humorously aware that he was but the snip end of a bargain. And at her touch Onkel Hans, who had been such a gay fellow in dark passages, collapsed, shrunk, lay in her arms with as much energy as a windless balloon. He could do nothing with the tough resilience of his wife. Her vigour drained his, sucked him dry: she was as tough a virgin as ever reached forty still intact. And a virgin she remained, disappointedly. But mirth followed disappointment: this was really too funny, thought Marie Hahnenfuss, who had an earthy sense of humour. Night after night in the apartment on the Breitestrasse she lay and laughed at him. The laughter of Marie Hahnenfuss rolled away through thick doors, down the clammy steps, out into the quiet Breitestrasse, startling there the scavengers who at dawn begin to clear up Berlin's debris. When she had done laughing she would flick on the light to look at him, to gloat over this mirth-provider, lying with his meagre old shoulders hunched over his ears, his night-cap (yes, he wore a night-cap) all awry, his poor rheumy eyes between papery lids rolling in vain away from the cruel electric.

131

"Look at me, Häschen,[25] look at me!"

A wriggle in the bedclothes, and our Onkel Hans almost sinks from sight, submerged in sheet.

"*Look* at me!"

"What, Liebling?" (as if he were just waking, as if he really didn't know what she wanted of him).

"Look at me!" she commands again, leaning over him so that her big firm breast presses his cheek, "open your eyes and look at me!"

Slowly, painfully, the old tortoise opens his eyes to blink at her.

"You're a fine husband, you are!" cries Marie, leaning closer to search him relentlessly with pale blue eyes. Pale killer's eyes with no depth, they stare at Hans Bleibtreu, raking him from crown to sole. The blankets, the sheets, the bloated down quilt which is yet not thick enough to keep him warm, are now no good. Marie's eyes have X-ray quality: they reduce him, as he shivers, to a heap of brittle bone, impotent flesh.

And then, when she has seen all she will, she lies back and roars with laughter till the bed heaves. Once again laughter rocks out into the street to tickle the ears of the patient horses, the lean underfed scavengers collecting rubbish by the dawn's light. They straighten up, listen a moment, then bend once more to the restless raking of Berlin's filth, thinking as they bend that someone is taking her pleasure in a warm bed behind those curtains. Marie Hahnenfuss's laughter, gathering insolent volume, rolls away to beat against the citadels of the Blümchen clan on the Schwalbenufer, at the Oranienplatz, in the Gertraudenstrasse, even as far as the mighty West End.

Marie had diddled the embattled clan, and well we knew it. For once a Gentile had got through the shrewd subtle defences of us Jews. It was cunning, no more: a cunning as insidious, as

---

25   German: Bunny, a term of affection.

restless, as our own. The low cunning of a peasant woman who knows what all men want and how to make them pay for it. For it was now painfully plain that she would outlast him: she was not going to die first, not she. We watched and saw with disgust how each week she grew rounder, harder, pinker, while Hans weekly shrivelled, crumpled, until he looked ninety at least. After but two months of marriage our Onkel Hans looked a corpse cruelly resuscitated for a witches' Sabbath: beside him the new wife bloomed with the insolent grandeur of a big red peony. He, who had been a tidy, pernickety old bachelor, now slobbered his food down his waistcoat, dropped crumbs on his chin, chewed his nails till the raw flesh bled. Never was a man so changed, sighed the Blümchen females, as that poor old Hans since She got him. Poor Onkel Hans! sighed the young ones, seeing their businesses, their dowries, go slithering away on the downward slope of Onkel Hans's marriage—poor, poor old Onkel Hans!

This was in early spring: in June our Onkel became tragic indeed. He was the first of us to crash in the new Nazi regime, to bring home to us what non-Aryanism meant. It was a time of seething unrest in Berlin: plots were brewing, counter-plots lay ripe for discovery; the brown S.A. and the black S.S. could hardly be kept from tearing at one another's throats.[26] One fine summer morning it was the misfortune of Onkel Hans, that ineffectual dotard, to fall foul of both.

It appears that our uncle went out as usual that twenty-second of June to shuffle along the pavement of the Breitestrasse towards the Public Library, now his refuge. Frau Knobke saw him go and remarked that the day was fine. To which Onkel Hans, whose regrettable marriage had not cured him of a weakness for women, replied that he thanked her, it was a fine day, and to-morrow, he

---

26   The conflicts between the *Sturmabteilung* (S.A.) and the *Schutzstaffel* (S.S.) that preceded the Night of the Long Knives.

hoped from looking at his barometer in the hall, would be finer still. "It's a strange thing about that barometer," bumbled Onkel Hans, standing over her with his hat still in his hand, "but I think it improves as the years go on. Its present prophetic accuracy is remarkable—truly re-markable!"

And he was going on to tell her some of the barometer's recent successes, when Frau Knobke, who has a shop, six children, and a disabled soldier husband who does nothing but smoke and spit, cut him short rather curtly and retired down the steps among her vegetables and Limburger Käse. I can imagine Onkel Hans sighing as he put his hat on again: so few people nowadays, he found, had time to talk.

So on he trod, carefully, very flat-footed, along the broad pavement past the Ermelerhaus, now a museum, where he remembered dining as a very young man. He had successfully got over the road and was already under the archway leading to the library when a noise from the Schlossplatz caught his ear. Something was afoot: life's tedium was about deliciously to be broken. People lifted their heads to look along the street, a few of the flippant lighter-footed young were running the same way, agog for sensation. My Onkel Hans paused. On the one hand the cool spacious reading-room, the bliss of a quiet almost perfect except for the squeak of a chair when some giddy young reader got up to go: on the other hand (Onkel Hans under the archway carefully balanced the rival charms) there was excitement, bustle, life, something really new to think and prattle about. Or so he imagined, hearing now a burst of laughter from the Schlossplatz, seeing a sober matron stop dead like a pointer, rigid with curiosity, then break into a lumbering half-trot.

So Onkel Hans plumped for Life, and made his way as best he could to the end of the street. Here, where the buses curve round by Begas' Schlossbrunnen, that bulging group of mermaids and mermen writhing plumply about the water, was a crowd so thick and dense that Onkel Hans was hard put to it to push his way through. Being, however, long and shrivelled, with a pair of spry elbows, he managed at last to arrive and stood there wheezing, peering.

A very slim, pink, fledgling S.S. man was getting into trouble with two ginger-shirted S.A. Onkel Hans never knew what started the affray, but when he arrived words had evidently led to words and the crowd, goggling, hoped that blows would follow.

"Bloody black-coated tapeworm!" remarked one S.A. man in a casual tone, his eyes hard and bright with rage.

At this the affronted S.S., gathering all his courage, shot back:

"You blasted skulking communist, you—! You bleeding beefsteak!"

His voice broke on the last tremendous insult: to call a man a beefsteak in those days suggested that he might be brown outside but was certainly red within.

Raising a hand like a side of meat, the S.A. man felled the Black Guard with a single stroke.

"Aah!" sighed the ecstatic crowd. All the women shrieked before beginning to claw their way as near to the front as they could. Everyone was glad to see the black dandy uniform with its silver trimmings lying limp as a sack at the foot of the fountain, just under the more than life-size toe-nail of a galumphing great sea-nymph.

Seeing that the audience approved, the S.A. gave one look east and west to make sure there were no more S.S. on the horizon, then went on to further flights. They took off the stunned lad's cap, his grand coat: they undid the great belt with holster and pistol, the black strap which had bound his manly chest. Everything was cast, with suitable bawdy comments, into the fountain: the crowd giggled shrilly as the objects plop-plopped into the tepid water. There was a pause: the crowd hung on every movement. Lifting up the limp lad they propped him over the fountain's stone rim and slowly, slowly, with hot excited grins on their faces, drew off his boots and breeches. The crowd pressed forward in dead silence. No sooner were the pants off, exposing long quivering pale thighs, than all the ladies present squealed shrilly. What they expected to see when the trews were withdrawn is not quite clear: what they saw evidently startled them, for with one accord they squealed, covered their faces with their hands, and peeked behind chaste fingers.

The fun might have become even richer, since the crowd shivered with a common delicious sadism: but at this very minute, catapulting from a tram at the Haltestelle, came five enormous S.S. men. What figures! What men! With black coats sleeked trimly to wide shoulders and narrow waists, with jetty boots curving over great round calves, they hurled themselves through the crowd (which parted affrightedly on seeing so much black) and whizzed into battle.

Of the action which then ensued our Onkel Hans could never tell us much: it was too close under his poor inquisitive old nose. The two S.A. men on a last mad impulse had thrown their quarry bodily into the water: the avenging S.S., coming like a thunderclap, had slung the S.A. after him in less time than it takes to say O. The water sloshed over the fountain's rim, splashing the crowd who wondered whether to go or stay: the water was thick, foamy with the threshings and splutterings of badly scared bodies above whom the stout bronze nymphs stared down with no surprise in their prominent teutonic eyes, and dangled in their metal fists fish, fishing-nets and other marine whatnots. A lust after murder was in the air: small independent fights began amongst the crowd. Before many minutes were over Schlossplatz was full of pushing, struggling, smiting figures, women screaming and tearing their way out to safety, small children bowled underfoot but still bellowing lustily, the police, tardily arrived, laying about them with revolver-butts.

And where was our Onkel Hans in this disastrous mêlée? Alas, he had gone down like a ninepin before the fist of a rescuing S.S. man who, seeing an aged Jew salaciously peering from the crowd, had reacted in the proper manner. Onkel Hans lay senseless under foot and was later slung, along with other inert bodies, into the police car which came screaming from the Polizei Praesidium at the Alexanderplatz.

Now the crowd melted like snow before the Law, leaving some human debris behind. The S.S. dressed their violated comrade and took him off in a taxi. The trams, buses, motors and brewers' drays which had stopped at the farther edge of the Platz to see what all this was about now saw that the police were in charge, made haste unobtrusively to go on their way. The police car with my Onkel Hans inside it, a hearse for the living, sped silently off in the direction of Oranienburg.

In the Breitestrasse Marie Hahnenfuss did her housework, went out to her shopping, came back to prepare a frugal meal of spaghetti with tomato sauce, and waited for her spouse. When he did not come she ate heartily, washed up, took off her corsets and her shoes, lay on the great double bed looking at the pictures in the *Berliner Illustrirte*, and finally (for the afternoon was hot) fell asleep. At five o'clock there was still no Hans to drink execrable coffee and crumble a few stale Waffeln with her: Marie began to get a trifle alarmed. She went to the library, but found no Onkel Hans. She walked into a café at the end of the street in the half-hope that she might catch him napping, wasting his substance on a cup of mocha and a pretty waitress. Here also there was no Onkel Hans. Marching back aggrievedly to the flat she sat down to wonder where the old goose had got himself. She hoped he was not with any of the Blümchen crowd, but naturally enough never telephoned to find out.

Anyhow, we should not have been able to tell her anything. We ourselves knew nothing till the next day, Sunday. It was very hot, even as Onkel Hans' barometer had foretold. We sat, Berta, Brigitta and I, in the tiny Erkerzimmer overlooking the Luisenufer. A little stale air wandered in now and again: the flat was heavy

137

with the exotic perfumes of the twins, who loquaciously read the weekend supplements lolling in the flimsiest possible clothing. They were neither of them silent readers: I listened vaguely, mended my stockings, and let my thoughts wander.

There was a trampling of feet below in the hot dusk, a scuffling on the stone stairs, a ringing at the bell. Berta squealed, drawing about two inches of wrapper over her bare breast. Brigitta, less transparently decked out, got up to go to the door. Now in Berlin you do not open-heartedly hasten to admit when the bell rings; you stop and examine whatever stands outside on the mat: and you do this through a small glass eye built into the doors for that very purpose. Through the open door of the living-room I saw Brigitta tiptoe to do this, saw her shoulders stiffen, her hand agitatedly turn the lock, and rose to my feet in a spasm of terror just as three S.S. men marched in, slumped down in the nearest chair a human body sticky with blood: Its feet were bare, the toes were pulped masses: down its bare chest a spurt of blood had dried among deep purple bruises: its head—oh, Christ! shall we any of us ever clear that head from our minds! There was a gape over one eye where the flesh curved back from a splintered bone: in the other eye-socket, rusty with dried blood, an eyeball dangled bloodily by one thread.

Brigitta, all as she was in her airy wrapper, gave one look and fell like a stone. The figure groaned, turned its mutilated head away from the light.

"My God!" shrieked Berta, "it's Onkel Hans!"

The S.S. men turned to us briskly.

"This your uncle?"

"Yes—Yes—What has—?"

"Fräulein, it was really unfortunate. There was a mistake. We mistook your uncle for someone else: it was a mistake anyone might have made, but we should like to express our regret. We found this address in the pocket."

It was Berta's business card, so chaste, so debonair.

"Heil Hitler!"

They clicked their heels together, saluted smartly, and marched out again.

That was all we ever knew of the affair. There was, naturally, nothing in the papers. Onkel Hans, after weeks of semi-delirium, could tell us very little. He babbled, at weak intervals, of Oranienburg.[27] "They took me there and made me take off my shoes. Then they trod on my toes—about twenty of them, all big men. They marched on my toes." He hardly knew that he had lost an eye, that the wound on his brow, reluctantly healing, curved in a great angry red scar over the other eye. He mercifully knew very little: only now and then, pathetically sticking up his feet at the end of the bed for visitors to notice, he quavered: "They trod on my toes, quite twenty of them." Adding, after moments of mazy thought, that it had all been very painful.

This horror, this mangled bloody ruin that had once been Onkel Hans, made us at once and intensely aware that we were Jews. All over Germany other mangled uncles, murdered sweethearts, insulted mothers were bringing home to Jews that they belonged to Jewry. All over Germany we were drawing together, not because we loved each other but because there was no help for it. We drew nearer invisibly, as blobs of fat in a saucepan tend to drift into patches, merging themselves, wavering across the surface to one another, towards a willy-nilly fusion which is none of their making. We saw now that we were Jews, unalterable: we turned almost without seeing what we did to the ancient shibboleths of our childhood, the pious flotsam we had once so fiercely cast away. Now our children (like ourselves, the poor brats, Jews) were put to learning Hebrew, to sitting at the Rabbi's feet as our fathers had

---

27   The town in Brandenburg, Germany where one of the earliest concentration camps was established by the Nazis in March 1933.

done, as we should have done had our fathers not been born to an era of individual freedom. In the Blümchen family, as in others, this naturally did not happen overnight: it was a slow growth of months, a thriving mushroom nurtured in those dark years between 1933 and 1935. Neither did we draw harmoniously closer. Like sisters bound only by family ties, by a family convention, we squabbled unendingly. We Blümchens, as Hitler settled down into position, made the air shrill with our strifes. The house on the Schwalben-ufer was as peaceful as a wasp's nest. On the first floor Tante Ludmilla, large, blonde, Gentile, not even German-born, became for our intolerance the very monument to Aryanism. Her stinginess, her dunderheaded obstinacy, her stupidity: all these became for us the hall-marks of an Aryan. The signs by which ye shall know them. She had virtues, but we looked on those with blinkers: they did not interest us. Poor woman, I doubt if any of us thought how she suffered, alien in her own family, clinging passionately to her half-Aryan, wholly Hebrew-looking sons, feeling them edge away under her clawing mother hands, knowing that they were truly in the Jewish camp. Anna, her Gentile dove, was married in Amsterdam: five enormous photos and the fortnightly visit each year were all Tante Ludmilla had of her daughter. Meanwhile, in 1934, Georg was poised like a swallow on the telegraph wires, waiting to go to Brazil: Bruno, she knew, worked away steadily with both eyes fixed on Palestine. And above this nagging unhappiness, in the flat on the second floor, came a layer of non-Blümchen life, a Herr Dr. v. Pattendorf and his Königsburg wife, a couple of stiff bulrushes from Ost Preussen with Heil Hitler! forever dribbling from their lips, in their hearts a mulish allegiance to that old rascal in Doorn.[28] They were freezingly polite to us all, stared us down with pale Gentile eyes, and stayed only because the habit

---

28   Ost Preussen: German for East Prussia. Doorn: the town in the Netherlands where the former Kaiser Wilhelm II lived in exile.

of twelve years was their master, and the rent was low. Above, on the dizzy height of the third floor, up three flights of stairs which she reviled daily as she climbed them, came Tante Lydia. In times of peace Tante Lydia was no olive-laden dove: in strife she was an arsenal, a festering wound, a nagging nuisance to all her folk. Her tongue cracked unendingly, a veritable stock-whip. We none of us saw in her an unhappy woman: to the elder generation she was simply Lydia who had been a thorn in the flesh as long as they could remember: to us she was Tante Lydia, in reminiscent mood a bore, in argument a pestilent menace.

She and I, the two spinsters, lived bound by a common darkness in our annals, a common bitterness of temper, a wayward affection born of our likeness. And daily rubbed raw, of course, by the knowledge that we were so alike. We fought monthly over the rent, which she ostentatiously lowered (kind aunt to orphan niece), which I persistently increased (proud niece scorning kindness). In the end pride drove me crazy: I paid Tante Lydia far more than my board and lodging were worth, was despised by the family as a fool, and suffered daily agonies from the cooking of my erratic aunt. She, as stubborn as I, paid back the excess rent in a stream of small Neuigkeiten;[29] knick-knacks from Hertie's, from Wertheim's, from Woolworth, bright gimcrack objects, made in Japan, which had caught her eye as she limped predatory among the merchandise. Small, brittle, useless objects which made me raw with irritation, and were never forgotten by the giver. Did I, mending my stockings in her room by the devilish iron stove, fumble in my work-bag for a needle-book?—"Where's that one I gave you, Charlotte—surely you haven't lost it?" came instanter from Tante, who sat opposite draped in all her woollens, and made a new lavatory seat out of the old lino by the kitchen stove. And

---

29   German. News, usually informal, positive, and about family or acquaintances.

then from the drawer where I had vexedly buried the thing, I had to produce it, a brilliant purple affair made in the form of a Scotch terrier. The needles have long since rusted and are anyhow useless, being unreachable: for the zip fastener which tours the belly of the hound has jammed, and nothing I can do will open it again.

"Tante Lydia, you really shouldn't spend all this money on me, please don't," say I in a false warm voice (for tonight there shall be calm, no rows, only the cooing of sweet reason).

"Rubbish, I can afford it," cries Tante Lydia airily, waving a dirty hand. "I don't see why you should grudge me the pleasure of giving you things, especially when you *will* pay rent and I don't want it."

"Oh, Lord, must we go into that all over again?"

It appears that we have to go into that all over again. We do so, exhaustively. Calm flees affrighted at the growing rawness of our voices. We end in an orgy of unreason, Tante Lydia casting the unfinished lavatory seat to the ground in a furious spasm, shrieking that I am impossible to live with, this must end. Away she stumps down the two steps into the kitchen, there to throw pans along the shelves, kick the rubbish bucket, break an old saucer or two and behave altogether like a one-legged maniac. I, with throbbing temples, burning cheeks and a tendency furiously to mutter, stay bent over my mending and do not one atom of it. While Tante Herta, who spends most of her waking hours lying on her bed with the windows sealed reading movie magazines second-hand from Woolworth's and chewing Woolworth toffee, knocks when all is over on the partition between us and asks in a snuffling voice if anything is broken? At which Lydia really runs amok and casts to the floor a salad bowl which we now use as a bread-bin: it came from Königsburg with greatgrandmamma Berta Blümchen in 1806. Only Tante Lydia minds about it being an heirloom but—what are we going to keep the bread in? We all wonder as we simmer down. At Abendbrot, over odd little saucers

full of half-boiled beetroot, Rollmops, mildewed Kümmelkäse and
Pumpernickel which won't be torn from its silver wrappings, we
become reconciled. Tante Lydia swears she didn't mean one half
of what she said, I protest I didn't mean any of it; and in spite of
Tante Herta's elephantine tactlessness we manage the rest of the
evening in something like harmony.

But something like harmony is never good enough when mind
and soul cry out for peace. Let Germany seethe as she might, I
wanted peace. Peace from the nagging need to earn money, peace
from my own restlessness, peace from the daily tautness of life with
Tante Lydia. But there was no peace. In 1933, Hitler; in 1934, the
ghastly affair of Onkel Hans. It made us all sick to look at, think
of, Onkel Hans. We nursed him in Tante Clara's flat, holding off
Marie Hahnenfuss. At intervals Berta or Brigitta, speeding from
the sick-room, shrieked to no one in particular, to the world at
large: "The brutes—the beastliness of it—poor dear old Onkel
Hans—what can we *do*?!!" To which Kurt, in a voice made deliber-
ate and quiet by life with strident sisters and a lachrymose mother,
always answered: "My dear, we can do nothing, we're Jews!" It was
true: we saw it now. We could do nothing, being Jews. Nothing,
that is, in Germany, which led us quite naturally to the idea that
beyond Germany were other worlds, other chances, other ways of
living. To some America promised much, to others Palestine, to
others England, or South Africa, or Brazil. Or, dizzily farther still,
Australia. Onkel Hans's tragedy had shaken Kurt and Gisela right
out of their domestic bourgeoisie: they were quietly considering
all lands, putting chance against chance. Georg Blümchen, the
first to go, wrote sombrely of decadent German settlements in
Brazil, but more sombrely still of Germany as seen, looking back,
from that exotic land. The idea of departure—call it flight if you
will—waxed furiously in our minds, came to lull growth almost
before we knew it. And suddenly Onkel Hans, whose mutilation
had first planted in our minds the seed of flight, now gave us also

the full-blown blossom, the flowering tree. He had always, I think, been fond of me: I was a comely lass with spirit, and he admired both. Kurt's face, Gisela's face as they bent ministering over him, must have seemed seraphic to the poor old uncle after the uncomprehending stare of Marie Hahnenfuss, the devilish leers of his tormentors in the Oranienburg prison. Berta and Brigitta he did not care for: poor strident twins, they lost many a man by that noisy sex-hungry restlessness of theirs. However that may be, on the Saturday before that Familiensonntag in August with which this rambling chapter in my life begins, Onkel Hans had weakly whispered to me that he had News. "News!" bumbled Onkel Hans, his old eye glistening already with tears of excitement. "News!" He managed, in his dry whisper, to make the word a winged one, a flying fowl whizzing through stirred air.

"Yes?" I said, putting his unwanted slippers tidily beneath the bed, humouring him.

"Bring Kurt!"

"Kurt won't be home till Abendbrot, Onkel. Can't you tell me?"

He eyed me mistrustfully. "You're a woman."

"All right. Tell Kurt when he comes home."

But the aged mind, like the aged bladder, has lost the strength to wait. Long before Kurt came, pale and tired, from his surgery, Onkel Hans had told me the news. Holding my hand in a grip as startlingly prehensile as a new-born child's, he told me he wanted to do something for me, give me something. "It'll help you to get a husband at last, eh, Lottchen?"

I loathe being called Lottchen, but the smell of a gift made me smile amiably.

"Don't tell your Tante Marie about this—she'll have plenty, anyhow."

"No," I soothed him, "this shall be a secret."

Now out it came plop! like a hot potato from the oven. Onkel Hans was bestowing money on me, on Kurt and Gisela. He had cash, we knew, though we had long lost hope of seeing its colour: but that he had property outside Germany we did not know. And this property, this snug gold-mine of houses in Brussels' very centre, was being willed in a wheezing whisper to me and to the Seligmanns. My heart literally stopped a second as I, bending to his lips, heard Onkel Hans at last! at last! bestowing wealth on me. Not wealth, perhaps, for there were seven of us to share it, counting Kurt's young brood: but wealth comparative, wholly unexpected, delicious and useable. For it was outside Germany, beyond Nazi reach, snug in Belgium.

"That's the beauty of it!" chuckled Onkel Hans naughtily, "that's the beauty of it! They don't know about it, and if they did they couldn't do anything. I've had it since 1913—you remember, that year Bruno Blümchen was so ill, poor fellow, and I had to go to Brussels instead of him. You remember, don't you?"

"Of course," said I, knowing nothing, remembering nothing, of the years before my life began to be interesting to me.

"And ever since it's grown; that block'll be worth a lot to-day. Eduard Delabibier looks after it—you remember Eduard? He wanted to marry your Tante Ricarda, poor fellow, but she turned him down for Doucet and she did well for herself too, she must have seen there was more money in Alfred than in Eduard. Your Tante Ricarda always had a good head, poor thing. Pity she died like that."

"She's still alive, Onkel Hans. Don't you remember she wrote to Tante Clara last year when Berta and Brigitta were in Paris?"

"You don't say so!" exclaimed Onkel Hans, "and I've been thinking of her as dead all these years! Well, well."

He brooded, mumbling into the hairs which now weakly sprouted from his unshaven old chin.

"What a fine bust she had, that girl! Max Liebermann[30] wanted to paint her in the—without any—well, you know what I mean,

---

30   Max Liebermann (1847-1935), a leading German impressionist painter.

tee! hee!—but she wouldn't. She knew that wasn't going to get her anywhere, though Max was a good painter in his time. I was a bit sweet on your Tante Ricarda myself when I was a young man, I don't mind telling you, that's why I felt it so when she died. Ah well, we can't last forever. But she did well not to marry Eduard Delabibier: he's never got anywhere, poor fellow. Just a solicitor, you know: comfortably off, I dare say, but certainly not rich. What was I saying about Eduard, now—how did we start talking about him?"

"The property in Brussels, Onkel Hans," I said casually, even managing a faint yawn as if the talk of money (oh release! release!) bored me excessively.

"Yes, yes, the property. It should be worth a tidy sum by now. Willi Ludwig knows all about it, he sees Eduard each time he goes over. And Eduard's looked after it for me, got it all tied up ready to hand over any time I want. Another Jewish swindle, eh?" cackled the old Onkel gleefully. "But you wouldn't understand how that's managed, you don't need to bother your little brain about that side of it, girlie. Let the old Onkel manage that."

"Dear Onkel Hans!" I murmured, really fond, "dear Onkel Hans!"

Poor Onkel Hans no longer, but dear Onkel Hans, our guest, our love, our benefactor, lay back on his pillows and wheezed exhaustedly. The excitement of the News had worn him out, left him deflated and more than a little peevish. I brought him broth, tidied him up after it, settled his pillows and left him sleeping.

To Gisela I sped, Gisela sitting suckling Konrad with her spawn riotously enjoying itself around her on the floor, over the sofa-back, in and out of loudly banged doors. And Gisela's reaction to the news was pure motherly. Her eyes shone, her pale cheeks warmed to a pale pink, she clapped one hand softly against Konrad's cheek as he tugged and cried: "Fine! now we can have another baby!"

Dear Gisela, with David, Käthy, Hedwig yelling around her, tugging at her clothes, voraciously battening on her presence, with

146

the infant Konrad voraciously taking his Mittagessen from under her worn blouse—dear Gisela, who hears she has come into money and, with all this nursery disorder around her, immediately plans to have more of it, to go through it all again, to bear another child!

This upheaving Saturday ended in a spate of plans not only Gisela's. The three of us sat up till morning discussing, arguing, warming ourselves on our brilliant futures, since the stove had long since gone out while we talked. It made me for a brief time sentimentally moist, unwontedly tender, to find how naturally Kurt and Gisela assumed that I, the sharer in their luck, should go on sharing their lives also, should make the fine new start with them. I had grown fonder of both cousins with a settled fondness, no passion: but hardly knew them to be fond of me. This is what I have lost, I thought, watching both eager profiles, this family warmth, this community of creatures who are dear to one another, hang upon one another. This is what I have lost and must find again. I have been playing a lone hand all my life, too long.

At once Onkel Hans's wheezing senile voice came back to me: "So now you can get a husband, eh, Lottchen?" But did I want a husband, a staying comfort? No! So I rejected my tender interlude, looked fiercely at Kurt and Gisela, those cooing doves, and cried:

"Now be sensible, you two: what are we going to *do* with this money?"

It was settled, somewhere about 3 a.m., that for the moment we did nothing. Above all, said nothing. We knew our family too well to believe in their disinterested love for us. Let but a whiff of our enriched state get around, and on its heels all the Onkels, Tantes, elderly cousins to the infinite degree, would be upon us wheedling, coaxing, fawning. Not for themselves, ah no! But for poor Georg struggling in Brazil, for Bruno about to decamp to Tel Aviv, for Cousin This (whom we had never seen), struggling on an ostrich farm in South Africa, for Cousin That (whom we had seen but never wanted to again), eating out his heart on a cane plantation in Queensland, he who had been reared in Berlin. We knew too well the importunate Blümchens and their newborn urge to scatter, flee Hitler, settle in fresh parts. The desperate urge was now hot in us, we knew how it burned the outwardly sober bosoms of our relatives.

"Say nothing," warned Kurt, "not even to Mama." ("Least of all to Mama!" murmured Gisela.)

"We have time to make sensible plans and look about us. The money won't rot. We can wait a year or two."

"I can't."

"Why, Charlotte?"

"Don't 'why, Charlotte' me. I want to get away, right away. I can't stand Germany, I—"

"Why, Charlotte! I never knew you felt like that!"

"Neither did I till this minute. But I do, really I do. Kurt, why can't I go to Brussels instead of Willi Ludwig and see this Delabibier? I must go somewhere and get away from the damned Touristen Büro and the S.A. on the streets and the noise of our Adolf's voice on the wireless and all the rest of it. I'm tired."

"So you are," put in Gisela tenderly. "I've seen it for some time. Why shouldn't you go?"

"She doesn't know anything about business."

"Of course not, dear, but you can tell her what to do. She can arrange what you think best with this solicitor and write to you—we'll have some sort of a code, Charlotte—and then go on to England for a real holiday. Who have we got in England now? What about Onkel Baruch?"

"Haven't heard of him for years: he's the one who stopped writing in the war."

"All the more reason why Charlotte should go and see him," cried Gisela.

I doubted my Onkel Baruch's welcome, but smiled on the scheme. To England, to England, sang my heart as later I lay abed.

It might as well have been Egypt, Estonia, Ethiopia—the name mattered not, nor the place, so long as it was outside Germany. At last I saw release, a spacious freedom, a chance of finding the real Charlotte who for so long, too long, had been both cramped and lost.

To the Familiensonntag next afternoon we all went, tidily clamping down emotion. Perhaps because of this brewing excitement, this burgeoning hope, I was more alive, more sensitive. I saw my family with new eyes, I who was so soon to leave them, I hoped, forever. For England would be but the beginning, the lowest step of a brilliant flight: my escape should be world-wide. Back now in the iron chair by the Karpfenteich where my breathless reader, panting back and forth through time, can rest for a space, I gather my thoughts (as I gather them now writing, seeing the pencil stream across the page) into some order. I have no excuse for this bounding to and fro, from 1933 to 1934, thence to 1924: the date matters not one tittle. I write of myself as I like, unchronological, higgledy-piggledy, dodging from one mind-phase to another with no apology except that I must. The brain does not work to pattern, but sees some milestones on its road, ignores others: leaps back a space to look again on something that has pleased it, leaps forward to something as yet unknown which may please it better. Sitting together on the iron chair, reader and I can now gather our racing wits, get our breath, and with it say goodbye to German Charlotte. She will not come again. She is a Jew now, not a German: she is bound by no narrow Versailles-drawn territory, bound to no town, no province, no land. A nomad Charlotte with her tent pitched nightly on some new patch, each night (pray God) a new Charlotte beneath its canvas. She is finished, the old static Charlotte rooted in, belonging to Germany. Farewell, adieu, never (save in these moments of diving back once more to catch a bit of her on a page, pin her with pencil and paper) *Auf wiederseh'n.*

Chapter 5
Escape

Looking back now on my year in England I see it as pure farce, a watery-blooded comic opera, a thin English joke (haw! haw! with the moustache bristling, the long reddish-blue face grimaced in crude mirth). The twelve months seemed at the time unending, stretching out with no hedges, no limits, but now, oddly, they telescope into a brief rather sour jest.

I went in 1934, in winter. The memory of Onkel Hans's torn dangling eye went with me, but none of Onkel Hans's cash, for that was still tied up with legal bands in Brussels. I went (so my visa remarked) "on a short visit to relations." The relations, circularised by the Blümchens in Berlin, welcomed me by letter and seemed of the same mind as the visa authorities: my stay was to be short. They asked me to be their guest for a week or two until I had "found something." An odd phrase, that; as if I were searching in bed for a flea.

This Uncle Baruch of mine, rechristened Flower by himself and Teddy by his wife (née Naomi Lewinsohn), had abandoned Berlin in 1900, married this blossom from Whitechapel soon after, pursued for a while the family fur trade, then abandoned it for food. He owned now a dozen good, expensive small restaurants in the West End, and lived in cushioned ease with his admirably corseted wife, his four children, Ron and Edna, Cyril and Iris, in Frognal Lane, N.W. I hesitate to describe the household of my Uncle Teddy lest I should not do it justice. I hesitate, but nevertheless will try. To begin with, there was luxury. At the end of one week Charlotte Herz was no more: she was a cat drowned in cream, merely a bloated body floating thick near the surface. In fact, it is a wonder I survived at all. The house, the cream jug, was big, red-bricked, white-painted, planted firmly in a quarter-acre of lawn with trees, trim flower-beds and an arbour miraculously free from all insects. A fat pink cook, an impassive parlourmaid, a neat shining house-maid and a gardener-chauffeur attended to the simple wants of the little family. For their wants *were* simple: they simply wanted the best of everything. They wanted meals of solid quality superbly cooked, four times a day: a house so scoured, vacuum-cleaned, dusted and polished as to resemble the innards of a voluptuous pink shell: a garden neat yet rich, providing all blooms in season: a family car gleaming with the earnest elbow-grease of Squires, the chauffeur: two smaller cars for Ron and Cyril (since young men *will* be young men, bless 'em), a runabout for Mum and the girls. For this the Flowers were willing to pay. For this the four servitors had been engaged. If at any time the quartette had failed to yield service for cash, out they would go, dismissed by the inexorable law of Value for Money. That, in truth, was the catch-phrase of the Flower family. "Good value for the money!" cried Edna, approving her mother's new foundation, a solid rich affair of apricot-pink satin and needlerun lace. "I do like to get good value for my money," cried Iris to me, exhibiting her new suit from Bradley's. "My dear chap, it's damn' good value for money," exclaimed Ron to Cyril as they inspected his new roadster standing like a little dragon in Frognal Lane. And because he knew it was, because he knew that no motor salesman, however suave, could put anything over on a Flower, Cyril agreed that the vehicle was, even as his brother said, good value for money. It was the one criterion, the acid test, which this comfortable, shrewd, superbly greedy family applied to life. Nothing shoddy, cheap or skimped ever got into "The Beeches," Frognal Lane, N.W. If such an object, such a person, had managed to creep in at the shiny white door past the masterful shiny white front of Banks the parlourmaid, it would surely have died of shame, withered with chagrin, before half an hour were gone. The whole house breathed out not so much opulence as luxury for the sake of comfort, a strictly practical luxury. The Flowers, and "The Beeches" glowed with a well-fed polish which was quite astounding. Every summer, during the family exodus to Scotland, Bognor Regis or Brittany, the Flowers got a coat of tan, "The Beeches" a coat of paint. Every two years Aunt Naomi had the curtains renewed by Hamptons, replacing the rich heavy damasks of the drawing-room, smoking-room, billiard-room, dining-room and library by other rich heavy drapes which differed from their forerunners only in being new. Every two years Edna or Iris, in a fit of calculated girlish extravagance, had her room done up while she was away, and came back in October to walls of lilac instead of pastel blue, curtains of tussore instead of grey brocade, a whole new bedroom suite if she had caught my Uncle Teddy in a mellow state. Every year the chaste polished radio-gramophone in the billiard-room, the smaller H.M.V. in the library, the portable in the maids' sitting-room, gave place gracefully to their natural followers, the current models. You didn't, with the Flowers, listen to a 1934 programme on a 1933 radio. Every autumn, at the motor-show, Ron bought a new roadster, Cyril (whose girl friends were more numerous and less exigeant) a new saloon. Every other year, after affectionate but fierce discussion, Dad traded in the family Nash for a Humber, a Pontiac or even, when business was good, a Rolls.

You might think that with such oil-smooth cars to save their legs, such a lavish supply of good rich food, such yielding, bouncing Vi-spring mattresses, the Flowers might grow fat, suffer from acute digestive disorders, gout, lumbago, kidney trouble and the like. Not a bit of it: the Flower digestion, like everything else in this superb family, was good value for the money. It never let them down. After four square meals, and any number of such unconsidered trifles as elevenses with cream cakes, cocktails before dinner and Horlicks at 11 p.m. to fend off the alleged horrors of night starvation, any Flower could go to its bed, bury its nose in the pillow as soft as a swan's breast, and sleep like a log. In case by any dirty chance sleep were for a while denied, each Flower had by its bed a little table bearing reading-lamp, the latest worthless fiction, and a chintz-covered box brimming with digestive biscuits. Iris and Edna, the comfortable girls, had a box of chocolates as well to steer them through the night watches. But these solaces were little needed: as has been said, the Flowers slept well. They slept well, they ate well, they dressed well, they played well, they worked (in the cases of Dad, Ron and Cyril) well: they enjoyed themselves. Their days were full, lavish: their months pleasantly progressed, their years went on from richness to richness. None of the four young ones had yet found mates, though they had playfellows almost as well fed, as rich, as beautifully shampooed, brilliantined, manicured and permed as themselves. That peculiar richness, that wedding of self-indulgence with shrewd common sense, was not to be found in anyone not a Flower. So the young things played, flirted, went through all the social antics, and came out unscratched by any emotion keener than pleasure. Perhaps they could not feel emotion, just as (beyond the keen Hebrew shrewdness common to all of them) the Flower minds were empty, innocent of thought. They did not think, for they never needed to. When they read it was for comfort, not because they felt any need for quickening. Reading was a soporific, a voluptuous languid exercise for those evenings when the fires roared in drawing-room, in library: when Dad was dozing over *The Times* and one of the boys was getting dance music from Florence on the radio and Mum was knitting herself a jumper in pure silk at five shillings a skein. Then Edna, Iris, Ron or Cyril would pick up a book from the well-stocked tables, finger it, dip into it, read perhaps as much as a chapter of it, yawn, eat a chocolate, smoke a cigarette, and if nothing better offered read another chapter. Since by some happy genius of selection the libraries never offered, Mum and the girls never brought to the house, anything of a subversive, revolutionary or tragic nature, anything which any of them might find "uncomfortable," this reading of theirs did them no harm. I verily believe that the peculiar alchemy of this wholesome brood would have turned a Left Book Club cover from orange to pure soothing blue, its contents from Leftism to a fat, succulent Toryism which would amaze Mr. Gollancz.[1] That the Poor suffered, that liberty of thought was in England perpetually threatened, that Earl Baldwin[2] had ever been or could ever be anything that was not wholly admirable, would have surprised the Flowers very much indeed. The Poor had the dole, they knew: liberty of thought they took for granted, having never in their lives expressed a thought lively enough to need suppression: and Prime Ministers of England, that upper crust of a rather dubious political pie, were by their office as sacrosanct as Money.

Dear me, I spent two weeks with my relations the Flowers. I seldom came into the upper air. When I did, England seemed odd indeed. In contrast to this full-blooded opulence of my relations (who, like most anglicised Jews even in England more English

---

1 Victor Gollancz (1893-1967), an English publisher and supporter of leftist politics.

2 Stanley Baldwin (1867-1947), three-time Conservative Prime Minister of the United Kingdom between 1923 and 1937.

than the natives), the other specimens I met in that first week seemed strangely watery. My Aunt Naomi tried to interest me in them, but could not. She introduced me, much as one introduces the new kitchenmaid from the country, to an institution known as the Y.W.C.A.[3] I could see hope in her eye as she remarked that there I should be sure to make nice friends. I was a Jew, but religionless—the soul of niece Charlotte was cleaned of one devil, swept and garnished: now was the time for the seven new devils to enter in. Unhappily the Christian Young Women and I were at cross purposes from the start. I was grimly determined to observe them in their strange sub-aquatic life, they were as surely but less scientifically bent on observing me. A mutual barrenness of spiritual comfort resulted: the Y.W.C.A. and I parted without much enriching one another. Aunt Naomi sighed and grew restive: I had been living on Flower bounty for a week and nothing to show for it but acute indigestion. At this moment, a heavenly portent, an advertisement in *The Times* struck her eye. (She never read anything in that paper but the front page and the engagements.) Someone in Cambridge wanted a refined foreign lady, Austrian preferred, in the capacity of Mother's Help. This was Auntie's help indeed: she packed me off hey presto to the address given, a club in South Audley Street. "You'll get this job, I feel it in my bones," cried Aunt Naomi girlishly, buttoning me with unwonted kindness into my coat. "If you behave yourself," was the unspoken coda: I felt like a girl at her first ball, watched by a ring of chaperones awaiting results.

The club was a dark building smelling of dirt, neglect and Englishwomen. Mrs. Blatchford rose limply to greet me from a leather chair in which she swam like some muddy fresh-water fish. At the end of ten minutes I was engaged, pledged to the care of her two little girls aged six and nine. "Intelligent, but rather

3 Young Women's Christian Association.

naughty," sighed Mrs. Blatchford; before the matter was clinched the children had been merely intelligent. She pressed into my palm, on parting, a sixpence for the return bus fare from Frognal Lane. The fare was eightpence and I told her so: blushing nervously, she dug up another twopence, laid it on the table littered with *Tatlers*, and fled, murmuring instructions about times of trains on Wednesday, the need for warm clothing, hot-water bottles and a good dictionary.

Well now, here was I, an independent woman, about to earn three pounds a month. Aunt Naomi was jubilant: she saw me already the departing guest, and seethed with auntly plans for making the last days pleasant for me. I would have given anything, as I trapesed about London in her wake with my poor head swimming with impressions, to be back once more in Berlin. My heart ached for the Dorotheenstrasse, the pawing tourists, the vivid squalor of life with Tante Lydia, the warmth of Kurt and Gisela. I would have given all to go back: a despairing pride kept me where I was, saw to it that when the evening train left for Cambridge on Wednesday I was in it.

If there is anything more coldly squalid than the station platform at Cambridge on a foggy day in early January I have yet to meet it. Dr. Blatchford was to have been there: a tall thin man, said his wife, with glasses and a dark suit. In the raw mist all the men were tall, thin, bespectacled, dark suited. Not one of them showed signs of wanting me: the blank English stare, the rotten English teeth half-bared in a grimace against the cold were all that I got from my peerings. At last, exhausted and wet, I hopped with what luggage I could on to a bus and told the conductor where I wanted to go.

"Orri," said he, swaying on a strap: with a spine-searing jerk the wretched thing got under way. Oh, interminable town of Cambridge, stretched along an interminable street, seen through an endless shifting veil of cold, raw, choking fog! I stared through windows steamy with foul breath and hated every brick, every dark blowing figure on a bicycle, every lamp-post. Unintelligible cries broke from the conductor each half-minute or so as the bus stopped: over my feet tumbled fierce, wet, muffled young men with wild forelocks who plunged from the exit, all but fell into the street, and vanished in the dirty swirling vapour. There came a Woolworth's, brightly lit, and a sombre church with pious ejaculations pasted on boards all over the churchyard: here we stayed a full five minutes while I painfully congealed. People fell out of the bus, more people fell in, glistening with damp. Life was a marrow-piercing nightmare of wet woollens, wet boots, harsh voices raw with fog, fierce shrieks of vehicles as they tore madly past us into streets as narrow as a virgin's bed. I, who had imagined all university towns like Göttingen, naïve, cheerful, tree-green places with pleasant streets, groaned inwardly and blew upon my fingers which were mere tallow candles, so pale, so bloodless, so stiff with cold. My God! I thought, to what hell has poor Charlotte come, where will she end, unhappy one, in this drear dampness of despair?

And even as I thought it, almost pushing a tear from eyes that never wept save in self-pity, a tall thin man with glasses and a dark suit leaned over me, smiled stiffly over dreadful teeth, and asked: "Are you Miss Hurts?"

I answered Yes, I was Miss Hurts. I never knew how he had missed me, how later found me. I was too glad to find him there at all. There were explanations, to me incomprehensible. Enough that I was no longer Charlotte the lost one, but Charlotte found, being taken somewhere, talked to by someone, her being at last recognised. Charlotte found, wavering to life, no longer a suffering icicle but a woman curious, observant, malicious. A woman, in the next few days, quivering with the desire to find out. To find out how these queer fish lived, how they thought, what they thought of, why? why? *why?* That was the question for ever ringing in my head about the English. Not why thus? why so? why not the other way? but simply WHY? Why *are* the English? would have summed up my attitude in those first few staggering days in Cambridge.

Perhaps I write thus spitefully because, remembering Cambridge, I remember also to be ashamed of myself. There happened in those months something I should like to forget, an intrigue of the kind most properly called "low". My only excuse is that I was soon vastly bored, watching the English. Their flat cod-faces bored me, their thin tinny voices bored me, the clothes of the women, the glances of the men, were alike sickeningly boring. I was bored and I was lonely, a fatal conjunction. In a fit of more than ordinary ennui I encouraged flirtation: in desperation I fed the first flicker, and then the thing was well alight, smoking to high heaven. Essentially he was such a nice boy, no brilliantined cad with a list of smoky intrigues to his discredit. A nice, simple-minded, intellectual baby, clumsy in his approach, desperate at the onslaught of his puritanical English conscience, an innocent haunted forever by the conventional spectre of guilt before which his Quaker grandfathers had trembled. The poor lamb was already married, that made it the more sordid. Like many another simple clean-minded Englishman he would never have minded ruining me were it not for the blasting of his own respectability thereby. But, once embarked upon blasting, he knew no middle way: there was no middle way, for unlike most English he could not compromise. And I? Clear-eyed, shrewd, ruthless, I saw where we were going, realised the end, and because in my parched state I had to have excitement, inexorably led him on. This had to satisfy me, this low, underground, mean yet pleasurably seething affair with young John Lae. I write "young John," "young John Lae," for he was very young. He and Clementy had known each other for only three months, were only twenty-two, when they married. Clementy was modern and enlightened: she desired everything and enjoyed nothing. John was also modern, but more vaguely so: he was always wanting something very badly, but never quite knew what it was. While I was still for Clementy a New Mind, not yet the Serpent and Lilith rolled into one loathsome whole, she confided to me in her bald, modern, staccato way the history of their marriage. They were both rather surprised to find themselves married at all. Clementy, having had her ego nicely developed at one of the more advanced co-educational schools, was determined to live with several men before committing herself to wedlock with any of them. John thoroughly approved of this in theory: they had made elaborate and naïvely youthful plans for living in what they hoped their elders would call Sin, when he suddenly got some minor university job and the whole scheme collapsed. You can live in sin in London but not, unless rarely strong-minded, in Cambridge: so the two of them were man and wife almost before they knew it, and had set up house in a yellow brick object, frequently mistaken for a public latrine, on Milton Road. John was but lightly attached to the University: otherwise, he wrote. That is, he had always wanted to write, and if editors were less ignorant of what is good for them he might, Clementy thought, have published quite a lot. But as things were he had to content himself with contributing articles of the deepest and most intellectual gloom to the various precious journals with which the place was littered. There were always a good many of these, all distressingly ephemeral in character. But they all had two common traits: each was convinced that it alone, like some undaunted glow-worm, maintained the light of true Culture in an otherwise murky world: and not one of them paid its contributors a sou. You knew the editor, or you were the editor, and you wrote, therefore, for the *Phalanx* or the *Vanguard* or the *Rising Phœnix* or for any one of the half-dozen frail ventures which flourished thinly for a time and then were gone. How strange, to the German-Jewish mind, this frittering away of intellect on the pages of journals read by nobody! I never ceased to marvel at it. But John knew quite a lot of editors, locally: so his little articles appeared, to be read by perhaps two hundred people in the University and then wholly forgotten. Clementy also itched to write: she had all the modern itches. Her line was poetry. She read me a great deal of it. I need not add that it was bad poetry, being thin, bloodless, agitated; and having much the same effect on the ear as the sound of a knife scraped on a tin plate. It, however, pleased Clementy very much: and a female friend, living the simple life in High Wycombe, printed quite a lot of it, for practice, on her little printing press. The two of them, John and Clementy, were regarded in Cambridge as a promising young couple, though what they promised God only knows. John lectured twice a week to a group of lads and lasses only slightly younger than himself, and spent his spare moments in growing a beard with the wistful hope that he might in time begin to look like a man named D. H. Lawrence. Clementy kept house sporadically, attended one or two lecture courses for the good of her mind, and belonged to all those societies (again, how un-German!) who in Cambridge meet every Sunday evening somewhere and set the world to rights, very satisfactorily, between the hours of nine and twelve-thirty.

They were at this stage and attending a meeting of this nature when I first met them. They had been married two years, and Clementy was no stayer. Of course, she and John had decided, with infantile earnestness, that each should be free. Erotically Free, naturally. It was a lovely theory, and had never met a test until John's eye, vaguely roaming, lit on my tawny hair.

He told me afterwards that it glowed like a new-peeled chestnut: Clementy, you see, had simply hair-coloured hair. The phrase pleased Clementy, she often repeated it in the early days of our acquaintance: later (alas! the poor modern!) she allowed it to drop, frowned, like any un-modern Eve, whenever my hair was mentioned. I, who saw as clear through her as through cellophane, that other modern product, felt faintly sorry for the girl. She was due for a cropper sometime, if not over me, over some other woman:

and I could salve my conscience a little with the thought that it might as well be I. Only the very young, the very green, could have talked such utter rubbish about erotic freedom, the right to graze in any pasture of love, as Clementy did in the first years of her married life, as she was still doing when I met her, as she is almost certainly not doing now. I think she really believed what she said. "Love," she would shout, at some semi-public gathering, opening wide her really fine eyes, shaking back lank hair, "love is like eating, just another appetite. Why should we always eat carrots? Why should we go on loving the same carrot, when there are parsnips? It's too bloody absurd. A woman is just as free as a man is to choose where she'll sleep, and who she'll bed with. I've no patience with the people who—" and then followed a tense, lurid description of the people with whom young Clementy Lae had no patience. She had little patience with anyone, poor child: it was not only the conventional view of marriage which roused her to such a tinny fury. Living with her must have been rather like embracing an aluminium saucepan. I often thought: all you got was the cold impact of metal and a metallic clang in answer to caresses. No wonder John found my hair and neat curves and Jewish femininity alluring: the wonder is that he had not strayed before in some other direction.

When he strayed in mine I had been in Cambridge three months and was, as already said, bored. Here was no adventurous leap into new life, as I had somewhat childishly hoped when fleeing from Berlin and the memory of Onkel Hans. Here was only a trivial round of jobs, people I found wholly "unsympatisch" and a little town I had not yet grown to love. It was spring, and Cambridge in spring is raw, very raw, on the nerves. I had not met a single man I fancied: the women were to my mind even more sterile, flat, unworthy. In contrast to my Flower relations the English still appeared strangely thin. I watched crowds of them, at debates, meetings, lectures, football matches: the rare Jews among them stood out like comets. Jews are vivid, alive; blood flows in them, you see at a glance: in the English it sedately ambles. Jewish hands, fluttering to the rhythm of vibrant Jewish voices, make Gentile hands look like so many dead fish laid chilly on marble slabs. We are more febrile: a phlegmatic Jew is a monstrosity, a horror. We express life, the English suppress it. And how thin, how bloodless, how mauve they are! I thought, sitting at a charitable meeting to which Mrs. Blatchford had led me. A Miss Amy Gates was to talk to us about a home for unfortunates, to wring our withers and our pockets in the same kind cause. "It'll be good for your English," said Mrs. Blatchford when offering the strange entertainment: I much doubted, but here I was. We collected in a college room lent by the philanthropic wife of a Master: it was old and oaky, smelt much of aged wines, aged men, and was so picturesquely dark that even our hostess said the days were drawing in and ordered lights. Like fowls in a hen-house we blinked astonished at one another when candles came. It was at this point I found my fellow females so mauve. And what hats! cried Charlotte, observing, to Charlotte, recording, after the second look. My English governess had favoured hats like these. Hats chosen without the slightest regard for the face beneath, nor for aesthetics generally: hats on which a large amount of garbage had been carelessly laid, as carelessly sewn; so that the dame who kindly tittuped to me while we waited for Miss Gates distracted the eye by wriggling at my nose's tip a brown velvet pancake from which a red velvet cherry with a pansy leaf in green velvet skittishly dangled. Under this laughable horror the woman squeaked at me. All the women squeaked: the room rang with it as if a conference of outsize mice were afoot. They all squeaked, they all looked like my English governess: it was impossible to believe that they had blood. If you pricked Miss Bailey, Mitzi always said, a rather warm, dishwashy liquid would ooze. We called her Dishwater Annie: and here was I, years later, Mitzi-less, in an English room full of Dishwater Annies.

I had reached the point of wondering why they draped their really nice ankles in such frightful hosiery, when the squeaking at my side took on a more urgent note.

"There's Miss Gates—*such* a fine woman, I always think she's an example to us all."

The example reared itself up by the fireplace, cleared its throat, and dangled mauve cold fingers among its necklaces of imitation amber. She also was a Dishwater Annie, but hatless. Her thin, cinder-coloured hair was parted in the middle and corrugated in mean waves to the ear-tips. Here it ended abruptly, and, as it were, complainingly, in a series of tortured frizzles which died off in a fiercely shaven neck.

She talked of rescue homes. Rescue from what? who? I idly wondered; then remembered that there is only one thing women ever want to rescue other women from, and that Miss Gates was interesting us in a home for prostitutes. But no brothel, oh no! They did laundry work, these flowers plucked from vice. Quite a lot of Cambridge people, Miss G. told us, glowing, were delighted by the way in which the harlots laundered their table-napkins. Not that such words as harlot, prostitute, were uttered: the inmates of the home were referred to throughout as Unfortunate Girls, and the nature of their misfortune left to us. I doubt if any foreigners less innocent than I would have known in the least what Miss Gates was talking about: they would have gone away still thinking that our threepenny bits and sixpences were for the good of little girls with hare-lips, bow-legs, moustaches or some other bodily ill.

Miss Gates rambled on, weaving her amber necklaces, wetting dry lips with a constipated tongue, warming shrilly to her theme. I could not listen, my mind and eye roved. And here suddenly, I saw the young Laes, Clementy and John, perched modestly on a single chair at the back of the room, interested and (I knew at once) malicious observers. Clementy was hatless as always, had her head thrown back to show a pale, pretty, pale-grey throat which (disciple of Joad[4] at this time) she strenuously kept unwashed: John supported his downy young beard in a large young hand, chewed on his pipe, and watched the assembly beneath a dark wild forelock. The two of them were so Cambridge, yet so incongruous in this gathering, that I gaped at them, positively gaped. And seeing me with my mind off Miss Gates, off the laundering Unfortunates, Clementy nudged John, our three pairs of eyes met, and slowly, impishly, the young couple winked. Then casting their looks demurely downwards, clinging to one another because the chair-bottom was narrow, they heard out the rest of the address.

There were no inhibitions about young Clementy. She bounded to me, upsetting tea-cups on side tables, so soon as all was over.

"You're a kindred spirit!" she yelled, seizing my hand, "say you are, say you're here just for a good clean laugh."

"I—"

"Good. I knew it. This is John. I'm Clementy. What's your name?"

"Charlotte Herz."

"Not a *Jewess*!"

"Yes."

"Hooray, how thrilling!" cried Clementy, opening her eyes till they looked like glass marbles, clear, depthless, and jiggling up and down on her dirty sandalled feet. "A Hebrew mind is just what I *knew* I wanted to round it all off."

If my Hebrew mind thrilled Clementy it was my Hebrew body which thrilled John. He watched me like a starved pup ogling a meat safe: blushed when I watched him watching me, fumbled in his young beard, coughed, wildly offered cups of tea, and as wildly forgot to bring them when accepted. What woman alive would

---

4   C. E. M. Joad (1891-1953) was a popular writer and lecturer of the 1930s. Among his many theories was that cleanliness was the enemy of beauty: "The creative artist is always untidy and often dirty, while hospitals, which are always clean and always tidy, are never beautiful."

not respond to, thrill to, male open desire? I responded in subtle woman-like ways, outwardly sophisticated, inwardly amused and excited (thank God) at last. Clementy meanwhile chattered, her popping eyes on those she hoped to shock. And when all was over, when the gratifying sum of Two Pounds Eleven and Threepence had been collected, counted, handed to Miss Gates, we three walked home together as if bosom friends. All friendships, for Clementy, began thus: fierce warmth outpouring, lavished on the new one—then a faint waning—then fresh warmth, hotter than ever, to atone for past chill—then chill striking in, spreading, till the fine new toy, the soul mate was as cold as wood-ash, and, to Clementy's vampire mind, just about as useful. And under this friend-making, friend-shedding process now crept, snake-like, the intrigue of Clementy's husband with the Hebrew mind. It was a brief fierce passion; neither of us really got the slightest satisfaction from the business. Content was a word we neither knew. We were left, when finished, with no more than a foul taste in the mouth, an uneasy greasiness: and yet we went on, we had to, for John was bored with Clementy and I was bored with single life. Furtive, restless, miserable, we fumbled our way to some sort of untidy conclusion: pierced by an occasional insane ecstasy, we fumbled our way for the most part in darkness. And through it all Clementy, poor Clementy, clinging to her modern illusions, stoutly maintained that all was well, that John was free even as she was free. Or, when John's freedom could no longer be borne, the silly girl as mulishly, as obstinately, asserted that she knew there was nothing between us, nothing that a wife could mind. Deliberately she threw us together, miserably decamped so that our tête-à-têtes might be perfect. Haunted by the memory of her haunted eyes we yet could not stop ourselves, keep continence, respect the wife's rights which she so defiantly threw overboard. One night she rang up to tell me she was going out, would I come over to spend the evening with John who was working too hard and should be entertained? In a voice raw with tears she brightly told me this, cried: "Good! Good! It'll be a darned good surprise, I won't tell him anything about it," and abruptly rang off. I went, loathing myself, to the horrid little villa in Milton Road. Clementy was no curtain addict: privacy was one of her bugbears, and anyone who liked to see straight in at her windows always could. Looking, as I came up the path, I saw John gloomily reviewing a book of poetry: and thought for the dozenth time before I went in how charming, how irritating, how abominably weak he was. But necessary—God knows how necessary.

"Hullo, John."

"Hul*lo*, Charlotte!"

We looked anywhere but at one another.

"Clementy's out, I'm afraid—gone to the New Peace Society Meeting."

"Oh, I'm sorry, I only wanted to borrow—"

"Have some coffee."

"No, I've had some."

"Have some more."

"All right."

Dead silence while with shaking hands John poured out the liquid. I saw in his head, as if it were an aquarium, the fish-thoughts racing by, clear behind glass as his own legs on the mantelpiece were at this moment to onlookers in Milton Road. Did she know Clementy was out? *What* a piece of luck!—but did she *know*? Oh God, if this is just another female game I'll—hang it all, if she *did* know then this means she wanted to come, to find me alone, to—"Sugar, Charlotte?"

"Yes, please, lots."

We smiled warmly.

Oh dear, I thought, what a nice baby head, so round and downy, so fitting to a breast! And at once my hand strayed upwards, fingering as if in a dream my round firm breast so hot with life.

John's eyes followed the hand, tracing its caress: his own hand shook as he handed me the cup.

"Make yourself comfortable—another cushion?"

"Yes, please, just there."

He fitted one into the small of my back, breathing as he did so like a man at the end of a gruelling race, spent, exhausted, only half-conscious. Then, abruptly taking his feet from the mantelpiece, lying full length at my side across the firelit rug, he fell to talking. We were reading Blake together, then: an exercise smiled upon by Clementy, who doted on the man. I, too, found in his windy, subtle madness something that made me also a little mad: but though John talked of Blake to-night, and talked of him well. I hardly heard. I knew the man who talked as one knows the fish upon the hook; forestalling wriggles, deftly pulling in the line, delicately but inexorably draining the little strength left, I landed my prey at last gasping, goggle-eyed, upon the bank. I had him, aha! he was mine, only mine.

Now his head was raised to my fire-warmed flank, lay there hot and heavy. The talk ceased.

"Charlotte."

"Yes?"

"Put down your head."

Two arms came up urgent, clasped the back of my neck, pulled me down. We met cheek on cheek, hot flesh on hotter flesh, and the pressing of his shoulder into my breast. Then as suddenly my head, released, shot up: an outraged John sprang from me, towered over me, cried:

"I shouldn't have done that!"

Ah, fool! I inwardly cried, modestly casting down my eyes, modestly acquiescing, ah, fool! to let the moment slip, the delight pass unsnatched!

"I'm sorry, Charlotte."

"It's all right, John."

I looked up at him with eyes wide and innocent, mouth half-open. My dress, I knew, fell open at the neck: he could see the pale beginnings of a breast, the wandering hand once more tracing its roundness.

And when once more he cast himself upon me it was to talk in hoarse whispers (but why whisper at all?) about a weekend together away, away from Cambridge, as far as possible from Cambridge. As far as London, no less: London, that cloak for a thousand small furtive vices.

"I'll tell Clementy I must have a few days at the British Museum."

"Why not tell her the truth?"

"Good God, I couldn't!"

"Clementy," I said spitefully, "is modern. She'd understand."

"No, but—"

"She might, but Cambridge wouldn't, you mean."

He looked acutely unhappy. "You don't understand; in England—"

"I know, I know. 'There are certain things' to which we must all conform, otherwise Society would cease to be society, would be mere anarchy."

"Shut your eyes and let me kiss you!"

So discussion ended, as always, on a wet kiss.

We had in London our weekend. It was August, cold and beastly as early March. The smell of sooty rain, of greasy pavements, of wet woollen clothing and cooked cabbage, haunts me yet when I think of those three days dedicated beforehand to delight. I don't think John had ever slept with a woman before: certainly Clementy had taught him but little. Like a starved man gobbling, vomiting in excess of food, then falling to gobbling once more, he made love to me on Friday, Saturday and Sunday. "Let's lock the door and get into bed!" was poor John's cry throughout that grisly weekend. Our lodging was a fit scene for the orgy, must have seen many such. A sneaking little Bloomsbury hotel in a street once famous, dignified, chaste, it breathed now rank amours from its genteelly unclean walls, from the very streets which stank still of stale scent and staler tobacco fumes. Here we locked the door and fell to loving, abandoned ourselves frenziedly to delight. A John Donne could perhaps have made tangible the story of those days, of those two tormented fools straining after joy, spasmodically tender, uneasily fierce, acutely miserable. I, being no John Donne, can tell no more. Mercifully, I have forgotten much. I remember lying half-naked on the bed while John, that super modern, read me bits of *Peter Pan*. It appeared he had a fondness for the lad. What Englishman, indeed, has not? He is the national emblem, more potent even than the swastika. Everything in the English fancy seems to lead up a blind alley to this nauseating child. The minds of young men turn towards him in the intervals of their lust: the minds of stringy virgins mismanaging teashops leap to him, hence the "Peter Pan Café", the "Wendy House", all decked out in blue and white gingham needing a wash, all purveying rock-buns of an incredible rockiness. The English as a nation have one foot in the grave and one in Kensington Gardens: neither is terra firma, since the Englishman prefers to balance on an illusion and call it common sense. They are all Peters and Wendies, Little Boys Who Couldn't Grow Up, Little Mothering Girls giving thimbles (or was it kisses?). This national legend is as dangerous as the fiction of pure Aryanism. You might say all legends are dangerous; but those of Germany, of Greece, are at least adult, while the English glorify with senile fervour the irresponsibilities, the erratic whimsy, of a child.

"Rather charming, isn't it?" asked John when he had finished, leaning over me lovingly. I could not hurt him, not yet. I answered yes, it was charming, it was sweet. Exit John Donne, the fiery realist: enter, roguishly, on tiptoe, James Barrie, the supreme dodger, the man who dodged reality for the whole of a long life.

And then we fell to loving once again, and emerged sated, irritated, into a damp muggy evening, into a music-hall where we listened, mechanically interlocked, to the shrill inanities of a couple of dreary wizened children back-chatting about Watt Street, Ware.

On Monday we returned through a wet mist to Cambridge, seething in its torpid August vapours, to a red-eyed, brightly epi-grammatic Clementy who had guessed everything. And there, for me, the affair abruptly ended. Not for me these sordid venturings: it was not for this I had broken away from the sterile old life in Berlin. Here was only a new sterility, a more nagging barrenness. I looked beyond England, now, to something wide and free, which must somewhere exist. And, looking, wrote impatiently to Kurt to say, "Why do we wait? Why can't we go? Soon it will be too late for all of us, we're fools to linger. I can't stand Cambridge any more, nor England either. Even if you and Gisela aren't ready yet (when *is* the baby due?) I must get away."

So, in spite of John, my months in England were vague, form-less. I do not think I left much mark in the place; I broke no hearts, though I punctured some vanities: I made no real friends, left no firm imprint behind: no one, touring the Eastern counties will cry "Cambridge—ah, that's where Charlotte Herz lived in 1936." Instead—"What *was* the name of that German girl we had?" I can hear Dr. Blatchford asking at the breakfast table.

"Herz, dear," says his wife, slitting open envelopes.

"Well, I wish she'd tell these wretched circularising people that she isn't here any more, I'm tired of seeing the things," and a halfpenny package whisks through the air to land somewhere near the wastepaper-basket. That is how I shall be remembered by the Blatchfords, as a woman whose mail still comes to irritate them, since all mail which is not for us is supremely irritating.

While, in the villa in Milton Road, tired of writing poetry but impelled to it all the same, Clementy sits behind new-curtained windows and pours out such words as these on to unoffending paper:

> greasy green the willows
> by the tangled river brim, instinct
> with hatred the birds as their droppings
> drop through fœtid air.
> breathing lust the virginal demi-vierge water lilies
> decaying on water-surface under the eunuch eyes
> of frogs grown from spawn like the sago
> my Auntie Min used to press on us
> it was always in glass dishes,
> loathsome,
> watery,
> and made me retch
> Now near the sago-spawned-ones
> comes a cry—
> What is that?
> Worse than the crying of an idiot child in a thunderstorm
> Worse than the wail of a new-born child with hernia
> worse
> much worse
> because it is the voice of sentiment
> it is the nightingale.

I am sure it is very bad for Clementy to write this sort of thing, because she and John, tired of boring one another, are now going to have a baby: but the two of them must hang themselves in their own rope, poor young Clementy, poor young John. Now I, returning tired to Berlin, have no more use for them, no more interest.

*****

Now see us once more in Berlin, Charlotte restored to her family. But not for long. As swallows perch in troops on telegraph wires, waiting for relations to join them for the long trek south, chattering to each other of the journeys' prospects, so the Seligmanns and I perched a while in Berlin before leaving it forever. The swallows come back next summer: not we.

I left England in October with no regrets. Had I lived there any longer I should have settled down, become covered with chilly ash like the natives. "Du!" wrote Kurt in the autumn, "come back to us for a while and we'll see if there isn't a job for you *here*: Gisela longs to have you: the child is due in October." The 'here' was underlined, as if casually: Kurt in his discreet diddle-the-Gestapo way was telling me that our plans were set, Onkel Hans' money now ripe for use. So I gave my Mrs. Blatchford notice, endured her reproaches with great calm since I cared not a button for them, and went back to Germany. For the last time. But I would not think "This is the last time I cross the frontier inwards."

Kurt met me at the Friedrichstrasse Bahnhof. As I stood on the top step waiting for the train to stop, looking down at him as he ran smiling alongside, I oddly felt that this had happened before. Ah, but when? It puzzled me so: the picture skipped about in the shadows of my mind as I greeted him, answered questions about the journey. In the U-Bahn at last, wedged between him and my suitcases, I remembered my dream in Grübl thirteen years before. Myself with a child in my arms smiling down on Kurt as the train drew in, drew in forever without reaching its end.

"When's the baby due?"

"End of the month. I hope a little earlier, perhaps: it'll make things easier."

Our eyes met. No more of plans now, in this public place, his said: wait till we are within our own walls.

At the flat Gisela stood in the doorway waiting for us. "Oh, Charlotte, how nice to see you! You've grown thinner—didn't they feed you? What sort of journey did you have? Now sit down comfortably and we can all talk and wait for Benno."

Which is precisely what we did. Benno, however, was in no hurry to come into this world. Few of us would blame him for that. We waited three weeks for that child: at the end of October he was still unborn. On the last day of the month Gisela withdrew to bed with a frivolous novel I had brought her from England. The day wore on and Benno made no sign. Next morning, after a calm uneventful night, Gisela got up and went about her usual jobs, looking rather foolish. David had been born too soon, arriving practically on the sitting-room carpet: poor Gisela had never got over the shame of that, and the family's witticisms. However, her next three had been quite normal. Now her last, her Benjamin, on whose coming the family plans hung (for there was a ship to South Africa on November 27th—could we catch it?), her Benno dallied exasperatingly and would not be born.

However, waiting for Benno during those wet cold weeks, we talked. Our plans were made, re-made, discussed, argued over, till they were shredded from sheer exhaustion. The family dropped in, singly, in pairs, threes, and quartettes, for coffee, for Abendbrot, in the evening, after supper, staying till midnight and saying good night to us all as if they never expected to see us again. But next time they came we were still there, Benno had not yet arrived, and we fell to once more with our well-worn plans. Georg was in Brazil: the family had got used to thinking of him there. Bruno and Sabine, with their two pale mournful little girls, were in Palestine raising chickens: the family had even got used to the thought of them among these unwonted fowl, under a sub-tropical sun. Berta and Brigitta were in New York, living, as they always did, riotously from hand to mouth: since Mitzi's marriage we had considered New York as just another Blümchen quarter, so the twins' emigration was quite a matter-of-fact business. But this move of ours to South Africa was mass emigration, no less.

"Think of it!" cried Tante Heidi, "seven of you going all at once. No, eight, if that baby of yours ever gets born. Eight of you all at once! There'll be none of us left here soon, not one."

And Tante Heidi, ever a facile weeper, dropped a few elegant pearly tears over her organdie ruchings and her necklaces.

"Now, Tante, be sensible. What are we to do if we stay here? I've as many patients as I have time for, but you know as well as I that Jewish dentists and doctors will soon be stopped from practising at all. It may come any minute. Hands off the pure Aryan teeth—German dentists for German mouths—Heil Hitler!"

"Sh, Kurt!"

"Nonsense, Gisela. There's no one next door, I heard the Ritters go out ten minutes ago."

"But South Africa!" moaned Tante Heidi, dabbing at her eyes.

"Tante, it's not so far. One of these days you and Onkel Franz will be taking a pleasure cruise to Capetown to see us all."

"*Kraft durch Freude*,"[5] put in Onkel Franz.

"Exactly. Only twenty days from Hamburg—you can't call that far, it's a mere Katzensprung."

"Far enough, in Heaven's name! And what on earth will you *do* there?"

"Tante Saschia seems to think there might be something for us."

"Tante Saschia!—we've none of us seen the woman, she's not even related—just a big fat Boer your Onkel Heinrich, poor soul, married when he was too young to know better."

"But she's written often enough. Anyhow, even if there's nothing for us on her farm I can find a job in Capetown."

"Capetown's full of exiled Jewish dentists. Frau Schröder's

---

5   German: Strength through Joy. Kraft durch Freude (KdF) was a leisure organization established by the Nazis. Among its many activities, the KdF offered discounted cruise trips to German citizens.

Willi is in a bank there and says you can't move an inch without stubbing your toe on one."

"Tante Heidi," said Kurt for the dozenth time, but still patiently, "there's no sense in waiting here till the axe falls and it's too late to get out at all. Don't you see we *must* go?"

"But *South Africa*!" moaned Tante Heidi, and popped into her wailing mouth, unconsciously as it were, another burnt almond from the dish at her elbow.

So it went on. But South Africa it was to be, none the less. I saw blue sky, negroes, mangoes, a sluggish stream filled with crocodile. Here was adventure at which my stale heart lifted, roused from the apathy of simply existing. Life, surely, would be in South Africa the vivid pulsing business it once had been in Berlin. Meanwhile, I had plenty of time to brood over the bright future, waiting for Benno, waiting for petty Beamter on hard benches in the Polizei Praedsidium with my passport, seeing escape written on every line of the well-thumbed leaves. The job of getting permission to leave Germany from the Germans who were booting us out seemed endless, hopeless. I spent whole days in the stuffy police headquarters which smelt of cuspidors, cold corridors and clammy sweat, in the emigration bureau which smelt no sweeter, in the offices of passport officials, currency controllers and the like. Endless were the delays, endless the repetitions, the questions, the careful answers. What will they have us do? I cried to myself, almost weeping with weariness as I sat there on aching haunches towards the end of another day, what will they have us do? We cannot stay, we may not go: surely this is bureaucracy gone completely mad-dog! "'Raus mit den Juden!'"[6]—all right, we understand that, the barbarians have been at our heels before; but this malicious childish hindering of our going, these endless small impediments laid in our way like glass marbles strewn over a slippery corridor—what is the *sense* in this?

6   German: Out with the Jews!

"Ah well, it gives even the smallest runt among them a feeling of power," said Kurt resignedly, when I at last got home with another armful of documents to fill in. "What would they be doing if they weren't tying red tape? They've got to have their minds kept off the National Socialist revolution somehow. The poor fools, they think this is *their* revolution, their new world: they don't see even yet that they've been sold right and left like slaves in a market."

At last, at last, I had my passport stamped and visa'd, my papers in order. Kurt and I went to Hertie's Travel Büro to buy, tentatively, the family's tickets to England. Officially, we were going to England: officially South Africa was to us a continent unheard of. Because, delving as beaver-like as they had done into our financial matters, the officials knew well we had barely enough money to get us to London. But there over the frontier from Aachen, in the safe of our old ally M. Delabibier, of Brussels, lay half Onkel Hans's fortune furtively assembled, trickling through in many an innocent-looking business deal, crossing the frontier somehow during the last three years to safety. Onkel Hans himself, a corpse with a living eye, lay flat on his back in the Breitestrasse apartment and was fed four times a day by a rough-handed Marie. We had a conscience about Onkel Hans, but could do no more than feel conscience-stricken. He had wanted us to have the money: he was himself now eighty-three and half dead: in a very few months now the age, the dates, the brief name, would be graven on stone. And were the living Seligmanns, David, Käthy, Hedwig, Konrad and the baby not yet come, to be squandered to our feeling of uneasy pity when we thought of leaving Onkel Hans?

"Poor old man," said Kurt as we left him one afternoon after a painful ten minutes of carefully-mouthed remarks made close to that pallid ear, of bright encouraging smiles, platitudes that sickened the heart, "poor old man. I hope I never live to that age. What a burden your body is when it begins to rot. No, I hope I die at a ripe sixty-five or seventy: that'll be enough. The children will be grown up. They won't need me any more. To die with no regrets at sixty-five: that's a sensible prayer."

We leaned over the parapet of the Fischerbrücke to look at the cold oily Spree, so sluggish and so choked. In the cold air above the gulls wheeled screaming, pouncing as soon as a window was opened, to catch in mid-air scraps of flung-out food. As we watched them Tante Lydia's window high up beneath the roof of the old Blümchen house on the Schwalbenufer opened with a noisy creaking. Tante Lydia's crisp shock of white hair glimmered in the dusk, her voice, plangent and unmistakable, exhorted the gulls in the purest Berlin argot to rally to this feast. They wheeled round, the ugly-headed creatures, squawking and flapping. Then she cast out, very slowly and impressively, a shower of stale bread and prune stones. The birds wheeled off disgusted, leaving Tante Lydia's debris to rattle on to the cobbles below. She swore at them, shook her fist, screamed a final insult, then slammed the window to.

"What an old girl!" said Kurt, laughing. "If I could be sure of getting to her age with all that vigour left in me I might feel like risking it. But there's only one Tante Lydia in each family. Her mantle'll fall on you, Charlotte: you'll be feeding the gulls like that in fifty years' time."

He looked at me quizzically, but with an unusual tenderness, leaning sideways against the chilly parapet.

"Charlotte!"

"Yes?"

"D'you ever remember the Grünewald?"

"Yes."

"I've so often meant to say to you—but it's hard to say—"

"Then don't try. You don't need to say anything at all, Kurt. It's all behind us."

"But I feel I owe it to you—"

"You owe me nothing. I loathe this resurrecting of things that are done with. Let's forget it and go home: I'm as cold as ice."

At home we found Tante Clara and Tante Cosima descended upon Gisela for yet another talk. The farewells of the family were by now becoming ridiculous: the Seligmanns and I lived in a state of acute sheepishness, longing to be gone, dreading the actual moment of going. This afternoon the aunts sat solemnly in the living-room with Gisela, who had been urged to put her feet up, wrap her shoulders in a woolly, put another pillow at her back. Resigned, mournful, knowing how much the old ones suffered at the thought of our fleeing, she had let them fuss about her as they liked. Poor Tante Clara dripped tears from beginning to end of these visits, watching the children as they romped and squabbled, knowing that in a month or two there would be no children to watch. Come with us she would not: though her Berta and Brigitta had long since gone, though Kurt, her firstborn, pleaded with her to come, she would not. "What, leave Berlin?" she cried when again and again he tenderly suggested it, "leave *Berlin*!" She had lived here seventy-seven years, she quavered, and there was nothing anyone could do to her now that would matter in the slightest: once Kurt and the children were gone there would be nothing more to live for.

"But, Mama, you've got years ahead of you yet: don't talk as if you had one foot in the grave."

"Ah, Kurt, you little know. At my age the least thing's enough. Look at your grandfather Blümchen: as sound as a bell at eighty-seven, then dead in two days from a midge-bite. And poor old Hans, too—look at poor old Hans!"

Wallowing gloomily in these reflections the old lady successfully side-tracked herself, managed to forget that by the new year her Kurt and his tenderly-loved little brood would be gone forever.

So the Aunts Clara and Cosima sat now solemnly about poor Gisela, giving her advice.

"A very warm bath and castor-oil, dear," urged Tante Clara, bounding back to the main subject so soon as she greeted us, "only a dessertspoonful of oil, that ought to be enough."

"I won't have Benno hurried," said Gisela placidly, "he shall choose his own time, most of it'll belong to other people afterwards."

"What a point of view!" cried Tante Cosima. "Gisela, are you taking the little Blümchen card-table with you?"

"We're not taking any of the furniture, Tante."

"What! not taking the furniture!"

The word "*Möbel*" hung in the air, evoking all the deep feminine instincts. To a Jewess of Tante Cosima's generation "*die Möbel*"—the furniture—was almost as sacred as the marriage lines. These great Biedermeier bookcases, desks and tables, those elegant awkward scroll-shaped beds, those cumbrous chests made for an ancestor determined to get value for his money, waxed and polished by generations of loving housewives and red-armed Mädchen: they were sacrosanct. When Berta and Brigitta fled to America with their passports barely in order, no money, and a future as problematical as a political crisis, they yet took with them a complete bedroom suite in mahogany. It was part of the dowry Berta Wachsberger, our great-grandmother, had brought Egon Blümchen from Warsaw in 1806: crated in 1936 at enormous expense, it left Europe forever with Berta and Brigitta. Suspicious officials undid all the crates at the frontier, causing the twins a whole day's delay: the American shipping agents in Paris could hardly be persuaded to touch them, so cumbersome were these antique gloomy pieces. But with what triumph Berta and Brigitta finally landed on Manhattan among their packing-cases! Marooned on a strange continent, they were still not wholly bereft: they had "*die Möbel*." We never heard what they did with the suite—it could hardly have fitted into the average American flat—but all the females in the family gave gusty, tender sighs of relief when that first letter came from the New World and we knew *die Möbel* were safe.

Now, calmly, Gisela Seligmann, who was doubly a Blümchen, by birth and by marriage, lay there on Grandfather Werner

Blümchen's sofa that he had bought in Königsberg in 1830 and announced that she would not take *die Möbel* to South Africa. Tante Clara, who had heard all this before, on whom the first sharpness of the shock had already been blunted, looked pityingly down her nose. Tante Cosima exclaimed and protested, but with less than her normal vigour. She had her eye on the little card-table—her voice lacked conviction.

"What will you *do* with the furniture if you don't take it?"

"Sell it."

"And the little card-table?"

"150 marks, Tante Cosima."

Tante Cosima squawked again.

"150 Reichsmark—you're mad! Who'll pay so much for a little thing like that?"

"Willi Ludwig offered us 170 for it before he left, but Mama thought she'd like to keep it. Now she's got no room, so it's going at 150."

Tante Cosima brooded. Willi knew what was what with furniture—if *he* were offering 170 R.M—! We watched, seeing her thoughts buzz.

"I should never dream of paying more than 100 R.M. for it. And even then it would be just sentimentality: I can see myself now playing picquet at it with darling old Opa years and years ago, when I was a tiny little child!"

We remained stolidly unmoved by this shameless appeal to family feelings. The thought of Tante Cosima as a tiny little child playing picquet with Grandfather Egon Blümchen years and years ago did not move us in the slightest. Tante Cosima sighed exaggeratedly, gathered up her belongings.

"I must go, dear: Cosima will be in early to-night for Abendbrot: she's going on to the Opera with Willi Salomon. Such a gay life that girl does lead! I'll send a man around at the end of the week for the little table: you'll be glad to be rid of it before you begin packing."

"150 R.M., Tante Cosima,"

"100." said Tante Cosima, sitting down once more.

"What'll you do with the money, anyway?" she demanded after a stubborn pause. "You can't take more than 10 R.M. apiece over the frontier."

"We're buying the children really good clothes to last them two years or more, Tante. And then we're leaving all we can for Mama."

Tante Clara, thus directly brought into the haggling, cast her eyes modestly to her embroidery, affected not to see Tante Cosima's eye upon her. Tante Cosima's indignant stare showed plainly enough that she thought this just another family racket, a put-up job to do kind-hearted aunts out of a meagre livelihood.

"Well, dear, we won't quarrel about it—such a trivial thing. It was really as a favour to you I wanted to take the little table. But I certainly can't afford 150 R.M., much as I should like my Cosima to have something belonging to her dear old great-grandfather. Cosima has such strong family feeling."

This affecting picture of the illegitimate Cosima clinging to the family of her illegitimate father was taken in silence: Tante Clara's thoughts on it were plain, but unspoken. In an air whistling with innuendo Tante Cosima rose, kissed us all twice (she affected the Latin habit of attacking each cheek) and left.

"She's had her eye on that card-table for years," said Tante Clara as the door slammed. "You'll see, there'll be a man and a barrow *and* a cheque for 150 R.M. coming round in the morning."

Which there was.

The flock's Benjamin, our little Benno, arrived neatly and quietly on the fourth of the month, the first snowfall of the year. He was tiny, but as strong as a young ape. Never was a baby so welcome: we set about in earnest, now, packing for our Odyssey. The family came in relays to sit moaning, poor things, over Gisela and the baby, who were both in the rudest health. With the three elder children I trailed around Berlin buying clothes, toys, books, suitcases. In those last hurried weeks I said goodbye to my little town in silence and in pain. Coming out of the Salamander store on the Oranienplatz after buying stout shoes for David I looked along the vista of the Luisenufer to the flat we had lived in before the War when mother and father were alive. There hung its balcony, high, bow-fronted, over the quiet street. There Mitzi and I had raised little roses in pots, persuaded yellow canary-creeper to creep over the green-painted iron and from an earwiggy refuge we called the "bower." There was water in the Luisenufer then where now the dull ornamental gardens are: placid beryl green water down which the maple leaves floated brilliant yellow in October. We played at the edge of the water, two stout little girls in white woollen stockings, brown button boots: Mitzi fell in, I had not the wits to pull her out, but ran yelling for home while my screaming sister was plucked to safety by a workman in a blue smock. He had one green eye and one brown: it astonished us that the grown-ups took this oddity so calmly, while Mitzi and I discussed it for days. Now, in 1935, with David ahead clasping his shoe-box, Käthy and Hedwig skipping alongside, I turned my back forever on the Luisenufer.

I never knew how much I was leaving till that bitter December as I pushed my little troupe through the crowded shops, in and off the crowded tram-cars, in the dirty slush, under the dirty sky, of a modem Berlin which for me had never really changed. Here at the Potsdamer Platz Mitzi and I had hobbled through the rain on her wedding day: now David, whom Mitzi had never seen, stood in front of us with arms spread-eagled so that his females should not dart across against the lights. There had been no lights then, fifteen years before.

"Now!" cried David, fiercely protective, waving us on.

And while the light shot to green we meekly crossed to the other side, to that side where, that cold spring day in 1921, Mitzi and I had watched the wagon burning.

"Charlotte?"

"Yes, Käthy?"

"Shall we be going to Woolworth's?"

"Yes, because we *must* get those drawing-pins."

The three wind-whipped little faces, so earnestly turned up to me, began a slow smile. This was our joke, going to Woolworth's to buy drawing-pins, coming out of Woolworth's blithely drawing-pin-less. Gisela had dispatched us with a list of serious shopping as long as your arm: yet see us now, as merry as larks, pushing in at these gilded doors, fighting our way through the fat smelly crowd, to our Eden at the farther end. Each of the children had five marks to spend, five marks recklessly bestowed by Kurt out of Tante Cosima's card-table money. Not a pfennig had as yet been spent, though we had been to Woolworth's every morning for the last four days. Even David, a nervous child given to disastrous decisions, had not yet squandered any of his five marks.

Käthy now stood in an exquisite agony by a stall full of domestic utensils.

"I think I've made up my mind. I'll even have a little money left over: I'll keep that. You never know."

And eight-year-old Käthy looked at me seriously, one woman to another.

"No," I said, "you never do."

She chose two aluminium saucepans with lids (making the bored assistant try them to be sure they fitted), a scrubbing-brush, three neat chequered dusters, three teacloths, a clothes-line and two dozen pegs. Each object was chosen only after passionately minute examination: if Käthy bought a clothes-line for 65 pfg. it had to be a *good* clothes-line.

David watched enviously. Half of him was proud that he had still his five marks while Käthy had parted with all but thirty-seven pfennige of hers: half of him was ashamed that she, two whole years younger, should have her parcel so firmly packed for South

Africa, her decision so incisively made. David was always struggling with decisions. "Oh, do make up your *mind*, David!" his father was forever urging him: and, urging, was guiltily conscious that David's nervous vacillations, this keen awareness of the perils that beset us, were his own troubles all over again, that David was himself, once more ten years old and tormented by the world's desperate uncertainties.

Still uncertain, David now drifted to the stationery counter. How fascinating the serried wares, pink and blue and pale swooning green! What reams he could write, what letters from South Africa, on those voluptuously smooth sky-blue pads! How gorgeous to lick stamps and stick them on those manly square envelopes with crinkled edges to the flaps. But all the same he could not wholly commit himself to writing-paper: he might later find that in South Africa an electric torch ("nur 4.50 R.M.") or a small bedside lamp in pink bakelite would be more useful. He was now among the electric gadgets, stationery forgotten. I despaired of him, hoped Hedwig at least would know her own mind. Alas, she did. So far she had not expressed herself much about the five marks, only stoutly resisted all Käthy's attempts to spend it for her. Now, with her pink button nose well below the level of the confectionary counter, she plumped for sweets.

"But, Hedwig!" (this from Käthy) "you can't spend *all* your five marks on sweets!"

"Why not?" asked Hedwig, reasonable enough.

"Listen, love" (this from me), "they'll not keep very well. It'll be a long time before we get to South Africa, you know."

"Besides," said Käthy, "there'll be lots of sweets there, anyhow."

"I shan't have my five marks there," answered Hedwig, thinking this out.

Käthy now became priggish. "Well, I've got something that I can take with me and use for*ever*!" she smugly cried, hugging her bundle that gave out a hollow tinny clank each time she moved.

Hedwig's large light brown eyes, as yet so tenderly unawakened to real woes, filled slowly with tears. Her nose quivered, her lower lip sagged: disaster was about to overwhelm her.

"All right, my chicken, buy your sweets," I hastily cried before those enormous pearly drops (Hedwig sheds larger, rounder tears than any child I know) should start falling slowly, slowly over her smiling cheeks. "Which are you going to have?—These big pink ones or—?"

But, thank heaven, David broke in on this weak-minded surrender. He came pushing his way past waddling matrons, under elderly elbows, round perambulators: his face was one blaze of triumph. He had found exactly what he wanted—*ex*-actly. It was over there, on the fancy-work counter (my heart sank): would I come and look?

We trailed across, Hedwig's infant mind mercifully distracted from lollipops. On the fancy-work counter, amid a hellish collection of tea-cosy transfers, skeins of crude wool, completed tapestries of a vulgarity quite unbelievable, lay David's choice. It was a cot-cover in blueish-pink cotton, with the design ready stamped for working; a chaste cheerful medley, this, of storks, pansies, bows of ribbon and swastikas. The mercerised cottons for the fulfilment of the vile project were pinned to one corner: the price was 5.35 R.M.

"David, it's more than five marks," squealed practical Käthy.

"I'll embroider it for Benno, on the journey," said David, ignoring her.

There was something in this. But why is the taste of the young so appalling? Are we all born vulgar? Alas, it would seem so, thought I, eyeing the thing and striving to cast out prejudice.

"You haven't *got* 5.35 R.M.," persisted Käthy. David looked unhappy. "I thought you could lend me the rest," he mumbled, scraping one toe along the dirty floor and keeping his eyes upon it. "You got thirty-seven pfennige left over."

"Yes, but it's *mine*."

"I'll pay you back when we get to South Africa."

"What with?"

"I'll save up my Saturday money."

This was so wildly improbable that Käthy prudently ignored it.

"If I lend you thirty-five pfennige, will you let me sleep in the top bunk?"

"No, Vati said I could."

Käthy said nothing, just shook her bundle gently, her eyes fixed, like Mrs. Jellyby's,[7] on farthest Africa.

David caved in. Even at eight our Käthy was already the merciless female, deadly in conquest. She wouldn't hand over that thirty-five pfennige to David, not she, but gave it triumphantly to the assistant when he had already counted out his five marks. It was a touch that made my heart shiver, seeing how deep the serpent is in even the embryo Eve.

Now there remained only Hedwig, and she was quietly dripping tears by the artificial flowers, desolated at having found anything so lovely when she had already made up her mind to sweets. We spent an agonising five minutes following her across the store from pink sweets to sham daffodils, from Mickey Mouse in liquorice to a glass bowl full of paper roses of a sunset violence. A dozen times Hedwig reared herself on tiptoe to hand over her five marks and whisper her wants to the interested maiden behind the sweets: a dozen times Hedwig remembered the daffodils, the roses, the poisonous green leaves, and trotted back to them weeping bitterly. We were all worn out, sunk in despair, when Käthy became smitten with a notion.

---

7   A character in Charles Dickens' *Bleak House* so blind to the woes of those closest to her that one character says of her eyes that they "had a curious habit of seeming to look a long way off. As if...they could see nothing nearer than Africa!"

"Why not buy a money box and put the rest of the money in it to spend on sweets in South Africa?" she wondered.

This had to be clarified for Hedwig, too young as yet to have a mind for high finance. Käthy cunningly led her to the counter where the choice of money-boxes was simply dazzling. Hedwig, lifted up by me so that she could see them all, stopped weeping: her eyes glistened. We held our breath, scarce daring to hope. She put out a fat hand and grabbed the biggest money-box of all, a model Hansel and Gretel house in bright tin, from whose upper window, wreathed about with an inappropriate verse concerning the joys of thrift, grinned the witch herself, deliciously horrible. It cost 1.50 R.M. Still swimming in my arms over the counter, Hedwig paid her five marks, got back her change, was set on the ground again. We were all as bright as could be, delighted with ourselves, and with each other. Unhappily this could not last. Käthy, seeing that she had but two pfennige left, that David had nothing at all and owed her thirty-five pfennige into the bargain, began to be jittery about the family finances. To anxious Käthy the Seligmanns tottered now on the brink of ruin. She urged Hedwig to put her change at once into the slot in the money box. Hedwig considered the slot: it was an oblong hole in the chimney, shiny with japan, black, mysterious, leading to what? Heaven knows. Led astray by Pandora's little failing, Hedwig dropped in two marks. They clinked pleasingly. The one mark followed. "And the fifty pfennige?" cried Kathy, hopping. Hedwig dropped in the last coin, rolled the box, smiled broadly, and handed it up to me with a demand for the money back. Ah woe, and we had none of us thought to look for the magic lock, the open sesame. There was none. This was the very latest kind of money-box, said the callous assistant, frenziedly appealed to: once the money was in it stayed there till the box was full or you had decided to smash the thing.

The meaning of the words seeped but slowly into Hedwig's mind. We watched her in an agony. With her eyes fixed on the little

188

slit through which her money had dropped from sight, Hedwig was silent for a long, long time. Then slowly, slowly, her face crumpled up and grew red; slowly her mouth dropped open. Raising her tear-filled eyes to heaven she uttered at last a roar which would have shamed all Bashan's bulls,[8] and cast herself full length upon the floor.

Every one of Mr. Woolworth's customers, charitably sure that I had hit the child, drew round and cried shame upon me as I picked her up. My arms were full of parcels: Hedwig is a stout little podge. Rigid with fury and despair, she yet collapsed limply so soon as I had set her on her feet. And once again upon the floor-boards she stuck there like a hefty young limpet. The crowd grew more indignant, David and Käthy more appalled at the situation. I was expecting to hear the whirr of fire-engines, the scream of ambulances, the heavy treading of a scion of Schupos sent to quell the riot, when Hedwig's bawlings suddenly ceased in a snuffle. She rose, looked at the circle of bending faces, her own smeared with dirt and woe: then slowly, blandly, gave us all a gracious smile.

Dizzy with relief, we rushed her out of the store before she could change her mind, rushed headlong across the Platz to Küntze's to restore, with their famous coffee, our shattered nerves.

*****

Now all was ready, packed, strapped, labelled. Now came the round of partings, nagging as the stabs of toothache. To Tante Heidi and Onkel Franz in the Landgrafenstrasse, newly decorated in spite of Hitler, and brilliant with chromium chairs, grey oiled silk curtains, and scarlet poinsettias in Chinese ginger jars. Tante Heidi, gleaming like a well-fed seal in her black satin, wept over us for an hour while the gay poinsettias waltzed to the vibration of her

---

8   From Psalm 22:12-21: "Many bulls have compassed me: strong bulls of Bashan have beset me round."

sobs. Onkel Franz, related to us only by marriage, controlled himself better: shaking our hands he bade us report to him if we saw any openings for synthetic wool (his latest project) in Australia.

"It's South Africa they're going to, the poor, poor lambs!" wailed Tante Heidi; and Onkel Franz, unruffled, said: "In South Africa then," and opened the door for us. Out on the wide white-painted stairs we carried still Tante Heidi's scent, the flame of the poinsettias. Noises of her sobbing farewell floated after us into the street. She flung up the window of her Erkerzimmer and moaned shrilly at us as we straggled away beneath the wintry branches towards the Tiergarten. If we had not known our Tante Heidi to be completely happy in these poignant partings, these lushly sentimental last minutes, our withers would have been much wrung, for she made a considerable noise. But we knew her, the excitable old egoist, and we smiled ruefully at one another as the last anguished hiccough came gurgling from the window before Onkel Franz, with a brutal practised hand, shut it smartly down.

Now, on the Schwalbenufer, farewell to Tante Herta and Tante Lydia. Chestnut skins crackled underfoot in the dark smelly kitchen where Tante Herta like some blowsy Fate sat among saucepans, pressed home-made marrons glacés upon us, and snuffling bade us godspeed. We took the sweetmeats, thinking how the gulls outside would enjoy them in a few minutes, and followed Tante Lydia into the tiny narrow room she so jealously kept as her own. Dear Tante Lydia, always so practical: she also had parting gifts, but such as we could cherish. For days she had squatted among her trunks, turning out treasures, sighing over them, laughing over them, cursing at the moths, that flew up in clouds, all alone with the door fiercely locked against Herta. For Kurt she had found a tiny beautiful "*Wahrheit und Dichtung*"[9]

---

9   Goethe's *Aus meinem Leben: Dichtung und Wahrheit* (From My Life: Poetry and Truth), an autobiographical work in four volumes (1811-1830).

which her unhappy father had bought in Paris in 1870: for Gisela a pearl brooch, one of the lesser stars of our great-grandmother Berta Blümchen's dowry: for each child some little German thing to take with them away from Germany. For me there was a fierce uncomfortable hug behind the door as we parted, a small package mysteriously wrapped, and inside the set of brilliants which Egon Blümchen, now so long dead, had given his Berta on the birth of their first child. The whereabouts of these gems had long been hotly disputed in the family, Tante Lydia joining in the verbal search as urgently as anyone: now they lay in my hand, the lovely heartless sparkling things, with a note scrawled in Tante Lydia's hand bidding me hoard them if I could, sell them well if I had to.

Laden with these parting gifts, heavy with the leaden horrors of parting, we embarked at the Friedrichstrasse Bahnhof for Hamburg. Pale, red-eyed, snuffling, the family, all in black, gathered like crows to watch us go. Wrung as my heart was by all this, I could not help seeing with a mocking sadness how truly Jewish it was. How Jewish the women, most of them stout, all of them sallow, each draped in the darkest, most woeful black, each a Bernhardt, a Duse, enacting a tragic part alone, herself the audience, the player and the play. And the men? Less subtle, equally Hebraic, they stood about in dark clusters, hat in hand, as if the grave of us departed yawned even now at their feet, and addressed to us portentous remarks in hoarse deep voices. The train drew in, the men of the family leapt ponderously upon it intent on finding us our seats, seeing our luggage stored, making sure that the railway company was not cheating us of anything: the women with one accord fell bolster-like upon our necks, bearing almost to the ground those of us who were not strong enough to resist, and broke with one accord into a bubbling chorus of sobs. The noise of our going must surely be echoing yet in the high dim girders of the Bahnhof, unless the noise of other, more desperate partings, Hitler-created, has since drowned it.

And now the whistle blows, the guard yells, the train slowly rumbles into motion. A wail goes up from the assembled Blümchens, mingles with the hiss of steam, the quickening grind of wheels, the loud bawling of a porter who still has his clients' luggage in a barrow at the end of the platform. A wail goes up from the Blümchens, a dove-cloud of fluttering handkerchiefs: and then they too are gone, the train rushes into speed, nothing now but the grey backsides of houses on the Kronprinzen Ufer, the grey hulk of the Lehrter Bahnhof, a dull bare swim of trees in the Tiergarten, more water, more slums, then Charlottenburg, Spandau—and now Berlin fades, ebbs like a greasy tide behind us. We rush, stony-faced, despairing, onwards through the last of Germany to Hamburg.

*****

From Hamburg to England we, the poor outcasts, had a ghastly crossing. The boat, tossing already in the harbour, tossed herself somehow out into the open sea, and had not been there ten minutes before Käthy, with devastating thoroughness, was sick. Poor Käthy! It was the first time, I vow, that the child had ever lost her precocious self-possession. One minute she was walking primly across the little lounge, primly asking the amused steward for a stamp to put on her postcard to Oma: and the next minute the whole of Käthy's excellent Hamburg lunch lay about her on the floor, right there under the eye of the steward and the pinched blue noses of two English ladies who said: "Poor child," but did not raise a finger to help. David rushed to her rescue, coaxed her, weeping, into the ladies' room where Gisela sat suckling Benno. Here Hedwig and Konrad were rolled in one bunk like two little hedgehogs: above the edge their little faces glimmered cheese-green. In a very short time they, too, were sick: the little Seligmanns, it seemed, had no stomachs for the sea. But they at last, empty and exhausted, could sleep: above, on the cold wet deck, under the tossing stars, Kurt and I could not. I watched him, seeing his thoughts torment him, not daring to speak to him for fear of hurt. He wandered to and fro, to and fro, trying to fit his steps to the motion of the ship, stumbling now and then, bringing himself up short against the rail to stare out hopelessly at the hopeless sea. I had never thought he could mind leaving Germany so much. As the last lights of Hamburg died over the ship's stern, when there was nothing left but the windy heavens and the grey lacy sea slapping at the ship's side, Kurt leaned his head on his hands, braced himself against the cold wet rail, and wept. I stood beside him, silent and constrained: he clutched my hand and suddenly, horribly, poured out all he thought, as if I were not there, were no more than the rail on which he leaned, or the heaving sea below. He knew, with a mournful sureness, that he would never see Germany again nor ever love any other land so well. Himself as a child, a boy, a young man, lay buried there: three selves as dear to him as limbs and, like torn-off limbs, leaving bleeding stumps behind. Together we remembered the Germany of our youth, the old solid simple Germany of music and good eating and honest thinking: the old house on the Engel Ufer with its wrought iron balcony looking over the water, and in the window of the Erkerzimmer two dark-green glossy rubber-trees that his mother tended like small children, sponging them with tepid water, drying them on a silk handkerchief, moving them into the sun, moving them out of the sun when they had had enough. Now he saw himself, in a peaked schoolboy's cap, shooting from the front door on to the Ufer at six o'clock on a crisp wintry morning, running desperately, bitten with cold, along the iron-hard cobbles into the Schmiedstrasse, along the cold formal old streets of the Friedrichstadt to the Kölnisches Gymnasium and the smelly clangour of another school day. He saw himself as a young man, a seventeen-year-old (filled, as all seventeen-year-olds are from time to time, with a sweet piercing melancholy, a yearning in the bowels for he knew not what) leaning his head against the cold glass of the Erkerzimmer looking down on the snow outside, and listening with inexpressible nostalgia to the voices of Berta and Brigitta singing "*Stille Nacht, Heilige Nacht!*" in the room behind him. His mother accompanied them on the piano, bent short-sightedly over the music; and the two girls, in square-yoked, finely tucked dresses of dark green and red plaid, edged at the hem with yard upon yard of narrow black velvet, stood behind her with their arms fondly linked about one another's firm waists, raised their thin girlish throats that worked convulsively above the lace at their necks, and earnestly warbled.

St-i-ille Nacht!
Hei-li-ge Nacht!

Standing with Kurt by the ship's rail, hearing him pour out himself, his memories to the whining wind and the sea, I could hear those voices still, raw with youth, wavering a little on the top notes: and could see the two girls reflected in the bright glass of the window, as he leaned his head against its chilliness and looked out on the snow. That was the Christmas before the War: next Christmas he was no longer seventeen, nostalgic, but eighteen, a man, and fighting on the Eastern Front: centuries away, in experience, from anything so trustingly feminine as Berta and Brigitta with their sentimental Christmas carollings. Now, listening to his musings, I saw him as a man, muffled in all the woollen clothes Berta and Brigitta and his mother had so lovingly made him, all his clothes upon his back, round his legs, swathing his stomach, and still cold. God, how cold! Kurt now cried, clutching the iron stanchion on the England-bound steamer and making me, too, feel the remembered chill of that 1914 winter as it struck deep once more into his vitals. That was all he could, or cared to, remember about the

War. Still in his gentle mind, I knew, there was the full memory of horror: but for sanity's sake he kept it dug under, snowed over with trivialities, though knowing that beneath these it germinated a foul warmth, a spreading decay. That Germany was dead, and the young Kurt Seligmann who had fought for it was dead too, another war casualty. There remained now Kurt Seligmann the Jew, leaving Germany, with nothing but despair in his heart. He had little trust in the future, and looking into the past he could find nothing in it that was worth much. Added to cold, the oncoming of sea-sickness and a bitter *Heimweh*,[10] my poor Kurt now suddenly suffered from conscience. We stood together by the rail clutching at it; he clutched at my hand (I do not know which was the colder) and murmured of his own worthlessness.

"Don't, Kurt, don't!"

"My God, when I think of the things I've done! The way I treated you, Charlotte!—I deserve to be more than kicked. Suppose there had been a baby, now—"

"Please, Kurt, it does no good remembering things like that. Please, please!"

We fell to silence while the wind moaned and the sea heavily slapped the ship's sides. And now even the last light had gone, there was no more Germany, no more Berlin. Farewell to all, to Kurt's missed youth and missed opportunities, to the old houses in the Friedrichstadt with their grace, their easy opulence, to the town we were both babies in, grew up in; to the baby I had, and lost, and cannot for the life of me forget, though to remember does no good. Farewell to all that: let us go down below, we brave adventurers starting a new life, and get into his bunk poor Kurt who already, exhausted by emotion, heaves also with sea-sickness.

---

10   German: homesickness.

Chapter 6

The Black and the White

In England we stayed once more with the reluctant Flowers, ate ourselves sick on Flower bounty, and left them unregretting, sped on our way by nothing more cheerful than brilliant smiles of joy at our going. We sailed for Capetown from Liverpool on a mad day in January, the wind tearing the heart out of the trees, bending them almost horizontal, slapping them brutally when they tottered upwards again, ripping grey slates off roofs, hurling them against a grey sky to fall on the apprehensive pates of bald old men, peroxided young females, anxious scuttling matrons: the wind bringing down telegraph-poles across the Midlands, wrecking scaffoldings in grim northern towns, seriously injuring a wireless mast (to the genteel indignation of the B.B.C.) and piling up the Irish Channel against Aberystwyth pier so that it collapsed, beaten. The wind did all this, and more unchronicled, on the day we left for Capetown. Left for Capetown!—it sounded so casual, so excursionish, I thought; and yet here we were on a ship at last, free at last (surely?) from persecution of the grosser kind. The ship lay at her moorings all night, for she could not sail: all night the wind screamed, feet rushed to and fro on the soaking decks, the screech of winches and the icy smack of water fought each other for the upper hand. Late, very late, I stood by one of the gangways, screened by flapping canvas, and brooded for distraction not on myself but on the human beetles for whom this ship existed, who were even now teeming in her bowels. Not as maggots teem in carrion, perhaps, but something very like. I was tired, so tired that my mind flitted bat-like, entered with uncanny stealth into other minds, dwelt there a space looking through other eyes. I had no heart to spare for my fellow travellers, being far more miserable than they: but the tired mind is keen in understanding, quiveringly alert to contact. So I watched and understood, rigid with weariness, there at the entrance to the little lounge in which palms waved wildly, straining at their brass pots. I saw the great ship-hulk crawling with life, life so various, so diverse that we might have been the teeming continent of Europe split up into races, languages, cultures, yet still a whole in which the small parts busily warred one with the other. As I had stood on a high Alpine pass watching the minute life below, seeing the woman hang out her clothes, the man bend to his reaping, knowing why the woman washed, why the man cut hay, so I now peered at the T.S.S. *Cerulean* and saw not only clean through the stout wood of her creaking walls, but through the bony walls of her passengers' skulls as they fussed and fretted at their settling in. I have never been so close, so intimate, to unknown minds, unknown hearts, as I was that wild night, myself black with the horror of leaving, and leaving for ever, the only land I knew. I saw in their faces the petty emotions which fretted them: god-like, relinquishing hope (which is earthly) I looked into their minds. "I shall be sick," thinks the little woman who has tittered nervously as the steward helps her down the gangway, "I shall be sick." And she feels like a doom in her nostrils the oil, varnish, fish and dusty palm odour of all ships. That smell alone sharpens nausea in the gullet, smelling it, she sees already the bland expectancy of lavatory pans, water silting back and forth in them to the ship's horrid motion: sees the assumed concern of stewardesses to whom vomit is all in the day's work, the scornful amusement of fellow passengers who sail well. "I shall be sick," thinks the little woman despairingly, and twitters onwards to find her cabin, a martyr already, the arena already sanded for her blood.

"Shall I be sick?" wonders the bride, stepping after, nineteen years old and still with the dew thick upon her; "*shall* I be sick?" How awful, how shaming, to be sick on your wedding night! And images crowd in her mind as she follows her very young husband—images of her best school friend who flew to Paris on her honeymoon and was sick into a brown-paper bag, held by the bridegroom, between Croydon and Le Bourget, could not even deposit her sickness decently in lavatory or tin basin but had (red at the eyes, pale at the nose) to drop it into the brown-paper bag held by those hands which but three hours before had clasped hers as she ineptly sliced the wedding cake. "Air sickness might be worse," thinks the ship-travelling bride; here at least there is a "Ladies": and she notes with faint melancholy pleasure the green illuminated sign, the magic letters, the curtain dangling coyly over the door. Green for the female, red for the male: Ladies, Gentlemen, let us be genteel even in our excretions, our sea-sick agonies: let us not be man and woman, human, but Ladies, Gentlemen, ultra suburban, too refaned to care.

"Aha! this is the right sort of start, fine capful of wind as a send-off," bawls the bluff man in the bowler hat too small for him. "Pity the poor landlubbers, pity the—"

"Don't, Charles!" says his wife sharply, carrying all the parcels. She is a magnificent sailor, and now remembers him as he was between Dover and Ostend, herself supporting (she was young then and in love) his poor head, wiping his poor bedabbled mouth.

But wifely pride, now a habit, makes her protest almost laughingly at his childish bluff: wild horses would not drag his shame from her. Bright, archly reproachful, inwardly sick at heart (this fool, this pantaloon, this fat constipated man trying to impress!) she smiles at the company and begs them to admire her husband, Neptune's pet, the Perfect Sailor.

"Howdy, Cap'n!" cries the Perfect Sailor to an undistinguished steward: and amid gales of merriment passes on.

And now the masterful woman, conveniently widowed, who has trotted the globe so often that Mars, feeling her feet upon him, must surely be quaking. There is nothing, believe me, nothing, which the masterful globe-trotting widow does not know about the globe, its habits, its weathers, its peoples, its tourist agencies, its beauty spots, its ships, trains, rickshaws, bullock carts, charabancs, cable railways and funiculars. She has chosen her cabin, and knows full well how choice it is. Far enough from the engines to be unthrobbed by them, near to the surgeon, whom she knew in Karachi and who will look her over, should she need vetting, without any mention of the usual 7/6: far, aristocratically far, from the vulgar brilliance of the barber's shop with its vulgar males being scraped inside, its vulgar yellow Kodak films, its vulgar lollipops in jars and brilliantines in bottles outside. She has chosen her cabin, she makes for it: and at her approach the lounge, that was filled only with two spotty understewards and a small rabble of passengers, becomes at once gladdened by the chief steward, the head dining-room steward and the purser, all racing to drop their gold and frankincense and myrrh at the fat feet of the globe-trotting widow. While they offer her all they have (or are prepared to sell, much the same thing)—the best table in the dining-saloon, her bath at any time she wishes, the safe for her two pearl necklaces—while they offer this, Mr. and Mrs. Sparling, behind, who have never set foot out of England before save to spend six days for five guineas in Blankenberghe, Belgium, scuttle past her like awed weevils, for their inconsiderable cabin, an inside one, right over the engines, next door to, and therefore orally reached by, the constant flushings of the gents' lavatory.

And now the young ones, the Born Flirt, the Dandy with violet essence on his hair, the Masher, the pretty girls who know nothing (official), and the ingenuous youth who has brand new flannels, a yachting cap, and much looks forward to deck quoits. Also, less young, already a trifle crow-eyed, the Life and Soul of the Party. He, too, knows everyone: he calls the stewards by their Christian names, nicknames the purser, back-handedly slaps the barber on the paunch and cries at him: "What, old careless! What, my bucko!" and shouts at him dark sentences about the cutting of men's throats and like matters. To which the barber, remembering a puny half-crown tip on the voyage from Cape-town, smiles but wanly.

And so to noise and clatter, to the frenzied slapping of water and shouting of wind outside, to the hearty man-handling and inane excited shoutings of the passengers inside, the ship fills up. It is already plain she cannot sail to-night. The sea without is a howling waste, there would be danger even for this broad matronly vessel outside. So the passengers troop into the dining-saloon, reprieved for twelve hours, and fill their delicate stomachs with *hors d'œuvres variés*, Surrey chicken *à la grand-mère, coupe Montmartre, biscuits et fromage*—and then surge like inquisitive fleas about the lounges, the smokeroom, the veranda. But avoiding the decks: for on the decks you can hear the sea. A few timorous ladies of sensitive habit lie them down at once upon their bunks, close their eyes, ring for stewardesses, and delicately render into the chamber-pot just to show they know what a sea voyage is for. When told that the ship has not yet left port they look slightly foolish, dab lavender-water upon themselves, and sleep.

Still the trampling of feet goes on, and the noise of passengers too excited for bed; of baggage stewards sweating under baggage, of bell-boys with bursting blue serge bottoms careering madly along gangways collecting telegrams, yelling for Miss This, Mr. That, Mrs. Another. Perhaps someone answers their cries, perhaps not: who knows? Certainly no one cares, least of all the bell-boys. Theirs not to reason why, theirs but to yell and fly, cannonading along the narrow ways, buttons as tight to their fronts as Brussels sprouts to the stalk, yelling insanely.

But long after midnight people begin to go to bed, soon all are bedded like tired children after Christmas. The tired stewardesses wipe the sweat from their faces, take off their monstrous caps, ease themselves from starch into winceyette, and lay themselves, without much hope of staying there, upon their bunks. A steward passes quietly along turning out lights: one or two tired electric bulbs glow feebly, making the murk infinitely sinister. The wind howls outside, flaps at canvas, tears at cables, rocks the great boat trussed up in the docks. The water rushes madly past, mottled with a wild spume. Across the harbour pool a few lights flicker and rock reflected in the wetness beneath: a steamer hoots once like a tortured cow, and all is still.

But there is no stillness in the brain. Even the sleeping ones dream, and those waking, only a few, revolve wearily within the slats and bars of their own cage. Whose brain shall I find here worth picking? thinks exhausted Charlotte, alone among the palms that still reel to the storm. In whose mind shall I now laboriously plough, turning up earth-worms, centipedes, hard flints, crumbling lumps of chalk, like dog's dirt, old trouser-buttons, greenish bits of bottle? Not in the travelling widow's, hers is but a travel brochure (inclusive fare up the Mount by motor-car, down by toboggan, afternoon tea, gentlemanly guide, 14/-: Hotel Bella Vista, H. & C. all bedrooms from 12 pesetas: Jamaica for winter sunshine, 1st class throughout, all outside cabins). Not in the mind of the Perfect Sailor shall I plough, there there will be nothing for a long time but such anguished small-boy thoughts as: "Oh, my God, stay still! Why must you heave?—No, this time I'll keep it, this time I will not retch—this time—oh, my God!" Nor in his wife's; hers is filled with accustomed wifely solicitude, tame and stale as all long-worn habit. Those coarse evolutions which go on behind the sunburned front of the Life and Soul of the Party are too obvious to need my digging. They lie all over the surface, like small mean pebbles washed clean of soil. And the Flirt thinks but of flirting, and the Masher of mashing, and the ingenuous youth of the crease in his new flannels. While the pretty girls, the gay chatterers, what is in their heads that I do not already know? Nothing. And to the very young bride and groom thought is hard, alien, feeling to them is all.

No, there is nothing here, thinks weary Charlotte, turning to go, there is nothing here, nor will be. Perhaps I will not search for mind any more, perhaps my seekings (now that I have left super-intellectual Europe) shall be pure bodily. I want above all to forget that I have a mind (what good is a mind?). I want to stop thinking.

*****

It was very hard to stop thinking on the boat. Firstly, our own problem, the Jewish problem, which we had thought to leave behind us. stalked now the decks of the *Cerulean* and met us at every turn. We were not the only Jews on board. "The 'ole ship's bloody well full of 'em." said a grizzled deck-hand to me, assuming me purely Aryan. Really, I had sympathy with the man, for we travelling, fleeing, exile Jews are dreadful. One of us as leaven in a small company is excellent: two of us are fatal. For wherever we combine we create a new Jewry, another Palestine, with all the hates, strifes, schisms of the old. The sight of us, so persecuted, so unhappy, so worthy (surely?) of sympathy, rouses at once the lowest instincts in every Gentile breast. It is our misfortune, we can do nothing for it. And we are peculiarly loathsome on board ship, because pleasant shipboard life demands content. Content with existing things (for they are ruled by the sea, they cannot lightly be changed) and content to some measure with oneself. This we unhappy Jews, flying from a country which has spurned us to another which may well do the same with equal violence, cannot reach. We are thoroughly discontented. Warped by all that we have suffered, by the thought of the things we may further suffer, we become shrill, touchy, aggressive. We speak and behave as we should never dream of doing in our native Berlin, Frankfurt, Wien. We demand sympathy and by demanding it dry up the source: there is nothing left but irritation. The world hears about us, sighs over us, imagines us as white-faced fugitives, picturesquely thin, haunted by horror: very well, let it be so, the Jews are persecuted, they suffer, they are poor: what a pity! Thus the world, reading about us only. Then we are seen, we travel from London to New York, from Liverpool to Capetown. We are not in rags, we do not hide in barrels or in dark corners: we are out in the open, smart, sophisticated, emerging boldly from state-rooms, from first-class cabins. Some of us even have rosy cheeks, some of us even ask to be treated as other humans. This is all wrong! cries the world, outraged by impudence, it must be all wrong! Look at these people travelling, even as we do, in luxury. Look at the clothes they have, the endless clothes! They can't be poor, hunted, unhappy: the things we have read about them are simply not true. And the world fulminates against us, never stopping to think. We have clothes, naturally. We spent in Berlin, in Wien all we could to fit ourselves out for years. We travel first-class—also natural. Are we, abandoning our homes to the Nazi beast, leaving him our native soil, also to give him our money? We are not mad. By low means or fair means we buy our steamer tickets in Germany, in German currency, so that we leave as little as we can behind. We are going to hard times, wherever we travel: to the Argentine, to New York, to Australia, to South Africa: would you really have us, with that struggle ahead, travel meanly by third class and abandon to Hitler the money we have earned in Germany, the money we cannot take out?

Well, the argument goes endlessly on. The truth is we have committed the cardinal crime: we have survived persecution. Our dead bodies would be wept over, lamented, eulogised: alive, we are an insult to common sense, for how come we to be alive? What right have we to be anything but dead? "There must be something *in* them," says one peaked Englishwoman to another, bending her wet nose over her knitting and staring, affronted, at two Jewish maidens in swim-suits who, beside the *Cerulean's* bathingpool, are positively enjoying themselves. And: "My dear, you find them *every*where!" answers the second, horrified, appalled at our ubiquity. But are we ubiquitous in Germany? Alas, she has never been to Germany, she knows only what she reads in the *Daily Mail*. It is useless to argue: I listen, inwardly protesting, and then go to another part of the deck where, perhaps, I shall have quiet.

Try as I might, on that journey, I could not find any peace for my mind. There were too many problems. The problem of Kurt, who was like a man shaken, inwardly bleeding, he who had so light-heartedly planned to leave Germany with never a look behind. The problem of David, who fell in love, poor mite, with a nine-year-old Aryan lad and followed him, moping about the deck, followed in his turn by the Aryan's mamma who commanded her lamb to shun association with anything so low as a Jew. The problem, lastly, of Charlotte, who was fast growing into a nervy hag. I watched myself, heard myself, and knew myself to be ageing in an unlovely way. There was an edge to my voice, a glitter in my eye, which had not been there in Berlin. Things irritated me beyond all expression. Poor moping David with enormous hazel eyes pursuing his love, Kurt sunk in gloom, Gisela, gentle Gisela, fussing over her babies: the noise and clamour of the young aboard the ship who, like all young everywhere, never seemed to be anywhere but around one's ankles, under one's feet. The ship gives a lurch, there is a yowl and there! you have trodden on another of them, the affronted mother springs from the deck-chair in which she dozed, grandmamma materialises from positively nowhere, the deck steward pants up babbling baby talk and you shrink away shamed to the very marrow, a very brute of a creature, a fiend in female form. Children should never be loose, I often thought, watching the deck which teemed with them: really, they should never be loose. Yet the brats survived, however weighty the feet that trod on them: they were like the Jews, they triumphantly survived everything.

Then not only the children, the Jews, my own folk, irritated me, but the English, who were naturally everywhere. Now revived an ancient grudge against the race that dated from my first Englishwoman, governess Miss Bailey. She was plain, unintelligent, had bad breath and was yet, in the family hierarchy, set above our Bohemian nurse, Anni, whom we adored. She was also set above us, put in authority over us. Why? Because she was English. My childish reason seized on this, there bred in my childish mind the idea that the English, however unworthy, demanded and arrogantly got, as if by birthright, the place in the sun. Cambridge had done nothing to overset this theory: the *Cerulean* made it concrete. For here were the English in all their arrogance, aboard an English ship, ploughing through waters which, if they weren't actually English, certainly ought to be: here were the English on their native heath, insufferable. I had forgotten, till I went to Cambridge, that the English in 1914 had been our foes: it was they who reminded me. Now, with another war impending, they sat about the decks with their knitting, their fancy-work, their snapshots of grandchildren and talked of the last war. It did not matter to them that I was German, that did not still their tongues, curb their lip-licking repetition of the old, old atrocity stories. The babies burned down for fat, the poison in Belgian wells, the influenza germ—I heard them all. The late war was to these harpies a vivid oleograph, Right triumphing over Swinishness. They all spoke of war as if they knew what it meant, as if they, not we, had been blockaded for years. The well-fed English, shuddering blue-veined lids over their pale shallow eyes, told me, told the little world of the *Cerulean*, how they had suffered. How *they* had suffered, my God!

"There was no bah-ter!" they bleated, "no sugar! Even our *meat* was rationed!"

"Our children died," I imprudently said.

"No sugar even to make jah-m!—and such a lot of fruit that year, just rotting on the trees!"

"Our babies had no milk—"

"And the *inconvenience*—just imagine, when vou travelled anywhere you had to take your wretched little meat-cards with you so that your hostess could take them to her butcher and get the ration. I mean, it was so low, so humiliating—"

"For ten months after your war had ended," I burst in, prudent and polite no longer, "ours went on. There was no food, though we grubbed like beasts for it. I saw a woman turning out an ash-can, in the early morning, by some flats in Charlottenburg. She went through the gutter-stuff with her claws and found some turnip-tops which she gnawed as she went on looking. There was nothing more. She sat on a door-step to suckle her baby: her breasts were just the colour and shape of parsnips. There might have been some milk but the baby was too weak to get it. That was in June, 1919, when you were so busy with your childish plans for hanging the Kaiser that you cared not a pin for us, still blockaded by your ships. You talk to me, now, as if you knew what war was—!"

But the party had broken up, the ladies scuttled, leaving the maniac alone with her ravings and one pink ball of knitting wool which had dropped in the flight.

Such outbursts (and there were others) gave me a name on the ship. I had the reputation of a shrew with a tongue. When they learnt I was also Jewish they shook their heads, murmured: "Well, of course, we might have known," and left me. Gisela they petted: she was the mother of many babies and laughed at them so subtly that they never knew. But me, the good-looking termagant, they abandoned to herself. I was very much alone. The exaltation of leaving for new continents, new worlds, faded before I had seen the last of the old. Even the word "Capetown" now ceased to titillate my mind. "When we get to Capetown!"—"As soon as we land in Capetown," babbled the children incessantly: to me the place was now but the inevitable ending to a dreamy avenue, no pearly gate.

In a blur of heat we landed at length in Capetown. The last off the ship, we had sat stifling for hours in the lounge while our passports and customs papers were pored over, the children counted and re-counted, by hard-faced men. At last we were free, we were desirable immigrants, thanks to Onkel Hans' money: we could go ashore. The children were by this time too stunned with heat even to chirp: we piled them into a taxi, little pale lumps, drove into the town, unpacked them into a hotel, and put them to bed. It was mid-afternoon, drowsy three o'clock. The heat lay bright and hard over everything, over the town sprawling up the bronze-green slopes; over the sea that gleamed like molten lead, unwrinkled; over the great bare cliff of Table Mountain soaring at our backs into a hard blue sky.

Gisela cared not a button for the Table Mountain but lay on her bed in her petticoat fast asleep. Kurt and I went out into the town. I had not thought it would be like this, so neat and tame, its elemental wildness pushed back to that astounding mountain closing the streets to the east. There's something charmingly parochial about the place, I thought, looking at the old, ugly, over-trimmed buildings with their iron-fretted balconies and veranda-posts. Desperate adventures have started out from here, ended here: yet in the sun the little town lies dozing like a housewife at a picnic, pleased to have done with house-work for the day, to be able to lie in the sun and snooze.

We wandered up and down Adderley Street taking in all its strangeness. By the post office coloured women sat in a blaze of flowers whose brilliance hurt the eye: they thrust big bunches at us and murmured: "Only a bob, missus." But their voices had no conviction, as if hope died twenty times a day. They were slack and muted, stunned as we were, perhaps, by the savage afternoon heat. On the pavements the coloured people passed up and down between the Europeans, slinking past, fluid-limbed and very careful, careful not to swing their arms, to come too close so that there was risk of touching. What would happen, I wondered idly, mooning along, if black touched white? An immediate explosion? A roar of falling masonry? That roof (it was the old Dutch church) crashing in a shower of bricks? No, but what *would* happen? Why do they thread their way amongst us with such mistrustful care, sheering off just six inches or so when we suddenly step out of line, swerving instinctively out of reach of the white flesh? Is it that they do not like to touch us, dislike the feel of us? Or is it that they know we shrink from them? An Englishman would say "yes" to the last, ignoring the first, but I was not sure.

By the Botanical Gardens we stopped to watch an ancient Indian fascinating three moribund snakes. They crawled in the hot dust, contemptuously ignoring him: and he, sitting cross-legged, turbaned, played excruciatingly upon a little pipe. A ring of coloured people stood about him as apathetic as the snakes, but upright. The old man drew from his bosom a sham snake, a bright spotted calico tube with a spring coiled inside. It waggled under his hand: at once there was a stir in the crowd, the dark faces lived, the lips fell open in astonishment, the eyes rolled. A pleased giggle went round the ring as the aged man waggled his silly snake, pattered to it, played to it. The live snakes crawled languidly about, looped exhaustedly in and out of their basket; in the dust the old man played his pipe, fiddled with his imitation snake. Then a policeman cleared the whole circus away, driving before him the snake-charmer, who wheezily protested and brandished in one hand his snake, in another his pipe from which spittle dropped. Even when he had gone the coloured people stayed just where they were, vacantly gazing upon a vacuum.

That night, when the children lay sleeping and a friendly chambermaid sat in the corridor cocking her ear for sounds of distress amongst them, Kurt and Gisela and I went out once more. A wind had sprung up, blowing away the thick midday air. High above our heads shone the soft ripe southern stars which in the last ten days we had taken as familiar. The air was scented with sea water, with a smell of wetness on hot dust, and a fainter, sweeter scent from some strange bloom we did not know. Against the dark sky darker palm-trees rustled their hard leaves: their stems were thick, gross, like pineapples. We took a tram out along a wide road under gum-trees to some suburb by the sea: then got out, wandered to a bench among rocks, and sat there wondering at the velvety softness of the air as it blew in little puffs against our faces. Gisela leaned on Kurt's shoulder, took his hand: I think she felt, as I did, that this was a land we could be safe in, and perhaps happy later on. We had a sense of great peace, of an enormous peaceful stretch of country lying behind that dark mountain waiting for us, ready to give us room to live.

Along the road at our backs went a couple speaking German. It was so natural that we did not notice till they had gone how odd it was, how strange, to be hearing our own tongue in this alien country. Then at once, like children torn from their mother, we were all smitten with a ghastly home-sickness. We sat upon that bench yearning for Germany, silent, struck dumb, helpless with our longing. It was February: in Berlin now the wind we always hated would be wrapping dirty bits of newspaper, tramtickets, and chaffy dried dung about the ankles of women shopping on the Leipziger. The little tin newspaper kiosk in the Potsdamer Platz would be moaning and creaking as the wind hit it in the ribs. At the

Spittelmarkt bulky figures well wrapped against the cold would be getting in and out of the endless tram-cars, clutching at their hats and parcels as the wind came at them. The Spree, sullenly flowing past the castle, would be peaked into a thousand dirty toppling pimples by the wind. And the smuts from the steamers unloading coal on the Märkisches Ufer would be blown away down the wind in a pestilential shower, hard rattling little pellets of grit. Now high up in the house by the water, the old Blümchen house on the Schwalbenufer, Tante Lydia throws open her window, pokes out her head that is covered in an old fur cap tied down over the ears with a dirty woollen muffler, and veils shrilly for the gulls. They come, poor hungry hideous creatures, mewing raucously as they wheel: and she throws out to them fish-bones, potato-peelings, a hard dry crust or two. They swoop and dive, catching in mid-air; the window slams shut again, the gulls wheel away to settle again in hundreds on the parapet of the Fischerbrücke.

In Berlin, now, Tante Clara like a lonely old crow will be drawing up to her stove, reaching for her spectacles from the case at her waist, searching through the *Frankfurter Zeitung* for the shipping news, trying to comfort herself by seeing the name of our ship in print. Next door, in the girls' room that resounds no longer to the bright chat of Berta and Brigitta, the new lodger, Herr Rabinowitz, clears his throat, spits noisily. ("There he goes again! I give him something to spit into and he spits on the floor!" Tante would cry at this), sighs profoundly and lies down upon the bed. Tante Clara hopes against experience that he has taken off his boots....

I was never very fond of Tante Clara, a difficult and often querulous old woman. But the old are necessarily pathetic, and this night in Capetown my heart was full of her. I saw her so clearly in her obstinate loneliness, her dull despair, crouched over the stove trying to get some warmth into her long rheumatic back. I saw from Kurt's face that he was thinking of her too, mourning over her, knowing as well as I that if she had come she would have made herself and us miserable. As for Gisela, she was quite frankly crying, snuffling against his jacket.

"*Du Kleines!*" he said, wrapping her closer, "*hier werden wir doch glücklich leben!*"[1]

"Don't speak to me German, Kurt, that makes it worse."

So we valiantly talked English, staring out at the dark sea so softly lapping, listening to the strange wind crackling in the palm-leaves, pushing the thought of Berlin to the back of our minds.

Next morning was more cheerful. Never since Grübl had I lain in such sun as now poured through my eastward-facing window. As I turned fully to it, feeling the dry warmth soak into my skin, David came scrabbling at the door to ask if from my window you could see the mountain. Yes, from my window you could see the mountain. Like the rock-wall beyond the Kännchen at which I had stared morning after morning in Grübl before Bärbel came, the mountain here sheered up, magnificently aloof from all foolish human doings on its lower slopes; sheering up, appearing endless, then ending in a knife-cut level against a brazen sky.

"*Ach Himmel!*"[2] cried David, skipping at the open window, forgetting to hold on to his pyjama trousers. They fell in blue wrinkles round his feet and he jerked out of them altogether, thrust his skinny little body out of the window, hung staring at the mountain and murmuring to it endearments in German. I realised then that he had never seen a mountain before: in the holidays they had been no farther afield, these children, than the flat sandy Baltic shores or the Lüneburger Heide. This was David's first mountain: I like to think that when he has long outgrown wonder he will still see in his mind's eye that cliff above Capetown: that the word "mountain" will bring to him his first sight of it, rearing its rocky crest so proudly against the hot morning sky. That

---

1   German: Little one, here you will live happily!
2   German: Ah, heaven!

was a good enough beginning for a little lad of ten who had as yet seen nothing higher than the round green hills about the Havel.

Not that this sight from my bedroom window was the end of the mountains for the day. There were other mountains, chains of them, blue and remarkable as we jogged by train to Tante Saschia Blümchen's farm near Malmesbury. The train, lined in a grass-hopper-green leather which the children found quite entrancing, ambled northward across the sultry flats, ambled unconcerned away from Table Mountain, past the Hottentots Holland all hazy in the afternoon heat. The children were at first inclined to gambol: but the deathly stillness of the air, the heat which pressed against them every time they stirred, soon calmed them down: they sat dumb, staring at everything, Now the flats were left behind, the country was thick bush of young wattles or slender naked-stemmed gum-trees with shining leaves that crackled dryly against each other though as yet there was no wind.

There were few stations, but many stops between. For at the far end of the carriage chattered a troupe of returning school-children, dark little Cape-coloureds in frowsty blue gym dresses or flannel shorts, very dirty. Every now and then the train stopped, there in the green hot bush, and a child or two shot from its doors, fell like a rubber ball from the high step. Gisela with sweat-drops on her forehead looked wonderingly after them, obviously imagining in her maternal way how their mothers would have their tea ready for them, be waiting at home to cosset them, the little things returning after another week's peril in school. But I doubted if they had mothers, these alien small animals: were they not simply spawned in the teeming bush (there goes another lot back into the bush, leaving the door ajar as the train starts up again), did they not simply live off wild honey and locusts each Saturday and Sunday till civilisation grabbed at them once more, rammed once more their wild bodies into alien gym tunics, and sent them off to school?

Now the train chugged crossly past a place called Elsie's River (what did the girl Elsie do, that she should have a river all to herself?) and Benno, waking, had to be fed.

David sat beside me, very taut and still. The others peeped now and then round the shining brilliant green upholstery towards the dark children: and the dark children, ceasing their foreign chatter, stared back boldly at our little Seligmanns until they took away their eyes, abashed. But David sat aloof, stared unblinking through the window. Sweat ran down the sides of his face and trickled in the collar of his new English shirt: he looked excessively hot, but happy, like a mystic practising Yoga under the fierce eastern sun. Beside his window, against a violently blue sky, the murmuring wattles marched backward, lovely feathery things like exotic birds, like plumy cockatoos. They quivered with life, vigorously rippling—the only things in the landscape not prostrated by the heat. Opposite David sat Gisela suckling Benno, who made loud smacking noises as his lips met the nipple: but David stared away from all of us out of the windows at his new land: ecstatic, tired, and a little scared.

When at last the train stopped at Minnaarskopjie, which was merely two corrugated iron sheds, a post-office-store, and a petrol pump, the wind had got up and was blowing strongly from the hot north. We descended: it caught us up, flattened with hot blasts our clothes against our wet limbs, tweaked off our hats, blew out our hair in wild streamers. It was a dry brute, a very beast of a wind. There was no escaping. We ran back and forth in it lugging our packages from the train: it smote us at every turn. When at last the train rumbled away down the single line into the heat haze, we were left a prey to nothing but wind.

So this was Africa. The station stood higher than the country round, on a little kopjie. Spread about it lay a wonderful variegated plain rippling off to the foot of the mountains: a checker-board of hot tawny browns, bronzes, yellows and sultry greens. Forty miles away to the southwest the Table Mountain reared its flattened crest against the heat, incredibly flat-topped, clean-cut like a slice of cake. We stood under two rustling gum-trees staring at it all, clutching our clothes against the wind, staring at this strange wild country. Three Kaffir women carrying on their heads great kerosene tins, another in either hand, walked slowly, superbly, up the slope from the petrol-pump; then, stepping from the road on to the rails, picked their way cleanly from sleeper to sleeper, swinging their haunches, and dropped over the brow of the hill to a camp of tiny pointed tents under a wattle grove.

Still we stood, un-met, unrecognised, strangers in a land that heaved with strangeness.

David took the children to the lavatory, for which they had been clamouring, and came back a little shaken to report that it was "full of a black man." We looked along the platform. There they stood, Käthy, Hedwig and Konrad, an enraptured posse by the door: when the embarrassed negro came out they tagged after him silently along the road to the top of the slope, and watched him unblinking as he lumbered loose-armed downhill.

Now far away on the tawny ribbon of the road appeared a cloud of tawny dust, a motor-car. Tawny as the landscape itself, a mere blob of speeding dust, it came fiercely towards us. Odd to see a vehicle approaching two or three miles away, clear, exact, certainly for us, when we had been used to no farther view than our tram-car turning the bend from the Gertraudenstrasse into the Spittelmarkt.

The car came roaring up the dusty slope, stopped dead under our noses. A young dusty man leaned out, brick-red, brown-eyed, so burned and roughened by the sun that his skin looked like warm morocco. He stared us up and down, spoke not a word, grunted, got out of the car, and began to stow away our luggage in the trailer that rocked behind it. A jerk of the thumb showed that we were to get in: we gathered up the children and got in, stunned by the first impact of Boer manners.

"I'm Jan," said the brick-red one, and began most violently to start the car.

Now we were speeding back along the road we had seen him come, catching up the cloud of dust that he had raised in coming and that still hung weary over the dried fields. The road was a hot rusty red, fearsome to the tired eye, so rutted and ribbed that, packed even as we were, we bounced painfully in a clutching heap from side to side. There were but two whitewashed, grey-roofed homesteads between Minhaarskopjie and Kraanvlei, each standing in a quivering grove of gums, each with its windmill creaking in the open veldt beside it. Pigs ambled from the gateless entrances: mules champed at the dry grass verge, frisking up their heels as we passed; ducks and geese cackled after us; and on we sped in a dust cloud, swaying and lurching. Before us the plain spread out, heat-mazed to the very foot of the mountains. On our north a humpy rocky heap with fantastic tops: "Paardeberg," muttered Jan reluctantly in answer to our question. Beyond, coming out now from behind the Paardeberg, an odd little peak like a firm breast and nipple, standing all by itself, rising alive from the flat treeless plain. "Bobbejaansberg, there's the farm on this side of it," grunted Jan: and from the look he gave it over the steering-wheel we saw suddenly what earth, land, *his* land, meant to this earthy oaf, this human clam. We stared at the square white patch of house among regimental pines: at the smaller white cubes, like English sugar-lumps, standing along a green sluit farther down the slope.

Now the road was behind us, we swerved between iron gate-posts to a rutted track lying among fields so dry, so cracked and gaping that it made the eyes harsh to look at them. The grass by the little sluit, jewel-green higher up by the farm, here died to wispy tussocks, stringy, rasping, juiceless, at which the cattle nibbled despairingly while whisking their tails at black clouds of flies. Halfway between the gate and the farm an enormous scar ran across the land, a yellow canyon some three metres deep.

Loose boards bridged it: it became a joke among the Seligmanns, that temporary bridge. Every time we went over in the car Tante Saschia, bouncing on the back seat, would yell: "Jan!" (or "Dirk!" whichever happened to be driving), "when are you going to fill up this dongha and make the road decent?" "To-morrow, Ma," the lad would mechanically answer, "to-morrow." When I left in June to-morrow had not yet come—for aught I know the dongha still gapes across the Kraanvlei road, still bridged by straying boards that heave and rattle as the car goes over. Ah, Africa! *More is nog'n dag!*[3]

But we are still speeding to Kraanvlei, our new home, our hope and Canaan. On the roofs of the little Kaffir huts melons were ripening, green and orange and yellow. Swarms of small black children rushed after the car, cavorting in our dust, as we drove beneath an avenue of Monterey pines, past a grove of tenderly green willows. With a grind and a shriek the car stopped in the farmyard: Tante Saschia met us with a dead hen, bloody-headed, in either hand. Hardly the plump comely Boer housewife we had pictured, this Tante Saschia, but a woman of a terrific tubular leanness, resilient as a bicycle tyre, with quick small eyes and dusty hair thin-braided.

"Welcome!" she cried, waving the hens as Jan brought the car to a stop within an inch of her. "Welcome to Kraanvlei!" And as she pounced to kiss us all, even Benno who woke at it and yelled, there spattered from the beaks of the strangled hens, on to the tawny dust, brilliant hot drops of blood, ruby red in the sun.

*****

With the reluctant Jan, pressed into politeness by his mother, I climbed the Bobbejaansberg a few days later to look at our new land. In Capetown, that first day, it had been hot enough: but

---

3 Afrikaans: Tomorrow is another day.

out here in this odd tempestuous hinterland between Capetown and Malmesbury, it was very hot indeed. Here, over the parched waterless plain, the sun had really come into his own. From a sky as hard as metal the hot light streamed down. The whole land heaved and shimmered in the heat. At our feet the apricot orchards were a neat pattern of pale earth dotted with dark green: on either side lay stretches of pale exhausted wheat-stubble. The colourless soil gaped between the brittle stalks, burning the eye. And away beyond rolled the plain, away to the feet of the mountains, to their pleated bronze-green foot-hills. The Drakenstein were not mountains as I, remembering Austria, knew them: here were no soft beauties of green hanging alp, dark pine, tumbling water. Twisted and pleated by some malignant finger, thrown up pell-mell out of the protesting earth, they edged the plain in a line of fantastic variety. Now in the late afternoon they were lilac-grey, sharp-edged, with flower-blue shadows scarring them from foot to summit. Below the bare rock, on these mountains, begins a meagre vegetation: clothed in dry scrub, the brown-green slopes strike down into a plain gaping with heat. All is savagely different from the pictuesque, the beautiful, in Europe's scenery.

"It's beautiful," I said to Jan, who now stood picking at the dust with his great boots, "beautiful!"

And Jan looked at me sideways out of small eyes, grunted, turned his back, and began to go downhill. His loathsome task was over: now he could get back to his real job, the farm. It lay below us in a pool of green pines, the old farm which two hundred years ago had been a mere cube of mud wall, whitewashed; to which in generations the children and the children's children of those who first built it had added something. A stoep, another bedroom, two more bedrooms, a new store, finally (O, twentieth century triumph!) a bathroom: all sprouting from the side of the parent like toadstools on an old stump. A higgledy-piggledy inchoate mass, this farm, with buildings sticking in all directions: and yet the whole pile, from which the whitewash peeled in strips and patches, had an air, a juicy character. Not only from the old Dutch gable that stuck out now lost and meaningless over the roof of the new incubator-room: it would need more than a Dutch gable to make a home in the Cape Province. And: "Here is a home," one thought, regarding the whole. "It springs inevitable from the soil, as inevitable as the six prim oaks that from their grassy plot shade the stoep: it is as much a part of the countryside as that craggy hill, this sprouting of dark pines."

And a home it was to us in those first few days flushed with gratitude. Unlike the Flowers, Tante Saschia made us welcome with no reserves. We were her kin: that for the moment was enough. Though she buzzed with practical plans for our future, it was not in eagerness to have us gone. This large hospitality of the colonial was something as foreign to us, as exotic, as the rearing purple heads of the Drakenstein mountains, as the little dark children who swarmed in and out of the kitchen as casually as blowflies. Tender and raw from the hostility, the stupid clumsy sympathy, of Europe, we bloomed in this new sun. "I could love this place," said Gisela to me suddenly as we stood on the stoep together a week after our first coming: and: "I could love this place," I echoed a little later, leaning over the old garden wall to watch sundown. Before me the mountains deepened to a cornflower-blue: the sky, one veil of colour shifting behind the other, grew rosy. The whole plain, stretched out so naked, glowed with the last warm light. Then quickly the shadow of the Bobbejaansberg ran down its slope over the pines, the orchards, the sandy bank of the dam, the farm-buildings, and raced beside the sluit to the road two miles away. Only high up, now, in the glistening tips of the gum-trees, on the grey blades of the windmill, was there still sun. Now in the garden beyond the wall on which I leaned Tante Saschia waddled brooding above her wilting lettuces. Between the flowers and the vegetables, like the angel with the flaming sword dividing innocence from sin, was a dark rich grove of naatjie trees: this evening, in the brilliant last light, the little mandarin oranges hung, small lanterns, from the branches. A few weeks later, with fruit still on the topmost boughs, those trees burst inconsequent into a starry tide of blossom, and the bees were busy among them from light till dark. Now there were just glowing fruit, deep orange: and in the deep shade beneath Tante Saschia moaning our lack of water. Here by the sluit the earth was moister, though there had been no rain for two and a half months and the stream itself had long since utterly dried up. You could grow nothing, now, in this garden, in this parched earth that fell apart, brittle as a kingfisher's nest, between the fingers. The lettuces lay limp and scorched, no heart to them: the cabbages that Jan had planted in thousands beneath the apricot trees in the big orchards were whiting, their small leaves spread miserably open, miserable with blueish-green rosettes panting for water.

"*Ach*, if we could but have rain!" cried Tante Saschia as I advanced down the neat path: and shading her eyes against the last of the sun she stared northward to see if there were by any chance a cloud on the Paardeberg. No cloud, no sign of rain: only the flaming glory of another sundown, the end to another burning, waterless day.

"When it does come it'll come from there," added Tante, pointing to the dark top of the Bobbejaansberg, so like a conglomeration of sitting apes. "Very often after the Bergwind from the Kalahari desert."

Now at last I was in Africa, hearing her, so matter-of-fact and commonplace, utter the exotic words. Kalahari desert—to her it was just a spot far north from which the hot winds came, as we in Berlin might say Lübeck or Rügen. But for me the words had wings, a fantastic shape, like some strange brilliant parrot. The Kalahari desert!—now at last I had left Berlin, Europe; was in new worlds. I gaped in the direction of her muddy hand.

"And when the rain does come," added she sepulchrally, "the old house leaks like a colander."

Yet she eyed it lovingly, the old house tender in the brief twilight, as if she revelled in its solidity. We both knew, as we looked, that inside those thick white walls the termite ant was devilishly at work boring endless holes, dropping from corners its dung, its refuse, its dead waxy yellow grubs, on to the aged floors beneath. But still the house *seemed* solid. In time the termites would have the whole of it: even now, every morning, the coloured girls as they ambled lackadaisically about their cleaning, found new heaps of termite muck everywhere, little triangular heaps, witness to the senseless industry of that model, the ant. And yet in spite of this, in spite of the roofs, which leaked, and the gauze on the stoep which was ridged and rotted so that the flies enjoyed themselves as much inside as out, the house was Tante Saschia's home, and a good one. She loved all of it, the mouldering passages, the crazy steps up, steps down; even the bathroom, a sordid spot added after the war and floored in concrete by Jan's prentice hand. While still wet, the concrete had been left unguarded: and the geese, ambling in inquisitively from their gobblings among the acorns by the stoep, had left a mosaic of webbed feet, permanent as the pyramids, behind them. Tante Saschia commented on this each time she went across the floor: but she would not have had unsullied concrete for all the rice in China. The goose-marks were dear to her, were as much a part of Kraanvlei as the mud walls, long ago thickly whitewashed, now patterned with the corpses of slain mosquitoes, flattened flies. Flies also rose in clouds from the pine-branches dangling in the dining-room: flies flew at you infuriated in the kitchen, and buzzed wildly in your hair, round your nostrils, about your eye-cavities. The small blue-black pestilential fly, so irritating, so filthy, had to be accepted at Kraanvlei. Occasionally Tante Saschia would bawl: "Letjie! Letjie!" as she beat them off with earth-stained hands: and Letjie, shambling in from the stoep, the bedrooms, would be commanded to bring the fly-spray, drive these brutes out of the kitchen. But after a few wheezy puffs the spray would give out: Letjie and Dora and Spaasie, the three kitchen girls, loved the stuff, blew it over one another's hair with joyous giggles whenever they found themselves away from missis' eye, and riotously exhausted each new can a day or two after its arrival. Flit or Flytox was lavishly wasted at Kraanvlei, as everything else was wasted, because the black slaves had not learnt to use it properly and the white masters, slaves to their slaves, had neither the time to show them or the wit to teach. Life at Kraanvlei was altogether lavish, hurried and wasteful. Perhaps in South Africa it is impossible to use time instead of frittering it: certainly the South African Blümchens were prime fritterers. The farm work was done (they said) by the ten coloured "boys," the three kitchen girls, the women who sporadically laundered, and the uncountable small fry who hopped up and down between house and Kaffir huts mishandling messages, fetching pennyworths of sugar, fat, curry powder from the farm store, or herding the goats on the pasture slopes of the Bobbejaansberg. But (in fact) that useful fool, the native, has long ceased to be useful. Labour is cheap, but the labour of seeing that it labours falls on the European, is expensive in time. The Blümchens spent their days from dawn, when old Solomon the cow-herd had to be watched separating the milk on the stoep, till dusk, when the boys went noisily beneath the pines to their huts, in seeing that work was done, in flogging on natural indolence to a most unnatural shiftless, reluctant industry. In the kitchen Tante Saschia gave her orders; did she then sit back in the calm certainty of results? Not she: she stood there, her little eyes darting like lizards, to see that the orders were obeyed. And while she did this in the kitchen, watching Letjie, who was to see that Dora and Spaasie were not making havoc along the stoep, in the bedrooms they were supposed to clean? So every now and again Tante Saschia darted out of the kitchen (having first locked all its eight cupboards) and descended in a wrathful bustle upon Dora (trying out Jan's hair-oil in Jan's bedroom), and on Spaasie (happily overwinding Mr. Grierson's alarm-clock). Jan's life, Dirk's life, Mr. Grierson's life, Tante Saschia's life, were thus one unending nag, one exasperating procession of scoldings, admonitions, threats, blows, abuse. Day after day the same thing: work shirked and badly done needing to be done again, sullen resentful dark faces looking up from a bungled job, dark hands swiftly furtive in rice-sacks, sugar-sacks, in pantry shelves, snatching all they could, insanely greedy. And dark suspicions everywhere—white suspecting black, black heavily, dumbly, hopelessly suspicious of white. Suspicion the keynote, the cornerstone, of that early morning scene: Mr. Grierson, the manager, standing over Solomon as he ground at the separator, dawn coming chill and lovely through the old gauze of the stoep, Solomon's eyes bent industrious to their task, Mr. Grierson's eyes bent industriously on Solomon: and under the table, hidden by an old dirty cloth, a cracked ewer pilfered by Letjie from the lumber-room in which Solomon, her grandfather, hoped to slip a quart or two of milk when Mr. Grierson's attention was for one second switched away. In the kitchen the same dirty drama: in spite of Tante Saschia's uncannily quick eyes sugar got stolen, bacon vanished, guavas mysteriously were not there when the pantry door was unlocked. Whole basins full of cream, at one stage, went down the road under Letjie's jacket, in the innocent billy-can Dora brought up with her for morning tea, wrapped in the old sugar-bag Spaasie bought with such self-conscious honesty at the store. And in the tea-cloths lying tumbled by the kitchen sink were other trophies: you picked up a tea-cloth to dry a cup, shook it out, and out flew a sticky handful of brown sugar, half a mutton chop, or a stinking relic of smoked snoek. Watch those dark faces bending over the steaming water in the sink as these things whistle past their ears: faces shining with bland, guileless innocence, the faces of three dark cherubs.

Here at Kraanvlei life flowed below life, things were anything but what they seemed. Everything in the landscape lying open, flat out, naked to the eye: everything in the life so underhand, furtive, creeping, mean. And with it all, sharp tang of contradiction, a curious child-like honesty, innocence. So that the young maiden Spaasie, eyed sharply by Tante Saschia for some weeks past, asked outright by Tante Saschia at last whether she were going to have a baby, could grin cheerfully, cheerfully answer: "Yes, missis," and with unconquerable cheerfulness remark that she didn't know whether Oum Solomon's Frikky or Oum Adam's Piet were the happy father. True, it was probably a waste of time to concern oneself with the future of the babe now so cheerfully burgeoning within Spaasie, since like most of them it would most likely be born dead: but this careless spawning, this easy waste of life, appalled me while it left Tante Saschia only annoyed.

"They *all* do it," she said crossly when Spaasie's state was made clear; "dirty little bitches, they all do it."

They all did it: they all lied, stole, fornicated: it was expected that they should. They always had, they always did, they always would. They were Cape coloureds, lower than the dogs who, laden with bloated ticks, mooched about the kitchen yard. Or were they not? Watching them, sickened by them, knowing that I ought to love and teach them (for is not this the white man's burden, his holy privilege?) I sometimes caught a gleam that was not pure animal. See little Dora, the most devilish of the kitchen trio, shyly bringing me a handful of Bobbejaantjies from the sluit; and the black hands of little Dora, seamed with unspeakable filthinesses, curling tenderly round the flower-stems, delicately parting the petals to show me the colour of the flower's heart. And this same Dora, twelve hours later, thrusting a handful of butter into the filthy bosom of her filthy jersey, protesting mildly, in spite of a warm spreading butter stain, against Tante Saschia's suspicions that butter has by her been filched from the dining-room table.

Strange, strange mixture, a Cape coloured: and yet more full of contradicting oddnesses than the superior white? No, only in all his little meannesses, little tendernesses, little dirtinesses, is he more shiftlessly child-like, more innocently deceitful, less sophisticated.

It was of no use to talk thus to Tante Saschia. She knew the coloured folk, had lived among them for fifty-five years. She knew them to be feckless, worthless, utterly undependable. One saw in Tante Saschia the fierce prejudice born of fear, the cruelty born of mistrust, which in her Boer forbears had made out of the coloured folk a wretched, downhill-slipping race. Ruthless and kind, she hummed with plans for Gisela's, Kurt's, my assured happiness: a brutal termagant, she treated her coloured girls as if they were outcast hounds. There was no liberalism in Tante Saschia: black and white were the colours she saw, they were inevitable, antagonistic, harsh.

And now, after only a few weeks at Kraanvlei, life began for us to be once more a matter of habit easily come by, the thing that was wild and strange now became utterly familiar. Our children played Kaiser, König, Edelmann, Dieb in the cool patch by the washing-troughs, under these alien willows, as they had played it on the Platz by the Märkisches Museum in Berlin. Watched by a dozen rolling alien eyes, they made for themselves a new nursery life which swiftly became as ordinary as the old. When they baked mud pies in the sun by the sluit it was with wild orange montbretias, wild waxy arum lilies, that they decorated the confections. Montbretia, arum—these were now no more strange than daisies. David began to chatter Afrikaans, to tag along behind Jan calling him Kleinbaas,[4] arrogantly scolding the small black boys for lacking in respect. Käthy organised the small girls into a miniature of Tante Saschia's kitchen hierarchy: herself the missis, the boss, doing all the interesting tasks such as cooking wild

---

4 Afrikaans: Little boss.

cucumbers in her new saucepans, and fiercely commanding little Tina, Guzzie, Betjie to wash those same pans when she had dirtied them. As in Tante Saschia's, so in Käthy's kitchen, there were two classes of napery: Käthy wiped her hands on her new tea-towels, the black minions humbly smeared another set of rags with their filthy paws. Race prejudice, colour prejudice: Käthy had suffered from the one, she now inflicted the other, as ruthless as only the unthinking young can be.

And we adults, supposedly reasonable? We fitted into Kraanvlei's scheme of things, echoed Kraanvlei's prejudices, as glibly as any. Gisela shrank from contact with black Dora, snatched her babies from the black hands of Letjie when that shiftless good-natured wench would have done some small service for them, fiercely scolded Hedwig for clinging round the black neck of Spaasie. Kurt meanwhile diligently learnt Afrikaans, and with it the Afrikander's brutal insolence towards the native. And I? Saddened, revolted by the unreason that I saw, I yet spoke to the girls in a voice raw with impatience (or fear, perhaps?): scolded Letjie fiercely for the small misdeeds with which the poor child's path by herself was littered: looked with loathing (or maybe envy) on the visible blossoming of pregnant Spaasie.

"Charlotte's becoming the best South African of the lot," said Tante Saschia approvingly, when I had just bowled over young Dora with a verbal broadside. "Wait till she's found a South African husband, then she'll settle down all right."

She smiled secretly at Gisela, who as secretly smiled back. It was the dream of these good women to marry me off, to find me some solid, earth-smelling, none-too-particular Boer with a prosperous farm who would take a Jewess and raise from her a brood of solid, earth-smelling children. Jan was too young: besides, fond though she was of me, Tante Saschia was yet shrewd enough to wish me anyone else's daughter-in-law. No, an unrelated Boer, living twenty miles or so away, near enough to be convenient, but not close, was the boon for which Gisela and Tante Saschia bombarded heaven in unison. It formed for them a fine hunt, a rousing tally-ho. One by one the eligible were routed out, produced, pressed upon me, told of my virtues, expectantly watched. But the eligible were as luke-warm about me as I about them: perhaps they saw in me the budding shrew. They ate the cakes I cooked, listened stolidly to Tante Saschia's lyrical accounts of how skilfully I cooked them, drank cup after cup of tea, and lumbered on their way unstirred. Gisela gave me gently reproachful looks, as if I were Hedwig in one of her tempers: Tante Saschia sighed, and advanced briskly upon some new sod, some as yet untried oaf. Now the victim was bidden to midday dinner, since tea was not (said Tante) a meal for a man. We cooked tomato bredee, meat-pie, a rich spread of vegetables swimming in grease, puddings of a large variety, all heavy. The victim arrived in a Cape cart, tongue-tied and hot: the men came down from the fields sullen with hunger. At the head of the long mahogany table (a Blümchen piece, made for the dining-room on the Schwalbenufer, not for a whitewashed room in South Africa, with termites dropping from corners their dung and discarded fruits) sat Tante Saschia expertly carving pie. Beside her, demurely domestic, I took each pie-laden plate, slapped on it pumpkin, rice, squash, potato, and handed it over my shoulder to Letjie who ambled sullenly down the table to slap it down in front of the victim. At the other end sat Jan and Dirk, those solid young Boers in whom not one of us could kindle a spark. "*Die Jungens,*" said Tante Saschia, with maternal pride, "*haben gar kein' manieren*":[5] unlike most maternal utterances this was true, manners had never come their way. They sat there almost dumb, disregarding the guest made so frantically welcome by Tante Saschia. Once Jan remarked to Dirk in Afrikaans that the Friesland cow might calve any day now: that the fence on the south side of Number 12

5   German: The young have no manners.

needed repairing. To both of which Dirk, through food, replied with the one word: "*Ja.*"

Near them another clam, our Scottish Mr. Grierson. In Mr. Grierson there rarely budded a social conscience: he felt he ought to say something, but the birth pangs of any remark were so painful that all united in wishing him forever silent. Flinging the last spoonful of squash on to my own plate I heard with distrust the strangled gurgling which meant that Mr. Grierson was about, in honour of our guest, to speak. Now, while we all uneasily waited, Mr. Grierson was seen to be in labour with a sentence. The travail was long and painful but the birth came at last: the newly-born shot out raw and hot from Mr. Grierson's intellectual womb.

"That's a verra sma' cat we've noo got in the grrrain-shed," said Mr. Grierson.

Then the placenta, or afterbirth.

"It'll doubtless be grrowing shorrrtly."

With this achieved, Mr. Grierson gave one blue, comprehensive glance round the table, then fell violently to work on his meat.

We talked for a while, frenziedly, of cats.

Life in Kraanvlei, in South Africa, I suddenly thought, glancing at the ring of chewing faces, was hardly likely to impose much strain upon the intellect. And once more I was wild with misgiving, studying the guest and the purpose for which he had come. Was I, too, to rot here, under this hot dry sun, in this parched, fiercely predatory land? Was I to rot, wedded to some oaf who married only because he owned Modderkloof and wanted a housekeeper, or had a good vineyard at Riebeeksfontein and wanted to leave it to sons, or had just planted a promising stretch of acres called Karnmelksvlei and desired a female in the new dining-room of the new house? I who had set out from Europe with the determination to be pure bodily, an animal seeking no more than a mate, was now suddenly and violently revolted by the sight, the thought, of the thing I had been pursuing.

With this sudden nausea, there at the greasily overladen dinner-table, began a blight which settled upon me, settled to some measure on all three of us, in this hospitable Kraanvlei. In a month, two months, the blight had become a pestilence. At first sight this had been God's own country, and ours: we were lucky to be here. What more could we ask? An air that was free, people who were not yet openly hostile, a chance to work. Kurt, from being a successful dentist among the upper middle class in Berlin, was now learning to be a store-keeper among poor whites, itinerant Kaffirs, Cape coloureds, in the dusty wilderness of Minnaarskopjie with its one gasoline pump. You could not say he had gone up in the world, but he was at least safe. They would not now knock at his door at midnight and beat him to a pulp because his nose-shape did not please them. Since he had work he had also the seeds of a new self-respect, had won once again the right to live as a human. Gisela, taking more kindly to an alien soil, saw her children blooming in the sunlight, bare-foot (this had a delicious novelty) in the dust, and was, for the time being, happy. Now after two months the family left Kraanvlei. After two months struggling with Afrikaans, itself a bastard speech, and with the wilder bastardisation of Afrikaans which was the local dialect—after two months giving out pennyworths of custard-powder, tickeyworths of sugar in the little farm store, Kurt moved himself and his new vocation to Minnaarskopjie, settled in under the corrugated iron roof of the store. Outside he had dust hotly swirling by, and the stupendous view across the plain to the Drakenstein. He had also the petrol-pump, unique in a radius of twenty miles. Inside, the store, a long low shed bounded by a counter, behind which, neatly stacked, lay overalls, cotton trousers, cheap boots, cheaper scents, soaps, groceries, hair-pins, castor oil which the Kaffir women were bidden buy for their babies and which they smeared instead on their blue-black hair, badly cured hams, slabs of salt fish, tins of canned food—all the mumble-jumble of every country store. Here came the Kaffirs from the camp of pointed tents by the railway: the men were quarrying stone for Capetown's new harbour, the women walked in balancing empty kerosene tins beautifully on their heads and, with the tins full, walked once more beautifully back again. Here came the poor-whites from the almost ruined grape-farms (ruined not because grapes were too few but because they were too many). Here came the farmer's wives, lean from eating dried salt fish, old chip-straw hats on their sun-scorched heads, to buy the week's groceries and then to jog back again, clasping an infant or two, on the hard front seat of the buggy. Here came passing motorists thirsty for a fill up of Pegasus: here came the real citizens of Minnaarskopjie, the pink Dutch station-master with his pink Dutch wife, the overseer at the Kaffir camp, the postmaster with his drooping dyspeptic stomach and a curiosity-mania fed by the sight of so many envelopes that even he had not the nerve to open. It was not a Hertie, a Kaufhaus des Westen,[6] that store; but the little bustle of Minnaarskopjie was minutely reflected in it, like life seen in a water-drop. Kurt would see more new things there than by gazing into the familiar mouths of Frau Glaspe from the Breitestrasse and Herr Apotheke Wernicke from Wallstr. 24a.

Behind the long fly-noisy shop were three bedrooms, a big kitchen, a stoep shaded by dusty gum-trees, and a water-trough in which the water ceaselessly dribbled. Mr. Abraham, who had parted with the shop to Kurt (and the last of Onkel Plans's money went with him, the Hebrew scallywag, as he drove off to retirement in Paarl in his disreputable buggy) was a bachelor: and had left the place filthy. Local gossip said that Mr. Abraham was a bachelor with a matured taste in Kaffir women; certainly Gisela dug out some loathsome feminine oddments from dark corners, abandoned boxes, and threw them furiously into the kitchen stove.

---

6 Kaufhaus is a famous Berlin department store, similar to Selfridge's in London.

This Abraham was the worst kind of Jew, the type we Jews would gladly disown. He had all our racial faults, was grasping, hard, aggressive and mean; Kurt would have a hard time shedding the bequeathed reputation, curing the local faith that all shopkeepers are Jews, all Jews out for the last drop of Gentile blood. However, just as Gisela, her face wrinkled in disgust, had cleared up the last traces of Mr. Abraham's filthy living, so Kurt, the cultured ex-dentist, would clear up the last anti-Jewish prejudice. Or so he hoped: and we could none of us be cruel enough to point out that anti-Semitism endures so long as the Jews endure, and will die only with them.

When the Seligmanns had gone, and were for a time happy under their hot corrugated-iron, the blight lay thick upon me at Kraanvlei. It had seemed such a heaven, such a sun-flooded Eden when I first came: there was nothing I could not do, nothing I could not enjoy, in those first delicious weeks. What a full, busy, purposeful life, thought I, rising at five to help Tante Saschia in the kitchen, to brew coffee for Jan and Dirk and Mr. Grierson who shambled through sleepy-eyed, dragging their big boots, on their way to the poultry runs, the cow byre, the orchard. One had a sense of something done worth doing as one filled those healthy hard-working stomachs. In the kitchen the coffee-pot, the enormous pan of mealies for the chickens, the stock-pot, all simmered noisily on the great stove that Letjie had raked and refuelled under Tante's fierce eye: outside, when I pushed aside the gauze door and went to fetch something from the store, it was dark as midnight, bitingly cold. Only in the east, behind the sleepy hump of the house, the sky was warming to dawn. The roosters by the grain-shed furiously crowed, cats rushed from dark comers of the store, from flour-sacks and mealie-sacks and sugar-sacks, to stream through the door yelling for food; on the sacks, by the light of my hurricane lantern, I saw the tender warm hollows the sensuous creatures had made for themselves in sleep. Later on, at half-past six when I went out once again to fetch the day's meat from the safe by the incubator, the sky was brilliant blood-red, fully dawning: the sun already dappled the upper leaves of the gum-trees as if they had been dipped in water. Everything was rosy and fresh: my hands pegging up tea-towels in a wire that ran blood-red across the dusk, my face in the glass of Tante Saschia's window, the walls of the old house, losing the night's bitter chill, warming to new life. Everything was starting afresh, hopeful. The blight had not yet set in: wait till later, till the hot mid-morning when the flies droned about us, settling on our hands, our faces, as we chopped the bleeding meat or sawed a forequarter from the new-killed sheep on an old scarred wooden block that reeked of blood and onions. Then was the time for the blight to begin, in the sudden thought: "Am I to be forever butcher, cleaving flesh to put into greedy stomachs, for the rest of my life? What am I doing, here in the great hot smelly kitchen, hacking meat for farmers?" And I looked slantwise at Tante Saschia digging rich sheep-tail fat from an old kerosene-tin to thicken the gravy in the stew: she put about half a pound in the pan, and at once the room was filled with the sickeningly intimate smell of fat mutton. Tante Saschia's face glowed with sweat as she bent over the stove, stirred in the flour, muttered: "*Allemaagte!*[7] that smells good!" Letjie, shredding onions, only too willingly stopped work to sniff the mutton-laden air, to mutter pleasedly to herself in Afrikaans. On the pink sweaty face of Tante Saschia and the black oily face of Letjie pure greed rested for a moment like a thicker oil: you could see them tasting already on their tongues the stew, swimming in sheep-fat, which would be ladled out at dinner. Then Tante Saschia shouted: "Get on with those onions, Letjie, d'you think I'm going to wait all day for them?" and the girl, shrugging her shoulders, hacked once more at the pale shining globes in her hand.

---

7   Afrikaans: Almighty!

Now it was time for morning tea, for blight to become more manifest. Letjie staggered under the great tray to the stoep, bellowing: "Du, Adam, glockerle!"[8] and an infinitesimal black shrimp in dusty trousers too large, its black face gleaming under one of Letjie's discarded Sunday hats (scarlet straw, much faded) streamed out across the yard to the old gum-tree, furiously hung on the string that pulled the bell. Up in the fields, the orchards, the men heard the clang and came ambling down the dusty roads, along the dusty paths, for their cups of weak sweet tea. For the South African does not want more than the name of tea. What he drinks is milk and sugar. I watched Jan at it, as he leaned against the gauze through which the flies buzzed and talked cabbages to Grierson. In went the hot milk, then a drop of tea: now the sugar. Spoonful after spoonful, absent-mindedly dug from the bowl, absent-mindedly stirred into the liquid, the same spoon doing both for digging and stirring, till the pale greyish tide slipped and frothed into the saucer. What a drink! What men! Healthy, all of them, and reasonably clean: but men so bound by and to the soil that any thought beyond cabbages was more than they could reach, abstract thought was anathema. The blight now settled dustily upon me as I considered these oafs. For this tea-mixing habit of theirs was but a symptom of disease: to take a delicate flavour, swamp it in the crass sweetness of cane sugar, and then drink it noisily, with enjoyment, was but the symbol of their daily, monthly, yearly life. Naturally only a fool would expect them, pruning the apricot orchard on the slope of the Bobbejaansberg or ploughing the western kopjie before putting in pea-seed, to pause and lean on the secator, the plough; to stay breathless, agape, admiring the last sun on the Drakenstein or the pearly blue edge of Table Mountain forty miles away. But to live, as they did, with no consciousness of Table Mountain or the Drakenstein, to see the wonderful tawny plain between as just

---

8   German: You, Adam, ring the bell.

so much wheat, so much lupin, so many acres of vine, seemed to me pure swinishness. The men were swine: they thought only, ultimately, of what would fill their bellies. When they thought of the coloured folk starving of malnutrition all over the countryside it was to call them niggers, to dismiss them as ingrate incompetents who would bite the hand that fed them. (Only there was no hand, they simply were not fed.) While on me, as I thought of the coloured folk, the blight settled heavy indeed. You can, of course, take them as one grand joke: how funny, how richly comic, to have a black skin! How droll to have frizzy hair sticking out like a bush! What can you do but laugh helplessly, confronted with such oddities? So the natural reaction of the European is to laugh, at any rate to smile. The coloured folk seem to him funny as a piebald horse, a white crow is funny—such a turning upside-down of nature. But to the thoughtful European, following the laugh, comes a worse topsy-turvydom: what if it is *we* who are funny, all pink and tender-looking like skinned rabbits hanging defenceless at the poulterer's? What if it is in us that Nature is turned upside-down? And for one hysterical moment thought makes havoc: in his own mind doubt is born. He eyes the natives in distrust: which, black or light-skinned, is nature's sport? He can no longer look at the native objectively as another man, another soul in whom skin-colour matters not. To God all races are the same, but he has not yet reached this stage of vague rather useless benevolence: he knows all men are not equal.

So went my mind, worrying terrier-like at this colour problem, tearing at it as a terrier pup rends a bedroom slipper. At the end, like the pup, I had nothing but a guilty look, shreds of slipper hanging from my mouth-corners. Shreds of a problem, and the idea, hardened at last to a certainty, that my blight came purely from this, this nagging unsolved question of the black and the white, the oppressed and the oppressor. There was no comfort for me in a land thus harried by hatred. Something un-Jewish in me, some startling small throw-back to the great-grandmother who had been an Englishwoman, forbade me to take the easy Jewish way out, to shut my eyes to the pathetic coloured face, my ears to the plaintive coloured voice, and settle down cow-like, pleasingly female, beside some comfortable South African bull. No, I would not do it. The nag of black against white, white against black was something bred in this land, something which I, living in the land, could neither dodge nor endure. The same cruel hostility that had sent me flying from Berlin would send me now flying, flying on, anywhere away from coloured faces and white arrogance.

*****

Still Africa had not seen the last of restless Charlotte. She hung about and could not go. Tante Saschia's stream of eligibles dried up: in a huff she washed her hands of me, fearing I would not mate and settle. Thus Kraanvlei lost an ingrate niece, the hotel Bona Vista, in a salubrious suburb of Capetown, gained a cook. It was a wild venture, a leap into blue uncertainty; but better, at any rate, than sitting out there in the shade of the Bobbejaansberg, with folded hands enduring Tante Saschia's reproaches, the injured eyes of Gisela who had seen me already the Boer Hausfrau tied to the South African earth by a horde of babies. The Bona Vista's advertisement for a European cook caught me thus on the rebound: I was European, I could cook, forthwith I took train to Capetown, and found myself, after brisk bargainings with the manager, a fellow Jew, engaged. Now for three pounds a week Charlotte the fastidious, the critical, Charlotte already conscious that she was also a failure, went from filling the stomachs of Kraanvlei to fill, just as wearily, the lower stomachs of holidaying bank clerks and their families, saucy lipsticked typists, withered old women, paunchy young men, at the Bona Vista Hotel. Now, hearing my tale of the interview, seeing that I was all set to go, Tante Saschia brightened considerably. "Perhaps," she cried with the old eagerness, "this Ludwigstein fellow'll take a fancy to you. That would be a match, eh, Charlotte?" To which Charlotte, agreeing for the sake of peace, smiled indulgently, kissed her kind auntie, and went off to her next matrimonial chance.

The kitchen of the Hotel Bona Vista was an enormous room among whose dim hot rafters the flies buzzed, swarmed, in midair went through the convulsions of mating, and left their spotty excrement. There were flies everywhere. "You can't," said Mr. Ludwigstein, "get them away." He flicked his fat yellow paws above a dish on the table, and the flies rose from it lazily, buzzed, and settled again. "Vunny things, vlies," he added, "they don't sit still—no, neffer, not even when they make luff." And Mr. Ludwigstein's laugh, a wet explosive sound like a smashed pumpkin, burst through the kitchen.

The kitchen staff, seeing that Master had joked, smiled eagerly. There was Charlie the cook-boy, lithe blue-black negro with hair shaved so close that you could see the skin rippling beneath the wool; Edie the dish-washer, who lounged in a sulky attitude against the sink in which a scummy tide lapped languidly over half-submerged crockery : and Adolph the house-boy, very stout, in a dirty blue-and-white striped apron. They stood there giggling at Master with their mouths, while their unlaughing eyes raked me from crown to toe. They patently did not like my looks: hostility and the flies seemed to buzz together.

"This is your little crew!" cried Mr. Ludwigstein, embracing them in one gesture, "this is your little gang! Treat them rough, Miss Herz, and they'll tchew your boots: be veak with them, Miss Herz, and they stap you in the back." Mr. Ludwigstein's metaphor was apt to stray, darting down surprising by-paths of misuse: his English, peppered with the explosive consonants of the German Jew who has learnt it late in life, abounded in the richly inappropriate, the slangy term just not right, the bruised cliché.

He showed me the pantry, the dining-room, from which at our approach the flies lazily swarmed upward: jingling keys importantly, he unlocked the dirty store-cupboard: and led me finally into a small court-yard where one squat and stunted palm, littered with Edie's drying teacloths, waved its battered leaves very faintly in the hot air. Here were two safes with great gauze doors behind which food left-overs, vegetables, eggs, and ants were piled in a grand confusion. There was a trail of ants processing stoutly from the safe to the kitchen door, a double line passing and ceaselessly repassing.

"Tsch!" cried Mr. Ludwigstein, spurning them with his foot. "Tsch! the prute-peasts!" And he led me hastily to inspect my bed-room in which, he vowed, there were no ants at all. I could well imagine it: there was hardly space. It was a small square hat-box of a room, thick-walled, spasmodically whitewashed, with one tiny window giving on to the compound which housed the coloured staff. A clothes-line, on which men's garments bellied, a hen-run full of nothing but waste-paper blown from the incinerator, two little pink houses, three stunted trees: beyond, the back of a large block of flats, and behind, brilliant rock under a dark hot sky, the bronze-green slopes, the final stony heave, of the Lion's Head. This was the view from my bedroom window. The room itself was still littered with the gear of the departing cook. A suitcase gaped on the bed, clothes drooped limply over the one chair. A cotton nightgown with a torn frill at the neck was looped half-way across the window as a curtain: behind another curtain hung still more clothes reeking of under-arm sweat. A chamber-pot with an old hair-brush, some slivers of soap, a packet of hair-pins and a coloured post-card of Groot Constantia in it sat smugly midway between door and bed. On the wall was a large photograph of George Raft hung by only three drawing-pins, so that one corner drooped loose, obscuring one eye, giving the actor the look of a waggish fox-terrier.

"Tsch!" muttered Mr. Ludwigstein again, spurning the chamber-pot as he had spurned the ants. The pot gave out a hollow groan, and Mr. Ludwigstein remarked that my "forerunner had not been a fery tidy woman, no!"

Thus I settled in at the Bona Vista. The hotel squatted, two low storeys, with a wide stoep, on an edge of rock rounding into the little bay. It was painted an enticing sugar-plum pink, and had a plot of coarse grass, four shining palm-trees, and a round bed full of the inevitable scarlet cannas between it and the beach road. Sitting on the stoep, one could watch the hot bright holiday life of Du Toit's Bay: watch the brilliant sea, the small green pool plastered with notices denying negroes approach, the flat rocks on which the bodies of the sunbathers lay all afternoon, motionless as seals. However, I never sat out on the stoep: my purlieus were the fly-black kitchen, the hot little pantry, the courtyard with its dish-cloths, the path to the safes along which the ants forever marched. The pink beauty of the Bona Vista ended at the diningroom: beyond, in what Mr. Ludwigstein called "the service quarters," all was desolation, crazily makeshift. The waitress-chambermaids, black as soot, did their washing, their ironing, their quarrelling and their crying in the square of roofed concrete just outside my room. Here Adolph, squatted on an upturned egg-box, smoked his pipe when Mr. Ludwigstein's eye was on someone else. Here Charlie conducted mysterious experiments in graft with the butcher, the greengrocer, the milkman and the baker. Here Edie had her famous hiccuping fits during which, affronted by man or circumstance, she whooped convulsively, bent double and dribbling over the concrete. The whole life of the hotel, far from being boxed in the select shade of the stoep looking out to sea, was concentrated here in hates and passions, loud yelps of laughter, a snatched kiss or two, a ringing smack. And through it all, past it all, day and night, the tiny moving ants went up and down. You brushed at them, trod on them, flicked them away:

Edie drowned whole battalions every Thursday when she cast a bucketful of water into the court-yard and listlessly pursued it with a besom: nothing made any difference to those creatures. They swarmed from every crack, dropped from every palm-leaf, seeped under the doors, forming yet another marching column in the direction of food: they were everywhere, and always. Adolph had orders from Mr. Ludwigstein to set little saucers of brown sugar and water in their way: the little saucers became black with ants in no time, ants thoroughly enjoying themselves: we kicked the little saucers as we rushed from kitchen door to store-cupboard, they went spinning merrily away across the concrete, to rock sharply up against a wall and there remain, still with their happy cargo of ants and sugar.

However, kicking saucersful of ants was not what we were paid for: our job was to nourish those vague, cantankerous, fickle creatures the guests. Do you know the story of the German sausage-maker who, rescued from drowning in the Spree by an unknown, said: "My friend, I cannot reward you with money but I will give you a piece of valuable advice: Never eat sausage"? After a month at the Bona Vista I was like that man. I wanted to button-hole every guest I met and cry in its ear: "Never eat in an hotel. Above all, never eat curry, stew or soup in an hotel." For those tasty-looking chunks of meat, rich in their rich spiced gravies—that aromatic Potage Julienne, chicken broth or cream of celery—what are these but the essence of the garbage can? A fussy elderly woman sends back her fruit salad from the dining-room: Milly, the head waitress, brings it to me, shocked. There is an ant in it. This is awful. I give another dishful, guaranteed ant-free. I think, My dear foolish woman, if you but knew the camels you had swallowed while straining at this gnat! You had for your first course soup, brewed from the bones of last week's roasts which had been fingered by the butcher, by the butcher's boy, by Charlie, by myself while carving. You then had a virginal chunk of Kingklip, smothered in parsley, from which the black hands of Charlie had torn the skin, impatiently fending off flies, but an hour before. Charlie's hands, my dear white madam, were in your fish. And after that? After that a tasty goulash, the meat chunks cut up by black Charlie on a board he had just knocked smartly against the kitchen floor, without, however, dislodging *all* the ants. It swam in a rich dark gravy, that goulash: if you did not take an ant or two in with it, I will eat my hat. And now, my purblind female, you complain of an ant, one single innocent ant, in your fruit-salad. If ants were yellow instead of brown you would have swallowed it without knowing and voted your fruit-salad delicious. What the eye don't see, etc., etc. Come into our kitchen one morning between ten and one, when we are getting your lunch ready, and I'll wager you'll eat out of tins in future. Though I doubt if even in tins lurks hygiene: it would surprise me very much if it did.

"Put a good portion of whipped cream on that and see if she'll eat it," I say aloud to Milly, giving her the new fruit-salad. And the merry game goes on.

Now lunch is finished, dinner looms. Since four o'clock when the kitchen simmers in afternoon heat, the hot smelly air presses like a blanket, the flies and the ants crawl languidly—since four o'clock Charlie and Edie and I have been toiling, with sweat pouring from head to heel, to fill the stomachs of the Bona Vista. Roast lamb and mint sauce: *Poulet à l'Anglaise* says every menu, typed by Mr. Ludwigstein, sweat-soaked in his shirt-sleeves, which stands demurely on the dining-room tables. The legs of mutton sizzle in the ovens, ten chickens are even now being gutted by Charlie. Charlie stands over the sink, his elbows red with blood, tugging from the pallid dome of each fowl's body a medley of pipes, kidneys, hearts, crops; a colourful mass of guts lie on the draining-board oozing dark blood, surrounded by glistening sponges of yellow fat which have also come reluctantly squelching from the bowels. That is to-morrow's giblet soup. "Only ve von't call it 'giblet,'" says Mr. Ludwigstein, "that makes them to think: ve call it Potage Ongarienne, heh?" The main body of the Potage Ongarienne, then, lies bleeding, like love, on the draining-board from which Edie has just snatched a cake of monkey soap, a sour-smelling dishcloth and two greasy soot-bottomed saucepans. Edie herself, after wringing out the dish-cloth and wiping her hands on her black apron, stands picking her nose at the kitchen door before getting down to the more serious job of peeling the vegetables. Soon, in an enormous washing-up basin, she has sweet potatoes, string beans, carrots and onions swimming naked.

Milly comes in languid in felt slippers, and washes up some tea crockery in the sink beside Charlie and the entrails. It is now so hot that every word falls muffled, foggy to the ear. Charlie and Milly chatter in Afrikaans, burst into song, their bottoms waggling in unison. "The greatest mistake of my life" is the kitchen favourite: they burst into it again and again, scuffling together at the sink. A giblet flies from Charlie's hand to skedaddle across the floor over which Edie has already cast potato-peel and carrot-scrapings, as is her habit. With one swoop, still singing, Charlie dives to pick it up, throws it on to the mound of Potage Ongarienne.

There are shrieks without: the kitchen door bursts open to admit Dora and Adolph in roaring pursuit. Sickeningly hot sunlight lies for a moment across the floor: shows the kitchen air blue with burning fat: for a moment the courtyard beyond is seen as a ghastly blaze of light, the palm-tree swooning beneath its harvest of grey tea-cloths. Then the door is slammed to. Dora, wriggling her hips, swanks through into the pantry to make a salad. Her black hands with their dirt-seamed rose-pink palms ply languidly between the leaves of the lettuces, picking off the corpses of slugs that have died in the heat.

I go to the pantry with an old tin plate to scoop up some flour. The flour is kept at the bottom of the big cupboard in its original sack: now as I open it the faint musty smell of mouse floats up.

There are little black droppings everywhere, in the corner crouches a small silky creature with shuddering ears.

"Aii!" screeches Dora, over my shoulder. "Charlie, Charlie, 'ne Mause!"

Charlie streaks through the kitchen, snatching up the pastry roller: before I can gather my wits the mouse is mashed with one cunning blow against the side of the cupboard. The pastry roller drips crimson. Charlie retires, wiping it on his apron; Dora gets on with her salad. This is so much a part of kitchen routine, all in the day's work, that I have no right to feel shattered. But I do, as I order Edie to come with a wet cloth and wipe away the corpse. The little droppings which I sift pensively from the flour have now a retrospective pathos. Out of my eye's corner I watch Edie slouching out with the body: who would have thought the little man had so much blood in him? But there is too much to be done: I cannot stop to mourn over what Mr. Ludwigstein calls "these plagueful mouses!"

At half-past six, when the heat in the kitchen is steamy, we gird up our loins for the real battle of the day. Mr. Ludwigstein can advertise the Bona Vista as having a "cuisine under the personal supervision of a trained European chef": if I do the carving the guests can eat at ease, seeing only white hands delicately separating their meat. What an odd fetish of South Africa, this belief in the inherent cleanliness of the European hand! "Of course," cried Tante Saschia, describing a friend's establishment in Johannesburg, "the Kaffir boys do all the other house-work, but they never touch the beds!" At what point does this become absurd? If the Kaffir boys may not make the beds lest they get Ideas, begin to rape the sheets, we can yet cheerfully hand over our girl-children to the care of Kaffir nursemaids. The dish we eat from has been washed and wiped by Kaffir hands, the silver we put into our mouths polished by Kaffir hands; the vegetables peeled by them: but tell a European that his meat has been carved by a Kaffir and he chokes on it forthwith.

Odd, very odd, think I, proceeding to carve the meat. The legs of mutton, the ten chickens, have been lifted from the oven by the bare greasy hands of Charlie, and lie cooling on the draining-board. The grease pales and hardens: they are cool enough. Tapping the ants impatiently from the meat-board, I take the carving-knife and slice up the meat. With the fowls no refinement: I merely tear them limb from limb. The hot juice, fat-speckled, pours from the outraged sockets: I wipe my hands on one of Edie's grey cloths and go on tearing. The livid drum-sticks squelch as I wring them away from the parent body. My fingers run under the rubbery skin and loop it off: more juice spurts, the flies descend in handfuls from their hot eyries near the ceiling and crawl everywhere. Now the mutton slices, the *Poulets à l'Anglaise*, lie in the oven ready to ravish the palates of our guests.

Quietly, behind my back, Charlie spits into the saucepan to make the beans boil faster. It is an old Kaffir custom. Perhaps if I bent my energies to it for a week I might cure him of the habit, but my energies are needed elsewhere.

Milly rings the gong, holding the brass dish proudly before her, sticking out her stomach, and waltzes through the building making the usual hellish din. Dinner is "on."

I hope the guests are hungry.

On the great centre table, spread with moderately clean newspaper by Edie, who is always going off into a trance over some picture in the *Cape Times* or the *Argus* as she smooths it down, and bending rigid over it till Charlie whacks her behind and commands her to get on, are piles of hot plates. They have been wiped over at the last moment with a greyish rag. When I bend over them I smell the warm greasy dish-water, the intimacy of Edie's sweating palms, the sickly dish-wash smell of the rags in which they have been dried. I hope no guest ever puts his nose near enough to get this too: evidently not, for about our plates we have had no complaints.

"Fish one macaroni cheese two piece mutton very well done no mint sauce!" screams Milly, shooting from the dining-room. It is all there. Charlie's swift fingers pick out a cube of fish, two slices of mutton, and a roast potato: they are slapped down on suitable plates, clothed in gravy, or egg sauce, whisked off by Milly. In the pantry she crashes into Dora and spurts gravy from her mutton plate all over the door-jamb. This means a mad rush back into the kitchen and a clean plate: the door-jamb can wait till later.

If I were in the oven with the chicken and the meat I could not be any hotter. A great drop of sweat splashes from Charlie's forehead as he stoops to hook out fish, potatoes, slices of mutton. The dirty dishes begin coming home to roost, and are piled one above the other on the far side of the table with knives, forks, potato remnants, grizzly meat scraps and other left-overs between each greasy dish. Edie at the sink swishes away like a maniac. Adolph whisks the food scraps into a pig-bucket with a finger which he licks between each manoeuvre. Some, in his abandoned haste, escape the bucket: by the end of the meal Edie will be standing in a Saragossa Sea of grease and garbage, slithering from time to time and cursing foully.

Now is the time of sweets, of coffee. "One sweet no cream two sweets plenty cream one cream no sweet!" yells Dora over her shoulder as she rushes past with four slopping plates full of rst. mutt., sce. and veg., as the dishes are now concertinaed in my distracted mind.

"No, me, cooky!" cries Milly, "me first. Two mutton no gravy one mutton plenty mint sauce one baked potato straight, dish of veg."

Charlie's hands are busy among the mutton slices twitching aside choice bits for Master, who always comes in late and likes "plenty plenty fat." Charlie's "plenty, plenty" is a cornucopia, a fatted calf, a complete harvest festival as he says it: his voice drops lusciously over the words.

Milly gets her orders filled, flies forth with plates balanced one above the other, gravy dripping richly. At the door between pantry and dining-room, where a screen mercifully hides the food-fount from the guests, she stops, cleans up the edges of the plates with a finger which she licks and wipes under her armpit, then issues demurely forth—"the best waitress, I swear you, in Du Toits Bay," as Mr. Ludwigstein often tells me. He has forgotten Berlin, Wien, Europe: his patriotism is now purely local, it embraces no more than Du Toits Bay and, at a stretch, Capetown.

"My sweets!" cries Dora, bouncing back. "Cooky, cooky, my *sweets*! One no cream two plenty cream one cream no sweet."

"One cream no sweet—rubbish!"

"Yes, she says so—Miss Gaskell with the little dog. She don't like trifle."

"Then she can have raw fruit. I'm not going to start serving whipped cream straight."

Dora retires sulkily: there is nothing a waitress more dislikes than refusing a guest: goddesses of plenty for a brief space, they enjoy bestowing.

Now the meal is nearly finished. Master has come in and chewed his well-fingered mutton, eaten his trifle. "Only two more," whispers Milly, making a drama of it, making me see two tiny shipwrecked figures in a waste of deserted tables laden with the crumbs of funeral baked meats. "Only two more, that Miss Gaskell and the gent with the wooden leg."

I do not see these creatures whose stomachs I feed four times a day: the wooden leg is a mystery to me, faceless, featureless, nought but a wooden leg stolidly eating trifle and the time now eight-thirty.

We begin to clear up. The eyes of Charlie, Edie, Adolph, Milly, Dora, glisten towards the pots still sizzling on the stove. Five plates are put on the table and under a fusillade of eyes I fill them up. "Gif them r-rice," Mr. Ludwigstein has advised me hoarsely, "not too many meat. Them niggers don't do no good on meat: it makes them vight." So I pile each plate with rice, with exhausted limp potatoes, cold carrots, and strew over each mound a liberal cupful of gravy. Charlie cleans the stove with an evil sack: the stench of burning hessian, charred fat, and scorched sugar rises in a blue vapour, wafts out of the open door to the yard now black with night but still hot. Still, like a rag-bag ghost, the palm-tree bears up its pale tea-cloths, rasps its stiff leaves in the waving breeze.

Release, thank God, release! sings my heart as I pour myself some coffee and take a plateful of fruit through to the dining-room. The coffee I made myself, the apple can be peeled: it is a safe meal. But the wooden leg is still there toying with trifle: I hop hastily back. In the kitchen the staff with its elbows well out is walking into the supper: neither fish nor fowl nor good red herring, *de trop* in kitchen, and dining-room alike, I stand waiting in the pantry and absent-mindedly roll my apple to and fro on its plate.

A stunning blonde with a blatant bosom sweeps from behind the screen. She wears a garment so perfectly vulgar that the eye cringes from it: a skin-tight cyclamen satin with black worms of embroidery on outlying parts. This is Miss Gaskell, who owns a little dog called Mac and (rumour has it) aims to be Mrs. Ludwigstein.

She makes eyes at me: like most blondes, she behaves as if she were a permanent fifteen.

"Can I have a wee bittie for my little doggie? He's *so* hungwy!"

"Charlie has some scraps, I think."

Miss Gaskell sallies into the kitchen, causing no end of a sensation: this is a drama that plays to a full house every night. At sight of so much blondeness and pink flesh demanding from him dog-meat, Charlie every night wilts and stammers, rushes to obey, can find (in his mad embarrassment) neither meat, plate or knife: under the sardonic eye of his fellows finds at last all three, manages at last to chop up some raw meat for Miss Gaskell's Mac.

"Thanks *ever* so much, Charlie!" cries Miss Gaskell, titillated by the twin dynamo of sex and race-prejudice. And she sweeps out again leaving Charlie enraptured, mazed, utterly discomfited.

At last it is all finished. The remnants of food are laid ready for the ants in the safes. Edie has drawn her wringing wet dishcloth over the last of the plates, the grey greasy water gurgles away, she does some desultory floor-sweeping. In the dining-room the tables are laid for breakfast by Milly and Dora, who yawn and stretch as they languidly cast down forks.

The lights are out in dining-room, pantry, kitchen. In the courtyard where mosquitoes ping and ants (doubtless) scurry underfoot, I stop a moment to look at the stars. In the front of the hotel a wireless burbles: upstairs a half-naked bosom swims to a window, cut waist high by the sill, and rather belatedly pulls down the blind. Behind in the compound there are amorous scuffles: Adolph is pinching Dora again, nipping her breasts in his large black hands. She escapes and goes winging off to the little hut she shares with Edie and Milly: back on the hot wind comes the noise of that infernal song that she loves: "The greatest mistake of my life."

Adolph noisily makes water against the wall, spits with enjoyment, and shambles off to his shack.

I lie exhausted on my bed stripped of all my clothes. The sour smell of the day's sweat rises in clouds. Full length on the dubious counterpane, watching two large overfed flies as they zoom against the ceiling, I see my days, fly-spotted and hot, yawning out in front of me. South Africa, this is South Africa.

Yes, it is South Africa. I have exhausted South Africa: there is a boat sailing for Australia on August 4th. Tomorrow, my half-day, I shall go to George Street and book my passage. That means (my fingers drum out the count on my hot tired stomach) only five weeks more. Thank God, thank God.

A knock at the door. Shuffling into a dressing-gown, I open. Mr. Ludwigstein is full of apologies: didn't know I was getting to bed, just vanted to ask if I had ordered the eggs from Lewis Sim.

This has happened before. Mr. Ludwigstein's mind never develops an egg complex till I am *déshabillé*. I reply coldly that the order was given, and bid him good night.

Mr. Ludwigstein's foot, by an odd chance, is in the door.

"Oh, Miss Herz, I haf meant to ask, haf you everything you wish?"

"Everything, thank you."

The door is brutally shut, Mr. Ludwigstein having to nip his poor foot away to escape hurt.

Mr. Ludwigstein lacks, I consider, originality. He is too obvious. I do not like stupid men: this has finished me with the Bona Vista. The thought that this man, my racial brother, is the complete twin of those revolting creatures on the cover of *Die Stürmer* does not make me love him or his establishment more. When I have bolted him out I open my drawer, look wistfully at a travel brochure from Cook's, a koala funnily clinging to a tree on its gay cover. Australia, that is the land for me. Not in Germany, not in England, not in South Africa, but in Australia, surely, shall I find what I desire. I do not know what it is, the form is still cloudy, but I know that I want it, that I shall not find it here.

So on, now, to Australia.

Chapter 7
The Journey

Now came a little life within a bigger life, twenty-seven days between Capetown and Sydney, a snip of time in itself round and eternal. It began for me with a bright morning in Table Bay. The *Ceres* lay outside the harbour about a mile off-shore, waiting. I do not know for what she waited. That is one of the charms of life at sea: the outer life impinges only vaguely. Stops are made, speed is increased or lessened, and nobody knows enough to care. If you ask an intelligent question about this you are handed a kind silly answer by the captain, chief officer, one of the engineers. This is not your province, this touching of the ship's life with the world outside: your mind, as well as your body, should be confined within the crystal dome of the journey like immortelles in the French cemeteries, divorced from living: your horizon should be that dark blue circle where air meets water, that circle which is the limit of your ship-board view.

So I did not ask why we lay swinging gently from side to side in the Atlantic swell. I carried my early morning tea on deck, balanced it on the rail, took my last gulp of Africa, thought of Kraanvlei. The parting from it, from Gisela and Kurt and the children, had been hard. My mind went back to the place, haunting it mournfully. In Kraanvlei now, I thought, the sun will be already scorching the useless gauze of the stoep, flooding inwards to the dark kitchen where Tante Saschia fights the flies, harries the girls, and bakes snoek for breakfast. In the greening oaks outside the weaver birds will be twining their grasses, weaving their bower, twittering excitedly. The Grünberg's western flank will be just catching the sun: round the tumultuous flanks of the Bobbejaansberg the goats will be streaming upwards, new-released from the byre, with little Dirk in wordy chase. Now at the back door, the kitchen door that gives on to the yard, the cats will be at their musical wailing, pressing against the fly-door, begging for porridge, showing mauve-pink cavities, woeful caves, as they open their mouths to mew again.

But here was Table Bay, Table Mountain with attendant hills, the town a confetti-heap of coloured roofs sprawling up its slopes, and Charlotte new embarked on another journey, another search. I sipped my tea (like all tea on board ship it tasted purple) and watched. An officer went past, gave me "good morning" with the careless politeness of a man whose life is made up of new faces, faces he has to greet. A steward approached, emptied an ash-tray adroitly over the side, and congratulated me on being up so early. He must have said that fifty times this trip, I thought, smiling at him. He ebbed away humming "Little Old Lady."

"Well," I thought, "I am finished with South Africa. *Wenn i'komm, wenn i'komm, wenn i' wiederum komm*[1]—but I shall not come again."

"Beautiful, isn't it?" said a female voice. I had noticed her the night before: a large, apple-faced woman with shining grey

---

1   German: When I'm back, when I'm back, When I finally return. From the lyrics to the Swabian folk song, "Muss i denn."

hair, clothed from chin to toe in articles that were patently hand-made. It is a common English type, as foreign as the kangaroo to us. Everything hand-woven, shoddy, amateurish: a false medieval roughness about the whole, a look of self-conscious rectitude on the face of the owner.

"Yes," I said, "it is lovely."

"Tell me, where are the Twelve Apostles?"

I pointed out the Twelve Apostles and we mused on them awhile, deciding which was Peter, which John. I wished the ship would start: it is easier when one has at least the illusion of getting somewhere.

An elderly man came up, stared over the side, and cried: "What, not off yet ?" in a voice of fierce reproach.

We all glared at the bay, as if the water itself should do something about the matter.

"No, not off yet," twittered my arty one. "Oh, Mr. Hobart, may I introduce Miss—I don't think I know your name, dear."

I gave it, thinking there was little enough reason why she should.

"Mr. Hobart—Miss Hurts. Miss Hurts is going to Australia."

"So are we all!" he cried. "When the blasted ship starts, so are we all."

His laugh rolled out with shocking heartiness, considering the hour. He was in pyjamas with a gaudy plum-silk dressing-gown about his corpulence: a big man, massively boned, with a healthy warm-coloured face. He laughed again, inviting us to join: and as he did so his full lips drew back over deplorable, much-stopped teeth.

A retired colonel, I thought, with nothing to do and energy still yeastily bottled within. Köln is full of them during the summer months: thus far and no farther, to see the whole of Germany. Hearty, I decided, considering him over my cup's rim, and unsubtle—full of anecdotes about batmen and Flanders in '17, and animals. To be avoided.

"Miss Lamb's the gay one," he boomed, jabbing at the new friend, "she's the gay one. There she was in Capetown painting the place red till all hours, yet now she's up with the dawn and doesn't look a day older."

"*You're* the man to talk about painting towns red!" she cried, delighted, making as if to push him away.

Smiling politely, I left them to their horse-play. There would, I hoped, be something more rich in surprises during the voyage than these elderly innocents.

But Miss Lamb had taken a fancy to me. During the morning she clung fondly, exclaiming over the beauties of the South African coast as we chugged slowly away from it, telling me of herself, her work, her aims, her politics, her struggle to keep Principles unstained by Expediency. It sounded an odd way of spending fifty years, but she seemed to have thrived on it. Man, she told me, was made to be Whole: the Holy Wholeness of Man, she punned happily, was her life's ideal.

I made polite gurglings. "Not for me," I thought, "Man's Holy Wholeness. As soon as I get away from this amiable imbecile I shall take my chair on to the boat-deck and seek me a corner where man is not, neither whole nor unholy."

Like all travellers, I mentally denied the right of anyone else to be on this ship. I should have the choice of every nook for my chair. To find any that I fancied already full of other passengers was a raw insult. However, by the captain's bridge was a space of deck unsullied by deck golf, coils of rope, tennis-nets or any other gear. Sighing with relief, I shed Miss Lamb and made for it.

This, I mused, is good. To lie stretched out in the sun on a deck-chair for which you have paid nothing, with your feet, propped between white rails, dangling over the sea, and your eyes absently searching its blueness.

But alas! Mr. Hobart had also taken a liking to me. He lumbered up in a doggy pale grey jacket with thin red lines, a cloth cap making him seem more rakish than was natural. He straddled above me with his stomach firmly ballooning. Even with the sea behind them his eyes were astonishingly blue.

"May I?"

He sat down upon the foot-piece of my chair.

Confound the man! I rumbled inwardly, must I talk of cocker spaniels and other canine whatnots to this limited intelligence? The Holy Wholeness of Man, I thought, politely smiling, shifting my feet away from his grey flannelled stem, were better.

The man, however, talked well, and not of cocker spaniels alone. Unself-conscious, he prattled on from one subject to another, sure of my listening ear. Should I not listen? Was I not a woman? Soon he was speaking of Australia as a man talks of his sweetheart, described a trotting race with rich detail; made me laugh. Delighted, he talked on. In a way which startled me the afternoon slid by. It was tea-time. We went down to tea and were immediately wedded to Miss Lamb, who made for our table buzzing like a purposeful bumble-bee with philosophies. Plainly the two were on good bickering terms and had been amiably annoying one another all the way from Liverpool.

Miss Lamb, proclaimed Mr. Hobart, was a blooming idealist with her head in a rosy fog.

Mr. Hobert, cried Miss Lamb affectionately, was not half so hard-boiled (with pride she brought out the modernism) as he would have us believe.

"On the contrary," shouted Mr. Hobart. "I'm boiled a great deal harder than you can ever imagine, my dear lady!"

The simple battle pitched on. I watched the elderly infants, myself now hoary with age. But somehow I liked them both: in a slick world they were strangely innocent.

The day passed with the usual petty businesses. Lifeboat practice on the boat-deck at five: cork squares in filthy canvas caressing the back of one's neck, and the older stewards only too eager to fasten the tapes on each female passenger. A visit to the purser to deposit cash and passport: the purser had a purple wart, like the holy Brahmin mark, between the eyebrows; and could by no means spell my outlandish name. A sports meeting at five-thirty which I let others attend. For me, the lower deck deserted of everything but spicy salt air and the light of the sunset.

"What, not at the sports meeting?" cried Mr. Hobart, looming once more. He cupped my elbow in his large fresh hand and guided me round the deck. We made a padding constitutional. The sun set and we uttered the usual comments: a green eerie light spread over the west, the wind suddenly was very cold. My spirit fled wistfully back to Kraanvlei to Minnaarskopjie, to Kurt and Gisela, my last of Europe. But Mr. Hobart would not hold with wandering spirits: something reminded him of a darned funny thing that had happened to him once in Kalgoorlie, and he tethered me to earth in the telling of it. There was not a doubt in his mind but that I should find it as interesting as he did.

Sad, cold, irritated, I made my evening bath the excuse and went below.

Looking back now across the stretch, not of time alone, which cuts me from that voyage in the *Ceres*, I cannot remember at what point I saw that I was spending all my hours with this man Hobart and enjoying them. He told me afterwards that he loved me from the moment when, coming on deck for his early airing, he saw me sipping tea at the rail, chatting with Miss Lamb. From that minute (he said) I knew you were the girl for me. Like most assertions after the event ("I *knew* something was going to happen to that train—I said to myself: 'There'll be an accident,' and"—triumphantly—"there was!") this one was thoroughly suspect. I tell myself often enough that the whole thing was quite simple: he was bored with the journey, bored with himself; any personable woman would have hooked his fancy. But what use now to argue about fact and may-have-been? We met, there by the rail, on a superb morning in August: within two days we lived in one another's pockets. I am the last person to know how it happened. It was for me a railway journey through pitch dark to a new country: you see nothing, you are merely blindly going there. In the morning you wake to light, to a foreign tongue, to the sound of an alien river.

This awakening came on the sixth night out, ourselves already divorced by æons of time from shore, land, normal life, Africa. It was a Tuesday, though why I should remember that and forget so much else I do not know. After dinner we walked the deck talking amiable nothings. For a heavy man he moved lightly, yet was slow. My own swifter feet, like my more nimble mind, took me ever ahead of him. I was forever stopping as we talked, waiting for him to lumber up. This became boring, like a cure at Wiesbaden. I was but thirty-five, not yet in middle age. So at last I said good night, made to step over the little ledge into the hall by the notice-board. Then he surprised me. He followed, clipped me to him with an arm as hard as teak, muttered: "Give us a kiss, old darling," and planted one wetly on my cheek before I knew it.

There are but two ways of dealing with this: either the frigid stare or the startled giggle. I giggled; it was too absurd. And, giggling still, I called once more: "Good night," and went below.

When I got to my cabin I stood some little time before the mirror and saw nothing. I had it in me to be very angry. The usual type, I thought: kiss-snatching, cuddling in dark nooks, the experimental hand laid on the female knee, then casually falling to the skirt-hem. creeping along the stockings while the owner brightly chats (they are all fine chatterers). All so friendly, so harmless, so furtively obscene. Where do you draw the line? At the hand on the knee? Every woman must know her own mind on that: I had thought I knew mine. But this time there had been no preamble: the kiss (I smelt its whisky yet) had shot out, positively shot, from the innocent blue of our relationship.

Standing there staring at myself I decided that I would be angry. Not angry in the conventional unhand-me-sir-you-insult-a-defenceless-female manner, but angry as one should be at infringement on individual rights. No, I said aloud, I am not the sort of woman who suffers this calmly. It is a trivial matter, but here I take a stand.

Taking on the face of an affronted woman, I undressed. In bed, with the light out and the sea slapping past my port-hole's glass, I began to giggle. Giggles led to roars of laughter, veritable spasms that had to be choked in the pillow. For indeed it was too foolish! To be seized upon and swung round like that by a hard male arm, pressed close to a barrel-hard male stomach, kissed like any peasant wench at a fair! It was too funny. The memory tickled me again, I whooped helplessly into my pillows. It was not worth being angry about, I said, snuffling with mirth: and at that composed myself to sleep.

We met in the morning as friends with no grudges. I could not but like the man. There was something so truly young in those heavenly blue eyes in the red fleshy face. I talked to him directly, as I would to a child. His gross lumbering body followed me up the stairs after breakfast: he asked if I would walk about the deck. When we came abreast of the door where we had last night parted he stopped, looked at me, not committing himself to a smile till I began it. I laughed, helpless against his simple humour. So we went on, admiring the fine fury of the waves as they rose and sank, the ice-blue sky, the Cape pigeons still wheeling about the ship's stern from which the Chinese stokers had put out their frail kites. It was a companionable morning, soothingly banal. I cannot remember one thing that he said and am very sure that I, too, uttered nothing noteworthy. The day passed in a pleasant blank, like a broad lazy river between trees which are all alike. The peculiar flavour of time spent at sea, when the mind has sloughed its past and resolutely refuses to take one blink at its future, wrapped us about. I do remember that we agreed, some-where in mid-afternoon, on doing some work: he had papers to sort, I letters to write. But at once, before our inward eye, rose up a calendar of days in which there was time enough: more than twenty days in which papers could very well be sorted, letters admirably written. So, sighing and smiling at our sloth, we eased more comfortably into our chairs, looked out once more to sea, and dropped on the peaceful air, from time to time, a remark which had no importance whatever.

Perhaps for the first time in my life I was content.

Next morning the rain beat against my port-hole, the ship wallowed in an evil sea pock-marked with rain. We sat after break-fast in the smoking-room. At what stage, I wondered, does one begin to drift in this easy shipboard fashion towards intimacy? At what stage do one's fellows assume that Miss A. and Mr. B. will be strolling together round the deck after breakfast, sitting together in the smoke-room before lunch, chatting together in deck-chairs during the afternoon? At what stage does the deck steward, quietly, unobtrusively, yet with that insolent faint leer so common to stewards, put the chairs of Miss A. and Mr. B. close together on the shadow of the awning, in that cosy hidden hole on the boat-deck? Time has so few mile-stones at sea. Seedling friendships that would on shore take months to grow into healthy plants, develop here in a day or two days, and, once back again on land, shrink in a moment, like a bee blown away down the wind, to a tiny point, to nothing. Here am I, I mused, talking to this man as if for years he had had the peep-hole to my mind and I to his. Was it yesterday we met, or a year ago? I do not know. For fifty years (so old I guessed him to be) he has led his separate life: for thirty-five years I have led mine. All time would not be long enough for us, now, to lay bare to one another those eighty-five years spent apart. And we do not need that time: in three days we knew one another.

"You know," I said idly, "when you came up to Miss Lamb that first morning I took it for granted you were her husband."

"My God!" he cried, "give us a chance! You remind me of the story of the old maid and the tramp—do you know that one?"

He told me the story. It was the sort that flourishes richly in smoke-rooms. It had neither wit, humour, nor point: it was purely smut. When he had finished telling it I laughed heartily.

Well, well, I thought, this had to come sooner or later. The straying hand on the knee, the snatched kiss, the dirty story—they are but stages. Now is the time, I thought, to break this off. Go away and write letters: find Miss Lamb and talk with her about Humanity. Rescue yourself now (for surely you cannot later) from the Siamese twinship which fate, your own indolence, the attitude of all the other passengers, is forcing upon you. Now is the time to go.

I looked at him again as he sat chuckling, toying with an ashtray, and stayed.

Cold salmon was on the luncheon menu. I remember that because, *àpropos* the salmon (Miss Lamb being mal-de-mer-ish in her cabin), the captain also told a story. It was exactly like the one in the smoke-room, and I laughed just as much with just as little reason. I had not suspected myself of this. Had I the face, the manner, of a woman who likes smut? Or, perhaps, does the hearing of one of these drearily obscene tales make a woman more vulnerable to others, as in love? Women fresh from lovers' arms invite more lovers, they glow with the need of them: perhaps the same is true of a woman who has just seemed to enjoy a smoke-room tale. True, the indecency of this one was no new thing to me: the field of improper stories among the German Jews is rich and inexhaustible. But, being Jewish, they are witty. I considered, now, telling one of them to the two men who gurgled still, flushed with the success of the captain's. But as I looked at them I knew it would be pearls before swine. Our stories are too subtle, too deeply witty, for any but a civilised mind to enjoy. They spring from the same root, the physiological differences between man and woman: but they have gone farther, branched out more delicately. They are, in short, too good for schoolboys.

So I told my schoolboys instead a clean cathedral-city jest from their own *Punch*. They greeted it with shouts of uninhibited laughter, and the lunch went merrily forward.

"Charlotte," I said to myself after the meal, renewing lipstick, "you are now up against the Anglo-Saxon mind. Remember there are two things it rejects out of hand: subtlety and innuendo. None of your Jewish double-entendres, if you want to be a social success. They are not understood: the hearers merely shift uneasily. If you can remember any of those jokes whose point has to be driven home with a sledge-hammer, now is the time to trot them out. If you can't—if all you can collect in your mind are the Berliner-Witzen[2] about the Witwe Müller, Rabbi Schnitzler in the butcher's shop, or the girl who terribly wanted to become a nun, better keep silent."

I drew the coral line firmly along my lower lip, smiled at myself and my double, went demurely on deck.

The afternoon was pearly and innocent, rain-purged. Small tender clouds drifted across its blueness: the sparkle on the dark clean waves was like breaking glass. We took our chairs to the boat-deck, where some fools were braying at a game of quoits, and lay close to the rail brooding happily over the water below us.

This will be the time, I thought, for the Life History. It was. One thing led to another, as they always will; before half an hour was gone we were well in the middle of it. I listened with a bright intelligent face. I subtly emanated admiration. In truth, the autobiography of Harry Hobart was delightful. It had a naïve freshness,

---

2 German: Berliner jokes, which often incorporated stereotypical figures such as Witwe Müller (Widow Müller) and were known for commenting on social conditions while also serving as comic anecdotes.

an innocent heartiness: it reminded me of those volumes of a boys' paper I had found in the Flowers' library. It reeked, as they did, of Lifebuoy soap, youthful sweat, and the honest obvious smell of sausages fried in the open. I learned now all about the old home in Worcestershire, the holidays at Scarborough, the schooldays at Sherborne. Then the clerkship in the mining engineer's office, the transfer abroad, Johannesburg, the Rand, the Boer War. And, after, Western Australia, Perth, Fremantle, Geraldton, Kalgoorlie, Coolgardie. The awkward names hopped about like grasshoppers: like so much that is British, they had neither rhythm nor melody, these names. "Aquapendente, O Aquapendente!" I murmured as the twin brutalities of Kalgoorlie and Coolgardie crashed into the monologue: the supple Italian name was like witch-hazel on a bruise. At this my attention must have flagged, for Harry, too, paused, fidgeted with the fringe of my rug, looked out, rather embarrassed, to sea.

"Go on," I said. "You were telling me about the gold mines."

"Yes, oh, yes. I was twenty-eight then, getting on, you know. A man can't—I mean, things were pretty wild out there then, and at that age you want to settle down a bit. Look here, did you know I was married?"

"I thought it more than likely."

He preened himself unguardedly, then took on an absurd serious frown.

"Yes, yes. It wasn't a great success. She was a magnificent woman—had the finest bust, people said, west of Sydney. We were like animals—in love that way, I mean—and when that was gone there was nothing left."

"Children?"

"Two boys. Both of 'em grown up now, of course. We don't see much of each other. She hasn't lived with me for nearly twenty years. By Jove, I don't believe we've even gone out together in all that time."

Stopping again, he laid his hand on my knee. "You don't mind my telling you all this?"

"Not in the slightest."

"Sensible girl. Ah well, it can't be helped. What I needed was an intelligent woman like yourself who'd help me along, and all I got was a tigress.

"With the brains," he added after a moment's deep thought, "of a louse.... Well, that's enough about me."

We were silent for a full minute, and then:

"You'll never see anything like that again—those early days in Kalgoorlie, I mean. There'll never be such another crazy town. Some of the things that happened—!"

He chuckled.

"Tell me."

"How modern are you?"

"1937."

"Well, there was a barmaid there at the 'Southern Cross' called Bessie. An awfully pretty girl she was and a darned good sort. There was a fellow there drifted up from Perth, a remittance man—I wish to hell I could remember his name—oh yes, Bob Astley. And he fell head over ears in love with Bessie. Used to lean on that bar drinking (when he had cash) and begging her to marry him or kiss him or at least tell him where her room was. Well, he begged and begged and made such a confounded nuisance of himself she told him at last he could come to her room. All the girls lived in, in those days, on the top floor of the hotel: and a very hot lot they were, too. So next night up creeps poor old Bob, dead drunk as usual and trembling like a leaf, and there was Bessie standing at her door in her nightie. (Mind you, a woman's nightie suggested more in those days, what with square yokes and lots of fullness and frilly doodahs and whatnot—I was sorry to see 'em go out of fashion.) Well, in he goes. But instead of Bessie all alone and trembling he found all the other girls there, too, and they laid him over the bed and stripped him naked, left him without a stitch. That wasn't the worst of it either: they put him out in the corridor just as he was and whipped him up and down the length of it with wet towels. My God, they were strapping girls, too. I don't know how he ever got home again, he must have been like a piece of bleeding steak. God, were those the days!"

We laughed together. Surprisingly good, thought I. The story, in a Jewish milieu, would have been sharpened to a finer point of impropriety; but for a Britisher this wasn't bad at all.

"There was another chap there," he reminisced, "who was living with a Frenchwoman. Quite a decent chap he was, but this Froggie had got her claws into him right enough. Well, one night when I was in the saloon with two other fellows (one of 'em's dead now, poor buck—shot himself after the Melbourne Cup[3]), in comes Basset (that's this other fellow's name) and he was as drunk as a lord. He came up to Lily, the other barmaid, and he said—"

Ah well, I thought as it went on, there was bound to be a falling-off. When the mental age is sixteen you don't often rise higher than this. So I stopped listening, just lay and watched. His eyes were bluer than I had ever thought possible, even in an Englishman. Underlined by a fine network of creases, by deep pouches drooped a little over his warm fleshy cheeks—surrounded by all the usual tell-tale marks of dissipation, they were yet youthfully and joyously blue. The little moustache, pure white, was as neat as a suburban garden plot. In fact, the whole man was virginally tidy. His linen, his handkerchief pushing one dazzling corner from a breast-pocket, his square purplish hands with close-cut nails, were all scrubbed and scoured and aired till they fairly shouted freshness. Here was the kind of man who bathes twice daily, carries his own towels about with him, and never washes but in running water.

---

3   The premier professional horse race in Australia, run annually on the second Tuesday in November.

SARAH CAMPION

"You know," his voice broke in, "I can't bear these basins on board ship. I like to have the tap running and wash that way."

I laughed.

"What's the joke?"

"Nothing," I said. But the feeling of oddity clung. How odd to have my thought and his speech crash in such sweet collision.

"Well, old darling, what about a spot of tea?"

He stood over me with his great belly hanging like a firm fruit and held out both his hands. I pulled myself up by them, was for a moment very close.

He made an engaging grimace. "I'd like to—but not in daylight."

"Not in any light," I answered primly.

"What, didn't you like being kissed?"

"No."

"I'll teach you to like it."

"Wait till you get the chance."

Odd how in parrying questions, innuendos of this type, most women plunge to the pert shop-girl level, I reflected, climbing carefully down to the lower deck.

It astonishes me still that for once I did not trouble to look clearly where I was going. Surely the young Charlotte had learnt a lesson? If so, the middle-aged Charlotte had as surely forgotten it. Perhaps even looking ahead would in the end have done me no good. Perhaps one is sometimes doomed to mindless drifting, and I, following my doom, mindlessly drifted. Loneliness makes us do strange things, seek strange comforts: I had been unbearably lonely for years.

So on we drifted, Harry and I. With him I flirted shamelessly, bringing all my guns into action. We went through all the usual stages of male kiss-snatching and female protest. The kiss-snatching became a fierce predatory game, in time a tedious exercise. I saw no way of stopping it but an utter refusal of his company, and this I had no mind to lose. There seemed still to be a vernal innocence about us both even in our worst moments. I was no longer the weary blasé Charlotte who had seduced young John Lae out of sheer boredom: I was a woman whose youth, the epoch at which this catch-as-catch-can game of sex is natural and good, had been wasted, sunk in the mire of that beastly war. Harry, so far as I guessed, had been chasing skirts for twenty years or more without ever becoming very apt at the sport. This lack of polish, this schoolboy roughness, utterly disarmed me. When, holding my coat for me to put on in a darkish corner of the deck, he swooped and kissed my neck before wrapping it around in the blue cloth, I could not help laughing.

"Don't *do* that!"

"Why, don't you like being kissed?"

"Not that way."

"We could have such fun."

"I couldn't."

"But, my dear girl, we must get *some* happiness out of life."

"That's not my idea of happiness, being cuddled and rumpled in corners. It doesn't lead anywhere."

"Where do you want to be led? Or are you going to do the leading?"

"Perhaps. No. I—Oh, well, never mind. Let's go and put our shillings on the tote."

And wrangling amicably about the number they shall back, the two idiots (old enough, both, to know much better) pass out of sight.

I was titillated, not yet fully awake, till that night on the boat-deck. I have always shunned boat-decks at night: I know their reputation. This night I was in an inquisitive, feckless mood: I don't drink, but there are other ways of getting intoxicated. I had been sitting watching him through my cigarette smoke as he put away two pink gins. My thoughts ran on, heady and inconsequent.

"If only he were twenty years younger. Not I, I'm the right age. But fifty-eight and thirty-five—there's too much difference. I am ripe and ready, he has gone too far into ripeness. Here am I with my girlhood lost, forever gone, my womanhood slipping away so fast that middle-age, the drying up, the ebbing of the sap, seems but a matter of the next few moments. I must snatch while I can. Indeed, why not?"

"What about looking for the Southern Cross?" asked Harry, getting to his feet.

"Why not?" I said again.

We go to look at the Southern Cross. In a few moments, only the climbing of the companion-way dividing our sanity from our madness, we are in darkness and fleshily clamped together. The Southern Cross, utterly ignored, beams above us. The wind whistles past our ears. Harry's firm heavy stomach supports my breasts, and with his lips on mine he mumbles:

"I love you."

"No."

"Would I be holding you like this if I didn't?"

"Would you be holding me like this if you did? Anyhow, I don't like being kissed."

"Nonsense, every woman does."

"Honestly I don't. When I was quite small—"

"Every woman says she doesn't, that means she wants more."

More followed.

"Give me your lips, darling."

"No!"

"Come on, give me your lips."

"No!"

But already his lips, too warm slugs, crawl luxuriously over mine.

"I loved you the first moment I saw you."

"Rubbish."

"I did. When I came out that first morning and saw you standing there talking to that old nanny-goat I knew I loved you."

"I don't believe it."

"Look here, if you don't believe me, what about this? I went straight to the dining-room steward and told him you were a friend of Miss Lamb's and it would be nice for her if he put you at our table. I wanted to be able to look at you all the time."

"So I changed hands for a ten-shilling note?"

"God, you're hard. Kiss us again, darling, put your arms round my neck and kiss me as if you meant it."

"But I don't."

"Yes, you do."

And he descends on me in a bear-hug while I despairingly abandon myself to a warm squeezing, the odd tickle of his coat-buttons between my breasts, two large hands finally and, I suppose, inevitably, beginning to stray in the same direction.

"Don't!"

"I say, *chérie*, you've got a fine chest!"

"Stop. That's something that I really hate."

"Why?"

"Because I do" (somewhat feebly).

"But you know you've got a lovely figure, don't you?"

"That's no reason why you should paw me and kiss me in that snatching way."

"I never kissed a woman against her will."

"You've just done it."

"That wasn't against your will."

"It certainly was."

"All right. I promise you faithfully I'll never kiss you again unless you want it. Will that do, darling? Say it'll do!"

I suppose I made some vague murmur. We fell apart and leaned against the rail, staring at the glistening sea as it slipped so silently away.

"Look, there's phosphorous."

"Where?"

"Down there, look—just under that jet of steam."

Frail, ghastly, livid, the phosphorous slipped away over the dark water, danced with the dark water out of sight. I craned after it and drew back, somehow, into Harry's arms. So long as he did not paw me I found his solid bulk very comforting.

"You'd never live with a man, would you?" he murmured at length.

"If I cared enough for him, yes."

"You're as hard as nails, aren't you? One of these days, my girl, you'll crash badly and know what it feels like. God, I'd like to be there then!"

"I crashed, as you call it, years ago," I murmured, thinking with sick brief pain of Kurt and the young Charlotte under the bare beech-trees many years ago.

"Did you, by Jove! What happened?"

"He married someone else."

"The fool! If I'd been there—! D'you mind my being so much older than you?"

"I can't see that it makes much difference."

"Thank you for that, darling."

I dreamed on, comfortably held to his breast. After a few minutes I heard that he was talking of a little flat in Melbourne. Sooner or later, I supposed, this sort of affair led to conversations about little flats in some town or another.

"Would you? Would you?"

"No."

"Why not?"

"Harry, I don't care for you enough."

"Say it again."

"I don't care for you enough."

"No, not that—you said my name."

"Harry," I murmured. This was hopeless. What was I to do with him? And honesty, echoing the question: "What are you going to do with yourself?"

"It sounds grand. Say it again. You've never called me by my name before."

The little flat in Melbourne dropped out of our ken as I repeated his name, trying to make it sound matter-of-fact.

After this tender interlude his mind with its usual simplicity went back to an incident in the smoke-room before dinner. Sitting there, he drinking and I smoking, we had been joined by a man I liked talking to, a fellow Jew, a doctor from Johannesburg. It was like fresh water to talk with him for a few brief minutes, to talk the language which was our own, the language of minds. Harry naturally hated it. This night, sopping up his drink, he glowered childishly at the two of us. We talked (why, I don't know) of the abolition of licensed abortion in Russia. Poor Harry, his bewilderment waxed comically. When Dr. Joachim had gone he leaned over, his eyes already showing the gin, and said:

"I suppose if that chap weren't safely married, you'd have him."

"Certainly not."

"But you like the same things. You're both darned clever sort of blokes. I like you better when he's not there: with me you're a woman, with him you're a damned intellectual.

"Why!" he brooded further, "the man actually listened to what you were saying!"

"Why not? I can talk as intelligently about abortion as anybody, I should hope."

"It's an awful subject for women to talk about."

"*Donnerwetter*,[4] man! If women haven't the right to discuss abortion, who has?"

---

4 German: Literally, thunder weather, but colloquially an expression of astonishment.

"But *abortion*!" he muttered unhappily.

Now on deck, remembering the absurd scene, he harked back to it.

"You'd rather talk about abortion and whatnot than kiss a man, wouldn't you ?"

"It's much more hygienic."

"Charlotte, you're clever!"

"And you don't like women to be clever: you want them simply to be cuddlesome, with their minds tucked well in and their ankles showing."

"Hold on!" he cried, appalled at my vehemence. "I *like* you to be intellectual and all that. I felt proud of you to-night talking to that fellow what's-his-name and he listening to you. But be a woman when you're with me, old darling."

So, with Harry I was to be a woman. Full well I knew where that was likely to lead. And yet, seeing by now which way the two of us were going, I could not draw back.

Was I in love with the man? No, not yet. Only lonely—oh, my God, how lonely!

The next night he was drunk. Not riotously, crazily drunk, simply a sot with a red face, loquacious, quarrelsome, not knowing what to do with his hands, ludicrously disgusting. Tradition evidently dies hard in an Englishman: it was Saturday night. We had had that most asinine business, a Tape Derby. Harry backed me heavily. I won my first heat, he nearly kissed me for joy. But in the finals the damnable curved scissors veered across the silly tape, ran off and severed it. Feeling vastly relieved at being thus out of a childish business I joined him where he stood jingling half-crowns in his pocket beside the betting table, and found him furious. He was already tipsy enough to sway a little as he stood on those massive oak-stem legs: he swayed to and fro glaring at me, saying, thank heaven, nothing at all.

It was all too absurd, so much furious energy wasted over a

bagatelle of this kind: I left him for Dr. Joachim, who stood philo-sophically mooning in a corner. We walked austerely, separated by at least a yard of chilly air, on the boat-deck. We talked of Russia and Trotsky. I enjoyed myself immensely; yet all the time at the back of my mind gloomed Harry's big figure swaying from foot to foot, thoroughly childish and very sad. It hurt. There was no reason why I should feel a tenderness for the man. He had behaved like a boor and a sot. Yet I wanted to put my arms round his neck, to comfort him, saying: "There! There! did its pretty balloon burst, then? It shall have another, so it shall!"

So strongly did this crazy impulse mount in me that I went back to him. When Dr. Joachim and I parted chastely by the notice-board I went to the smoke-room instead of going to bed as any sane woman should. There he sat, redder in the face, talking to a neat little gay little elderly widow from Bayswater or some such place. I was glad to see her there: making my peace with Harry was going to be easier under the sharp unintelligent eye of Mrs. Farrell.

He greeted me as if I were a friend of his boyhood. He was by now gloriously drunk. It distressed him that I would drink noth-ing. Mrs. Farrell sat there with her black velvet neck-band, her bright knowing old face exquisitely rouged, tippling genteelly at her whisky and soda. I merely smoked cigarettes, watched Harry. This seemed to bother him: the flow of his chatter was made choppy by such remarks as: "But look here, old darling, you're not—have a pink gin?"

"No, thanks."

"Oh, I say. Don't like it, really don't like it, you not drinking. Have a—What was I saying?"

"So the old man got married to a girl of eighteen," I helpfully prompted.

"Oh, yesh. He marries the girl and he brings her out of the reg-istry—registrar's office and he leans on her shoulder—you know, like this" (a great hand, hot as July, smouldered for a moment on my shoulder) "and he gets into his Rolls-Royce. And another shover comes up to the first shover—you know, the old man's shover—and he says: 'What's that your old man's got?' And, do you know what he says—what the first shover says?"

"No!" we trilled together.

"He says—he says—my God, but this is funny, I laugh every time I tell this one—he says: 'Can't you see that's a Stepney wheel?'"

Whoops of laughter crashed through the almost empty smoke-room. Harry leant back until his stomach was a quaking hill, and roared with laughter, wiped feebly at his eyes. Mrs. Farrell and I shot at one another the look, amused, faintly provoked, patiently tolerant, of women whose menfolk can't hold their liquor.

"My God!" cried Harry, scrambling back to a sitting position, "I don't believe you either of you know what a Stepney wheel is? 'Fess up, now, girls—you don't know, do you?"

No, we didn't.

So he told us. The point of the story is still wrapped in mystery for me, but I dare say there was one somewhere. Almost certainly indelicate: no Englishman would be telling a clean one at that hour in a ship's smoke-room. The English are very odd: everything with them has an appointed time and season. Saturday night: get drunk. 11.30 p.m. Saturday night: tell, if you still can, a dirty story. I got up to go to bed. It seemed that he bore me no ill-will over the Tape Derby: there was no need for reconciliation. Mrs. Farrell, still bright, birdy-eyed and intact despite the whisky, got up to go too. Harry protested, but shepherded us nevertheless to the door, upsetting chairs largely as he went. He had reached the stage at which a foolish smile drifts across the features, leaving blankness behind. As I turned to say good night over Mrs. Farrell's little head he gave me a look, a gesture, which took my breath away. I had never before been so silently and unmistakably commanded to go to bed with a man as I was now by this ruddy leering creature swaying on his great feet.

Cold, furious, deciding: "This is the end," I went down below.

The maternal instinct, long misused, undid me. He came to breakfast next morning, sheepish of eye, wearing a white silk muffler under his jacket. He had not dressed properly, he explained: he was just going to have a spot of breakfast and then straight back to bed.

"Is this what they call a hang-over?" chirruped Miss Lamb, deeply interested.

I laughed. "Is it a hang-over, Mr. Hobart?"

His eye met mine: a ruby eye it was, bleared and exhausted. For a moment I exulted frankly, wiped out last night's disgust.

"You wouldn't like to hold my poor head?" he facetiously pleaded.

"I would not. Lie down and sleep it off: see you again at lunch-time."

"A dear man!" sighed Miss Lamb when he had gone, "so full of beans, so experienced—and yet such a schoolboy!"

"Oh yeah?" I vulgarly replied, and left her to her romantics.

*****

Harry! How well the name fits! I thought that afternoon, watching him on his ponderous way towards me.

Harry, Hal, Bluff King Hal; he straddled the deck benevolently watching the neat ankles of two American girls as they played Bullboard. Bluff King Hal who exhausted five wives and was beaten finally (if Mr. Korda is right[5]) only by Katharine Parr and anno domini. Bluff King Hal with an eye, a roving blue eye, for female parts, and a large careless tolerance for such female frailties as did not seriously incommode him.

---

5   Reference to King Henry VIII as portrayed by Charles Laughton in Alexander Korda's 1933 film, *The Private Life of Henry VIII*.

King Hal came carefully on, eyeing me from afar with a sideways look. Little Robert Cresswell, hurling himself and a skipping-rope across the deck, fetched up smartly against those stout legs and burst into affronted roars. His nanny plucked him off and bore him away, apologising. Harry raised his cap to her: he prided himself on his deportment to such lower orders as nursemaids.

"If that child goes on as he's started he'll soon be one of the lads of the village," he remarked jauntily, settling in comfortably beside me.

"He will."

"It's scandalous, the way these nurses shirk their jobs. Look at that child now: no one's really got an eye on him; if the ship gives a good roll he'll roll with her and hit his head on something. And there sits the nurse-girl knitting and gossiping, never looking at the kid."

He blew himself into quite a little fury over it. I watched him and waited.

"I say, *chérie*, did I make a complete ass of myself last night?"

"Oh, not quite *complete*."

"No, but seriously, was I very awful?"

"No worse than most. How's your head?"

"Ghastly," he groaned, remembering it.

For the rest of the afternoon he was docile and subdued, coming to life only after dinner when, with our stomachs full, we leaned against the rail and talked to the chief officer about negroes.

"Don't call them niggers, please!" I cried, goaded by the familiar, contemptuous, white-man word.

They both stared.

"All right," said Harry, taking my arm (here under the eye of the chief officer, under a bright light, after dinner, such gestures are quite in order), "we won't. This girl," he explained, "has been having a set-to with the old man about Bolshies. She got the old man on the run, too. She's got all sorts of red ideas. We're all

273

brothers, and the nig—negro's as good as you are any day. She'd walk down the Strand with one if she got the chance, wouldn't you, eh?"

And filled with the first glow of a good meal, he chucked me tenderly under the chin.

"Seriously, *chérie*, I wish you wouldn't," he said as we settled once more in our chairs facing the starry night.

"Wouldn't what?"

"Get so het up about politics and all that. Politics are all very well, but when I see a woman leaning over the table arguing (as you did to-night), with her eyes sparkling and her face flushed, about Communism, or Soviet Russia or some such unsuitable flapdoodle—"

"Harry, you make me furious."

"It's not a woman's job to argue about politics," he muttered obstinately.

"You make me *mad*. What would you have me do?—Stay at home over the cook-pot thinking about nothing but baby's nappies?"

"You could do much worse. That's a job every woman should tackle instead of getting worked up into a red-hot temper over Stalin or some such bounder. What you want, my girl, is a husband."

"Harry, I shall scream. You're going to tell me next that I should find some go—ood man and marry him."

"Well, why not?"

"*Gottes Willen!*"[6]

"Hi, where are you off to?"

"I'm going to walk round the deck and cool off a bit."

"Don't be an ass, old darling."

He laid a hand on mine: symbol of solid security, warm comfort, all the thought-saving tradition of a man-made world, lay over my hand in a curve. I thrust it off and got up.

---

6 German: For God's sake.

But what was the use of charging round the deck like a wasp in a bottle? New arguments flowed into my mind, but this was no time for argument. And, anyhow, to some male minds all women's arguments are suspect from their source.

When I got back he still lay there watching for me, and put his hand once more over mine as I settled into the chair.

"You've got lovely legs, old darling."

My laugh pleased him. The woman had flown off the handle a bit but here she was again, come to her senses, warm and quiescent under his caressing hand. With the expertise of long habit the hand ran up my arm under my loose coat-sleeve to rest in the crook of my elbow. His fingers beat a gentle tattoo there, rhythm to his thoughts.

"What about it, old dear?"

"About what?"

"Our sleeping together."

"Harry, why do you want it? You know this will last only a few more days, till we get to Sydney, perhaps."

"You know I'd marry you if I were free."

"That would be a mistake."

"Why?"

"I've got a hell of a temper."

"I like women with tempers. Can't bear those spineless fish who say: 'Yes, Harry: No, Harry' like blasted penny-in-the-slot machines. What do you do when you're in a temper?"

"I once threw a little cousin of mine against the stove and cut her head open."

"Good," said Harry approvingly. "You'd be a wonderful woman to sleep with. Listen, Charlotte: we'll go ashore at Melbourne—separately, of course, I wouldn't for the world do anything to harm your good name—and spend the night at Mackenzie's. It's a good hotel. More a man's place than a woman's, but good and solid. They do you well there."

He put his hand suddenly on my shoulder, his head very close. The familiar smell of whisky and Pears' soap tickled my nostrils.

"You must know by now how much I want you, *chérie*."

"Look out, someone's coming."

Grumbling, he withdrew his hand, cleared his throat, stared with brassy innocence out to sea. The chief officer came round the corner wearing the bland half-smile of a man who won't see spooning couples unless they want it.

"Captain, what of the night?" called Harry.

The chief officer stood over us and talked. We talked of the wind (veering to the north-east), of the rain (which had stopped), of the ship's run (which was satisfactory). Mr. Arbroath then passed on, sweetly tactful: there is nothing the chief officers of the "Classic" line don't know about the blind eye.

"God, I've got a head on me!" suddenly groaned Harry when he had gone.

"Better go to bed with a wet towel."

"I'd rather go to bed with you."

One could only laugh at this.

"That's another thing about you," he murmured contentedly, snuggling down in his chair: "you always take things pretty well— you never take 'em the wrong way. I can say the most awful things to you and you only laugh."

"What do you expect me to do—slap your face and yell for the police?"

"Lots of girls would."

"I'm no longer a girl. Let's dance, Harry—they must have started by now. We'll get Mr. Arbroath to lend his 'Lambeth Walk' record—I love that."

"Because I don't hold you in my arms for it, just clasp you chastely round the waist, eh?"

"Not entirely. Do you remember that bit in *Vanity Fair*?"

"Never read it."

"*Haven't* you?—it's the only English novel I ever enjoyed—except *Dorian Grey*, of course. There's a sentence in it about that new dance, the waltz, and how shocking it is because the man and the woman are almost in each other's arms. I suppose all dances are mirrors of the love-act, really."

"Charlotte!"

"What?"

"You do say the most frightful things. I don't like a woman to talk like that."

"Don't be a fool, Harry."

But he was genuinely shocked, shaken. He looked at me reproachfully, pulled me up from my chair without a word, and reluctantly lumbered at my side towards the dancing deck.

On the starboard side those solid objects miscalled "fairy lamps" (how quaintly the English mind dwells upon fairies) glowed inanely. The flags were up, tacked under the lights by an enthusiastic deck steward. A few streamers hung dejected from odd corners: the festive spirit on the old *Ceres* had mainly to be supplied from within, by the passengers.

We never danced the first dance together, Harry and I. It would be too marked, it would make people talk, said Harry solemnly. I thought as I watched him guiding the prettiest of the nursery governesses around, myself demurely penned in by Mr. Arbroath's official arm: "How little we can say to one another that can be understood!" Perhaps that was one of the charms of our intimacy.

Because of his insensitiveness, his lack of subtlety, I could talk to him as to no one else. Because I knew I should not be understood, I could say what I liked. He took all my jests seriously, not knowing that I have wit: their flavour, for me, was quietly enriched thereby. Still there were jokes that we shared: warm obvious jokes, maliciously human. Often, across the table, our eyes met and held for an appreciative minute: often, sitting at Housey watching Captain Rogers, that tight Welshman, painfully parting with small silver, our elbows lived in one another's ribs, ecstatically nudging. Dancing, as now, clasped in the arms of separate partners, we would pass within a few feet and shoot a joke (like a hot chestnut shuffled from hand to hand) by eye-signal across the space between. That these jokes were mainly improper made our joy in them sharper: the Knight and the Nut-brown maid,[7] we gloried in our twin outlawry.

The dance ended, Mr. Arbroath released me, Harry lumbered up as if we had met but a few minutes before. That glorious ostrich, man! His eyes were bright and moist with desire: smugly certain that no one noticed it, myself least of all, he asked me to dance.

He danced beautifully. Leaning on him, upheld by the massive dome of his stomach, resting my hand confidently on the muscular spring of his shoulder, I was a little ship. Buoyed up by fathoms of sea, I was a little ship gladly floating on the firm waters, trusting in them to bring me at length to port. We swung blissfully together, our knees lightly brushing now and then: when this happened, without thought our happy eyes met, unspoken words passed between. I knew without doubt to-night, waltzing to the looping strains of "Sympathy," that I should be sleeping with this man soon. My body had decided it, brushing away all moral-intellectual pros and cons, speeding like an arrow to the inevitable conclusion. Remembering seventeen-year-old Charlotte in the Grunewald, her pain and rapture, I drew my fingers softly across Harry's vast shoulder-blades. Softly, softly. Once again our looks were welded. He had understood the touch: there was no need for me to say "Yes."

I—want sy-ym-pathee
Sy-ympathee—just sympa-thee—

---

7 Reference to the 15th century English ballad, "The Nut-Brown Maid," a dialogue between a knight in disguise and a maiden on the theme of fidelity in love.

"What an insane song!" I cried, tossing back my head, laughing into his face. "*What* a silly song. Sy-ym-path-ee—just sym-path-ee!" I mimicked and at that the record ended on a whirring protest, the dancers stood still.

*****

Now Australia, the Land of Promise. Or just another stepping-stone, I wondered, looking at the land-line on the eastern horizon. Just a dirty line of humpy land against a sky that was melancholy and green: no more—Australia.

"There's Rottnest Island," cried Harry, pointing.

I looked at Rottnest Island, dismissed it: but took advantage of the moment to press closer. New land, new continents, were now nothing to me. My mind was bounded, these mad days, by Harry's large comforting body. Since we danced to the banal lilting of "Sympathy" a few days ago there had been an odd strangled pause between us, the constraint of waiting: by touching him, pressing my elbow under his as we leaned together to look at Australia looming, I could for a moment cheat myself into thinking all was well.

"So that's Australia," I said glibly, pressing as it were a casual arm to his.

He squeezed me absent-mindedly, his thoughts on something else.

"We'll go ashore, won't we, *chérie*? It'll be dark but still I can show you the little old town of Perth, Pride of Westralia. Only thing is I've got to talk business with this man Andrews: he'll be on the quay to meet me. Tell you what, I'll get Baxter (that's our agent, and a damn' decent fellow) to take you on to the 'Fair Maid' in his car and amuse you till we come. Andrews and I can get our pow-wow done in half an hour, then I'll be free to paint the town with you."

Australia—Fremantle: as we drew near it was a dismal sight, this new world. Flat it was, and monotonous: a dead lake of corrugated-iron roofs. On the quay a silent crowd stood, mere shapes in the dusk. It was almost dark when the *Ceres* dreamily slid to her moorings. Now the crowd moved a little, breathed a little, spoke a little. A pale egg-shape was pointed out to me as Baxter: another, longer, paler, as Andrews.

"What ho!" yodelled Harry, waving his grey felt hat. How odd he looked in shore clothes: a neat grey suit, gloves, cane, a hat! I marvelled at him, letting Australia look as she liked for the moment. First impressions of Australia: for me they were a tall stout man in a suit I hadn't seen before, a hat that didn't, I fondly thought, become him, waving to egg-shapes on a foreign quay, calling to them: "What ho!"

"What ho!" called the hearty boyish voice again (we're to be boyish to-night, are we?): and an answering wheeze came from below as the gang-plank rattled down, as we touched Australian soil.

Mr. Baxter greeted me with surprise. He looked me over, decided in the obvious way men have that old Hobart knew how to pick 'em, and with nervous familiarity shook hands. He was a pale, sandy little man, easy to handle: the type that inevitably gets handled by some woman who is not too particular. Mr. Andrews was inconsiderable, except for a hot and roving eye which seldom rose more than thirty inches above floor-level: knee-height, that is.

I was driven off in Baxter's car, chattering brightly, leaving Harry and the Andrews ponderously talking their business by the gangway. We purred along a wide desolate street edged with the inevitable colonial arcade, fretted iron-work its trimming: crossed water by a clanking bridge, came out on an empty highway spattered at its rim with tin-roofed bungalows. It was a dark moaning night, starry: the river on the right shimmered, catching a few stray lights.

"This the first time you've been to Australia?" babbled the amiable Baxter.

Yes, I had never been here before.

"Pity it's dark, you won't see much."

Yes, it was a pity.

"I'll tell you what, we'll drive round by the Univ. buildings: they're flood-lit, they look bonzer at night."

We drove round. Against the floodlit stone a single tree shone brilliant red, leafless, naked, tasselled with great startling red flowers.

"Oh!" I cried, shocked out of my pleasant platitudes.

"Pardon? Oh, that's a flame-tree—do you mean to say you've never seen a *flame*-tree before?"

"Never."

The flame-tree, the lovely thing so quivering, so gay and tender with life, was dismissed. I had to listen to the story of the University buildings, the old man's dream, as the car slid under archways, past blank windows, by shadowy vague spaces.

"Fine, isn't it?" said Mr. Baxter, completing the tour and the tale together, stopping the car for one more moment at the floodlit front.

I saw only the flame-tree, the bare smooth branches sprouting, like my own life, so suddenly into colour, into singing fiery flamelets of flowers.

We drove uphill through King's Park. Strange antipodean branches swished against the car's roof, the headlights silvered one tree after another, each stranger than the last. Perhaps all vegetation thus sucked into the flood of headlights, thus swiftly left behind again, belongs to another hemisphere, another world. Perhaps by day King's Park would look as familiar as the Tiergarten. But for me, that night, these trees and bushes were new as fresh eggs, making their debut for me alone.

"What is that tree, there—the one with the feathery boughs?"

"That's a pepper-tree. D'you mean to tell me," asked Mr. Baxter, goggling from behind his rimless lenses, "that you've never seen a pepper-tree before?"

This was growing monotonous. What did the man expect me to know of Australia after but forty minutes on Australian soil? I decided against more questions. But Mr. Baxter was in a gallant mood. He got from the car and picked a branchlet of pepper-tree, gave it to me as one gives edelweiss culled from perilous precipices. The fine delicate leaves smelled of verbena, of marjoram, of thyme, but had, more piercingly sharp than all these, the tang of a new continent. I held them dreamily to my nose while I heard the history of King's Park.

At the entrance to the "Fair Maid of Perth" Harry straddled benevolently. He had made good use of his time, was already pink with beer.

"What on earth have you got there?"

"Pepper-tree—smell it."

I held it to his nose, rather consciously arch under the speculative eyes of Messieurs Baxter and Andrews.

"Where d'you get it?"

"Mr. Baxter picked it in King's Park."

"Oho—Baxter doesn't waste time, does he?" giggled Andrews cheerily.

Harry shot me a suspicious look. "Whatever did you want to go through the Park for?"

"We drove out that way. Are we going to stand on this step all night? I'm cold."

In we went, Harry and the Baxter eyeing each other like unfriendly dogs. Half the *Ceres*'s passenger-list seemed to be gathered together in the plushy lounge of the "Fair Maid." Mrs. Farrell in parma violet sat sipping whisky with the chief officer in one corner: the two American girls yelled with laughter in another, showing teeth as full of nuggets as the Yukon. A fat frog-like man whom nobody had much noticed on board was now making an infernal nuisance of himself at the far end of the room under a photograph of the M.V. *Wanganella*. Giving him and all the other men in the room a look of hearty dislike, Harry shepherded us into plushy chairs and ordered beer.

What had I imagined myself doing this first night, doing to salute Australia? I cannot remember. What I did, to my undying astonishment, was to sit in the lounge of the "Fair Maid of Perth" from eight-thirty till half-past one the next morning drinking beer. The beer was very bad: Harry must have put away quite ten glasses of it. I toyed with mine, sipped, rebelled, sipped again, resigned myself to the doom of it, and lit a cigarette. Harry was quite happy: to him it was good beer. For Harry, as the evening dragged on, the beer got better and better. Mr. Baxter and Mr. Andrews became the best of fellows, the "Fair Maid" the best hotel in the world, Australia God's own country. He began to sweat, to shout, to show off.

"Come and see what they've got here, Miss Hurts—here's what I've been wanting to show you—'member me telling you about the python that swallowed the ole man kangaroo? 'Scuse me a minute, you fellows—I wanna show Miss Hurts the photograph."

He led me off, decorously not touching me, to the bar, which was now stale with fumes and pitchy dark. Before he switched on the light, he pressed me behind the door and fumblingly kissed me.

"Harry, don't be silly! What were you going to show me?"

The light went on: he straddled by the wall gesturing largely in front of a photograph which showed a snake extended, a sheepish lad in the trousers of 1900, standing by with a yard-stick.

"Well?"

"Don't you see—it's the photo I was telling you about, the python that swallowed the old man kangaroo. Look, there's the kangaroo in its stomach, that bulge—look at it, by God that *is* a bulge!"

Only Australia, announced his broad beer-pink face, his straddling legs, could show you a bulge that size.

"Bless me," said I to please him, "what a sight!"

He turned off the light again and put his arms around me in the beery dark.

"Tell me something, *chérie*!"

"Yes?"

"Did that swine Baxter try to kiss you?"

"Kiss me—? You must be crazy, Harry; of course he didn't."

"Honest?"

"Of course not. What on earth would he be kissing me for? We weren't together more than about twenty minutes, anyhow."

"Forty-five, my girl, and the drive from Fremantle takes about twenty-five. What were you doing in King's Park picking pepper-trees? Didn't he even try to kiss you then?"

"Harry, this is absurd—let me go."

"One more kiss!"

"No."

"By Jove, you're going to get kissed now whether you like it or not."

Which I was, extremely wetly.

We then walked demurely back to the lounge, exchanging banal pleasantries about the snake.

Someone had turned on a wireless: it only needed that. Behind the shouts of laughter, the clinking of glasses, the noise of twenty people each trying to impress the others, this infernal machine screeched and cackled. "My God, it's awful!" a man would cry, leaping from his chair, hurling himself at the apparatus. "I can't stand this stuff, let's have something *decent*!" And bending unsteadily to peer into its face he would twiddle knobs, adjust pointers, till the first noise had been conjured through the usual stages of Morse, cat's concert, loud shattering scraps of orchestra, to something equally bad. We twitched thus from the Frühlingslied[8] to a boxing match in Sydney, from the boxing match to a talk on Lithuania: from Lithuania, squealing through the tail-end of the Frühlingslied, to a military band playing "Colonel Bogey." No one said: "My God, this is awful, let's turn it off!"—oh, dear me, no. The wireless stood there, the infernal cabinet: it must speak, at all costs make a noise else why was it there? The new barbarism, I thought: the new tribal noise—and the same here as in Berlin, London, Capetown. Do we need to drown our thoughts, or have we none to drown? Difficult to say: as difficult in Berlin, London, Capetown, as in Perth, Pride of Western Australia.

At last, however, the preserved noise gave out. At 11.30 the cabinet gulped and was silent. A frenzied chase through ether by two men who were too drunk to know music if they heard it yielded no more than pippy conversations between ships or loud shattering crackles. There was nothing, nothing more to be heard now: only our own voices shouting from habit where before we had shouted in competition with the radio.

What we shouted for those five hours I can mercifully not remember. Everyone seemed happy enough. I smoked and smoked, dreamily abandoning myself to watching Harry's face, to sinking farther, farther into a haze of affection, cigarette-smoke, and the all-embracing warmth of a pneumatic chair.

At midnight, Mr. Andrews, in whom we could almost hear the tide of beer slopping, stumbled up and left us.

Half an hour later Mr. Baxter rose, shook hands, murmured something about a wife, and was gone.

"Don't you believe him," said Harry, leaning forward, his eyes very bright; "wife my eye! He's off to a tart shop or my name's not Hobart. Wife, indeed!"

---

8   German: Spring song, a type of folk song celebrating the end of winter and the arrival of spring.

"Oh, well, it makes as good an excuse as any other. Harry, are you going to sit here swilling beer until to-morrow?"

"Yes. Anyhow, it's to-morrow now. Hi! you! another beer!"

The waiter, with a face damp and weary, took away empty glasses, brought a full one.

"Harry, I don't want just to see Australia as a series of pub-crawls. Let's go out and get some air and look at the town."

"What a restless girl you are! You'll see nothing: it's as black sh my hat outside. Besides, 's probably raining by now," said Harry morosely, eyeing his glass as if he had begun to dislike beer.

I left him to it, wandered out into the hall. Such a hall—all crimson plush, thick balled fringes, dense curtains; heavy wall-paper in dark green embossed with gold pineapples; the furniture thick, dark, heavy, immovable; and on the walls photographs of interstate steamers and deceased publicans. The wan clerk smiled as I bought cigarettes, yawned wearily under the counter as he fumbled in a cigar-box for the change. Why had I come thousands of miles for this, this weighty mediocrity, this vulgarity, so smug, so international?

"What are those flowers?"

"Them? They're kangaroo paws."

He brought the vase nearer, smiled indulgently as I sniffed. I saw that the flowers were the summing up of the plushy lounge, all that in essence this hall was: great green and red plush fingers, woolly, thick, hideous. They were not flowers, they were hotel sofas, hotel drapes, torn into finger shapes to be stuck flower-like on wire stems covered in hotel plush, stuck flower-like in a vase to deceive trippers. Nature's attempt to provide the ideal hotel flower, plush, indestructible, which collected dust and endured forever.

"So those are Kangaroo Paws," I murmured, fingering, staring.

"Too right they are," said the clerk, and yawned again.

Harry came out of the lounge, his face hot and bloomy.

"Here you are, old darling. Wash wondering where you got to.

Wanna go home? So do I. Hi you whashemame, a taxi!"

In the taxi he put one hand out to mine, yawning heartily behind the other.

"Enjoyed youshelf, *chérie*?"

"Yes," I lied.

"Good. Good fellows, Baxter and Andrews. Dam' good fellows, the swine. That's the Swan River over there: very pretty. Pity we can't—ah—oh—aah !—sorry, I'm sleepy—pity we can't see it in the dark."

He cuddled closer.

"You're looking lovely to-night—in fact you're a very wunnerful woman. Sure Baxter didn't kiss you?"

"Harry, don't!"

"Well, he was a fool not to, that's all I can say. Charlotte—"

"Yes," I whispered, watching the weary lights dance on the Swan River, watching the sway of the frail pepper-trees.

"What about it—about Melbourne, I mean?"

"Yes."

Through the smell of beer and tobacco that he pressed on me with his lips I got, faintly, from the branch I still held, the sharp fragrance of pepper-trees, the acrid aromatic smell of the new continent.

*****

Next day we both suffered somewhat from the "Fair Maid's" ample beer. We sat tired in our chairs watching the southern tip of Westralia go past. It was a grey day, depressing. Now that Melbourne was settled between us, less than a week away, we were suspended on a single string of impatience. The six days would never pass, never. Meanwhile, here was nothing but leaden sea, driving rain, slumped passengers with red noses lying in deck-chairs, and decks awash with cold wetness.

"I can't stand it," muttered Harry, "let's walk a bit."

We walked round the wet deck: some disagreeable spring in his mind had been touched upon, he told me in detail about his duodenal ulcer, his hæmorrhage. A dreary monologue, fitting the rain. The shrouded figures still sat, rolled like damp cocoons. We looked at our empty chairs and shuddered, skidded once more along the slippery boards, did the complete round once more to the tune of another instalment of the ulcer story. When we came back the other chairs were empty, the other passengers gone.

"Thank heaven!" cried Harry, "those people give me the pip. Christ, I've got a headache! You're looking a bit under the weather, too, old darling."

"I'm tired."

"So'm I. Come and sleep in my cabin this afternoon. There's no one about there."

"Harry—"

"Yes?"

"No, never mind."

How say that the thought of day-time love-making sickened me, brought back to me the sordid vicious filthiness of my weekend in Bloomsbury with John? Would Harry understand? He would not. So that afternoon I went creeping like guilt past the flapping curtains, the half-closed cabin doors. The curtains in his cabin were drawn to: we were not the same creatures there in the damp half-dark, peering oddly, searching one another's faces.

"Let's sleep off our beer. It's nice and quiet here when those blasted kids are having their little rests. We've got to whisper, though: the smoke-room steward's in the bar polishing glasses."

His hand was on my breast. I lay still beneath it, letting the experiment run on.

"Charlotte—Charlotte!"

"What?"

"I want you."

"Harry, not now, not here."

"All right, darling."

"Do you mind ?"

"No—I'd like you less if you'd said 'yes' right away. There are dozens of women who can be got that way, but I hoped you weren't one of them. Is my head too heavy on you?"

"No, I like it. You've got more hair than a man of your age has any right to. I'm very comfy. Let's go to sleep."

Deep breathing silence for perhaps three minutes.

"Charlotte—"

"Yes?"

"I can't sleep like this, so close to you. You'd better go, old darling. Will you come to me to-night?"

"It's so horrid and furtive, creeping along corridors hoping there'll be no stewards about."

"Will you at Melbourne?"

"Yes."

"To-morrow you'll say no and run away from me and look at me as if you hated me."

"I won't, my darling."

"How much do you love me?"

Coquettishly, hating myself for coquetry, I measured half an inch with my two forefingers held between his face and mine. Unsmiling, he stared down at me.

"Look out and see if there's anybody in the corridor, Harry."

"Never mind if there is."

"But I do mind. Please look out and make sure."

He got up and looked out, grumbling gently.

"All right, *chérie*, coast's clear. Just give me a kiss."

The kiss given, away I sped like a wild thing.

It was strange meeting again at tea, seeing him sit there so demurely eating bread and butter, talking to Mrs. Farrell about the Melbourne Cup. The strangeness of it, remembering him as a warm pressing body, a voice in the stuffy half-dark. Not the same man, I thought, smiling falsely, saying: "China, please," to the bending steward. We were both different. How can I sit here and look the same? How can he? Will no one notice? Has no one eyes? But it seemed that no one had. And so now it seemed to me (calmly taking a macaroon, calmly saying "Thank you") that the fumbling incident was above all natural, inevitable. Why had we been born, if not for this? In six days, in Melbourne, two blindly fumbling creatures, fumbling through life, will for one night be blindly and mindlessly happy. So Melbourne was now our Mecca, our Paradise assured. So we said to ourselves, to each other: "Only six days to Melbourne—," "When we get to Melbourne..." and, more rarely, with a newborn chill: "*After* Melbourne..."

Six days passed. We stood on the boat-deck under the bridge watching the sailor by the fo'c'sle send up a rocket for the pilot. It was about eight o'clock, pitch dark, cold and windy. A few lights at the river's mouth, a few lonely sparkles from light-ships and buoys—otherwise there was nothing but dark air, dark water, and dark figures toiling half-in, half-out of a pool of light. Now up she goes, the rocket, hissing and roaring, a clear gas-blue flame rushing triumphantly heavenwards, pausing to take breath, then slowly falling, falling in a stream of brilliant sparks, hissing to a hundred small deaths on the water.

Harry was absorbed and happy. We hung propped close together, his arm around me, neither of us caring what people thought. The wind blew clean through us, making our teeth chatter, whipping up our blood: Harry's big body pressed closer to mine as we leaned over the rail and looked out on the moaning waters. This was the famous Rip, this dark boiling tide seen only as a hiss and a foam by the ship's sides: this was the Rip, beyond lay Melbourne swathed in sooty darkness. Why can't we always stay like this, just here, just so? I wanted to ask Harry: but knew before I spoke that it would be vain. He would not understand. Besides, his mind was now fixed on the pilot's coming, the engineering of the pilot's boat round the *Ceres*'s broad stern, the casting off of the ship's row-boat from the mother ship's side.

"Look, Charlotte, they're bringing her round to make a lee for the dinghy—d'you see?—so that it can be lowered into calm water. See her bows swinging round? Now they've got it down, there, in the light. Jove, that was neat, the way they made a lee and lowered her into it! That was real watermanship!"

Darling Harry, so stirred by watermanship, by the sight of men doing things. I snuggled closer and wished he would forget the boat for long enough to kiss me. But he was much too absorbed. So absorbed that he probably wouldn't notice if I dropped clean out of the circle of his arm, clean into the cold waters below. For the moment I, Charlotte, vividly warm and living, pressed absent-mindedly to his side, simply did not exist. I could fall into the water right now, I thought dreamily, and he wouldn't notice. Which was a humiliating but healthy thought for a woman in love.

The pilot reached the *Ceres*'s side, swung over it on a rope ladder. He was dressed, as all pilots seem to be, in a bowler-hat and dirty raincoat: he looked like a doctor hurrying to a confinement, as he stood under the arc lamp with his little black bag.

"Harry, I'm cold."

"Are you, old darling?"

"I think I'll look at the rest of the Rip from the lounge windows."

"All right, *chérie*, see you there later." And without a pang, he let me go. What it must be like to be married! I thought, stumbling in the dark down the companionway.

What am I doing on this ship, intimate with this oaf? I wondered, sitting dejected in the chintzy lounge, a woman who has shed her male and found to her outrage that he doesn't mind being shed. What am I doing, giving myself to this insensitive large beast? I wallowed for a while in a pleasing sentimental warmth, asking myself this sort of question. All sorts of delightful clichés rambled through my mind as I sat there in deep self-pity. I had almost decided to have no more of this, to tweak myself out of Harry's arms back into my prowling spinsterhood, when Harry's face appeared at the window, red-nipped by the wind. He peered in at all the windows, having a horror of the lounge's feminine smell and stuffiness.

"What on earth are you sitting here all alone for, *chérie*?"

"I was cold."

"Poor little one—by Jove, your hands *are* cold. I'll rub 'em rosy in a trice. Give us a kiss, old darling, I haven't had one for ages."

I kissed him somewhat frostily: I was still Outraged Woman.

"Hi!"

"What's the matter?"

"Don't kiss me as if I weren't there."

So I kissed him as he wanted, outraged woman no longer, but woman with a horrid, humiliating urge to be warm and cuddled.

"To-morrow, eh?" he murmured with his lips on my cheek.

"To-morrow!"

So, to-morrow came. I waited for Harry in the smoke-blue lounge of Mackenzie's Hotel. "There is nothing to be thought of but this present, this living present as warm as a bird's breast between my hands. No more than this night, nothing before it, nothing after," I thought happily, watching the stout men of Melbourne come in. They blew in jauntily on a cold draught from the swing-door between the potted palms. They twitched off their bowler-hats, smacked dust off their trouser-hems, joked with the hall porter, all while their shrewd well-fed eyes roved round the lounge for their meat, their female prey. Then when they had found it, they went through into the hotter, noisier cocktail-bar, padding like grand jungle animals a little past their prime over the soft carpet. There was a great bough of almond blossom artily poised in a blue-and-white jar at the door between the lounges. I laughed to myself seeing the fat ones bend their shoulders, duck their sleek baldish heads, to get under it. If they had had any wit they would have moved the thing. One, blundering gallantly forward to greet a scented blonde, crashed among the blossoms, swore softly, glared and pranced on his heavy way, Geisha-like, with pink petals on his hair.

This was too foolish. Soon all the city fathers would be gracing Mackenzie's Hotel beflowered like Geishas. I thought of Hedda Gabler,[9] of her longing to see at least one man roll home with vine-leaves in his hair. Ah, but I was not Hedda Gabler. I crossed over to the almond-bough and swivelled it round so that the door space was clear.

And going back to my place, impatient that it was I who had to wait for Harry, not he for me, I heard a shrill, self-conscious female voice uttering these remarkable words:

"My dear, it was *sinful* not to tell us anything—why, on my wedding night I—well, anyhow, the window wouldn't open so I couldn't get out that way—but I should of, if I could—They told us *nothing*! I said to mother afterwards: 'Mother,' I said, 'if you'd only *told* me it was like that it wouldn't of been so—I mean, if *that's* what being married means then give me a convent every time,' I said. And mother really had the grace to blush a little, really she did. I think she felt she was a bit to blame and really I reckon she ought to of."

She ought to of, naturally, I reflected, sitting in my dusky corner and regarding the hens as they confided. What veil-peering secrets, what intimate blush-provoking details get shouted by strong-lunged females in hotel lounges! Particularly on the subject of wedding nights, as if that generation, coming through the various crises of gestation, childbirth, motherhood, grandmotherhood, climacteric, had still only that to remember, that first introduction to the innate predatory fieriness of the male.

---

9   The heroine of Henrik Ibsen's 1891 play of the same title.

So mused I, sitting in the lounge of Mackenzie's Hotel on *my* wedding night. For it was that, no less. The Grunewald with Kurt, the hay-hut with my unknown yodelling wanderer, those squalid Bloomsbury lodgings with poor young John—those had been incidents, small inconsiderable milestones soon to be forgotten. But this, this with Harry, was real, solid, sculptured in the round.

Suddenly, without warning, with a sickening suddenness, panic smote me. Panic at the thought of the unknown, the suddenly-to-me-unknown Harry Hobart. Wrapped in panic, smitten hip and thigh by panic, I sat miserable and stared about me. The noises of men talking, men drinking, men clinking glasses, crying: "Here's how! Here's luck! Here's mud in your eye!" to their fellowmen came faintly, muffled by cigarette smoke, from all about me. The lounge air was blue with smoke: through the stale haze I stared across at the smoke-blurred image of my own face, mad Charlotte seeing herself as the image of all insanity. Then, calling "Excuse me" to no one, to no one at all, I rose and wildly fled, scattering an ash-tray as I went, bumping into a thin man who had trod cat-like with a cocktail delicately balanced. Scattering apologies I rushed on, leaving him with bright beads of cocktail spilled at his feet, and a confused affronted face.

In my bedroom I behaved as all women do: locked the door and cast myself upon the bed. Then I remembered it was a bed and flung myself into a chair, staring at the odious thing. It was bland, pale, secret, as all hotel beds impersonally are, innocent as yet of human touch: to-night a snowy bank, to-morrow a rumpled ruin warm with flesh.

I pressed my face into my hands and deliberately thought of Harry as I had seen him that first day: a large coarse man in loudish tweeds, the male brute, the swaggering male who looked (I then had thought) upon all women as acres to be ploughed. Was he really no more than that? And I no more? But straight on the heels of my disgust came Harry as he had tenderly caught me one day as I stumbled down the companionway, tenderly set me upright again: of Harry's face, absorbed, maternal, as he tucked me in his overcoat against the bitter South Atlantic blasts. But could I go on expecting tenderness from him, from anyone, in a world so crazy with disease, misery and well-planned savagery? Perhaps I was mad to expect it, but mad I then would be. Away with the ghoulish confidences: they were wrong. Wedding nights were not all agonies of outrage. We are more also, higher, than cow and bull mating in a field. We are in love—or think so, which is perhaps even better.

So now must I forswear thought, this cold torture by the intellect, and be animal only. This is what I wanted, for this I left Europe, to sink with animal abandonment to pleasure pure and unrefined; to be body, no more than body: above all, dearest bliss of all, to stop thinking.

Now to Harry, poor Harry, perhaps waiting down below, fretting for his cocktail, poor Harry waiting aggrieved in the entrance hall with watch in hand.

"Thought you were never coming, old darling."

"I'm sorry, have you been waiting long?"

"Only half an hour or so."

"I've been listening to two cows talking about their wedding nights."

"What—!"

"Women do, you know. I've been button-holed by more than one on the subject. I don't know what on earth makes them dwell on it so."

And whatever makes them do it, I thought, fondly watching him put away his pink gin, they don't frighten me. There's no frightening me from this.

Harry raised his glass.

"Here's to you, old darling."

"And here's to you, my love."

"Here's to us! I suppose you won't drink anything better than that filthy orange-juice?"

"I will not. It doesn't alter the spirit of the toast. I'm happy to-night, Harry, I want to run all down Collins Street."

"You shall," he answered indulgently, only half hearing me, "you shall."

So outside the hotel we took arms and galloped along like a pair of young horses, kicking up our heels as horses do in April, laughing for pure joy. There was no one to tell us we looked foolish, and we cared not one button. Up the hill we went under the hard electric lights, a stout elderly man and a woman who was certainly no chicken. At the top Harry stopped, out of breath and wheezing. "Wait—here—a second—old darling—I won't—be—long."

He popped from sight into a shop. I watched the crowds go past, happy crowds bent on pleasure, but none so happy as I. He came back in a moment or two looking almost bashful. Tucking my arm under his he slipped a little chemist's package into my pocket.

"Take care of that, *chérie*, eh?"

In Königin Luise's time, I thought as we walked more soberly on, the chaste nosegay, the frilled posy: now, in 1938, the tube of contraceptive. Wooing *à la mode de* 1938, and I pressed his hand, touched by this sudden absurd shyness that made him stare away over the heads of the crowd, sternly and self-consciously staring at nothing at all.

We had a cosy man-chosen dinner at Scott's, laughing a good deal at a little table in a corner. We sat for two hours in a cinema, ravished by Ginger Rogers and Fred Astaire. Because the film was so young, so carefree, my thoughts went back to Kurt and our days in the Grunewald, my own young days. The young Kurt and the young Charlotte were in my mind all evening so that at times I hardly knew if it were the roof of the Alhambra or the beech-tree branches of the Havel above my head. It was all so long ago, surely I could safely speak of it? As we went back along a now silent Collins Street I took Harry's arm.

"Harry, I want to tell you something."

"Tell on, old darling."

"I fell in love when I was twenty—"

"That's a good age."

"Don't interrupt or I can't tell you. I don't think he ever loved me, but we slept together."

"Where?" asked Harry, always practical.

"In the Grunewald—it's a wood by Berlin. Do you mind?"

"Don't be silly—why should I mind? Is that the fellow that married someone else?"

"Yes."

"Well, he was a fool. Give us a kiss, *chérie*."

So I kissed him, right under the lamp, a faintly disappointed woman. Harry had taken my romantic confession as something that might have happened to anyone: so it might, but I did not care to think so. I was piqued, wishing I had never yielded to this silly urge towards unbuttoning. Why had I? The Grunewald incident was over, Kurt, as I knew him then, as dead as mutton, more dead than Bärbel's little memory which sometimes stirred within me. I had no right to try my hand at resurrection.

Lying in bed waiting for Harry, staring at the ceiling which held a great mellow moon of light from the bedside lamp, I thought again of Bärbel. She would be thirteen now, herself almost a woman. Did she look like me? I was vain enough to hope so, since Kurt, except for his eyes, had never been a beauty.

A cat-like scuffling at the door and Harry lumbered round it looking rather flustered.

"Put out that damned light, *chérie*."

He sat on the bed in the dark, fondling my feet.

"Listen, Charlotte."

"Yes?"

"Do you really want me? I mean, it's all very well for me but what about you? It's not too late to say so."

"It's all right, dear heart, I want it."

He bent down and kissed me, full and warm.

"Move over, then."

The comfort, after chilly years, of lying in warm arms, a warm breast pressed on mine. I saw the beech-trees of the Grunewald above me, netting the dark October sky. I put my arms about his neck as I had done so many years before, and whispered: "Kurt!" But it was not Kurt, it was Harry whom I loved. Or did I not? No matter now.

"Harry, be gentle with me, don't be impatient."

"My little dear, I promise I won't hurt you. Not," he amended honestly, "more than I can help."

With Harry at last asleep on my shoulder, a happy man, I saw that I should never know more than this. This was all, the peak, the summit. Perhaps a rather flat summit, with the view not so glorious as has been supposed; but, they say: "There is no more. Why are you not content with this, you craving woman?"

Harry snored in my ear. I smiled, turned so that my breast hollowed a nook for him, and slept.

Later to wake, to find him restlessly turning.

"Move over a little, darling, I've got cramp."

"I can't, the bed's too narrow"—and I laughed softly, thinking of the hotel single-room bed made so chastely narrow for virgins.

Shocked, he implored me to remember the people next door. It was a jarring note. We had loved, had taken our ease of one another, satisfied one another, were now happy—but the people next door must know nothing, the conventions must be honoured, bliss, however sharp, must be hidden. What an odd jumble love is! I had wanted to lose myself, to cry "Take me, I am thine, I have no thought of my own, no corner of my flesh that is not yours." But I couldn't manage it, quite: I had been watchfully aloof. While Harry, who a while since had been blind to everything, now suddenly prattled of the people next door. As if we lived in an aquarium, I thought, moving as best I could while he lumbered against me and slept again.

Pressed up against the wall, I was still aloof and separate. Is this what they can't forgive us, is this the root of the ancient grudge? That even in passion we can be coolly detached, observant. Here in bed they lose their minds, are no more than fumbling animals, while we lie back and experience it all sharply, dispassionately. Even in this last extremity I am still invulnerable. Whatever hurt my body had from lust, whose tool man merely is, I am still inviolate. It is for this, this withdrawal, that they can never forgive us.

I watched the light of late cars, far below in the street, swaying above the curtain-tops across the ceiling, each a pale fan gliding from corner to corner, dropping down the wall. The gentle hiss of car-wheels on the hill, the rasping of gears, the fan-lights across the ceiling: and away in the harbour the hoot of a steamer. Like a cow moaning, like a cow. Perhaps we are in this no more than bull and cow. It is a pretty question: do we, in love, drop down to their level, or do they, mating, soar up to ours? A pretty point, I sleepily thought, moving closer so that Harry's breath came warmly whiskyed on my cheek, a very pretty metaphysical point.

*****

See me next night, once more aboard the old *Ceres*, creeping along the passage to Harry's deck cabin. We have but three nights more, we elderly lovers; and are set on taking what we can before our enchanted ship reaches Sydney. There is a certain thrill (of disgust, if you will) in sneaking thus, chastely dressing-gowned, at dead of night, carrying in my hand a hot-water bottle. Harry's idea. "Bring your hot-water bottle with you, then if you meet anyone you can be looking for a hot-water tap." Dear ingenuous Harry, what a brain! So I creep along dangling the thing ostentatiously, and meet no one. Harry's door is ajar, Harry himself pyjamaed just behind it, ready to lock us in. Here is our little fortress, our snug nest, with port-holes open to the salty air, and no one to hear us now that the Gillespie family has disembarked at Melbourne.

"Charlotte—Charlotte—"

"What is it, silly one?"

"I thought you weren't coming."

"You know, I think this bunk's wider than the bed in the hotel."

"Probably is. But don't spend all night just looking at it."

I laugh, he looks acutely anxious.

"Oh, Harry, let me laugh, there's no one to hear. And if there is, I don't care. Laughing is part of loving: I hate having to do everything solemnly, in whispers."

"You're a silly girl. Now are you comfy or will you have the extra blanket?"

He tucks the blanket in at my back. At once with frightful clearness, I am bending over a strange pram in an Austrian train, tucking in blankets to a baby's back, covering lightly a little face. My God, and I have not yet been punished—there is that to come. Still to come and my lost Bärbel's sleeping face clear before me, clearer than Harry's as he looms above.

In a frenzy of despair, clutching at a last hope of human comfort, I must have yielded in a way which startled him. I clung to him desperately, for my punishment, my Doppelgängerin (who till now, I knew it, had stalked at my shoulder) now pressed close with Bärbel's face.

"Old darling, I really believe you're a passionate woman after all. You were so cool before, almost as if—as if you were watching."

He mumbled at my ear, all barriers down, a man released and drowsy. "God, they're awful, the cold women who lie back like flat fish and say: 'Let's get this over with and go to sleep.' But they say the worst ones to sleep with are the ones who want a child and can't have one."

"Harry, don't, don't!"

"What's up?"

"Nothing."

The universal answer of a woman too deeply hurt for words. Nothing. It's nothing, dear, nothing.

I burst incontinently into tears, crawled upon him desperately, still crying.

Harry, I think, was pleased and flattered by this tempest. His Charlotte was growing from a cool woman, brisk with her tongue, into this warm passionate creature who clung to him like a hot vine and would not be dislodged. That was as it should be, she was behaving at last as a woman should. He clasped me closer and mumbled loving absurdities into my ear, biting the lobe gently. But still I cried and quivered, straining myself to him.

"Hold on, old darling, you're strangling me."

"I'm sorry."

"What's up—nerves?"

"No."

"You'll get used to it," he assured me comfortably. Poor dear Harry, he supposed himself to be the root and source of my emotion. I was reacting to his love-making, behaving exactly as I should, being, for once, pure womanly.

*****

How quickly, once the top is reached, one slithers down on the far side. I had always heard, now I was to know, how a man's interest fades when once a woman has become a habit. Her feelings may still be mounting to the peak, not yet there: slower, more tenacious, less easily satisfied after pure rapacity, she climbs only to find that he has left the summit, and is by now a mere speck in the distance. He would have denied it hotly, but even in our last few days it grew plain that Harry was within sight of satiety. All that he wanted to know of me he knew: boredom would soon set in. No one but a woman taut and nervous would have seen it: to the little world of the *Ceres* we were as before, all was as it had been. Mr. Hobart and Miss Herz came joking down to lunch after a morning spent in their private nook on the boat-deck. Miss Herz and Mr. Hobart vanished from human ken after lunch and came down joking once more, patently well pleased with one another, to tea. Mr. Hobart and Miss Herz sat in the smoke-room before dinner, he drinking, she smoking. (And why does she watch him so? a perceptive woman might have asked. But in the smoke-room, this last night, there was no perceptive woman.) Miss Herz and Mr. Hobart, looking as if they had no care, walk arm in arm around the deck after dinner. Now you may catch them kissing, if you will, in that dark little stretch forward, under the bridge. They always kiss here, under the bridge, after dinner: it is quite automatic.

"Again, Harry!"

"Thought you didn't like being kissed, you humbug!"

"Kiss me again!"

Kiss me again and again, lay me the little following ghost of Bärbel.

"I say, old dear, we'd better be getting on. People will notice, you know, if we stay here too long. And" (an afterthought, this) "I wouldn't for the world have them talking about you."

"Wouldn't you?"

Now the gay conversation, the affected carelessness as we emerge arm-in-arm into the light under the pallid eye of the chief purser sniffing the night air by his little door.

"What are you going to do in Sydney? You never told me much about yourself."

"Oh, find a job of some kind."

"You, a job! Don't make me laugh."

"Of course I'm going to get a job. I must earn my living. I've got some introductions from people in Berlin. Harry, do you know a man called Henry Freudenberg in Sydney?"

"You mean the milk-combine man? Don't you go near him, my girl: he's one of these bloody grasping Jews: he'll have the kidneys out of you before you know it."

"Harry, stop! I'm a Jewess."

"You're what?"

He goggled at me, stopping dead.

"I'm Jewish—didn't you know? But of course you knew."

"How on earth should I know? Not that it makes any difference, of course: I hope I'm as broad-minded as anybody."

It seemed incredible to me that he should not have known. But, indeed, why should he? The name Herz—does it mean anything to an Englishman? I remembered the British officer at Mitzi's wedding: he was just such another innocent. And my looks? To the average Englishman a Jew must have yellow skin, black hair and eyes, hooked nose: he waves his hands fin-like when talking, and always misuses his w's.

"I'm sorry—I never thought of telling you."

"My dear girl, don't apologise. It doesn't matter—why should it? Don't let's think of it again—just enjoy ourselves, on our last night, huh?"

But all that evening he came back to it again and again, as one scratches at a swelling flea-bite.

"Coming to me to-night?"

"If you want me to, Harry."

"Of course I do, old darling. Now look here, you're not worrying about this silly Jew-business again, are you? Don't be such a silly girl—why, in Australia, nobody bothers about that sort of thing at all. You'll find" (with impressement) "that there's *no* feeling of that kind at all.

A man's a man, whether he's a Jew or a Jap, and a woman with your looks and brains is bound to get on all right."

Merci, mon cher! thought I bitterly, smiling with false gratitude at the complacent oaf: not before have I been so casually linked with the Japanese, nor further linked, by implication, with all those coloured folk you British so prettily call "niggers."

We stopped walking and sat in the little veranda by the smoke-room that so often before had harboured us. The atmosphere was resentful, gloomy, yet fond.

"It's this damned gastric trouble again," said Harry, groaning and laying a hand on his waistcoat. "They cut me about like anything last time they operated: I was in a nursing-home for fifteen weeks. I—"

"Yes, you told me."

"I'm sure I didn't tell you this."

I resigned myself, heard it all over again.

"Harry, you ought to be more careful what you eat."

"Not on your life. A short spin and a merry one, that's my motto. What's the use of going on year after year drinking nothing but Benger's Food? I'd rather be dead."

"You don't need to drink Benger's all the time, you could just be reasonably careful."

Heavens, I thought, while he rambled on, we might have been married for years. Husband and wife with nothing in their joint future but two familiar faces, two nauseatingly familiar stomachs.

"Oh, let's walk!"

So we walked. It was a beautiful night, the stars huge, brilliant, threatening, over-ripe southern stars in a thick, dark southern sky.

"D'you remember the first time we walked round here?"

"Yes."

How futile and how dangerous these do-you-remembers! Already the sated mind looks wistfully back to the days when bliss was still to come, was not yet overpast. Already the sated mind yearns back to those happy days when what it now knows was still thrilling, unknown.

We leaned over the rail as we had done a dozen times before.

"*Chérie*, I don't want to lose you. I'd marry you if I could, but a man in my position—"

"I know, Harry."

"You wouldn't live with me if I found a little place?"

The little flat in Melbourne reared its seductive head once more between us. Once more, in a mental flash, I was a happy woman saying: "Yes, Harry!" For indeed it was such a comfortable picture: Charlotte waiting for the footstep she knew so thoroughly, seeing the door of the little flat open, then falling once more into Harry's comfortable arms. The snugness, security and warmth of it to a woman who had never known security! Then forthwith I saw as clearly the other way, myself going on alone, always alone, from country to country in this savage southern hemisphere, this alien stretch: myself lonely, free. But was not woman's freedom, like virginity, made to be sacrificed?

"Harry, I can't tell you now, I must think. Will you give me time to think it over?"

"As long as you like, *chérie*."

"No, I'll tell you to-night. Now I must go and pack: so must you, my dear, if we're docking early to-morrow."

When I had finished packing I sat down and wrote to Tante Lydia. It may have been my fatal leaning towards the dramatic, it may have been the orderly instinct to get things clear: by writing them, I found, one often came to a decision without knowing it, as it were painlessly.

Liebe Tante Lydia!

I met a man on this boat whom I like better than any other. I won't say "love" because you know as well as I that to be in love means nothing until you can look back after years of it and say, "I'm still in love." He is fifty-eight, but very young for it: after all, I'm not a girl. He's married but lives apart from his wife: there's no question of divorce. Tante Lydia, shall I live with him? It looks so easy. We could be happy for six months, perhaps even a year; I can keep him in love long enough for that. I don't want happiness so much as security: perhaps at my age they're the same. But I must be used: I can't go on like this as empty as a rattle with my body idle and my mind spilling on to nothing. I could make him happy for a short while, anyhow: he's a simple soul. I needn't talk about morals: you know better than I that if I feel it right to do this it is right and what other people think is no more relevant. It's the conflict in my own mind I want to resolve, not the doubts in other people's minds about what I choose to do. Can I live with him and still be free? You see, when I am with him I am in love, I guide my life by his. That, I suppose, is slavery, but it's still new enough to be exciting. If I say "no" and go on without him I condemn myself to a loneliness which gets harder as I get older. I daren't think about children, though perhaps this world is kinder to bastards than the old one. But it's such a risk. I don't want to take any more risks. I want to be safe. You don't know how lovely safety looks now I have got my first peep at it.

Dear Tante Lydia, I can see you being bored to death with all this, but I must talk. And I can't to Harry. For him it is all too simple to be talked about. Either I'm content to be his mistress for as long as I can keep him, or I'm not. He can't see that for the women there may be more to it than that: he never will see it. His mind is very male. He can afford a flat with a mistress in it, he's met the woman he fancies for the job, if she says "yes" there's nothing but the actual moving-in to be arranged. Like most men he thinks of every arrangement as being permanent until he himself in a passion decides that it is wholly intolerable and ends it.

But will the woman say "yes?" I really believe he's impatient for the answer, though he's pretty sure he knows what it will be.

You too will know, when you've read as far as this, that I am saying "yes."

*****

There was no melancholy about our love that night. We were beginning, not ending. I had deliberately put away doubt: looking forward, I deliberately saw nothing that was not rosy.

"Harry, Harry, do you really love me?"

"What do you think, old darling?"

It didn't occur to me that now, after a brief three weeks, it was I who asked the question, he who parried it. I lay there content to feel him dropping into sleep, to see his half-sleeping face in the faint starry light that came through the port-hole. He slept so like a baby, so trustful and unwitting: we shall have many nights like these, many gay comradely days. Loneliness can be shelved.

"Charlotte—Charlotte—!"

I woke to feel him leaning over me, fumbling.

"Darling, I'm so sleepy, I want to go on sleeping."

"Charlotte—!"

He choked on a hot tide: it was a hæmorrhage. Blood dribbled on his chest: his ruddy healthy face was drained of it, ghastly in the light of the bedside lamp. I wetted a towel in cold water and wrapped it round him: the choking stopped, he lay back and feebly thanked me. In the corner another bloody towel lay crumpled up, thrown aside.

"Harry—! When did this happen?"

"Never mind, it was only a slight one."

"My dear, why didn't you tell me?"

"I wanted you to come—I wanted this—the two of us—I thought it was going to be our last night."

"All right, don't talk, just lie still. I'll fetch the doctor."

"No, no! Don't do that. I tell you, *chérie*, I'll be all right in a jiffy. This has happened before. Just stay here, don't leave me."

"But, Harry, you must have a doctor."

"No: stay and talk to me, I'll go to my doctor tomorrow, I promise you. It'll be much better than going to this sailor chap. There's some brandy in my flask, old darling: give me some of that."

I sat on the bunk with his hand in mine, sick with fear. It was such a ghastly face lying on the spattered pillow.

"Charlotte, do you know what I'd do if I were really rich?"

"No, dear."

"I'd make you have a child—I'd have enough money to provide for you both. He'd have your chestnut hair and be a champion prize-fighter."

"Red hair and blue eyes," he murmured after a little while, "and a grand little pair of fists."

"What makes you so sure he'd be a boy?"

"I dunno. He'd be a lovely kid, anyway: children of passionate lovers always are."

"Oh, my dear!"

"You're crying."

"Yes, I am."

"I'd no idea," said Harry with a fatuous satisfied expression on his poor pale face, "that you could cry like that."

"Harry, now we must think about you and be sensible. Let me fetch the doctor and get him to make you comfortable."

"You can't—how will you explain being in my cabin?"

"Oh, good heavens, as if that mattered! I—"

"It matters very much, I'm well known in Sydney."

"Oh!"

It was a shock that we were both such egoists, even in calamity. Harry's poor blood might flow, but we must preserve our reputations.

"All right, I'll go back to my cabin if you'll promise to ring for the night steward as soon as I'm gone."

"I'd much rather you stayed here. Look, it's all over, I'm better already. Grand stuff, brandy! Why don't you have some, *chérie*?"

"No, not now. Don't be silly, darling one—just lie still and ring in five minutes when I've had time to get back."

"Kiss me. This isn't going to be serious, Charlotte," he

murmured as I laid my cheek to his. "It won't make any differ-ence to us. I'll be all right as soon as I get ashore to Urquhart: he's a first-rate chap. I'll be all right in the morning."

"Yes, darling."

At my cabin door I paused, waiting. After a heart-rendingly long time, when I was about to rush back to him and damn the scandal, the bell rang. It rang a second time: at the end of the corridor I saw the night steward struggling into his white jacket as he shuffled to the stairs.

On my dressing-table lay the letter to Tante Lydia in its bland envelope. I tore it up and dropped it through the port-hole to the slapping sea beneath. Already the first light was spreading, the water slipped past with a free, rosy, oily glow upon it, the first warming of the sun to a new day.

*****

I parted from Harry in the nursing-home a week later. There he sat, guarded by a simpering nurse redolent of disinfectant.

"Well, Mr. Hobart, how are you?"

"Much better, thanks—this is very nice of you," he said with incredible primness, sitting up there all mauve pyjama and white sheet and slicked-down hair, like a monument to Mother's Good Boy.

"It's nice of you to come and see me," he said again with con-viction gathered in an uneasy pause.

I smiled politely. "I brought you some brown boronias."

"Do you remember—oh, you can't have forgotten already!" cried my panting heart, "how you bought me three bunches of these in Melbourne and made me smell how sweet they were, one large warm hand pressed on the back of my neck to make me sniff closer, get the fuller fragrance?"

Over the boronias our eyes met, mine wild with memory, his stonily sheepish, their clear blue dulled by embarrassment.

"Thank you, thanks!" he muttered.

The nurse smiled too. "How lovely—what a lovely smell! Let me put them in water for you, Mr. Hobart. Now if I leave you alone for a minute you'll remember he's still weak, Miss—Miss Hurts? Don't let him talk too much. The naughty boy," carolled the nurse, officiously flicking at non-existent dust on the sheet, "he does *love* to talk!"

She bustled out, clutching the flowers: and at once Harry flashed on the sickliest smile I had ever seen on any human face.

"Tell me what you've been doing since you landed—what do you think of our Sydney?"

"It's a nice city," I answered politely.

"Yes, isn't it? Isn't it a fine place? New York's got nothing on us when it comes to skyscrapers—*nothing*," he repeated with violent conviction, brushing his moustache up with the swaggering gesture I knew so well.

"Harry—"

"Yes, old darling?" and half reluctantly his hand crept out from the sheet to meet mine.

"Harry, it's all right, I'll never give you away!" I wanted to reassure him: but instead I remarked: "I'm off to New Zealand on Friday."

"New Zealand! Well, you *are* a fast traveller. You'll like New Zealand, it's a fine country, a grand fishing country. I was up at Taupo once with a coupla fellows—Monty James who was with me in Kalgoorlie and poor Basset who shot himself for a Frenchwoman—you should have seen the fish we got! Why, one day—"

He told me the story again. I, who had heard it twice already, listened with a sickened heart to the familiar rambling tale, watched his familiar face as he relentlessly forged ahead. When its pointless conclusion was reached I laughed as heartily as ever, avoiding his eye as I laughed. Indeed, it was all over now. I was no more to him than an embarrassment, a visitor, a bringer of brown boronias.

310

The nurse came back sniffing effusively at the flowers in a vile mauve vase.

"There—aren't they too sweet! Aren't you the lucky man to have so many visitors and so many flowers! Look, Miss Hurtch, at what he's had already today. Mrs. Hobart brought him these gorgeous carnations, and young Mrs. Tommy Hobart brought him these daffs, and—"

"I must go—really, I've stayed too long as it is. I mustn't tire you. Have I tired you?"

I looked at him directly, challenging him to meet my eye. For one bitter second the familiar blue flashed in them again as he looked up at me from the bed, holding out (too readily—had I really bored him so much?) a hand to shake. Then the eyes clouded over, once more the polite smile glazed his face, he became once more poor old Harry Hobart who'd had that nasty hæmorrhage, had had to lie up after it, was now getting better, thank you, and saying good-bye with relief to yet another of his female visitors. One of those women he'd met on the boat coming out: old Harry was really rather taken with her. These little affairs on board ship: pretty hot while the going's good, you know—but of course they don't mean a thing really.

As I walked away from the hospital in the dull grey heat of a Sydney day I argued with him still, argued in my mind with the common-sensical male. "What are you grumbling at?" he asked. "You said yourself it was just another shipboard flirtation."

"Yes, I know. But—"

"But what? My God, you women are unreasonable. When I told you I loved you, you laughed and said: 'Yes, till we get to Sydney.' Now we've got to Sydney, it's all over—and you're girding at me because I take you at your word."

"I know, Harry, I know."

"We had a grand time together—surely you didn't expect it to last?"

"In my heart I believe I did."

"Well, of all the silly little fools! A woman of your age—!"

And so on, *ad infinitum*, logic against sentiment. Realism against the romantic fallacy of all womankind, that love will last unaltered for their unalterable joy.

Chapter 8
Siege and Fall

Beginning now the last full chapter, looking back from the garden of the Welquik Nursing Home (yes, I am recovering, I can write now in the garden) I see my life as no evenly flowing stream but as a jerky rush of incidents, remembered faces, voices that remain, all tied together by the one thread of Charlotte Herz like stray bits of paper on a kite-tail. Looking back to that September of 1937 with Harry lost, myself making yet another start, I think: Truly this is a portrait of a woman hunting. Hunting for some anchor which would weight her to one place, for some interest (Oh, hopeless hunt!) which would keep her content to stay there. This curse, this restlessness, this fugitive Jewish fate, had plucked me from one land to set me, faintly hopeful of better things, in another. And then that other, too, proved hopeless and off I went again hunting for my peace. Germany had not had it, nor England, nor South Africa. Australia was only a blur in the mind, a night's boredom in a Perth hotel, a night's brief fearful joy in another hotel in Melbourne: Sydney finally as a background to despair. Into that background I had seen vanish from my port-hole on the berthed *Ceres* a blanketed shape on a stretcher that was Harry lost, Harry gone forever, since the Harry I saw later in the nursing-home was no concern of mine.

Now, in a last despairing throw, New Zealand. And some change in Charlotte, too, to make her from within less impossible. As in September, 1937, I walked alone on the *Awatea*'s deck with the ghost of Harry's arm under mine growing chillier every minute, I wondered what it was that made my discontent. A contempt of my fellows, perhaps: I see too deep into them. Or a still naïve and adolescent faith in the ultimate perfect relationship, the perfect mate. Small day-to-day relations are easy enough—one can always be charming—but when it comes to fitting this fierce ego Charlotte Herz to another ego equally tigerish, then, then, there is nothing, no more than frustration. And yet, I thought, I wanted my ego yoked with another: I had no pride in being solitary. But if not solitary, what was I? A creature fumbling, unsure, drably experimental, forever trying out the mould of this one or of that one: forever unfitting, unsatisfied, chagrined. At each new place, in each new land, I had said: "Here! Here is what I seek." And there had been a day or two of happiness, planning life again. Then, drearily regular as morning sickness in a pregnant woman, the knowledge that here was not what I sought, I must go forth and look again. Why could I not have endured South Africa, Kraanvlei for a few months, a year or two, then marriage with a comfortable farmer, and a little folding of the hands to sleep, to the good, earthy sleep of the intellect women enjoy in that fruitful land? Why not? Why this fastidious loathing of man as a husband? My Jewish ancestresses had not been so pernickety, had not looked too hard at the men to whom their fathers married them. Each was content to find him sober, industrious, moderately wealthy, with the hope of more, likely to be a tolerable father to the sons they all prayed for. So the marriage portion was settled, the marriage contract drawn up, another marriage (surely the most desperate of adventures) common-sensically and prosaically begun. Why should I, having so much less to give, demand more than they? My answer to this had been Australia, the search renewed: and now Australia, briefly tried and discarded, was ebbing away westwards over the choppy waters of the Tasman Sea.

And Mrs. Wyatt's new nursery governess, neglecting her charge, strode furiously about the deck in the cold sunset air while all around her normal people, normal satisfied comfortable people, wrestled good-humouredly with bow-ties, sequinned gowns, tight evening shoes, in the various state-rooms. As I walked by the windows I saw this nightly human drama: here a solitary male holding up a dress shirt, wondering if it would do for another night: there a young girl callowly eyeing her new rouge-pot; now a corseted dowager, bulging over the top of her armour-plating, petulantly poking a comb through the greasy rat-tail of hair on her shoulders. And from the final window, the end state-room, a fierce hot "Blast!" as I went by, something bright shooting through the window to tinkle at my feet.

"I say, that's my collar-stud!"

I gave it to him, too absorbed for any polite smiles.

"Thanks awfully. The damn' thing leapt clean out of my hand. Lucky you were passing, or it might—"

But his words fell on air alone, for I had gone on: I was not interested in his collar-studs and their habits. Oh, Harry, Harry, at this time you and I watched the sun go, leaning together over a rail like this: and then parted briefly to meet again in the smoke-room, rosy with warm sea-baths; to smoke and drink till dinner-time, mindlessly content with one another.

Such wistful mooning, I scornfully thought, does no one good. And I went to my cabin to see if little Bubbles slept. For the next four days *in loco parentis* to little Bubbles, I bent now over the cot lashed to the spare bunk. He opened one eye mistrustfully, as if to venture both at once would be too hazardous; we studied one another for a full minute, cautious, non-committal, two people who had to make the best of one another for some time to come. Then standing suddenly in his cot, still tottering in a half-sleep, he pushed me away. The effort, and a lurch of the ship, sent him rocking back to his pillow. There he sat, two fingers in his mouth, eyeing me wrathfully.

I dressed for dinner, deeply depressed by the thought of tending children once more for a living. But luck was with me in the job: I approached New Zealand as an employee, no longer as a pleading emigrant. Not many could do thus. How sickened I had been, how affronted by the state of my fellow Jews in Sydney. In the new ghetto, in Darlinghurst and King's Cross, I watched the dark crowds of faces familiar by their race go surging past, dark faces that were so racially familiar, the faces of my own family almost. Faces that should have been alive, vibrant, and were yet pallid, grim in resignation. Why should they be resigned, in heaven's name? Why were they not happy? Were they not the lucky ones, the fortunates, to be here in God's country, free from Nazi foulness? All this is true: they are fortunate, yet still unhappy. Look at my father's cousins, the Ludwig Herzes, with whom I stayed, whom I mercilessly watched. Happy Herzes! They had in Potts Point a neat bright apartment looking over that heavenly water of the harbour—a flat which was a modest collection of little pale bedroom-cubes, a balcony living-room, a kitchen brilliant with tiles and chromium. Papa Herz, my Onkel Ludwig, was now no longer a successful lawyer; he bid fair, beginning afresh at sixty-one, to be just as successful a hawker of women's most intimate toiletries, strange little packages, discreetly and seductively wrapped, for which women or their complaisant men friends ask in whispers, in chemists' shops. A brother in Budapest had bequeathed him the first recipe, native talent had done the rest. With the help of a second cousin in Melbourne who compounded the things and an unrelated Jew from Warsaw who designed the wrappers, Papa Herz was in the way of becoming a benefactor to womankind. Mama Herz meanwhile sold corsets, herself stout but streamlined in black satin, in David Jones's store. She, who had had in Wien a modest salon for lesser wits, who had known Thomas Mann, been loved by Manfred Reichenbach the poet, and played duets with the old Brahms! Now Tante Rosa brought three pounds ten home every Friday to the flat in Potts Point, and was on all sides accounted a lucky woman. And Lotte, the Herz daughter, the hope of the Herzes? She, clever one, had smuggled from Wien a dozen hat-blocks given her by a Jewish lover who then flung himself, the successful milliner, from a top storey to the horrid concrete of the Kärntnerstrasse: with these as her stock in trade Lotte had in Sydney gone into partnership with another Wienerin, employed two ripe young Jewesses as extra hands, and modestly throve in a tiny hat salon on the top of the State building. Lotte now had nothing in life to yearn for but a husband: and that, in a Potts Point teeming with fellow refugees, should be easy enough. But was Lotte happy with her hats, was Mama content with her corsets, was Papa satisfied with his contraceptives? Not she, not he, not they. Rootless, restless, in essence homeless, they inhabited their new land, grimly set teeth into their new jobs, and endlessly talked of the Austria they had left. They were all three harassed by the sick nostalgia, the despairing *Heimweh* which attacks Germany's sons and daughters, be they Jew or Gentile, when they are away from home. The longing, in a parched brilliant land like this Australia, for Germany's meadows and dark cold woods, for the running of a brook through Alpine grass—here, even in mountains, there is no running water—for the farm-houses, thick, mellow and solid in their yards, yards which are ankle-deep in the dung of many years. More than anything, perhaps, these Jews who in Austria had despised the peasants, now passionately longed to see peasant life about them. The heart ached to see a narrow dusty road edged with wild cherry trees, with granite stumps to mark the field boundaries: and, beyond, the neat squared potato-fields, corn-fields, bean-fields in which stooping figures toil. Men in faded blue shirts, women in worn old black skirts and red blouses, tend the earth with infinite care: it is their life. Above, larks trill in a blueness that is tender (here, in Australia, it is scornfully hard): the ripe dark cherries drop into the dust, starring the dazzling dust with blood-dark juice. A peasant trundles along in the broiling sun on an old bicycle, a scythe dangling dangerously over his shoulder, and yodels, as he goes, to the figures in the field who straighten, wave, yodel again, and bend once more to earth. With this in their hearts, the memory of a land which in spite of Hitler is still theirs, the Ludwig Herzes looked at Australia, at New South Wales: with the memory green in my mind, I and the Ludwig Herzes took an extremely costly, efficiently organised trip to the Bulli Pass. We drove, that is, out of the clang of the city into the fearsome bush. Mile upon mile the green stuff stretched, featureless, monotonous, appallingly old. Mile upon mile, hundreds of miles upon hundreds of miles, of a green that is neither fresh nor young, no, never, not even at the changing of the seasons: a green that is forever abominably the same. Seated in padded luxury in a sight-seeing coach we exclaimed over such beauties as we knew needed exclamation, such as the guide-book told us were admirable. "Isn't it lovely?" we all cried, ecstatic: while our eyes, with appalling honesty, said: "Isn't this frightful in the full sense of the word, the old sense: isn't this the most frightful thing we have yet, any of us, encountered?" Which it was. So we returned, bouncing pneumatically, at the end of the day to the noise of the city, sped in all haste to the more familiar sounds of Potts Point.

So the Herzes were not happy. It was not only the bush which appalled them. They were, and knew it, a small troop of men hostilely surrounded, facing whichever way they turn a bristle of bayonets, the sinister glint of guns. Among this they recognised, with sick hearts, the all too familiar faces of their fellow Jews. For this also Hitler's victims have to fight: the furious resentment, the hot fear, of those Jews who are by now Australians, their roots securely in Australian soil, their jobs, their reputations, now threatened by these swarming refugees. They see, the Australian Jews, a mounting tide of anti-Semitism in the land they have till now found free from such: they read disturbing little newspaper paragraphs about immigrant Jews who have broken their bond, betrayed their guarantors: they read indignant letters about sweated alien labour, back-yard factories and the like. Rooted as they thought securely, as they thought now solid Australian citizens, these old established Jews feel the rock under them quiver, see splits appear. At their very feet the rats nibble, the rabble of newly-come Jewish rats. And how they swarm, the newly-comes! Up and down the William Street hill, along the already crowded pavements of King's Cross, in and out of the delicatessen stores along Darlinghurst Road—in hordes of four and five, in close clusters of three, in intimate arm-linked couples, the Jews swarm. The perfume of the women lies heavy on the air; the cigar-smoke of the men adds a headier flavour. The air smells of Jewry, the air hums with it. And everywhere the German voice, the Jewish voice, dropping like ripe fruit among the harshnesses of the Australian whine. No wonder Australian Jews, Australian Gentiles, are affronted by this invasion: no wonder the invaders, escaped from one horror, walk now with horror in their eyes cautiously among the hostile antipodean natives.

Meanwhile, Onkel Ludwig sells his gay packages, Tante Rosa her peach silk corsetries, Lotte her insouciant little hats. They madly sell, they madly spend: racial thrift was cast overboard in mid-Pacific, somewhere between Honolulu and Suva: now they will spend all, have a good time, while the chance is theirs. It will not, they think, be theirs for long. Already war can be sniffed in the air coming rotten from Europe: already the horrors of intern-ment close, like some dark single yew, the avenue my poor Jewish cousins have just found.

"We shall all be interned," says Onkel Ludwig, gloomily put-ting down his *Sydney Herald*. "There's war coming and we shall all be interned."

"From concentration camp to internment camp," think I somewhat flippantly, yet knowing that the poor man says truth. They cannot leave us loose, we the alien rats newly come from a country at war (or soon, surely, to be at war) with their Empire. We are worse than the rats who carry bubonic plague: we must be isolated.

So, at any rate, said Onkel Ludwig.

"Don't be so pessimistic, Onkel."

"I can't be anything else, *meine Liebe*. It's all right for you. You're a woman and can marry an Aussie and make yourself Aus-sie too. That's what you must do, and do it quickly. But for God's sake don't marry a Jew: you might as well fling yourself over the Gap right now as do that. Marrying ought to be easy, with your looks. I could arrange for you to meet a few decent Gentiles, I think: there are some good bureaux here."

Shades of Berta and Brigitta, my young days on the Luisen-ufer. Courteously I thanked my Onkel Ludwig, courteously I said "No" to his Gentiles. How many people burned, I wondered, with the desire to see Charlotte married? All, it seemed. And Charlotte herself, stunned cold by the impact of the affair with Harry, was beginning to be of like mind. I could not forever, I knew, go on hanging up my hat on strange pegs: I must have one of my own, a wall at any rate that I knew to be mine. So quite deliberately, now, I looked for what I wanted—security. To a Jewess, that is but another word for husband. Seeing clearly only Harry's remembered countenance, I yet searched every male face I saw for traces of the Good Husband. Scenting my search, romantically helpful, my

Tante Rosa in Sydney egged me on. When it became plain that I had not, in Sydney, found what I sought, she pinned her eager hopes to the boat, to New Zealand now teeming, surely, with Good Husbands for Charlotte.

"You'll meet someone on the boat, *Liebling*," said Tante Rosa archly to me on parting. But, once more at sea, remembering other seas, other starry nights, I was dogged that first night only by Harry's ghost. No man meant anything to me, I vowed, as I wandered that first night alone about the smart *Awatea*.

The young man of the collar-stud, however, seeming to think no further introduction needed, broke blithely in on my sad after-dinner reverie. He could not possibly be English, I thought, as he talked to me over execrable coffee in the lounge. This easiness, this certainty that he was acceptable to any female, could only be colonial. Dishing out the usual banalities, a Charlotte sick to death of being sociable yet mechanically so because she could not help it, I watched him as he talked. He seemed a nice young man. Not so young, either: about thirty-five, I thought, seeing one of his well-made hands go time and time again, furtively, to a pale spot of baldness on the crown of his dark head. Thirty-five, and conscious of the years going, as I knew them to be going, on to a probable nothingness, an old age empty of any memories that brought richness in the remembering. Poor old young man, I thought, agreeing in a sprightly chatty manner that Sydney was a nice place—poor old young man so conscious of his pale bald patch, his urgent need to keep young, his middle age so loomingly, so unpleasantly close. His name, he told me, was Adrian Lovat: he lectured in German at Auckland University: he had never been near Germany nor, indeed, farther north than Suva: he would like to travel more, but spent, somehow, all his vacations in Sydney or the Islands. I could see that the idea of a really foreign land, an alien country on the other side of the as yet untraversed Equator, fascinated and appalled him: he was one of those travellers who wistfully travel in the fancy only, timidly refuse the real adventure of travel. All the same, I found him charming, as he meant me to: he found me charming, as he was meant to do. We parted in a gay friendly way, the young man pouring out, as he left me, a positive bucketful of charm in a manner so accomplished that I knew him to be no novice at the game. But my role had better be that of novice, I decided, if I wanted to keep this Adrian as companion on the voyage, a spiritual buffer against the sharp memory of Harry: and this Adrian was not the type of man who likes his women too clever. If they knew more than he, they had better hide the fact.

So I played yet another role; we got on nicely together, Adrian Lovat and I. Our days (with painful intervals of tending Bubbles) passed in a suave easy manner, most companionable. Our days were pleasant: my nights were hellish. For the blow of losing Harry had fallen suddenly: the wound developed slowly like a bruise, blue, fatal, sinister, darkening under a sensitive skin, spreading, becoming not blue but an ominous thunderous green, then gangrenous yellow at the edges, and spotted with smaller red where the outraged blood had clotted. Nothing, not my loss of Kurt, of Bärbel (so self-inflicted, stormily impetuous, bitterly regretted), not the long-drawn-out squalor of John's seduction had hurt me as this loss of my warm, vital, irritating Harry now hurt as I left him (or he left me—oh, vanity, there's your deepest wound!) and was transported a captive, stricken dumb with grief, to another new land whose newness brought no excitement, no hope. God, how I suffered! At night (there were but four of them, they were endless) I lay awake watching the shift of reflected water pale, on the studded steel of the cabin, hearing the glass-muffled roar of cold, inhuman water, the occasional tramp of feet unknown and therefore also inhuman, the rare ringing of a bell, the lackadaisical answer of a steward thereto. Above all, through all, the steady infantile click-click of Bubbles' breathing—Bubbles, a baby, a mind, though living, yet wholly unresponsive to my own, utterly cold in sympathy or succour. This horrible little thing, this Bubbles, lived, moved, yelled, ate, digested, went through all our common functions, yet was as alien to me, as useless, as exasperating as a little lizard. As if I bedded nightly, seeking therefrom comfort, with a little gila lizard cold-blooded from the hot strange Arizona desert, or with a dugong, a sea-cow even more disgustingly cold. So ghastly remote, so far away, was little Bubbles, my charge, my sleeping companion, as I lay awake dumbly mourning Harry. Not altogether dumbly: at times there welled up in me a sorrow unbearable, and I groaned, moaned, wept; beating the pillow, turning my hot head this way and that, scarifying the *Awatea's* linen with scalding tears, writhed in an agony that was unstilled by writhing, and wept the more in that I knew weeping to be vain, and sorrowed the more over my impotent stricken self.

Meanwhile Bubbles innocently slept, innocently woke to demand the pottie, innocently eased himself, was mechanically put back to bed, and was at once asleep again. Meanwhile the sea heartlessly swished as if no hearts suffered, the foreign footsteps battered on the deck above my head, the night bells imperiously rang, life went most heartlessly on to another day, another wholly heartless dawn which knew nothing, and cared nothing, about poor Charlotte. Sick with self-pity (and what is sorrow more than this?) Charlotte dozed towards dawn and woke greyly to another day. Another day of struggle, of blank mechanical duty, of more chats with other governesses, of a brightening interest, towards noon, in the prospect of a chat with the young Mr. Lovat who never, he solemnly told me, got up before twelve o'clock. So there there *was* something to my afternoons: the sun of young Mr. Lovat's kindness was regularly shed from the time of the before-lunch cocktail till late at night. But no walking on starlit boat-decks with this man: he shivered at sundown, vowed cold nights would be the death of him, and never stirred from the cosy thickness of the smoke-room air till it was time for bed.

On the last night, still (but perhaps, a horrid thought, less poignantly) mourning Harry, my dramatic Jewish mind was suddenly illuminated, dumbfounded, by a picture of myself wedded to this Adrian. Oh, Harry! My mind moaned, by now mechanically, as I mechanically sobbed into my pillow: and at once echo replied, not "Harry," as it should, but "Adrian," as it certainly should not. So perfidious is the female mind, so instinctive in perfidy, that I could think the two names in one moment and feel only a faint guilt. If pursuit of Adrian, his ultimate, inevitable capture (since what man pursued by Charlotte had ever stayed long at large?) would still this nagging ache for Harry, then pursued Adrian should be! "And suddenly there was a great light"—where had I read that? Had I heard it perhaps in London, in the fashionable false church to which long ago my fashionable false Aunt Naomi Flower had driven me?—and suddenly there was a great light which showed me Charlotte, not mourning forever (as she picturesquely should) for warm Harry, but triumphantly manacled to chilly Adrian. It was all so simple. The young man's interest in me, his casual sophisticated interest in a woman, handsome, piquantly foreign, ripely mature, was the string to which the rope, the hawser, the cable should be successively tied. And at the end of the cable, a triumphant Charlotte, Mrs. Adrian Lovat. "Marry an Aussie, *meine Liebe*, marry an Aussie as fast as possible and make yourself safe," said Onkel Ludwig's voice once more. Well, Adrian was no Aussie (I saw his fastidious mouth grimace, his fastidious hands instinctively curl at the idea), but he was safe. Once caught, he would be my safety.

As if I had known this for years, as if the prospect of safety in Adrian had been with me since girlhood, I abruptly ceased struggling over Harry, and to the tune of Bubbles' snores planned my campaign. To-morrow, as early as to-morrow afternoon (said the captain, that day charmingly interrogated by charming Charlotte on the boat-deck), we should dock in Auckland. There, unless charming Charlotte used her wits, Adrian would cease to spell safety, would be merely a nice man met on the boat, no more, and no use. The little flame of interest must be fed, quickly and most skilfully fed.

Thank God, I thought, for this swift sure female wit so sharpened by many a campaign, never allowed to rust even in victory. Part of the way I knew instinctively, as one knows a remembered path which has often led to pleasure: only part had yet to be mapped out by a nimble mind made sharper still by sleeplessness and the coming of dawn.

Impossible to put into words the subtle undermining, the tenuous wizardry, the frail insidious flattery, by which a woman skilled in such convinces a man (without, naturally, his regarding it as anything but his own conviction) that he would like to see her again. Even (the bottomlessly false Eve!) that she would be willing to see him again. Impossible to pin anything so smoke-like, wispy, on to solid paper, bludgeon it into writing. Enough that after a whole day's cunning (and the *Awatea* helped by docking not in the afternoon but late that night) Adrian Lovat was pledged to "see something" (odd Anglo-Saxon phrase!) of Charlotte in Auckland. A hearty hand-grip at parting, the gleam of a knowing wink in grey-blue Lovat eyes, a demure half-promise in the bluer eyes of scheming Charlotte, and the thing was done. Finally done, moreover, under the snub, slightly black-headed nose of Mrs. Wyatt, who met her Bubbles and his new governess on the wharf. Desperate military engagement, this: Charlotte at one and the same time making Adrian's gay "I'll be seeing you" sound to him a pledge, to Mrs. Wyatt no more than the casual parting of a stray young man from the governess she so patently hoped would not stray. I achieved it; exhausted, the female Napoleon glowing with the victory of Montenotte, I turned my forces to Milesimo. For Mrs. Wyatt must not be made at once suspicious: I became, therefore, as soon as Adrian's debonair figure had vanished, no longer a woman charming, to be seen again, but a woman trustfully grateful to, determined to do her duty by, the kind Mrs. Wyatt who had rescued her from the Nazis by engaging her as Little Bubbles' fond guardian. A titanic task which left me shredded, unable for one night more to sleep, but triumphant.

Triumphant, that is, until those nasty hours of early morning when doubt becomes gigantic, hope microscopic. Then Charlotte wept again, no longer for herself abandoned by Harry, but for herself about to be abandoned by Adrian. Suppose he should forget? Suppose he should remember, see me again, find me not what he had yesterday so patently hoped, and vanish as men do, skilfully, beyond the wistful horizon of a woman's grasp? Suppose anything, everything that is dismal: at this time of morning when the night grows cold as forgotten love, all that can be supposed is catastrophic. So once again I wept and once again Bubbles abominably snored: while next door in the strange hotel strange Mrs. Wyatt equally, but more loudly, proclaimed that she slept while I could not.

I woke next morning after an hour's sleep to a wide stretch of harbour as milkily opalescent as my remembered Isar at München, to sun, and fresh wind, and hope blowing through an open window. Lovely harbour, so strangely pastel-shaded, so delicately fresh, so new: and lovely hope, new since last night, sharply welcome as spring. So I leapt from my bed, performed briskly, cheerfully, as Mrs. Wyatt's new governess ("Such a nice girl—what a piece of luck!") all morning, most cheerfully endured Bubbles even when he whined; and cheerfully leapt to the telephone, innocent of guile, when Mrs. Wyatt, with suspicion dawning once again, told me that a Mr. Lovat wanted to speak to me.

"Don't be long, Miss Hurts," she added (suspicion sharpening her polite voice), "because I want you to get Bubbles ready to go with me before the shops shut."

Miss Hurts was not long.

"Hullo!" said Adrian's voice.

"Hullo!" (quite non-committal).

"Remember me?"

"Y—yes."

"Not quite sure?"

"Of course!"

"Good. What about to-night?"

"I don't know if I—"

"Oh yes, you can. Tell her I'm your cousin, or your stepfather's best friend, or your stepmother's gigolo—I don't mind which. I'll call for you at seven."

"Do. I'll try to be ready."

"You *will* be ready. Good—o! Seven o'clock. I'll get the girl to ring you from the lounge when I come in."

"Good-bye."

And Miss Hurts, pink-cheeked, puts the receiver down a second before he does (sound strategy, this!) and girds up her loins to do battle with Mrs. Wyatt for the evening's bliss.

I learnt all about Dorothy Wyatt in that ten-minute interview. Married an unremembered number of disappointing years, wearily a mother, sexually outraged and wholly unsatisfied, bitterly jealous (as drearily married women are) of an unmarried woman still sexually free, yet gloating (as drearily married women do) over the prospect of what this one, the still untethered, has yet to endure from sex, and bitterly envious, too, of the attraction this very untetheredness of the spinster has for men. So Dorothy Wyatt, politely listening to my bright girlish plea for an evening off, as politely refusing the boon. So Dorothy Wyatt, getting faintly purple in the cheeks as I persisted, more sharply replying that it was impossible, losing bit by bit her courtesy, her very English manners.

And suddenly, watching her grow purple, seeing her mind so meanly at work, so nourished on mean jealousies, I glimpsed my way out. I collapsed suddenly, dropped my eyes, murmured: "Yes, Mrs. Wyatt, I quite see, I'm sorry I bothered you," in answer to her sharp "I'm surprised, Miss Hurts, that you should even consider leaving me to put Bubbles to bed this evening."

There was then silence. She was faintly flabbergasted, winded by my collapse. Then, in a kinder tone: "You'd better telephone this Mr.—ah—ah—Lovell at once and tell him you can't go."

"I don't know where to find him," faltered I, still with my eyes on the ground, on the stubs of Mrs. Wyatt's broad ghillie shoes, so unimaginatively English.

"Oh!"

A silence, while I silently but powerfully suggested to Mrs. Wyatt that it was her turn next. Powerful is the suggestion which a headstrong woman can bring to bear (not a word spoken, not a look exchanged) on the mind of a woman less strong-willed, more unhappy perhaps or merely emotionally tired! At the end of a pause which racked her nerves hardly more than my own, I raised hypnotic eyes and Mrs. Wyatt spoke.

"Would you—perhaps I *have* been a little—would it be easier for you if I spoke to Mr.—er—when he arrives?"

"Oh please, Mrs. Wyatt, that *would* be kind!" The simple Charlotte, no longer thirty-five, a woman ripe and therefore challenging Dorothy Wyatt's ripeness, but an innocent green harmless twenty-five, regards her employer with eyes in which the dew of gratitude already glistens.

"He'll be in the lounge about seven," I added softly, folding up a little blouse of Bubbles' tenderly, as if I wished for no better task to the end of my days.

He was there, so was Mrs. Wyatt. I never knew what happened but imagination supplied the scene. Adrian, self-willed and made more so by obstacle, turning the undimmed headlight of his charm on Dorothy Wyatt who, sexually titillated by the odd self-possessed young man, advanced upon him in the nasty role of a dragon, a gorgon guardian of governesses. And charm, like Hitler, winning another bloodless victory. No, I did not go out with Adrian that night, I did far better: I met him, with Mrs. Wyatt and Bubbles, at Court's Restaurant for morning tea next day. Mrs. Wyatt, leaving us half-way through the feast, leaving us to our walnut bread and assorted indigestible savouries, gave me one coy backward glance over Bubbles' head, a friendly glance. In Dorothy Wyatt's unimaginative female head jealousy, curiosity, a great desire to be well thought of, had had an odd three-cornered battle in which jealousy had been utterly routed by the sudden alliance of the other two. She was now curious to watch romance budding, she was most anxious to be thought a nice woman by that charming young Mr. Lovat: and so here were Adrian and I, looking down on Auckland Harbour from the heights of Karangahape Road, at last tête-à-tête on terra firma.

No need to detail what passed, how we talked, how parted. I spun my web: the fly, half-knowing that I spun, and why, still wanted, when he left, to see more of me. To-morrow the Wyatt troupe took service-car to the Wyatt home, Te Pohutu: not the next day, he was too busy, but at the weekend Mr. Lovat would also take the road to the Waikato (in his own car—my heart lifted at the words), to see how Mrs. Wyatt's new governess did in her strange new home. Victory, a victory she had not dared to dream of, for the new governess, that odd yet somehow strangely beguiling Jewish Miss Hurts. So Miss Hurts parted from Mr. Lovat at the bottom of George Court's lift and went, delicately picking George Court's walnut bread out of her teeth, to rejoin Mrs. Wyatt. "So long, be good!" he had cried at parting, and she, brightly: "Oh, what a thing to wish on a woman—good-bye!" Now brightly grateful, charmingly willing to help, I speed towards Mrs. Wyatt: the rival in sex replaced in Dorothy Wyatt's mind (at any rate for the moment) by Miss Hurts the new governess, who seems a *really* nice girl, though foreign.

So, we select play-suits for Bubbles, since summer is coming and who knows when we may be in town again. Dear little Bubbles, already whining with weariness, drags on his mother's hand.

"Let me take Bubbles, Mrs. Wyatt: you must be tired."

"Thank you, Miss Hurts, I should be glad. Did you enjoy your first morning tea in Auckland?"

"Oh, yes, Mrs. Wyatt, thank you." (Blast this gratitude, this voice dripping with it as butter drips from overloaded toast—but how useful, how devilishly useful, can assumed gratitude be to a woman who has won one battle and ruthlessly means to win many more!)

Now the play-suits, and the impassioned discussion as to whether yellow or blue suits Bubbles best (neither suits him in the slightest, but let that pass), and Mrs. Wyatt and Miss Hurts, a few hours earlier mortal enemies glaring at one another over a river of jealousy, now friends, cronies, warm with comradeship, soon (unless my instinct be at fault) to be Dorothy and Charlotte to one another, soul-mates.

*****

Now, play-suits and other matters being settled, to Te Pohutu, the home of the Wyatts. My home for how many years, oh, Lord? thought poor Charlotte, entering it for the first time with young Bubbles, hot and sticky from the long drive, clinging like a discarded lollipop to her hand. It had a look, that house, not of welcoming me but of accepting me, churlishly, resignedly, for the next half-century at least. It was old, ramshackly old, and it lay as if flattened in a grove of enormous mixed trees, gums and macrocapas and high glossy-leaved magnolias. You reached it by an avenue of chestnuts, stunted chestnuts thickly planted and now, in September, struggling once more after a brief rest into weedy leaf. The gums, native to this strange, non-European soil, rioted: the trees brought in by home-sick Scots and Englishmen some fifty years ago achieved no more than a weedy half-life, finding the growing pace too swift for their bewildered caution. Only the weeping willows at the back of Te Pohutu over the washing lines and the dog-kennels were as luxuriant as the gem-green tree ferns, rosetting round the wide lawn. As for the house, that was entirely native. A veranda straggled around two sides of it, and like it was wooden, with a curved corrugated-iron roof once painted red and now a faint drained pink, curving over like a disapproving lip. Some native creeper scrambled over its hideous tinnyness on the eastern side: looking dismayed from my window that first afternoon I saw a vista of ribbed iron, edged with this herbage, littered with hair-combings, cigarette-packets, burnt-out matches, and the impertinent bright pink caps for Bubbles' pistol. The whole house, inside and out, had an insolent untidiness, a colonial don't-care untidiness, which I hated so much that I could never simply ignore it. It had hit me first in Fremantle, this native disorder: corrugated-iron roofing carelessly used for everything, carelessly clamped together, great chunks of it painted different colours or not painted at all, but left in its sullen zinc-grey: a packet of Player's finished with, dropped by some Aussie on the wharf like a baby's toy, lying there in the dusty wind till some other Aussie, equally careless, as if he resented the job and were as likely as not to abandon it the next minute, negligently and slouchingly swept the filthy thing away. Or did not sweep it away: left it there to moulder, rot, soften into filthier pulp. Who cares, anyway? Who cares? No one, obviously. In the Antipodes we mind our own business, thank you, and a large fierce disregard for the amenities is no one's business at all. So all over the continent, as far as I could see: shacks, themselves rubbish-heaps, firmly established in a desert of rubbish, rubbish blowing past their collapsing doors, whenever the wind blew, rubbish blowing in, out, in again to stay, at the whim of the fierce, hot, frolicsome wind. As in Australia, so in little New Zealand, the gem of the Empire, little green New Zealand. So at Te Pohutu the house squatted, carelessly untidy, littered with creepers which no one bothered to trim, the veranda roof filthily littered with rubbish which no one bothered to clear up. Even the varied blue hydrangeas by the broken front steps were also littered with blown paper, dirt flung out from dust-pans, spatterings of paint from the brush of the handyman who had once begun to paint the fretted wood-work of the veranda and had left it unfinished so that half was a dirty grey, half a flaking white, and the dull netted hydrangea leaves spotted with paint-flecks. Though, when I first saw that veranda, Bubbles had been away three months, his toys lay as he had left them there, in a sordid heap by the family's upturned Wellington boots. And having lain there, were now mildewed, rotted, rusted, ruined by the prevailing damp. All this was evidently so commonplace that as we mounted the steps Mrs. Wyatt, the returning housewife, did not even notice it. And inside the same tale: nothing had its accustomed place, was simply cast down by someone in a hurry, left there till found again after frenzied and noisy search, or, if not needed, left there forever. On the corner of the desk in the study lay a crumbling maggot-ridden slab of chocolate, furtively gnawed at by Bubbles' animal-like front teeth whenever he was left alone with it. That chocolate became for me the spiritual sum total of Te Pohutu—it stayed there, the tiny maggots busily chewing, from September till the following August when I left, and how long it had already been there no one either knew or cared. A duster was flicked over it when Ruahine the Maori girl was in the mood to dust: it was shifted slightly when Mr. Wyatt rummaged on the desk for lost necessaries: but there it stayed, unaltered save by the inroads of Bubbles' front teeth and the tinier busier maggots, to my certain knowledge for eleven months.

So in the same way life at Te Pohutu was of a topsy-turvyness I had never before met. Dorothy Wyatt was always saying "When we get settled" as one says "When the milennium comes." I doubt if in all her twenty married years she had ever been settled. It was not a physical rooting, but a spiritual, that one lacked. Here at Te

Pohutu was the home of the Wyatts for three generations, the very house which old Rattray Wyatt had built in New Zealand's early beginnings, the house in which his grandchildren now lived, in which his great-grandchildren would most probably also live. The old house had housed nothing but Wyatts, yet every morning when I came down to it afresh I felt that all was packed for flight, that to-day would see the last of us all. It may have been the inveterate untidiness of the place which made it, to the newcomer, look like the last day of a rummage sale: it may have been something less tangible, a large sense of unrest, a spirit of insecurity. After twenty years of marriage Dorothy Wyatt was yet insecurely married: her husband, one felt, would be hardly surprised if he awoke one day to find himself a bachelor. The two elder boys had no sense of sureness, no roots in the home they had never left: Bubbles was a small malignant soul forever wandering, forever unsafe, his elfin malice sprung from this deep uncertainty. Conscious only dimly of an aching hollow in themselves, a void where living warmth should be, the Wyatt family were yet to most eyes a normal, healthy, happy family. Or perhaps they really were so: perhaps only to my jaundiced eyes were they inwardly rotten. I don't know. I cannot see them clearly, only through a haze of misery. Misery at first acute, then merely aching, finally only no more than a habit. And to get into a habit of misery, to bed with misery, wake to misery, is of all states the most pernicious. In the end I hugged my pain as St. Lawrence hugged his grisly gridiron,[1] for the sake of the release it would one day surely bring.

For though the pursuit of Adrian, the chase, was feverishly thrilling, though the winning of Dorothy Wyatt to my side was a

---

1   St. Lawrence was a Christian martyr tortured and executed by the Romans in 258 AD. Legend has it that he was burned alive on a gridiron and that he declared at one point, "Turn me over: I'm done!"—for which he is known as the patron saint of cooks and comedians.

matter of Machiavellian subtlety, though I bent my fierce Jewish energy to both day after day, unrelenting, unrelaxing, I yet had time to mourn for Harry. It had been so bitterly sad, leaving Harry as I did. If he had gone from me I could have borne it better: but I had gone from him. I was the one on the ship waving, choking into a handkerchief, yearning over its salty wet edge at the face of the one on the quay growing smaller, dimmer, more irrevocably lost in distance. As weeks at Te Pohutu dragged on I would have given all to go back, to be also on the quayside, never parting: but I had chosen to go on, must go on. Letters I had: the letters between us, in those months, were a study in diminuendo, the loud notes dying, dying to mere whispers, the soft notes fading, piercingly sweet, down unguessed-at vistas to an end, a silence, like the last atom of a sigh. He wrote at first loudly, blusteringly: he revealed, through piled-up half-truth, as only Harry could, the truth. Why had I only come to see him once when I was in Sydney? Why had I not written at once from New Zealand? I must know he would be anxious about me, longing to know what I did, whether I was happy. The woman Harry had briefly made of me would have responded to this with dog-like eagerness, protested in a thousand subtle female ways her unhappiness away from him. I was no longer that woman of the *Ceres*: I was by now too old, too sad, too honest. So I wrote briskly back giving news, matters of fact, enquiring (but without passion) how he did? ending his sincerely. His next letter, in a warm spurt begotten of reproach, began: "Dearest," and went on through sentences of an odd but touching literary baldness to protest how much I had misunderstood him if I thought he had for one moment been neglectful of or forgotten me. He wanted nothing from me, he wanted me only to be happy. To this I responded in a sprightly chatty way, loathing myself for caring so much, for working so hard to hide from him how much. Against my will a real warmth must have crept in: I was still his dearest in the next letter, hot on the heels of mine to him. "Yours of 20th to hand today and I was awfully glad to get it for to tell you the truth, your last letter seemed so very cold and distant that I felt you had fallen for more than the scenery in N.Z., not that I could hold it out on you if it were so but it caused a pang." And then prosaic news of the Melbourne Cup, as if, shamed by his outburst, he had plunged desperately to horsey matters as a stepping-stone to firm ground. Had I been ten years younger and more foolish I should have gone winging back to him, dared everything, cast myself into his arms, so moved was I by this belated *cri-de-coeur*. But I was thirty-five, a woman who had been through both lust and love, who now was no longer in love with anything but her own comfort, her own assured future. Adrian meant both: poor Harry, who could give neither, must now be shed.

So I shed Harry. I never wrote to him again. Other letters came: I was female enough to read them, strong enough to leave them unanswered. Slowly Harry faded, poor stout fleshly Harry who had been so warm and close: after three or four months (but how long those months were!) I could regard, calmly, a picture of Harry now sporting with some toothsome blonde in Melbourne, offering her pink gins, little flats, himself as chiefest prize. I have no doubt that is what he is at, even as I write: that is what he always will be at.

So off with Harry, on with Adrian. "Tally ho!" I inwardly cried, a middle-aged Diana still fresh and frenzied in the chase. It was no fleet ecstatic pursuit, this bearing down of Charlotte upon Adrian: it had its exhilarating moments but was in the main a grinding, nagging business, a struggle daily renewed, as much a part of life as washing wax out of one's ears (how the stuff accumulates, this self-raised beeswax!), or seeing that Bubbles did not tear his food limb from limb with his fingers. The only difference lay in this, that by catching Adrian I added something to my life, in admonishing Bubbles I achieved nothing at all. There was no changing Bubbles, now. Though only six years old he was already moulded to his life form, already the obstinate, malevolent, flinty little man he will be at twenty-one, thirty-one, fifty. Little man! Mrs. Wyatt called him that, fondly: her last born, her baby, her little man. She was right: there was something foully, precociously mannish about this child. I watched him, in those early days, at nursery meals with the nanny he had so long outgrown. As far as Bubbles cared, Nanny was finished, used up, done with: but still she stayed on, arrogantly sure of her place, to nurse the baby now due in the autumn. "Our English Nanny," Mrs. Wyatt called her proudly, puffed with pride at having anything so English as a Nanny: and the starched lump of stupidity smiled, always self-conscious, preening herself over the flattery in the title. Me she resented, naturally, as being neither English nor Nanny, as being the foreign interloper who took from her her Bubbles. From this nursling of six years she had little comfort: he now clung to her not at all. Meals in the nursery, before I became more mother's companion than Bubbles' governess, were one long bicker, bicker, of sharp exasperation from Nanny, quiet insolence from Bubbles.

"Now, Bubbles, you don't need to eat the pattern off your plate!"

"Don't I, Nanny?"

Always the same: "Bubbles, you don't need to do" this, that or the other thing, in heavy sarcasm from Nanny, heavily in authority: and Bubbles' clear, rather deep, subtly insolent little voice saying "Don't I, Nanny?" Though aggressively on the look-out for insult, what she called "sauce," Nanny never grasped that here was sauce of the deepest sauciness, an utterly blistering contempt, in the grave question of the little boy. When he raised his grey, black-fringed eyes to her, she never felt a shock of uneasiness from the disdain they showed: not she. To her they were just eyes, Bubbles just a little boy. He was still a baby to her though to his mother he had stopped being one when she weaned him: after that curls were disallowed, tiny frills of knickers, trim-tailored, took the place of frocks. Bubbles at eight months looked raffish in a tam-o'-shanter: a year later he wore an infinitesimal checkered shirt with a miniature tie dangling in front. Gravely beating his spoon on his high chair (which also would soon be too babyish) Bubbles, I doubt not, stared at his adoring family, at brothers Ned and Tom, at Daddy, at Mummy, at Nanny, with pale grey quiet eyes: while on his little manly chest the little tie, bedaubed with egg, bobbed and danced. "He was the dearest little man!" cried Dorothy Wyatt to me often, recounting these episodes in Bubbles' early days; "such a little man!" I have no doubt the little man's tie always ended up under his milk-strewn chin, giving him a roystering club-man look: but at two years old he *had* a little tie, shirt, trousers: he was no baby but a real little man.

But, though at six the little man wanted companionship and I had been engaged to provide it, it was as confidante to poor, middle-aged, vaguely unhappy, wearily pregnant Dorothy Wyatt that I put in most of my time. Bubbles might be her Benjamin, her baby treasure, but she had not the slightest desire for any more such: and here she was at forty-three, a woman with three difficult births and two miscarriages to her credit, once more enceinte. It was long before she admitted, even to me, that she hated the thought of the new baby, the recurring sickness, the weariness and heavy discomfort of the whole process. She knew there was no pleasure in it: not in its conception, forced upon her by Edward, that devoted model husband: nor in its coming, nor in its birth (oh, horror, remembering those other births!) nor in its actual self. She was sure it was going to be a girl, and she loathed girls. "Silly things," said Dorothy fiercely, sitting with me in the big untidy living-room and jabbing most ineptly with her needle at a petticoat for the little unwanted, "I never did like 'em, never. Of course, I don't mean you, Charlie dear, you're different, and I don't know how I ever got on without you—but little girls are such idiots."

"Never mind, it'll be rather nice for a change to have a daughter, won't it?"

"No!" cried Dorothy furiously, and burst into tears.

I had many tears to cope with, many weak wailing fits, in those first few months. Poor Dorothy, I pitied her profoundly even while I despised her, trying to be patient with her endless sickly whimsies.

"I've never been like this before!" she often wailed, when I had once more persuaded her upstairs to take off her shoes and frock, lay herself upon the vast double bed. "I've *never* been like this with any of the other babies!"

And then she would go on to tell me *ad nauseam* how as a bride she had gone straight off from morning sickness to a meet of the Waikato, mounted bravely on her dear Chestnut, bravely smiling (after retching behind a held-up hand gloved in yellow leather) at Edward in his pink coat (he was Master then: it was all very English, admirable) as he smiled encouragingly at her. I saw it all so plainly as she told it: the whole grim scene repeated through the winter till the hunting ended and Edward belatedly put his foot down. Poor Dorothy, really one could not help admiring such British grit—or could one? And now all through this awful pregnancy, hearing her tell of the others, I remembered my own, my young unheeding ecstasies among the grass and flowers of Grübl, Bärbel's birth to the tune of the zither and the concertina in the echoing Saal below my room. A youthful, gay, unthinking business it had been, compared with the grim despair, the petulant effort to make the best of a very bad job, the middle-aged lassitudes of poor Dorothy's. She was too loyal to blame Edward for her state: but we all knew, Nanny knew, Miss Blood the cook knew, even Ruahine smirkingly knew, that this baby had been forced upon her. The baby was but one result of this charming family's deep urge to cruelty. Quietly, unobtrusively, the whole Wyatt family indulged its frenzy. To kill, if possible; but if not to kill, to maim, injure, inflict hurt. See young Ned, that loutish nineteen-year-old, going off to shoot quail with lust for blood in his dull eye: see him, when quail proved too elusive, sitting thwarted on a stump aiming at, and as often as not merely clumsily wounding, inoffensive little widow-birds or the bright shining cuckoo who sang so proudly in October. See Dorothy herself, when one of her Scotties had misbehaved, advancing upon it with her riding-crop; doing a painful duty, of course, yet the eyes betrayed her, gleaming with lustful joy as the blows fell, as the dog writhed and yelped. And so her Edward, with the thrill of killing foxes[2] over, irrevocably, for another season, advanced upon her (I have no doubt with the family gleam in his eye) and begot another child.

But in Bubbles, that little drop from the family bucket, this family taint came out darkest of all. Bubbles loved a killing, none enjoyed it more than he. It was to his mother evidence of his little mannishness that he haunted the hired man when there were ducks to kill, hopped excited around the yard as the creatures, beheaded by the handyman's unhandy axe, leaped among the debris headless, blood spouting from the severed stump of neck. The axe-blows sounded, the heads flew, the ducks rushed madly about the blood-spattered yard, and now behold little Bubbles carting the corpses triumphant to the kitchen, himself spotted with hot blood on his little feet, his arms, his face: and gleaming in his pale eyes that unholy gleam of cruelty, the lust to see pain, which his elders managed only to show less nakedly. And sitting enraptured by the English cook, Miss Blood, as that poor girl, queasy of stomach, plunged a hand despairingly into the duck's bowels, brought out a slipping handful of bleeding guts, Bubbles quietly enjoyed himself for another ten minutes or so. Things which did not suffer in being killed had no attraction for little Bubbles.

---

2   This is an error on Campion's part. Foxes are not native and were never introduced to New Zealand.

"What are you doing, Miss Blood?"

"Skinning peaches."

"Are they dead already?"

"Yes."

"When did they die?"

"When Bates picked them from the tree, I should think."

"Won't they squeal when you put them in the saucepan? Won't they, Miss Blood?"

"Won't they what?"

"Sque-ee-al!"

"No, of course not."

"Oo, but I want them to squeal, when they get too hot. Don't they feel *anything*?"

"No, don't be silly, Bubbles."

So Bubbles drifts off, losing interest in peaches since they die painlessly. This has been a bloodless day, disappointing. I find him ten minutes later on the veranda, running his Hornby train madly around its tracks.

"Bubbles! If you put it on the lines that way the engine will fall off."

"I want it to—I like to see it go all wrong and funny, like this."

And the engine, plunging along the curved rails, plunges off to lie on one side with its wheels racing madly, the spring whirring madly to a stop. If it had blood, nerves, feelings, this train, Bubbles would cherish it dearly, torment it daily: as it has only a spring, coiled iron, no lungs to shriek with, no flesh to be torn, his fit of fury exhausts itself at once. When the engine is silent, lying outraged upside-down, Bubbles drifts off in search of other matters.

Yet sometimes, still too young to be completely hardy, utterly a Wyatt, Bubbles was overcome by horror. In early summer the lambs at Te Pohutu were docked of their tails. Frisking singly through the wicket into the pen where men seized them, snipped, released them, they came away wiser lambs, each bloody little stump a tribute to efficiency. The lambs also, conforming with the Wyatt code, were now no longer babies: they, with this forced shedding of their tails, grew up to little sheep. Bubbles, the little man, stood by his father's side as the men snipped. His eyes opened wider, wider, enormous pale grey pools in inky lashes. A white ashy line grew around his mouth.

"Daddy—"

"What, Bubbles?"

"Daddy, I—"

And Bubbles, the little man, jerked his head sideways and was sick.

This was disgrace, public under the sardonic eye of the hired man. Mr. Wyatt took his retching son away, disgustfully handed him over to Nanny, who wiped him up as she would have wiped a dish and fulminated over the messy shirt.

"What made you do it, little man?" asked Mummy in a forced, brisk tone.

"The lambs—their tails—" hiccuped Bubbles.

"Oh, but the lambs have to lose their tails, and anyway it doesn't hurt!" cried Mummy blithely, encouragingly, slapping her son on his shirted back and despising him for his sickness as she despised herself, every morning, for hers. Every morning, before breakfast, a yellow-faced Dorothy heaved over the enamel basin in the bathroom: every morning, when Margaret Blood violently rang the bell, Dorothy, still yellow-faced but bravely smiling, came down the dusty staircase to face the morning bacon. See her now at breakfast, facing it, appalled at the sight, the smell, of glossy fried eggs, grease-fringed bacon: yet determined to go through with it to prove once more, gratuitously, her grit. No breakfast in bed for Dorothy Wyatt, the soldier's daughter, be she never so pregnant. And thus, in an air heavy with grimness, we begin yet another day. The mystery of breakfast-time! I often thought. All these people who had just spent six or more utterly solitary hours, unconscious or dreaming (of what?), wholly alone, wholly and unbrokenly themselves, now coming back to consciousness and the world again, coming back to take up a new day, to face other people's eyes (so hostile when off-guard), to face a breakfast-table fringed with hostile eyes—"Good morning, Miss Hurts,", "Good morning, Mr. Wyatt"—to come in battling for their own egotistical existence—"Good morning, Charlie dear!", "Good morning, Dorothy"—since every ego, however weak, fights for its life from cradle to coffin—"Good morning, my little man!"—All this beginning again, the night-peace sloughed like a snake-skin, the renewed, desperate, silent struggle taken up once more around the breakfast-table. The breakfast-table typical, redolent, of the life of these strange unlovable Wyatts. Mr. Wyatt deep in yesterday's *Auckland Star*, which he reads, always twenty-four hours late, as solemnly as if it still breathed hot from the press: Tom eating steadily through two large, grey, greasy mutton chops (with mutton all about him, his livelihood and his landscape, he still cannot face the day without a lining to the inner man of mutton): Ned, less carnivorous, puts into himself eggs and bacon, great slabs of toast thickly strewn with Opotiki butter and home-made marmalade. Both lads, thank God, are silent. Dorothy sips bravely at strong tea, vaguely, fondly, eyes her youngest whom I control. But there is no controlling Bubbles. Plump on a red cushion designed to raise his chin above table-height, he forges his way through breakfast like a Diesel caterpillar mowing down scrub. Debris and destruction litter his wake; on he goes to a future as yet uncertain but sure to be destructive. Whistling through the two new gaps in his front teeth, he squirts oil from the mandarin peel at the cat who gets it in both eyes, yells and bolts.

"Don't do that, Bubbles."

"What?"

"Eat your fruit properly or I shall have to feed you like a baby."

"Feed me like a baby, I don't care. Mum—mummie!—oo, mummie, look! Charlotte's going to feed me like a baby!"

"Don't be silly, darling," murmurs Dorothy fondly, gazing away from me and showing, by the uneasy twitching of an eye, that she sees trouble ahead, and is set upon dodging it. I am as determined that she shall take her share: why should I alone wrestle with Bubbles and his swinish habits ? I neither begot nor bore the child, thank God he is none of mine!

"S'Blood's burnt the toast," says Bubbles through a mouthful of milk.

All too true, Miss Blood has burnt the toast. But she is English, so nothing will be said. Except by me, who must work off some of the ire bred hotly in me by Bubbles' breakfast frolics.

"Toast's burnt again, Margaret," chirrup I, fetching bread from the kitchen.

Margaret looks up hot-faced from the stove, blushes even more, opens her mouth to speak, pinches it to again, and slaps down a saucepan fiercely on the shelf. How plain she is, poor creature! A very short nose and upper lip give her a look of nibbling innocence, but oh me! she is very plain. It is fatally easy to be unkind to anything so homely. So we are all unkind to her, even stout greasy Ruahine who cheeks her from the kitchen sink, blandly ignores her orders to wash again a cup that is still dirty. Margaret endures it all with a fatalistic despair which has dignity. She knows she was made to be cheeked by Maori hirelings and nasty children. A snub-nosed, red-haired virgin, she is proud of having knocked about the world a bit; and looks as if it were the world which had done most of the knocking. She is only thirty, but everything about her is battered, worn, much the worse for wear. Even her hair, which never stays up, and from which an unending dribble of hair-pins daily descends: even her weathered complexion, her sunburned freckled legs scrawled over with the scars of many thorn-bushes, her bare arms criss-crossed with oven burns, her hands raw from endless washing. Her name, too, can have brought but little blessing to the poor girl. No one could say: "My cook, Miss Blood," without embarrassment. Even though Dorothy consoles herself by maintaining that she is very English, very well-connected (was there not a Captain Blood in some bit of English history?—Dorothy thinks so), she always says the name faintly, in distaste, and only when she positively has to. And Margaret herself, horribly self-conscious about her horrid name, never fails to blush violently when it comes out into the open, when Mr. Wyatt, forgetting, yells from the study: "Miss Blood, can you bring me a cup of tea?" or one of the boys, the careless oaf, bursts into the kitchen with: "Mum says, anything you want from Te Aroha this afternoon, S'Blood?" Then, quivering furiously at the onslaught of the name, she blushes, thrusts her head down to the oven, to a saucepan, mutters thickly: "No, thanks," or: "Yes, Mr. Wyatt," and suffers, poor girl, agonies of shame which do no good at all. Only when Tom yodels at her in his raw young voice, new-broken and uncertain on the top notes, does Margaret cease sulking: she has a horrid weakness for Tom, a secret excited fondness for the rough colt so violent with life.

I often thought, looking at her, spiteful from my own misery, that Margaret Blood was very English. Under her proud certainty that, being English, she was also All Right, swelled a frightening flood of uncertainty, a wonder, a misgiving, the horrid question Am I All Right? In her light English eyes the two currents swam pursuant, changeful as an English sky; so that the poor girl (whom I grew to like, mildly, though she irritated me and spurred me on to cruelty) was ever in a state of flux, one moment arrogantly sure, the next moment blushingly unsure: always knowing which Margaret Blood she wanted to be, forever knowing that she was not that but another one who fumbled, was clumsy and ridiculous. Only in her cooking lay her safety, bliss. Though she flung herself upon her pots and pans, as Nanny said, "like a mad 'un," she made meals of a toothsome quality one does not expect from the English, she sacrificed her energy to this end with a passionate joy, tending, like some fierce vestal virgin, the flame of her kitchen range. The burnt toast was a sign, an omen, a daily lapse: Tom had taken to fetching the duck-bucket from the kitchen just before breakfast, and, tremblingly not looking at him, Margaret charred the bread and cast it, despairing, into the toast-racks.

What bubbling currents seethed, what passions rioted, in the musty, dirty, untidy house at Te Pohutu! Living there was like struggling (as often in nightmare I have struggled) through a pond filled with snakes, always with some writhing thing, some wriggling awful coldness, some boneless body, between the legs, beneath the arm-pits, round the neck. Dorothy's furious despair at pregnancy, Edward Wyatt's frustrated months of single-bed-dedness, Ned's bursting, never-granted desire to kill plentifully throughout his waking hours, the painful stirrings of sex in young Tom, Nanny's rioting jealousies, Margaret's ungainly emotions—all these, in a house old, neglected, rotting; under a roof pitted with holes through which the cold New Zealand rain pitilessly dribbled. And through them all, like the harsh wail of violins, my own loneliness, regret, disillusion, my own unceasing need to forget Harry, to pursue Adrian. Though now I write of it in a brief half-chapter, swiftly read—though to you it may seem but an episode, a little happening in this rambling tale of one woman, for me it was a bitter business of weeks, months, which kept my nerves stretched taut to snapping point, drained my restless energy, absorbed me utterly. When all was over, Adrian won (or as surely won as an engaged man can be), I was a woman bled, sapped of her juices, spent to the last drop, tired beyond words. A woman in whom nothing stayed but a faint triumph, an unspeakable weariness. How hard I worked, how remorselessly I toiled, from September when I met the man till July when he was mine. Worked to titillate his fancy, to keep him interested in me, to keep his neat little car always bowling along the road between Auckland and Te Pohutu, to keep his mind so fresh regarding me that this journey through the lush green Waikato country should be no boring duty but a glad adventure with reward at its end. To keep him, above all, interested. Interested in me, in the affair: never bored, as I was, with the sameness of the game. Is there any man who does not, as the game goes on, grow desperately boring to the woman who must net him? No, not one. Boredom is the price we pay for security, I told myself as I listened to Adrian talking of himself. All men love to talk about themselves, that is why they bore: the wise woman, her soul yawning, leans back and brightly seems to listen. With Harry I had never had to listen very hard, but with Adrian I must. His mind, as quick as mine, as femininely pouncing, would catch me napping if I so much as slackened by one hair's-breadth my strained, bright, flattering attention. I must never be caught napping. I incline to think that I got Adrian in the end because I listened to him so well, because he saw that, once his wife, he had in me a resident ear. A resident, decorative ear: recklessly abandoning all to this last hope, I spent Onkel Hans's money on decoration. It had to be subtly done. If I dressed too well, Adrian's alarmed cautious mind would shy from the thought of what this woman cost to keep. If I dressed ill (which is not one of my sins) he would not look twice at me. Whenever he saw me I must be a woman well-turned-out, a woman in whom a fastidious man would take pride. My clothes must be elegant, not too expensive-looking, never young, never matronly, composedly chic. One or two old pets I garnished up again and let him know I had done it, that I was a woman who could use wits and needle to make ends meet. For the rest, my clothes, my gloves, shoes, hats, beauty-parlour bills, mounted quietly higher. I thought of them at night, listening to Bubbles' childish chick-like snore, and blenched. But in the end I got, as Flowers would have said, value for my money. I got my man.

The struggle was harder because, from the very beginning, we were on such easy terms, treated one another with such a fluid intimacy, as if we had been cradled in the same suburb, as if we knew one another like friendly cousins. This familiarity is the colonial way. We had early reached the Christian-naming stage: in the free British Colonies where conventions are as rigid as anywhere else, but different, Christian names are *de rigueur*. So it was Charlotte and Adrian, Adrian and Charlotte. Such an easy intimacy, so warm, so friendly seeming, so meaningless. I learnt it, I learnt the language, swiftly: so swiftly that he never guessed I had to learn it. "That's dinkum, Adrian!"—"Adrian, you're a skite!"[3]—"Good-o, Adrian!", and all the rest. A new language, and a hideous one, as new-born babies are hideous, but I learnt it. So much he took for granted. He was surrounded by girls who called him "Adrian," said this or that was "dinkum," exclaimed "Good-o!" They were as attractive as I, though not so intelligent: but oh! how much younger they were. There lay my nightmare. A man of thirty-six is much more likely to fall for a twenty-five, than for a thirty-five-year-old. And the twenty-fives swarmed about him, their pretty confident little noses hot on the scent of eligibility. He *was* so eligible, so very much the husband for any twenty-five-year-old a little brighter than the rest. He knew them all, he had known them as girl children, as flappers, as students at the University. Wistfully he saw in them frail beautiful traces of his own youth: he might any day wistfully take any one of them to wife. Though always on one of the weekend days he came out to me, there were, I knew it, gay weekdays in between on any of which he might take one of these beguiling hussies, these bright dewy flowers, out to dinner, to a cinema, to a bridge-party, for a ride in the little car. And I must never ask, never want to know, whether he had done so. What right had I to ask, what right to know, how my casual charming friend of Friday, Saturday or Sunday spent the

---

3 Dinkum: Australian/New Zealand slang for something that's true, skite for someone boastful.

days between? If I were lucky enough to have the charmer once a week, let that be enough. I knew that if he scented possessiveness, be it ever so faint, in my voice or manner, he would shy off at once; he would dash away, I knew, as the half-wild horse out at grass, hearing suddenly the bridle jingle behind the back of the human who coaxingly offers him bread, throws up his fine free mane, snorts down his fine free nostrils, and is away, away, plunging away through the high grass. So I suffered agonies, in my imagination picturing all, from Monday till Friday: and from Friday to Monday suffered agonies again at having him with me, his life so apparently open to my eye, and knowing nothing, daring to ask nothing, of what he had done since last we met. Other women, I knew, had tried their seductive hand at Adrian and failed: not without reason was he now wife-shy, though fascinated by the female presence. It was darkly deep in him, this fascinated horror of the huntress. Once, only once, he suddenly showed me how he felt, how careful my approach must be. We walked along the fine pale sand at Tauranga, Dorothy, jealously reluctant, having granted me a whole day for this seaside spree. The whole day, and Adrian to myself, Adrian in a gay boyish confiding mood, a very larrikin[4] of a man. Here we were disporting ourselves, chattering middle-aged children who would wot not of years past, on the lovely beach. The hot long summer was over, now the bleached downs, tawny, dry, brittle as straw, lay exhausted to the west of us, above the cliffs broken here and here by a dark pohutukawa clinging sturdily to the rock face, jutting out, sturdily dark, from its grey strong roots embedded in the crumbling rock. Eastwards the sea lay heaving silently, a silent flat of steel-pale water hissing where it met the sand. We had the beach to ourselves, mere specks upon it, and clambered over the rocks searching for oysters, eating them (oh delicious oyster so rare and cold, eaten so guiltily

---

4   Larrikin: Australian/New Zealand slang for a boisterous young man.

crunched between cliff and rock!) and hardly bothered to think of spying ships at sea. Now we energetically tramped nowhere in particular. The day had been comradely, soothing: we had never, Adrian and I, spent so long together in such easy harmony, in such a lack of tautness for me. For once, even with Adrian, I was at ease, relaxed, a woman restful, not stretched like a catapult ready to let fly. For once I felt young, younger than my foes the twenty-five-year-olds. For once I was young Charlotte again, carefree, carelessly hunting: no longer a grim-jawed woman intent only on the kill with no time to enjoy the chase.

So we trudged across the sand, scrambled among the rocks. I took off my shoes and stockings, slung them across my shoulders, strode gipsy-like along. Adrian at first hardly cared for this: eyeing my feet, he made to disapprove. Then, seeing that they were shapely, clean, well-tended, he shrugged (mentally) his shoulders and decided to let the woman go gipsy if she would. But his own neat shoes stayed on his feet: not for Adrian the thrilling discomfort of bare soles pricked by little limpets peaked like the Kaffir huts of Minnaarskopjie. Not for Adrian, either, the pagan joy of plunging from the bitter chill of autumn sand into a half-warm pool: he grimaced slightly as I splashed, and neatly skirted the water with unwet feet. All the same, though these little exasperations were undercurrent to our comradeship, there *was* comradeship, a budding peace.

"Funny," said Adrian, lightly dipping his hand under my elbow as I scaled a rock, "how one remembers things. I suppose I should give you my whole arm at this point, invite you to cling to me—but I'm damned if I will. I've been had that way once! It was fifteen years ago, but I've never forgotten it."

A silence in which I, knowing my Adrian, silently invited him to go on. He went on.

"It was when I was a student in Christchurch. We lived in a boarding-house, about five of us all doing Modern Languages.

My lord, it was a place. The old hag who kept it made a practice of sleeping with her lodgers in turn—all that were weak-minded enough, that is. I suppose you got let off a night's rent if you gave in to her, she was a regular old Potiphar's wife. But that's got nothing to do with the story. There was some sort of a fair there once a year, everybody picked a girl and went to it. I was very young, and I picked something called Lily out of a café. Pretty little piece she was, but clinging. She took my arm at the beginning of the day's enjoyment and never let go of it once, not even on the merry-go-round. I never felt such a fool in my life, I must have blushed for something like five hours on end. Since then I vowed I'd never take another woman's arm nor let her take mine, and, by cripes! I've kept to that."

"All right, I won't expect it."

"You'd better not."

We laughed merrily, brightly, leaping over the rocks so light-hearted and gay. But I had not missed Adrian's quick eyeing at the tale's end: here was a warning adroitly given. "Don't you go expecting anything from me, my girl, not any more than you're getting at present," said Adrian's laughing well-cared-for face as he made some indelicate remark about the seaweed. "Take what you've got and be thankful, there'll be no more." Indeed, I knew that: I needed no reminder.

The story of clinging Lily stayed to irk me. I saw so clearly the young Adrian, already fiercely fastidious, clawed at by the tactless lass, nauseated by her, too young still, too polite, to shed her as he now would never hesitate to do. I saw in him the nervous fear which this little happening had begotten, the uneasy horror of rapacity in females, the fear of being caught by one more ruthless than the rest, caught and pinned down for life. He knew himself to be so eligible: the knowledge bred in him an absurd self-consciousness. He could not now see any woman in any attitude save that of pouncing. Anything between the ages of eighteen and thirty-eight, as yet unwed, spelled danger most drear to Adrian's shrinking, fascinated mind: he dreaded them all, feared them all, yet could not for the life of him keep away. See now his seeming attachment to me. The Wyatts treated us already as an engaged couple, looked upon us indulgently as united for all time—yet I thought that Adrian's resistance to me grew daily deeper, stronger, as I became daily for him more of a habit. From habit he now drove out in the little car on Friday, Saturday or Sunday: habit kept him with me, the amiable companion, the gay diverting friend, for the whole day: habit (so quickly bred) sent him back to his other life, his other female habits, when the brief weekend was over. I had to endure this, there was no changing it. Endure it for months, for what looked to me like years, all through the spring, summer, autumn of that unrestful year.

*****

Now Christmas had come and gone; a baking hot Christmas, roast goose, plum pudding and other traditional British atrocities gulped down in a temperature of 80°, lying like hot sand in our affronted innards till tea with rich Christmas cake came to complete our ruin. The New Year, much like all Old Years, had come and gone. Strange, now, to watch the year waning in March, April: strange to face the coming of winter in June. Bubbles changed play-suits for jersey and little flannel knickers: in the kitchen Margaret Blood's bare brown legs grew goose-fleshy, purple, mottled, shapely firm calves on which the chilly hairs stuck out at right-angles: signs of the times and seasons, these: of times much out of joint and seasons all antipodean, awry. A sodden peace wrapped poor Dorothy as April marched into May. She was now, it seemed, resigned to the baby, kicking no more against pricks. Resigned, apathetic, enormous, she no longer braved the breakfast bacon but sipped tea in bed, rose at noon to flap languidly about the neglected house, climbed the stairs painfully towards six o'clock, and was no more seen except by me. To me she clung, nauseating and pathetic. I read to her, I played Beggar My Neighbour with her (it was slightly above our intellectual reach, but we played it): I sat and talked to her in the stale foetid bedroom: I even at night held her hand while she went to sleep. It was a servitude so galling that I marvel at myself: but as I sat there my mind was somewhere else. The hulk of Charlotte, gently stroking Dorothy's hot arm, arranging Dorothy's pillows, persuading Dorothy to eat scrambled egg or drink hot milk, did well enough: the hulk only was at Te Pohutu, the vital Charlotte pursued in fancy, as in fact, Adrian Lovat wherever he might be.

Now in the middle of May Nanny went about with pursed lips, self-important eyes, a stout bustling body to whom birth was a commonplace. Miss Hurts the foreign interloper might hold Mrs. Wyatt's hand while she dropped off to sleep, but only Nanny knew how many pilches were needed, or where the cotton-wool was kept. In the coming drama Nanny would be the chief character, we the stand-ins humbly crowding near the wings.

"She makes me feel as if I were going to have this blasted baby," muttered Margaret tartly to me, watching that stout starched backside waddling from the kitchen door. "Wouldn't she have the time of her life if we were *all* pregnant!"

"It's not worth trying just to see her reactions, though."

"No, I suppose not. Though, mind you" (Margaret was always "minding" us in this deprecatory way) "it must be an experience worth having. Virgins like you and me have obviously missed a lot—or aren't you one?"

"One what?"

"Oh, never mind!" muttered Margaret, blushing warmly and diving her head into that cavernous refuge, the oven.

Poor Margaret, how obsessed she was just now by virginity, with the futility of her own smiting her afresh every time she peeped hungrily at Tom's rough young face as yet unawake, but stirring. As if the stir of Dorothy's coming pangs were not enough, we had also this surging unrest in Dorothy's cook to cope with: for in May, with the hot numbing summer over, Margaret was set on having Tom and patently didn't know how. Never was a girl so coltishly clumsy, so obvious, in her approach. Hot in my own tally-ho after Adrian I yet had time to pause in the chase and watch her at hers. "*Gottes Willen!*" I thought, "do the English never grow up?" For she had no subtlety: it was all exhausted in her cooking. She went after Tom as a woman chases a hen in a back yard. How wildly she flung herself upon him, how wildly missed, while her alarmed prey squawked, dodged by a hair's-breadth! How hot, how flurried, how ungainly she looked as she still flung herself after, barking her knees, grazing her elbows, losing her hair-pins and her little store of self-control! It was a piteous sight, grossly ludicrous. If we had not all been so absorbed in Dorothy and the baby, this low comedy would have been public. As it was, only I, maliciously sharp, observed it: and had a perverted pleasure in seeing unfledged Margaret doing so badly what I did so well. There was nothing to separate us but this: that she bungled her job, I brought mine to a neat conclusion. Contemporary, parallel, the two hunts went on: the one to the tune of loud cries, raw despairing hulloos; the other silent, deep, dangerous, terribly serious.

Into this emotional maelstrom Dorothy's baby was born, after a long sordid agony, in the middle of June. Two weeks overdue, an unpunctual babe, she was tiny, frail, miserable, wringing the heart with her vexing hopeless wail. Dorothy wearily turned her head away from the little thing, who thus became Nanny's baby, and in an odd way mine too. A woman must have something weak to love: loving is her chief, her only legitimate job. This little scrap, this unwanted mite, became Bärbel once again, Bärbel whom I had forsworn but now had once more. I knew it to be sentimentality of the grosser kind, but never cared. Most women make fools of themselves over a child or an animal when they have finished making themselves fools with men: I had a baby again in my arms and anyone who liked might mock.

"Look, Bubbles—come here and look."

"What?" said Bubbles, suspicious.

"A new baby, a sister for you."

"What's a sister?"

"A sister? Why—!" Good heavens, how explain a sister? But before I began Bubbles saved me.

"I don't want it," he said, and was gone.

"Silly little boy," remarked Nanny, preoccupied with nappies.

That was the attitude: silly little boy, not to like his dear little new sister. How wildly unreasonable grown-ups are: we who had freely aired our resentment at the coming of this infant nuisance, now sweetly, reasonably (but with what acidity behind the careful sweetness, what prejudice behind the reason!) rebuked poor Bubbles for not being overjoyed at its arrival.

"I really believe he *hates* Baby!" said Dorothy weakly, the convalescent mother flopping on high-piled pillows. "Silly little man, I really believe he's jealous!"

Bubbles hunched a shoulder and turned away. How our children betray us! The hunch, the averted head, were pure Dorothy: so Dorothy had looked, had turned, when we first showed her the unwanted baby. So Dorothy still behaved, when the child was thrust upon her. She would do anything rather than touch it, hold it, nurse it.

"You'd better take her, Nanny—I don't want to be awkward with her and hurt her!" whimpered Dorothy, giving the babe one brief murderous look before turning from it, "my arms are so weak I might drop her. Take her *away*, Nanny!"

But this in Dorothy was natural: in Bubbles we all found it unnatural, inhuman, deeply to be condemned.

"Look at Baby, Bubbles, look what darling little tiny feet she has!"

Baby's blue flat soles are thrust out to Bubbles, who looks at them with loathing, turns from them. And then, when no one is by, steals back to nip them fiercely, so that Baby wails on a more maddening note than usual.

"Bubbles! don't! that's dreadful, you *mustn't* hurt poor little Baby!"

"Why not?" asks Bubbles, reasonably enough.

We are all shocked, outraged, at the unnatural child's behaviour. We yell shrilly at him, pepper him with admonitions, besiege him with moral precepts. And the little boy, whose first thought of Baby had been no worse than bored, now begins secretly, malignantly, furtively, to loathe her. His little soul becomes hot with hatred: he broods over his hate, nurses it, fosters it. At Bubbles' age loathing must out, there is no polite burial of it. So now a drawing-pin, strategically point-upwards, is found in Baby's cot.

"Well I never!" says Nanny, shocked, unsuspicious, and she casts it out of the window to join the haircombings and other human litter on the curved tin of the veranda.

Next day there was a needle where the drawing-pin had been, and now even Nanny's dull mind began to stir. She taxed Bubbles, who flushed indignant red, opened enormous innocent eyes, burst into tears. The flinty little fellow could always turn on these waterworks for Nanny, who was always humbugged by them. So for days there were no more needles, no more drawing-pins, and Nanny's mind went once more comfortably to sleep. Then Bubbles, quietly over-blown with triumph, over-reached himself. He aimed with his little catapult at Baby (murder written in his young eye), and hit her full on the temple. There was no chance that this would be put down to a wayward Fate: Bubbles was dragged before his father, who, more in sorrow than in anger (and purely for the good of his soul) thrashed him till both were white with fury and Bubbles' little buttocks almost raw. Then having (perhaps) walloped the devil out of his little son and released the pent-up grudges of the past celibate months from himself, Edward Wyatt handed the shaking child over to me, mixed himself a drink, and went back to the *New Zealand Herald*.

Bubbles had still enough spirit left in him to rip up his pillow-case before he went, dry-eyed, stony, to sleep. Of the two, he came best out of the battle. Not for a moment, no, not even when his pink vulnerable bottom, bare for all to see, was being heavily belaboured, did he lose his strange aloof dignity, his eerie detachment. How Bubbles had outgrown those two adult infants, his parents! Now his malevolence was heated, sharpened by the whole wretched business: now he would murder Baby if he could.

"Don't be absurd, Charlie—such a little boy! And he's got to be punished when he does dreadful things like hurting Baby."

"Dorothy, you don't realise—"

But how try to tell a mother anything about her own child? It was hopeless.

"Bubbles has been very, very naughty, but he's sorry now, he'll never do it again, will you, little man?" said Dorothy briskly: and Bubbles, raising for one instant those shocking light eyes, murmured: "Yes," scrabbled with his little toe at the floor, and looked to any mother the picture of deep remorse. And was so quiet, so mouse-like, so good for days on end that Nanny claimed he must be sickening for something. "Measles, perhaps, everybody's got it," she said hopefully, lustfully, seeing Bubbles prone and pimpled, her helpless baby once again. But it was Nanny who first sickened, reddened, took protesting to her bed.

"Measles," said the doctor briefly. "There's lots of it about. Might be dangerous, at her age."

Nanny snorted. "Measles!" she croaked. "It's no such thing! It's a nettle-rash, I've 'ad 'em often," and weakly fainted.

These tough ones are always frightful to nurse. How I cursed the woman as I laboured to keep her in bed, to make her eat the things she should, to keep her from believing that Dorothy and I between us would kill Baby with neglect. We knew nothing of babies, either of us. Nanny said so plainly enough in her weak mutterings about boiling milk properly, three-hourly feeds and the like. Tedious it is to nurse the sick, but how draggingly tedious when the sick also rebel and by rebelling make themselves tiresomely sicker still. A woman's best is supposed (by poets and such) to come uppermost at these times: not with me, definitely not with me. Rushing to and fro from Nanny's room to kitchen, from kitchen to Dorothy, from Dorothy to Bubbles, from Bubbles to Baby, I was a peevish hag of uncertain temper, a hasting Fury, a vile-tempered woman, a pest (but necessary) to the whole household.

"Darling Charlie, do sit down and rest!" pleaded Dorothy from the pillows on which (it seemed) she meant to spend the rest of her life. "*Do* sit down a minute and relax."

"Can't, it's time for Baby's bottle."

"Let me give her her bottle."

"No, Dorothy, it's all right."

"Charlie, I insist! You're wearing yourself to bits, and anyhow you seem to forget I *am* the child's mother."

So sullenly I gave in, sullenly brought both child and bottle, put them in Dorothy's arms, jealously watched her handle both. Really, *I* might have been the mother, so desperately it hurt me to see Dorothy holding the bottle to the little greedy lips. I might have been the child's mother in Grübl, watching my Bärbel on Frau Prandtl's lap take milk from a spoon instead of from my own breast.

"Suck, my little one, suck!"

Was it I who murmured it, or Dorothy? No, not Dorothy: with the face of one who does distasteful duties she merely held Baby and bottle in a slack embrace, let Baby do the rest.

"She's not getting anything, Dorothy!"

"My dear Charlie, as if I didn't know how to feed a baby!"

"But you don't, you don't!" I inwardly cried.

"You're getting nervy, my dear."

"I'm not."

"Yes, you are. I don't blame you. This is an awful nuisance, Nanny and me being in bed at the same time. I don't wonder you're thoroughly tired. But it's no use my getting up, I'm not fit for it. I should only collapse again and give you more trouble."

For though Baby was now six weeks old Dorothy still lay flaccidly abed, getting stouter every day and still (to her own eyes) a woman prostrated by childbirth. It was as if the violent resentment, the fierce revolt, in those early months of pregnancy had drained her of resistance: she lay now, a greyish flabby heap, day and night upon her high tumbled pillows, and, when rarely forced to it by conscience, slackly held her child, vaguely peered down at its dark red face. She exasperated me, now, even more than poor wooden-headed Nanny with her prattlings of nettle-rash, her cravings for thick white bread and butter, her unhealthy greed. God, how they exasperated me, these ailing women!

"Charlie, why don't you get Adrian to come and take you out to-morrow? Nanny's on the mend, Miss Blood and Ruahine can manage all right for the two of us."

"He'll come at the weekend: he only didn't come last Saturday because Nanny had such a temperature."

"Telephone him, darling, and get him to come and take you for a spin. It'll do you all the good in the world."

"No, I'd rather not."

"Then I will. Now don't be obstinate, Charlie: I'm going to be firm with you."

So Adrian was asked to come. Was this the fatal end, or a clever move? I wondered, as I listened to our side of the conversation. Would he be flattered that worn-out Charlotte wanted him, or merely nauseated by women and their endless ills?

Impossible to tell, with Adrian. Impossible to glean anything from that suave charming face. I searched it next morning for signs, and naturally found nought. He was just as usual; carelessly kind, subtly selfish, taking me (who yearned for the sea) to Helensville, whose thermal baths he himself preferred. No question of what would be best for a tired nervy woman: Adrian felt like taking a thermal bath, so to Helensville we went, undressed in clammy sordid wooden hutches, sported dismally together in tepid waters. My bathing-cap leaked, the wave in my hair (natural but temperamental) went wildly astray. I sat, a dank miserable woman, in pale winter sunshine among cannas and other sub-tropical whatnots, conversing gaily with Adrian and cursing the day I was born.

He was remarkably, offensively gay. The tight ornamental flower-bed atmosphere of Helensville seemed to exhilarate him, make him bubble insouciant like the geysers of his native land. My head ached with the strain of answering his sallies in kind. My head, still damp, ached vilely: my feet hurt from the endless traversing of Te Pohutu's stairs and landings: my eyes revolved uneasily in beds of red-hot grit: my nose still dribbled Helensville's healthful waters. Never was a woman less prepared to reach her journey's end, her desired goal. But so it was: suddenly, calmly, sitting there among the blazing cannas on a hard white bench, Adrian asked me to marry him.

"I think we should hit it off pretty well together."

"Yes," I murmured, blinking and sniffing.

"We're both too old and sensible to be romantic."

"Yes."

"That's settled, then. I won't kiss you here, in public: there might be someone I know around."

"No."

In the car, safely on the road to Auckland, he kissed me. It was not a passionate kiss, neither was it cold: simply a firm business-like peck designed to keep me quiet, nip in the bud any leanings towards nonsense. I allowed it passively, too spent even for the mild thrill of middle age at being kissed, at being (oh hotly-desired end!) at last engaged. The car swerved not one inch from its firm course as Adrian kissed me: perfectly controlled, utilitarian, it calmly pursued, like Adrian, the way which was best for it.

In this state we reached Auckland, had a quiet celebratory dinner in an hotel, smiling quietly at one another across the uninspired New Zealand food. In this state, only a little closer together because the night had grown bitterly cold, we drove back to Te Pohutu. It was late, well after midnight when Adrian, depositing me, deposited also the second kiss. It was as if he kissed himself, as if, as the Frenchman said of the cat, he caressed not me but himself on me. Then, smiling, he pushed me gently through the aged door. I crept upstairs, a stunned woman yearning only for bed and oblivion.

*****

But see how crisis mounts upon crisis, in this disordered chapter of poor Charlotte. How weariness, surprise, pain, disaster, ruin almost, pile up, up, till a veritable funeral pyre is builded: a pyre on which the corpse of the old Charlotte (no better, merely new) rises like a gaudy phoenix. A bird, the phoenix, who has been here before and knows all the answers: a weary bird, though bright in looks. For this night on which I gained Adrian after long siege was the end of the old Charlotte. The month and Charlotte died together: it was the thirty-first of July. "A year ago I was leaving Bobbejaanskopjie," I thought wearily as I fumbled up the stairs. A year ago I was within a week of meeting Harry, soon the dreary little notes in my diary will begin to be twelve months old. *Aug. 7th*: Harry. *Aug. 12th*: Evening with Harry (how laconically had I described that first fierce hungry kiss so rudely snatched beneath the notice-board). *Aug 15th*: Harry on boat-deck. And so on. Soon, as I write Auckland shopping-lists in this innocent-looking New Zealand diary I shall see these pitiful little reminders in a neat hand at the page-top. To-morrow is August. To-morrow I shall be on the way to become Mrs. Lovat, safe for all time. Perhaps to-morrow I shall realise it better than I do now: now I am too tired.

At this moment, my nerves sharpened by fatigue, I saw suddenly that Te Pohutu was not as I had left it that morning when I went off, a weary woman with no lively hopes of pleasure, to a day's junketing. Something now was deeply wrong. My mind leapt at once to Baby, but all in the nursery was quiet, she slept in her cot with one purple-reddish hand curled upward. The house was very still: no signs of life. Only under Tom's door at the end of the wide shabby landing a pale glimmer leaked. And even as I thought dully that this was odd (for Tom slept like a log, like a drugged man, like the healthy earthy sot he was), Tom's door opened charily, Tom's face poked out.

"Miss Hurts—!"

It was a hiss so urgent that it made the skin prickle. I followed his finger, went in. On Tom's ruffled bed, in a wild disorder of tossed sheets, dented pillow, lay Margaret Blood with a chalk-white face, an open gasping mouth. Spattered over the white her freckles stood out ghastly, a dirty greenish-brown.

"She came—I didn't ask her—she would come—said she'd got to and pushed in," babbled Tom behind me.

I hardly heard him. My eyes were fascinated by her nightgown, the nightgown (oh pathos!) of a woman who slept alone. Not the dreadful face, the dreadful stertorous breathing of Margaret in her swoon, was as dreadful as that sad, humble, ludicrous nightgown. Floss silk embroidery it had on it, and machine-made French knots in pink and apple green, and at the neck a line of coarse glossy lace.

"What happened?" I asked, pulling myself together and beginning to chafe her hands.

But it did not need Tom's uncouth shamed mutterings to tell me what had happened. Margaret had thrust herself upon him, a woman crazed by underground desires: had forced herself in upon him, roused him to what bovine passion, what savage young lust. So here she now lay, battered into senselessness by what she had so desired, a creature with all her defences down, utterly vulnerable, wholly pitiful, completely ridiculous. How ridiculous the poor girl looked, laid out there like an ungainly corpse, with her eyes only half shut, her mouth altogether open, one leg hanging over the bed's edge, one hand futilely clutching to her breast a dirty handkerchief!

Twitching my eyes away from the contemplation of Miss Blood at her very lowest, I did what I could to bring her round, despatched Tom for water (since really I could not bear the oaf breathing his clumsy young excuses down the back of my neck) and briskly set to rubbing her cold freckled hands. Mercifully she came to while he was still downstairs (I heard him plainly) fumbling for the kitchen tap.

"Charlotte—what are you—?"

"Hush, my dear, keep quiet." (How pat the kind phrases came, how mechanically the kind hands chafed still, while my malicious eyes, shocked but still unalterably malicious, took in all of Margaret's prostrate figure. And I noted while still kindly rubbing her hands, what Tom has also noted uneasily of late, uneasily growing aware of his need for such—Margaret's full, soft, strangely matronly breasts. Even as they stirred under the common nightie I thought "They'll get her into trouble time and time again, the poor creature." That and Margaret's mind, nurtured in the good old English tradition, hush, hush, learning the facts of life from the sniggering whispers of dirty-minded little girls in school dormitories. Poor Margaret, poor, poor, hot-minded creature, so unsafe and so unsure).

"Hush, my dear, lie still. Would you like an aspirin?"

"No!" cried Margaret fiercely, and plunged her shamed face into the pillow, broke into loud fierce sobbing.

SARAH CAMPION

What good were the conventional soothing phrases to a grief like this, a shame so hot? There was nothing I could do but get her back into her own bed, slip two aspirins into the drink I gave her, and stay till she was asleep.

Then a dead Charlotte, numb as a corpse, crept to her own bed and prayed for sleep. Sleep came, but what a sleep! A wild disorder of all the old nightmares with some newer, more poignant horrors to add sharpness. I dreamt that I had measles, that Baby had died of measles, that Bärbel, in a borrowed pram in an Austrian train, lay stricken with measles. I dreamt that Tom had violated me: and woke for a brief sweating moment to cry "Harry!" weakly into the dark air. I dreamt that I was in labour again, in that inn room at Grübl, while the peasants bounced, clapped, shouted to their barbaric rhythms in the Saal below. Pang upon pang, pain upon pain, and Frau Prandtl holding me down in the bed with great hairy arms, hands filthy with soil, fingers threaded through with writhing blueish earth-worms. The labour never ended, the pangs never ceased, I passed on simply to a nightmare in which mere bodily pain was followed by something far worse. I smothered, I choked in an air of ghastly fear, a fear so pressing, so livid, its cause so unknown, that my screams rang out as unbridled and bestial as the sobs of Margaret Blood. I was choking, so was all the world. All around me hands clutched throats, heads turned vainly this way and that, legs vainly threshed the air in an effort to free choking mouths from suffocation. But what was it, this universal choke? At times it was a dainty little cot-cover with embroidery on it; at times the filthy bedsheet of a mean Bloomsbury hotel; at times two great black hands shining with grease; and then I smelt again the dirty kitchen at the Bona Vista. And the hands came down hot and greasy, the little cot-cover swelled to a bloated acre of horror, a thing abominably and blindingly white, a cot-cover still but made to cover a nightmare, nightmarishly to smother.

Then abruptly one scene, clear as mosaic, sharp-edged. Bubbles in the nursery in his little striped pyjamas gravely standing by Baby's cot, gravely pressing down over her face the firm white edge of her blanket. With firm cruel little hands he steadily held down the blanket: Baby's hands, dark red and curling, as I had seen them that night, came slowly up, waved feebly. Slowly, slowly the curved fingers straightened, starfish-like the little hands were splayed against the first light of day, then fell, already growing cold, to the pillow. Bubbles, standing there, gravely waited a few minutes (long, how long, while my stricken heart congealed), then took the blanket down, straightened it, tidied it, turned it back as it had been, and tucked it in round a dead face. Peaceful, dead, little Bärbel's face that had been suffocated, lost its suffocated flush, paled to its normal pink, paled further to a livid white, while Bubbles interestedly watched, his grey eyes calm as water.

Now came the true frightfulness of my nightmare. For as I stood there, watching, sickened, horror-struck, I saw that I had done no more than watch, that I had not stopped the horror. I had stood by watching while Bubbles killed the child: I could have stopped it, but had not. Had even, in some subtle poisonous way, egged him on to the deed. There stood Bubbles and I, murderers alike, not a pin to choose between us: there lay the murdered tiny baby, our common victim.

It was terrible to wake, after this, to a meagre half light, a reluctant dawn: to lie awake sweating, trembling in a ghastly bed, watching the grey of one more dawn sink like water down the walls. Ghastly, as real consciousness came back, as normal things took on their normal shape, to see as I lay the fleas hopping back from me, their hot reluctant host, to their daytime lairs in blankets and pillowcase. For Te Pohutu was alive with fleas, fleas glistened in the old floor-boards, leapt gaily on one's ankles as one walked across the old carpets; they made here one of the minor horrors of life. Often, waking early to brood over Adrian, I had caught the creatures leaping back, as they now leaped, to their burrows: had nipped them between finger and thumb, as I now nipped one insolent fellow on my forearm, and felt the hard little skin crack, felt my own blood burst from it. Wearily, a woman once more taking up the burden of the day, I now after my nightmare might lay awake catching fleas. As I uncovered myself, threw off the heavy sweat-damp blankets, I raised a thigh and saw on it, pricking across the tawny smoothness like proud Barbary steeds traversing the desert, two enormous fleas. Arched they were, rich brown, glistening with sustenance. How grand they must look to smaller, emptier fleas, these great creatures returning gorged after their feed, returning blown with pride and with my blood to their safe havens! But they did not look grand to me, me they simply nauseated. With one savage jerk I nipped them both, squashed them between my finger-nails, flicked the corpses away in loathing. How loathsome these parasites who suck life from other lives, who live only to batten! How loathsome these fleas, these Margaret Bloods, these Charlotte Herzes! For we were all alike, I thought; alike parasites, alike loathsome. Margaret sucked Tom's young blood, I drained what I could from Adrian and meant through long years to drain more, fleas in their turn sucked, drained blood from us both. We were all alike loathsome, disgusting, parasitical: we could not live alone, nor did we wish it. Born parasites, we lived as parasites, and would doubtless die as such.

So I killed another flea or two, fellow parasites, and wearily got up. It was early, but there was much to do. Margaret was my first care, poor Margaret probably waking bemused and hot from her horrific night. She must be cajoled, bullied, flattered into coming back from her dreams and nightmares to the normal job of living. There should be no censure. She had done only what I had done, but more nakedly, more honestly, because her need, being physical, was fiercer. I must be gentle with Margaret, pitying her more than I pitied myself.

But prickly Margaret was not in the mood for gentleness. Heavy-eyed, surly, violent, she banged about the kitchen. The air rang with the noise of affronted saucepans. Over them Margaret eyed me sourly and asked me what I wanted. There was to be no revival of last night's grisly scene, no memories. I should have felt exactly the same: pulling myself together I asked for Baby's milk.

"Blast Baby, it'll have to wait a while till the fire gets up: and while we're on the subject you might tell that Bubbles of yours not to go sneaking round the house before everyone else is up. I was asleep and the brat woke me."

"He always wakes early."

"You look as if you'd never been to sleep. Out late with your young man?"

"Yes. Margaret, I think I've got these measles."

"Rubbish, you're just imagining. Though I must say you look lousy."

I remembered last night, my false pity, Margaret's poor cold hand in mine, my sympathy oozing mechanical while my eyes gloated. Boomerang-like it now came back, that sympathy, in the curt comment that I looked lousy.

And lousy I felt, heavy headed, heavy legged, burning, as I went upstairs to my nursing, to Dorothy fretful in the stuffy bedroom, Nanny surly in her odious red woollen bed-jacket, Bubbles vilely blithe and troublesome, bouncing over the rails of his outgrown cot, Baby sure to be querulous and peevish in her little cradle.

Under her covers, the blanket laid high across the pillow (how had I so exactly known that the blanket lay thus?), Baby was dead.

Chapter 9
To a Safe Landing

Now after long helpless agony, infantile measles spotting, beating, racking a tired middle-aged body, and the mind's agony riddling through the body's, worse, more subtle, more gangrenous, I begin to come back again. Now after long beastly weeks in the nursing-home, the boredom of convalescence, the languors of relapse, the renewed boredom of having once again, in spite of one's own sick horror of the world, to prepare for it once again, get ready to face it, I am a released woman. The Welquik has seen the back of me. I am pronounced fit. August, September, October, November have gone, so has half of December. Now it is Christmas, 1938. In Germany, in Berlin, despite the obscene trinity of Hitler, Goering, Goebbels, there is still some gaiety. The Advents Kranzen, dark green spiced with the red of berries, went up weeks ago: now it is the turn of Christmas, of blood-red candles in pine-leaf skirts, of the festive meaningless card, the polite bouquets glazed in cellophane, the Gänsehals, the gay ribbon bows, the looped tinsel, the little wooden angels holding yet more candles, the gilt five-pointed stars. Homes glare with electricity: Gentile children with faces bright as little lanterns crowd to the tables, to the Christmas trees, shout over the patterned wrapping paper, the wonder revealed in the maw of a parcel. In the streets there may be snow, crisp and startling: the shops along the Leipzigerstrasse and the Friedrichstrasse have died overnight, are now on Christmas evening no more than pellucid oceans of glass across which the mirage of a frost-bitten wanderer, a helmeted Schupo or a cat swim uneasily from time to time. Above, the sky swings frosty and sharp, spattered with the clear keen stars of the north. The wind blows soughing through the Tiergarten, ruffling the leaves of 1938.

In this damned country it is also Christmas. Under a sky of fearful blue, cloudless, the hot yellow beaches swarm with half-naked life, with the perambulating bodies of the tanned, the sunburned, the pink-inflamed, the peeling, or the merely scorched. One such lumbers past me now: a red-head like a nightmare prawn, the skin flaking from her in a leprous shower, the skinned patches angrily glowing. In Europe, now, the pure sound of bells echoes across the snow: here Christmas is the sound of hot feet dragging through hotter sand, or the squawk of the mother voice vainly calling its young from the water.

I have no idea why this reversal should anger me as it does. New Zealand's red peeling back is no worse than Europe's blue dripping nose. Perhaps it is the sight of so much unlovely life which frets my nerves. Lying in the pale austerity of that nursing-home I mused much upon humanity, liked it less and less, but looked at it very little. Now that I am out again I have to look at it a good deal. Perhaps I had hoped too much of the antipodes. Here in these vast sunlit countries, thought I, there will be a new race, near super-men. But the New Zealanders in their lovely land are not super-men. They all look as if they lived on sweet pastry, pickles and potatoes. When they are not knock-kneed they are bow-legged: their teeth appear to be false. Small peaky children swarm about me now, as I write, in the hot sand: New Zealand's hope. What a puling, scrawny, rat-tail generation in which to lodge one's hope! The children of Berlin are like this, but Berlin has had to tighten its belt every winter since the war: here in New Zealand the belt has never been tightened. It is an odd thing that a land with all material chances should be so placidly and contentedly peopling itself with C3 citizens.[1] As if mediocrity and sub-mediocrity were something to be aimed at, thankfully achieved. As if physical mediocrity in a spiritual vacuum were a blessed state. But after a year in the land I am used to vacuum, I am resigned to arid stretches, intellectual drought. There is so little here on which to brace the mind. The mind goes meanly humming on, a trivial mechanism, employing itself in such exercises as housework, matching wools and ribbons, choosing between two brands of tinned peas. Peas which, like the intellectual food, are probably imported. The senses, here, batten and grow fat on choice scenery: but there is nothing for the mind. The average New Zealand mind is a tram-line leading from small stop to small stop, past government-built houses, factories with award wages and the forty hour week, Plunket restrooms,[2] a hoarding brightly pictured with the faces of George, Elizabeth and the little Princesses; past a Presbyterian church, an Anglican church, a Methodist chapel, a convent, a hospital—to what? To the inevitable end, the grave at Hillsborough (monumental wall and slabs as illus: to order £10), and the rotting of that which has never fully lived. I cannot take to the simple life so simply. Mental jerks for five minutes every morning over the headlines in the *New Zealand Herald* do

---

1   C3 was the classification for recruits of considered to be of the lowest grade of physical fitness for military service and used by eugenicists to refer to the least mentally and physically able members of a population.

2   Plunket rooms were clinics established throughout New Zealand by the Plunket Society where mothers could take babies for weighing and exams and get advice on health and diet.

not keep my mind alive. I want more: I have exiled myself forever from that "more." Music? But here in New Zealand we have the radio. Drama? What on earth do you want with Ibsen, Reinhardt, when for one and sixpence at the "Civic" you can see every pore on Myrna Loy's face? Literature? You can buy all the books you want, at staggering prices: they won't take more than three months to come from Europe. But, remember, we keep our literature in New Zealand pure: banned are your morbid neurotic Boccaccios, Schnitzlers, Zweigs, Joyces, Lawrences. Apart from these and a dozen others deemed by the authorities obscene, read, my dear girl, anything you like. Read the Elsie books, the *Star*, too, has a nice weekend supplement full of wholesome short stories and recipes for ice-cream. And life, the painfully lusty, taut, reckless life of any European capital? What, I cry in despair to these enlightened kindly New Zealanders (whose expectation of life is longer, whose social services better, whose labour conditions are higher than in almost any other land), what are you going to give me for my life?

And they lead me to a modern, airy, well-planned museum set in a beautiful domain of grass, virgin bush, carefully preserved ornamental lakes on which black swans, red-billed, glide; they show me tea-kiosks in which all the scones are home-made and excellent—they lead me to this museum and they show me their exhibits. A model dairy farm providing the world's best butter; a sample of superb cheese; a man who works forty hours a week at a rate of two and sixpence an hour and retires on a pension at sixty; a woman whose motherhood (apart from the pangs of labour) is all at the government's expense; a state-educated child (rickety, but never mind that), a dignified Maori not yet killed by tuberculosis; an old pensioner who draws twenty shillings a week till he needs it no more. Stuffed, nicely dusted, grinning with the bovine contentment of stock-yard beasts, the dummies spout in chorus: "Here we are—New Zealand's best. What will you have, you that have fled to us to escape death in Europe? Cease your questions, you querulous female: settle down among us here, in our blessed twin islands, and be a good citizen."

But I can't, I can't.

And I must.

Beside me, now, on the sand lies Adrian, my future. Everybody else offers me sympathy, he is much too selfish. They rush to put cushions at my back, run to me with food in bowls, harass the new strength out of me with offers of broth and sympathy. But Adrian merely comes in his car, says: "We are going to the beach," and bears me off without so much as a rug for my knees. For the last ten years he has spent Christmas morning on Takapuna beach, there is no reason why getting married should change this. So here we lie in the sand, two aloof bodies. Flat on my back, no cushions pneumatic beneath, I lie limp and relaxed. My body flows like water into the sandy mould. Turning my eyes from the sky, which hurts, I see the panorama which will hedge my married life: a flapping half-acre of the *Auckland Star* gripped in Adrian's pale brown hands. Below the *Star* stretch Adrian's pale brown legs, firm, passionless, fanatically cleaned. My tawny limbs, smooth and pale from months of burial in sheets, please him almost as much as his own. He, like my English Flowers, likes value, quality, for his money: vigorous intelligent Blümchens have bred for two centuries to produce at last, for him, this flowering aloe, this sterile decorative Charlotte. He appreciates it, from time to time, with a connoisseur's eye.

"Adrian?"

"Yes?"

He comes promptly out of the *Star*, always the perfect gentleman, and smiles up at me as I lean on one elbow above him.

"What would you do if I had thick black hairs all over my legs, or freckles, or warts?"

"My dear girl, I shouldn't give you a second look."

True, but so unsatisfying. He laughs indulgently, showing perfect teeth that he scours after every meal. Through the years

I shall see Adrian scouring his teeth, a neat back bent over the bathroom basin.

"No, I suppose you wouldn't. Give me a cigarette."

He lights it deftly, but they are Harry's hands that cup themselves about the flame, not pale and long but broad, scrubbed, pinkly coarse. Harry's voice, so blithely unsubtle, says: "There you are, old darling: you smoke too much, but I suppose you've a right to poison yourself as you like." And he jerks the match too near, as he always did, so that my eyebrows are in peril.

I think with a shock that Adrian knows nothing about Harry. Though he has the air of knowing all that a man needs to know, he still knows nothing of this. I have laid so many ghosts, scribbling, propped on my pillows: now for final peace I had better lay this one too.

Pouring myself once more into the receptive sand, blowing out smoke and seeing it blue against the bluer sky, I rehearse what we shall say.

"Adrian, I don't know how deep the conventions go with you, but I'd like to be honest. I'm thirty-five. I've not lived a sheltered life. It's only fair to tell you—"

"That you're no angel?"

"That I'm no virgin. There was a man—"

"My dear girl, spare us both the details."

"You mean you don't want to hear—you don't want to know what happened?"

"Why should I? We're not babies. I don't think it in the least necessary to tell you of my experiences."

The rebuke would be light, but stinging: I should have offended his good taste by showing flaws in my own.

No, I decide, puffing at my cigarette, there is no need to tell. Adrian comes to me, as I to him, with no questions. What was it that Mrs. Cheveley said?—"Questions are never indiscreet:

answers sometimes are."[3]

For a moment, surprising as a bird's flight, Adrian's hand and forearm lie lightly, caressingly, over mine on the sand.

"I think January the eighteenth would be a good wedding date: that gives us almost six weeks' honeymoon before term begins. Any ideas about a honeymoon?"

"None."

"The Thermal district is disgustingly hackneyed, but Wairakei might be worth seeing if geysers are new to you."

Then he picks up the paper and is once again no more than the *Star*, two supporting hands and a pair of fine legs.

That is all you will ever hear of my affair with Harry, Adrian: and we'll not go farther back than that, to England, to the Grunewald. At their rare best all three were lovely and tender, those groping experiments into what is called love: the heart can remember that, throw out the rest.

Secure, flooded with a sudden spurious peace, I relax once more into the sand. Adrian shall be security: I can hug, as such, the pallid creature to my breast. Now my planned life stretches, orderly as a gravel path, into a calm unemotional future. I will grow roots into this before my climacteric. The soil had better not be looked at too closely: it is soil, that is enough.

We shall do very well, Adrian and I. We have known each other sixteen months, sixteen years, all time: there are no surprises. I think of his work, and see how mildly admirable it is. Lecturing on German poetry of the nineteenth century, he is yet popular. He knows his subject, is not unduly enthusiastic, does not expect anyone else to be, and teaches good-humouredly as much as he can without straining himself. It is a business matter, no more: to make an easy living he lectures, so that, in order to make later a living of their own, his pupils can listen, take notes, ask questions.

---

3   Quotation from *An Ideal Husband* by Oscar Wilde.

It is wholly a reasonable affair: none but the captious would cavil at it. He will go on like this for twenty-five years. He will then be sixty and retire. Meanwhile, I shall tend his home, oil his track. We shall not have children: they are so untidy, so disturbing. We are both neat folk, worshipping more, as we grow older, the lingerie ranged creaseless in drawers, the dress shirts on the fresh paper of the closet shelves, the snowy bath in the speckless bathroom. Litter and destruction follow in the wake of every young child, distressing order: rude pencil scribblings on walls, flower-heads nipped off in the intoxication of handling shears for the first time, scooters abandoned in the hallway, are not for us. Adrian does not actually dislike children, and they perversely adore him, flock about him, call him by his Christian name. He talks to them as to equals, dandles the baby in pale muscular hands, delights adolescents by saluting, wordlessly and in perfect tact, their adult dignity. The pregnant wives of his innumerable friends he treats with a tender brotherliness which makes them flow proudly in and out of rooms, no longer women swollen, but vessels burgeoning with rare freight, unutterably precious. As a pre-natal influence he is therefore much in demand. There is no one in Auckland quite so suited as Adrian to the quiet *diner à trois*, the friendly after-dinner talk, the little jokes, frankly improper, about conception, gestation, birth. When he goes, a little early ("for it's time you were in bed, Mavis—no, don't get up—good-bye, and thanks for a grand evening"), the woman's eyes follow him lovingly. "What a father Adrian would make!" she says to her husband as he returns from farewelling Adrian on the doorstep. "What an adorable father!"

In this nice aroma the adorable father goes quietly about his bachelor ways. He likes children well enough, as one likes things which never come too near. But with children of one's own there is no peace. A parent is of all humans the least secure. Astride a volcano of his own begetting he spends his life apprehensively looking this way and that for flames.

Really, as I write, I feel quite a fondness for Adrian. He has such an Oscar Wilde charm, is such a perfected pussy cat of a man, so expert in selfishness, so engaging as he subtly robs you of the right to your own way. A stupid man I could never stomach, but he has a keen, malicious, oddly female mind, the small perfect mind incapable of greatness. His standards are what mine shall be: a refined modest comfort, no show, no cheese-paring: an expert cultivation of comfort for its own sake. Imagine us, soberly settled, for the next forty years. A small neat car, a small neat house in a small neat garden. A gardener three times a week to make gardening a pleasure to us: a maid from nine to six daily so that there shall be no rough work for me. Breakfast at eight: at nine a kiss on the door-step coupled with an exhortation not to forget the fish. My day, between his going and return, an ambling from one small duty to the other; a luncheon at Court's with a friend, perhaps, embedded like a jewel in the sober matrix of the week. At six-thirty the whirr of the car on the gravel, the click of the garage door, the returning kiss as cool as a bird's feet on my lips. Then tea, modest, home--made, toothsome. And after tea? In summer, the veranda until the mosquitoes come ("There's no sense in sitting here to be bitten, I'm going in"): in winter our own fireside with a book for each of us, and titbits read aloud to me from the *Star* or pink gossipy *Observer*. Bridge on Saturdays at home or at a friend's house: a movie now and again when Adrian feels inclined to get the car once more from the garage. And after the movie, the fireside reading? Bed. Twin passionless oblongs covered with fine linen: bed, and the clicking out of the bedside lamps, the murmured unemotional dispute about the open window, the sigh of well-sprung mattresses, the first snore, the second, mounting in a pæan of sensible living to that heaven we care about so little.

I shall not think of Germany as I drop to sleep in New Zealand: at least, I hope not. It would be too uncomfortable. For in

Germany, in back streets, in wretched lodgings hurriedly found, the ghettoed Jews lurk. Though I am banishing the Jews from my future, I must now think of them. This is Christmas, the anniversary of that prince of peace whose birth has meant death, through how many generations, to how many Jews. Tante Lydia and Tante Herta, two harmless crumbling old women who have lived for the last five years in the faith that barbarism cannot last—what are they doing now? We know nothing, we have heard nothing. We only know, increasingly, that the German is but a very few years removed from the painted barbarian licking his great chops over the sight of blood and loot: he can slip those meagre generations easily enough when he smells blood and loot again. All the German wants is a leader, an ape more mad than himself, more reckless in insanity. He has him: Heil Hitler! Now what is there the Huns cannot do to the Jews, who, when Germany was a land ravaged by barbaric hordes, had their walled cities, their arts, their culture, their religion? It is no use, here, thinking that the German can do what he will with the Jews, that we can do nothing. I cannot go back: if we all went back, we scattered ones, it would do no good. Though the Jews suffer they will endure. When the Germans are no more than a trifling name in history books, learnt languidly by small children among other names as unimportant, the Jews will be a living race. Courage must survive. That is the only comfort we can take, we who have escaped from the European mad-house.

But this New Zealand is a peaceful country: surely Adrian and I can kill ourselves in peace peacefully enough. We shall have our joint life, an avenue of small perfected comforts stretching out to old age. I shall lose my figure and not care, grow fat and sleek and mindless as a cream-fed puss. Adrian will grow slightly more fussy about the laundering of his bed-linen, the pressing of his trouser-pleats, the toasting of his bread. Together we shall amble down the avenue, two grass-gorged beasts. At the end of the avenue is retirement, wise investments bringing in a comfortable annuity, more security. We slide into our comfortable twilight, barren of regret. No passion spent, for there was none to spend.

So our easy future. But on the open newspaper he holds now between us I read: "Further anti-Jewish measures in Berlin." I am one of the lucky ones, I think. Is it any use to get excited over Jews, over Berlin, now that Judaism and Berlin are thirteen thousand miles away? If I think any more on what has happened, what is happening, I shall go surely mad. Lying here in remote snug New Zealand looking back at Europe, I see on all sides a cruelty so gross, a malice so venomous, that it would crush me if I let it. Read your newspapers as I for my sanity's sake dare not do, read them steadily each day, sparing yourselves nothing. Is this a world of humans, or not? What sort of people are these whose doings shout in our headlines? Divided, they are, into three flocks: the persecutors, who are mad; the persecuted, who suffer madness; and that large, silent, amorphous mass, the spectators. These last know they look upon evil; but as long as they only look it is quite all right. "Oh well," they say, "evil is always with us. Until the millennium, of course, but no one believes in that. You can't ignore facts, my dear fellow: human nature is human nature all the world over." So while the spectators sit around in a sodden mass, no more than mildly uneasy, the bull is slaughtered in the ring, the blood flows, the torn flank gapes, the entrails drop sluggishly. In Wolfenbüttel the maddened Jew rushes upon barbed wire, away, away, anything to get away, and hangs there, a screaming bloody mass, till there is no more noise. In Berlin there is a pogrom to avenge the death of one man killed by a youth as mad as Hitler but more obscure. So once more, in Berlin, blood flows from the Jews. The smell of blood—oh, my God, the smell of blood!—once more fills the air.

"Comfy?" asks Adrian, putting down the *Star* to light another cigarette.

"Yes, thanks."

"What's the time?"

"Ten-thirty."

And at once Berlin fades, the cries of Jewry fade. For at this time, sitting with Charlotte on the veranda, looking aft to the little Chinamen lolling off-duty on the poop, Harry was wont to say: "How's the time, old darling?" Then she held out her wrist to him silently, because she wanted him to touch it. He took it in his warm clasp and studied the watch. "Only half-past ten"—the hand dropped her wrist, patted his stomach—"still thirty minutes to wait for me beer 'n' cheese." And at that, at the facetiously assumed speech, she regularly laughed. Not because she found it funny, but because she loved him. Vulgar the scene, witless the joke: but how warm, how deeply warming, to a chilly heart! Had it perhaps been no more than that, a vulgar intrigue between a woman emotionally avid and a gross elderly man in whom lust flared like a greasy flame for the last time? Perhaps it had been no more. Perhaps, throughout, she had been a fool, that Charlotte, and is a fool now to remember? But remember she does, at Christmas, in the antipodes, lying on hot sand staring at a hot sky.

"What's the time, old darling?"

"Harry, you asked me that only five minutes ago. It's twenty-five to eleven."

He sighs exaggeratedly. "Tempus won't fugit," he mutters, brushing up his moustache. She laughs again, loving him, doting on him, her eyes raised a moment from her knitting to gloat over his warm fresh face, the fleshy fold beneath his chin, the endearing tufts of hair which sprout inconsequent from his ears, the sea-blue of his eyes. Ah, Harry, darling Harry, so childishly impatient for your body's ease, your biscuits and your gorgonzola at eleven, the foamy beer over which you smack your lips, and once again, with that swaggering gesture, wipe your crisp moustache! Surely the two of them, foolish Harry, foolish Charlotte, will go on forever sitting waiting for Harry's biscuits, beer and cheese, waiting for eleven o'clock on the old *Ceres*, living happily in their present, happily sure of one another and the warmth that flows (but how frailly!) between them.

Meanwhile an older Charlotte lies on this alien shore looking sadly at the hot strange red of pohutukawas in full bloom, bound for another embarkation: watching the bright waves frilling at another sea's edge, beginning in sorrow, but how safely, yet another journey.

Afterword
by Sarah Shieff

Charlotte Herz has a problem—a world-historical problem. She's Jewish, she's intelligent, and she's female. She was born in a place and at a time when those things, taken together, would foreclose most futures. Sarah Campion imagines a life for Charlotte as an archetypal wandering Jew, thrown into a self-willed exile, just ahead of the apocalypse. At least to begin with, she is motivated by laudable, impossible ambitions: pregnant and alone in the Austrian Alps, she imagines she is blazing a brave new trail for womanhood, establishing the right of every woman to mother-hood without any of the boredoms of marriage. If men could be sexual freelances, she asks, why not women? That fantasy soon meets a fatal economic stumbling-block, and her ambitions take a material turn: she needs security, which means a man. By the time her narrative ends, in December 1938, she appears to have found both in the person of the sexless Adrian Lovat, a lecturer in German who has never visited Germany, and resigned herself to a life of passionless twin beds, unemotional disputes, and parasitism. The setting of this dreary future: New Zealand, with its promise of mediocrity, scenery, and spiritual vacuum.

But, as other readers have noted, Charlotte Herz *is* a problem, as a narrator, as a character, as a creature utterly selfish, sneering and insufferable.[1] Her favourite emotion is disgust, closely followed by its minor relatives, distaste, dismay and disdain. Disgust registers powerfully from the outset. Its first objects are the "wholly sickening" arum lilies that have tracked her from South Africa to New Zealand, and on to the nursing home where she is recuperating impatiently, disgustedly, from a nasty dose of the measles. The woman who has employed her as a nanny for her disgusting son brings an unwelcome armload to her bedside:

> [A]s she bent to kiss me a whiff of death, no less, floated up from those bleached trumpets. When after half an hour's chatting she was gone I made the nurse put them in the lavatory. For to the lavatory they certainly belong.[2]

It's easy enough to read those waxy blooms as a kind of objective correlative. Despite her physical attractiveness, and what she likes to think of as her worldliness, her intelligence, her fearless independence, time and again Charlotte falls victim to what a new-age therapist might tell her are self-sabotaging behaviours: her terrible choice of lovers, her self-hatred as a Jew, her shiftless yearning to be anywhere other than where she is. She likes to nip at those flowers, those pale other selves, spoiling their impeccable whiteness, loving to see them bruised and browning. And there's

---

1   Utterly selfish: Brad Bigelow, "*Makeshift*, by Sarah Campion (1940)" The Neglected Books Page <https://neglectedbooks.com/?p=9498> [accessed 21 Nov 2024]; Sneering and insufferable: "New Novels", *The Spectator*, June 28, 1940, p. 870.

2   *Makeshift*, p. 20

at least one good reason why she might feel she too belongs in the lavatory: when blazing a new trail for motherhood proves less than idyllic, she abandons her new-born daughter on a train, cooly and unhurriedly tucking her into in another woman's baby carriage.

It could be that self-loathing is so fundamental to Charlotte's sense of herself that it contaminates almost every observation, but it isn't an especially obvious part of her character—that is, until it's associated with her Judaism—and it's not her most characteristic mode. Rather, her disgust registers in relation to other people's physicality, to food, to predatory single women (herself included), to babies, to her lovers, and, most pervasively, to Jews. Its unsettling persistence makes it a useful lens for thinking about this makeshift character, and this awkward—and sometimes distasteful—novel.[3]

Disgust is visceral, an unwilled but deeply cultural response to dirt, disease, bodily secretions. It registers a fear of contamination or pollution, what Mary Douglas famously called "matter out of place."[4] Although we recoil from disgusting things, the things themselves are mostly not inherently dirty: dirt, as Douglas reminds us, is a by-product of a systematic ordering and classification of matter, the system that produces clean selves and dirty others. Unlike the related but distinct category of the abject, disgust is never ambivalent. If the abject and its pleasures oscillate around the interfusion of the subject-object boundary, "disgust strengthens and polices this boundary."[5] Disgust, as Sianne Ngai

3   My thinking here is indebted to Maud Ellmann's wonderful essay "Powers of Disgust: Katherine Mansfield and Virginia Woolf", in *Katherine Mansfield and Virginia Woolf*, ed. by Christine Froula, Gerri Kimber, Todd Martin and Aimee Gasston (Edinburgh: Edinburgh UP, 2018), pp. 11-28.

4   Mary Douglas, *Purity and Danger* [1966] (Abingdon: Routledge, 2002), p. 44.

5   Sianne Ngai, "Afterword: On Disgust", *Ugly Feelings* (Boston: Harvard University Press, 2005), p. 335.

has it, is insistent and intolerable.[6] It's the sign that something repulsive has come too close—up the nose, in the mouth, on the skin—something that threatens a clean and proper self, and must be urgently and forcefully rejected.

Charlotte's disgust amps up in step with her need to flee her family and its expectations, the claustrophobic world she knows, and its increasing personal and political dangers. The baby she abandons is as loathsome to her "as an infant vulture is loathsome while it pecks naturally at rotting flesh."[7] For a moment she bends—"but now in a mad tenderness I hugged my baby vulture, my carrion crow: she was once more the helpless wee thing, my little crumb, my dove"[8]—but "common sense" prevails in the form of a vision of her future: disgust at the man who might save her from the shame of single motherhood. "He would unendingly want gratitude. I hated gratitude then, I hate it still. The thought of it nauseated me."[9] It's nausea for herself and her child that impels her to leave Bärbel on the train.

She is repelled by other people's physicality. Tante Lydia, a single independent woman, is another possible future for Charlotte. Lydia unquestioningly rescues Charlotte from her Austrian ordeal and doesn't challenge her story about the baby—"She's dead, Tante Lydia. Croup"[10]—but Charlotte disdainfully describes her as "an exasperating old harpy";[11] worse, Charlotte disgustedly notices her "pettishly picking wax out of her ears."[12] Next, in South Africa, in search of another future, Charlotte becomes complicit

---

6 Ngai, p. 333.

7 *Makeshift*, p. 85.

8 Ibid, p. 85.

9 Ibid, p. 85.

10 Ibid, p. 115.

11 Ibid, p. 115.

12 Ibid, p. 17.

in another aunt's plans to marry her off to a "solid, earth-smelling, none-too-particular Boer who would take a Jewess and raise from her a brood of solid, earth-smelling children."[13] Food signals her revulsion for the plan, the place, the people: she slaps vegetables swimming in grease, tomato bredie (a thick mutton stew), meat pies and heavy puddings in front of hot chewing faces. "I who had set out from Europe with the determination to be pure bodily, an animal seeking no more than a mate, was now suddenly and violently revolted by the sight, the thought of the thing I had been pursuing."[14] And although Charlotte is apparently alive to the absurdities of racism—"What would happen, I wondered idly, mooning along, if black touched white? An immediate explosion? A roar of falling masonry?"[15]—her disgust registers fully, and as fully racialised, in the kitchen. "In spite of Tante Saschia's uncannily quick eye sugar got stolen, bacon vanished, guavas mysteriously were not there when the pantry door was unlocked. And in the tea-cloths lying tumbled by the kitchen sink were other trophies: you picked up a tea-cloth to dry a cup, shook it out, and out flew a sticky handful of brown sugar, half a mutton chop, or a stinking relic of smoked snoek."[16] Nothing marks the distance between the self and a contaminating other more than the other's food.

Here, and in many similar examples, Charlotte's disgust produces an inadvertent and disconcerting effect—an effect that is itself a property of disgust: as William Ian Miller has observed, "the avowal of disgust expects concurrence."[17] The reaction to a stink—"God, that's disgusting"—expects to find agreement,

13 *Makeshift*, p. 226.

14 Ibid, p. 228.

15 Ibid, p. 209.

16 Ibid, p. 223.

17 William Ian Miller, *The Anatomy of Disgust* (Cambridge, MA: Harvard UP, 1997), quoted in Ngai, p. 335.

or, as Sianne Ngai suggestively has it, "there is a sense in which [disgust] seeks to include or draw others *into* its exclusion of its object, enabling a strange kind of sociability."[18] Ngai then makes a related point: throughout history, disgust has been appropriated "as a means of reinforcing the boundaries between self and "contaminating" others that has perpetuated racism, anti-Semitism, homophobia, misogyny."[19] But what happens when disgust fails to find concurrence?

Charlotte saves her most disgusted rhetoric for other Jews: Jewish eating, Jewish physicality, Jewish grasping, Jewish cunning, Jewish shrillness and self-pity, the "racial" traits that persist even among the assimilated Jews of North London. On her hunt for an anchor that she hopes will weigh her to one place—an anchor that might free her from "this curse, this restlessness, this fugitive Jewish fate"[20]—she stops briefly in Sydney. There, she finds yet more relations who appear to have made peace with their "Jewish fate." These prospering Australians feel threatened by the swarming hordes of refugees who have already unleashed the antisemitism they thought they had left behind them. Charlotte too feels threatened: in her urgency to escape her uncle's plans to marry her off to a decent Aussie Gentile, she, like the other prosperous Jews, turns Hitler's victims into a pestilence she must escape to save herself:

These old established Jews feel the rock under them quiver, see splits appear. At their very feet the rats nibble, the rabble of newly-come Jewish rats. And how they swarm, the newly-comes! Up and down the William Street hill, along the already crowded pavements of King's Cross, in and out of the delicatessen stores along Darlinghurst Road—in hordes of four and five, in close clusters of three,

---

18   Ngai, p. 336.

19   Ibid, pp. 338-39.

20   *Makeshift*, p. 313.

in intimate arm-linked couples, the Jews swarm. The perfume of the women lies heavily on the air; the cigar-smoke of the men adds a headier flavour. The air smells of Jewry, the air hums with it.[21]

Disgusted, Charlotte sets off again.

This is a disgust that a modern reader—or, at least, this modern Jewish reader—cannot share. Despite the narrative's ostensible sympathy towards the plight of Jewish people in Nazi Germany, the racialised tropes have curdled, and themselves disgust, rebounding against the narrator: in Maud Ellman's neat formulation, disgust disgusts.[22] Charlotte's grimaces repel, partly because they unreflectively recycle hateful stereotypes, and partly because hers is a ventriloquised Judaism. The self-hating Jew is a familiar psychological and literary trope;[23] deployed by a non-Jewish author, however, even an undoubtedly sympathetic one, it risks shading into the very thing it deplores. Again, Sianne Ngai is helpful: "disgust blocks the path to sympathy."[24] Disgust at Charlotte's racialism contributes to distaste for her as a character. The readerly qualm—resisting concurrence—is part of what makes the book feel awkward.

Unsurprisingly, that racialism was invisible to the book's first readers. "The shadow of the swastika falls more or less darkly across these pages," wrote one reviewer, who goes on to distinguish between the "outward and obvious forces" arrayed against Charlotte—"the rise of Hitlerism, and the gradually growing oppression of the Jew"—and an "inner instability," which is racialized as restlessness, makeshiftness, as "this fugitive Jewish fate." For

---

21   *Makeshift*, p. 319.

22   Ellmann, p. 17.

23   See, for example, Sander Gilman, Jewish Self-Hatred: Anti-Semitism and the Hidden Language of the Jews (Baltimore: Johns Hopkins, 1986)

24   Ngai, p. 335.

that reviewer, as I think for Campion, Charlotte's endurance as a Jew "becomes something strong, life affirming," but they nonetheless characterise Jews by essentialised ("typical") traits. Although relatively innocuous, it's a view that exists on a continuum with the genocidal racism of those who believe Jews have no place, who would stamp them out like cockroaches.[25] Time would not be kind to the hopeful message of this novel, but its problematic innocence, its historical ironies, and Charlotte's disconcerting ambivalence are among the reasons it is worth reading today.

There are many others. It vividly evokes bourgeois Jewish life in Berlin between the wars, and the rise of Nazism—a world Sarah Campion knew well from her years as an English tutor. Charlotte, in turn, is a merciless and satirical observer—the sister, in many ways, of the narrators of Katherine Mansfield's *In a German Pension* stories. On a shopping trip to the Berlin branch of Woolworths, Charlotte's small nephew David finds exactly what he wants to take with him to South Africa: "a cot-cover in blueish-pink cotton, with the design ready stamped for working; a chaste cheerful medley, this, of storks, pansies, bows of ribbon and swastikas."[26] Her niece Käthy, at eight years old, is in training as a hausfrau: she chooses two aluminium saucepans with lids, a scrubbing-brush, three neat chequered dusters, three tea-cloths, a clothes-line and two dozen pegs. Charlotte is unsparing about lives of aspiring Cambridge intellectuals—a life Sarah Campion also knew well. John Lae, soon to become Charlotte's lover, contributes articles "of the deepest and most intellectual gloom to the various precious journals with which the place was littered," each "convinced that it alone, like some undaunted glow-worm, maintained the light of true Culture in an otherwise murky world."[27]

---

25   *The Scotsman*, 18 April 1940, p. 9.

26   *Makeshift*, p. 186.

27   Ibid, p. 160.

John, she observes, is growing a beard in "the wistful hope" that he might come to look like D.H. Lawrence.[28]

Sarah Campion also knew rural South Africa: she had spent nearly two years in Cape Province, 1938-39, working on a farm "up-country," and in a hotel kitchen in Sea Point, Capetown.[29] *Makeshift*'s set piece in the kitchen of Capetown's Bona Vista hotel is marvel of zestful, disgusting detail. Charlotte's view of provincial, self-satisfied New Zealand is also informed by Campion's own experience: she spent a few months here, 1938-39, before settling with her husband Antony Alpers in 1952. She was clearly struck by the false teeth so typical of New Zealand men of that generation.[30] She wasn't alone. The short story writer Frank Sargeson, with whom she later became friendly, also made fun of what my own father called porcelain choppers: "I imagine that after this war the Wandering N.Zder will replace the Wandering Jew in Europe—no home to go to—he'll always be recognised by his water-bottle khaki shorts & false teeth."[31] Sargeson met Sarah Campion soon after her arrival in Auckland. She made strong early impression. "She's quite amusing about N.Zders—said she got terribly sick of burning Chapter 1 of Antony's book about Katherine Mansfield to boil the copper, when, having done the washing, she'd have to knock off reviews for *John O'London* to keep the pair of them while he wrote it. I asked her if she had any trouble getting started on a novel, & she said if she did she just headed a page Chapter 10 or 20 & started there. She's pretty nice in fact—doesn't

28   *Makeshift*, p. 161.

29   See Sarah Campion, *Father: A Portrait of G.G. Coulton at Home* (London: Michael Joseph, 1948), pp. 155-56.

30   See Ibid, p. 368.

31   Frank Sargeson to John Lehmann, 10 March 1943, Lehmann Family Papers Box 44 Folder 77, Department of Rare Books and Special Collections, Princeton University Library.

believe in worrying, has a pretty good time I think." [32]

It's nice to think of Sarah Campion enjoying a good time. Charlotte Herz really doesn't. The very range of her disgusts command attention. She relishes the repulsive, courts it, savours it, and appears to seek it out in her lovers: her first lover is her first cousin Kurt—a coupling with a distasteful whiff of incest. In England, there's John Lae with his wispy beard: their affair is "furtive, restless, miserable" and leaves "a foul taste in the mouth, an uneasy greasiness."[33] There's Harry Hobart, who Charlotte meets en route to New Zealand—gross and lumbering Harry, with much-stopped teeth and a great belly hanging down like a firm fruit. Then there's little Herman Metzger, the hairy-kneed tramp. Despite his rapey come-on and his disgusting personal habits—he pares his nails with a long knife, humming as he scrapes—Charlotte sleeps with him in a foetid hayloft. The reader's discomfort escalates, along with Charlotte's desire to escape. Thank heavens, she bolts, returning briefly to her old life in Berlin.

On the eve of her next escape, to England, she third-persons herself, setting out in search of what she hopes will be "the real Charlotte":

> She is a Jew now, not a German: she is bound to no town, no province, no land. A nomad Charlotte with her tent pitched nightly on some new patch, each night (pray God) a new Charlotte beneath its canvas.[34]

From now on, this narrative strategy will mark every departure. That third person signals a transitional state between a self no

---

32   Frank Sargeson to E.P. Dawson, 13 October 1952, MS-2404/003, Hocken Collections, Uare Taoka o Hākena, University of Otago, Dunedin, NZ.

33   *Makeshift*, p. 166.

34   Ibid, p. 149.

longer fit for purpose, and a new and differently unsatisfactory "I." Her last self—which shows no more sign of sticking than any of the previous versions—is the one she invents to catch Adrian Lovat: well groomed, attentive, not too clever, not too Jewish. But this isn't the fragmentation of identity we might recognise in modernist fiction: although Charlotte's desires and anomie are modern, Campion's narrative is conventional in its treatment of character. "Yuck," Charlotte seems to be saying. "That was her. Now let's try something new." Her taste in lovers may be execrable, but she runs when she has to. Her makeshift selves are left in the dust, along with her lovers, in her headlong and entirely self-aware lunge for the future.

Although Charlotte may not always be the best or most comfortable companion on the page, Sarah Campion's vivid, problematic creation lives beyond her time. Mired in the era's racialism, she can nonetheless see how its most toxic effusions are about to consume Europe, and, quite possibly, Europe's Jews. That did not require special insight in 1939, any more than its resurgent dangers should require special insight today. The point at which Charlotte seems most emphatically of her time, and most uncomfortably of ours, is in her complacent belief that though the Jews suffer they will endure—that the tenacity of the race will somehow see them right. "When Germans are no more than a trifling name in history books, learnt languidly by small children among other names as unimportant, the Jews will be a living race. Courage must survive."[35] She agonises about the futility of action, and turns a blind eye: is it any use to get excited over Jews, over Berlin, she asks, now that Judaism and Berlin are thirteen thousand miles away? "Lying here in remote snug New Zealand looking back at Europe, I see on all sides a cruelty so gross, a malice so venomous, that it would crush me if I let it. Read your newspapers as I

---

35 *Makeshift*, p. 376.

for my sanity's sake dare not do."[36] The price she will pay for her own safety is boredom. For those who cannot escape, courage must survive. History will see to it.

Sarah Campion herself had no such faith. From the 1960s, from "remote snug New Zealand," she threw herself into campaigns for human rights, for social justice and for peace—campaigns against racism in New Zealand, against sporting contact with South Africa, against the Vietnam war, against nuclear testing. It was the need for purposeful activity, for not shuddering and turning away, that most distinguishes her from her fictional creation.

36   *Makeshift*, p. 377.

Sarah Campion was the pseudonym of Mary Rose Coulton. Born the daughter of a Cambridge don in 1906, she taught in Germany from 1933 to 1937, when she was expelled for refusing to collaborate with Nazi authorities. This and her encounters with apartheid in South Africa instilled in her a lifelong dedication to political activism. She spent a year in Australia, in which she set her most famous novel, *Mo Burdekin*, then returned to England at the start of World War Two. She published 11 novels between 1936 and 1951. She married the New Zealand writer Antony Alpers in 1945 and they settled in Auckland, New Zealand in 1952. After their divorce in 1962, she worked as a journalist and organizer in social movements. She died in 2002.

Diana Wichtel's memoir about her family's Holocaust history, *Driving to Treblinka*, won the Royal Society Te Apārangi Award for General Non-fiction at the 2018 Ockham New Zealand Book Awards. She worked as television critic and feature writer for the *New Zealand Listener* from 1984 until 2020, and was a columnist for the *New Zealand Herald's Canvas* magazine from 2020 to 2024. *Unreel*, her 2025 Ockham Book Awards longlisted memoir of a life viewed through the lens of too much television, was published in November 2024.

Sarah Shieff is Associate Professor of English at the University of Waikato, where she teaches New Zealand literature, food writing and the literature of trauma. She is the editor of *Letters of Frank Sargeson* and *Letters of Denis Glover*. Her current project is an edition of the letters of the New Zealand poet Allen Curnow.

Other Titles in the Recovered Books series from
Boiler House Press

Gentleman Overboard by Herbert Clyde Lewis
Introduction by George Szirtes, Afterword by Brad Bigelow
ISBN: 9781913861230

Pull Devil, Pull Baker by Stella Benson
Introduction by Julia Blackburn, Afterword by Nicola Darwood
ISBN: 9781913861605

Time: the Present – Selected Stories by Tess Slesinger
Introduction by Vivian Gornick, Afterword by Paula Rabinowitz
ISBN: 9781913861582

Two Thousand Million Man-Power by Gertrude Trevelyan
Introduction by Rachel Hore, Afterword by Brad Bigelow
ISBN: 9781913861858

Quarry by Jane White
Introduction by Anne Billson, Afterword by Helen Hughes
ISBN: 9781915812001

The Sanity Inspectors by Friedrich Deich
Introduction by Sinclair McKay, Afterword by Chris Maloney
ISBN: 9781913861872

To Test the Joy: Selected Poetry and Prose by Genevieve Taggard
Introduction by Terese Svoboda, Edited and with commentary
by Anne Hammond
ISBN: 9781915812025

Other Titles in the Recovered Books series from Boiler House Press

Solitary Confinement by Christopher Burney
Introduction by Ted Gioia, Afterword by Hugh Purcell
ISBN: 9781915812469

Trance by Appointment by Gertrude Trevelyan
Introduction by Louisa Treger, Afterword by Rebecca Bowler
ISBN: 9781915812742

And So Did I by Malachi Whitaker
Introduction by Catherine Taylor, Afterword by Valerie Waterhouse
ISBN: 9781915812742

Forthcoming Titles

Vengeance is Mine (Mein ist die Rache) by Friedrich Torberg
English translation by Stephanie Ortega
Introduction by Menachem Kaiser, Afterword by Marcel Atze
March 2026

An American Journey by Ethel Mannin
Introduction by Joanna Pocock
May 2026

We Too Are Drifting by Gale Wilhelm
Introduction by Sheila Liming
September 2026

Season's Greetings by Herbert Clyde Lewis

Introduction by Kathleen Rooney, Afterword by Brad Bigelow

November 2026

Makeshift
By Sarah Campion (Mary Rose Coulton Alpers)

First published in this edition by Boiler House Press, 2025
Boiler House Press is part of the UEA Publishing Project
Makeshift copyright © Sarah Campion, 1940
Introduction copyright © Diana Wichtel, 2025
Afterword copyright © Sarah Shieff, 2025

Proofreading by Hannah Jones

Photograph of mid-1950s Sarah Campion by permission of
Philip Alpers

The right of Sarah Campion to be identified as the Author of this
work has been asserted by her in accordance with the Copyright,
Design & Patents Act, 1988.

Cover Design and Typesetting by Louise Aspinall
Typeset in Arnhem Pro

ISBN: 978-1-915812-48-3

9 781915 812483